DEVILS, DEATH
& DARK WONDERS

ALSO BY RANDY CHANDLER

Novels

Bad Juju

Daemon of the Dark Wood

HELLz BELLz

Dime Detective

Angel Steel

Novellas

Dead Juju (in DEADCORE)

Howler (in MALCONTENTS)

RANDY CHANDLER

DEVILS, DEATH & DARK WONDERS

EDITOR: CHERYL MULLENAX

A Red Room Press Book

First Red Room Press Trade Paperback Edition
July 2013

ISBN 13: 978-1-936964-56-7

Visit Red Room Press on the web at:
redroompress.com
facebook.com/redroompress
twitter.com/redroombooks

Red Room Press

The stories first appeared as follows:

"The Stain" in *The Dream People* (2004)

"Kudzu Man" in *Books of Flesh* (2003)

"Manchine" in *EOTU* Ezine (2002)

"Devils" in *Sick Things* (2010)

"River Rats" online at *Randy Chandler's Oddities & Entities* (2003)

"Twister Man" in *WriterOnLine* (2003)

"The Handyman" as an Amazon Short (2006)

"The Spook" in *Shivers* IV (2006)

"Deadside In Bug City" in *Bare Bone* 6 (2004)

"Terra Incognita" in *Damned Nation* (2006)

"Death Comes Calling" as an Amazon Short (2006)

"The Grind" in *Thuglit* (2008)

"Lipstick Swastika" in *The Death Panel* (2009)

"Devil In 206" in *Darker than Noir* (2011)

"Flesh And Word" as an Amazon Single (2013)

"Deathless" in *Books of Flesh* (2003)

"Jacked" online at *Randy Chandler's Oddities and Entities* (2005)

"Fungoid" in *Vile Things* (2009)

"Halloween Bash" in *EOTU* Ezine (2002)

"The Bone Train" at *Horror World* (2000)

"Manhunter" as an Amazon Short (2007)

"Miss Thang" at *Horrorfind* (1999)

"Hogbutcher's Heart" at *Horrorfind* (2000)

"The Kitchen Witch" in *Grue* (1986)

"A Witch In Faerie" in *EOTU* Ezine (2003)

"Split Finger" in *Bizarre Bazaar* (1994)

"(3-D)" in *EOTU* Ezine (1988)

"The Coffin" *deadlines.com* (2010)

"At The Edge of the World" as an Amazon Short (2006)

"Undertaken" in *Death Grip: Exit Laughing* (2006)

"Life After Living Death" *deadlines.com* (2010)

"The God of Broken Worlds" *EOTU* Ezine (2002)

"Mortal" first appears here (2013)

"Hellbent House" in HELLz BELLz (2005)

CONTENTS

THE STAIN

It found him in the dark.

A cool droplet smacked his forehead and misted his lashes. He switched on his bedside lamp and there it was above him: a wet stain marring the ceiling, another liquid bead bulging from its center like a pink eyeball.

He heard water droning through the pipes in the flat above him, number 10, where *she* lived. He stared at the stain, fascinated by the pattern it was creating on his ceiling. He watched the pink eyeball detach and fall. It splattered on his forehead.

He phoned the landlord and reported the leaking water in number 10. He pushed his rumpled bed to the side, then lay on his back and studied the ceiling's stigmata.

Events unfolded above him. He listened. He stared at the stain.

They found her dead in a bathtub overflowing bloody water, wearing countless cuts. He tried to imagine how her breasts looked when they found her. Did they still float with puckered nipples above the surface of the water?

The detectives questioned him the next day. How well had he known her? Had he ever had sexual relations with her? Had he heard any unusual sounds coming from her flat? They seemed satisfied with his answers. They looked at the stain. They looked at him. They said they would be in touch. He moved his bed back to where it had been.

He spent hours staring at the dark blemish. He didn't go to his job. Didn't answer his phone. He spent his nights with the light on so he could contemplate the discolored blotch, its spiderlike tendrils reaching out from a dark center. He slept very little, if at all. He stood on his bed and touched his fingers to the stain's rust-colored hub. It was soft, damp, like cold mottled flesh. *Her* flesh. He licked his fingertips. Tasted her, tasted the damp blotch of her life's culmination, a sad summation of mortality.

But she *wasn't* dead. She was alive in the stain. She lived for him and no one else.

She was his.

He stared into the stain's density. Night and day. He poked his finger into its mushy center. Punched through. Deflowered, it began to whisper to him. On tiptoes and a stack of phone books on the bed, he pressed his lips to hers. He licked her jagged edges. Tasted menses-flavored sheetrock.

He pushed his bed aside and moved his writing desk directly beneath her. She whispered to him and he wrote down her stories. Tales of dark wonder and awe. Of flesh and fantasy. Of black dogs and gargoyles and cranial holes opening upon other worlds. She showed him wondrous geometries far beyond the four-cornered world of his drab room.

The stories accumulated as his body withered. He drank cheap red wine and pissed blood. He didn't bathe. He shrank to skin and bone. He wrote longhand on a legal pad. His fingers grew as thin as his Number 2 pencils. Flesh diminished. Fantasy flourished.

The stain crooned and cooed.

They banged on his door. He ignored them, scribbling frantically.

They broke in and threw him to the floor. Snapped steel bracelets on his wrists. Arrested him for first-degree murder.

He laughed at their stupidity.

"You can't murder your muse," he shouted at them.

They locked him in a cinderblock cell. He wrote out his confession, recounting weeks of stealthy stalking; in graphic detail he described how he'd sculpted himself a muse out of feminine flesh. "I didn't murder her," he concluded in scrawling hand, "I created her."

Now he writes his tales in crayon. The blemish on his forehead darkens every day, and he feels the way opening. Soon there will be a true *in-breathing* and his muse will set up shop in his skull.

Then he will create his masterpiece and they will know he killed no one.

KUDZU MAN

Jack Talley pulled into Babylon at sunset. He should have been there hours earlier, but he had dallied in his favorite Atlanta watering hole for several hours, tossing back his afternoon quota of vodka-on-the-rocks and brooding over his humiliating assignment in this hillbilly town.

It was his punishment, to be sure. You didn't lip off to the Almighty Maxfield without paying penance. Still, it had almost been worth it to see the look on the City Editor's face when Jack told him he had his head so far up his own ass he couldn't see the forest for the bullshit. Notwithstanding the mixed metaphors, the zinger had been absolutely on target, within the context of their argument. Maxfield had wasted no time in placing him on temporary assignment to the Features Department, which meant Jack was the ditsy Feature Editor's flunky until further notice. Hence his assignment to cover this Southern-fried Bigfoot story in Babylon, Georgia. It was sure to be 100% unadulterated tabloid crap. Junk-food journalism, guaranteed to clog your brain's arteries and make you into a flabby-thinking fathead.

"Alas, Babylon," said Jack. Population: 3,133—give or take a hick or two. A rock-quarry town nestled in the rustic bosom of the North Georgia hills, Babylon was a prime exporter of marble for tombstones and monuments all over the Southeast. Beyond that, it was little more than a hillbilly hamlet for descendents of moonshiners and semi-literates.

"Payback is hell," howled Jack, tossing the smoldering butt of his last cigarette out the window of his elderly Honda Civic as he pulled up in front of Tudrow's General Store. He stepped out of the car with the intention of buying a fresh pack of smokes from a local merchant, but was stopped short by a lady cop. A meter maid, he presumed.

"Sir," said the shapely woman in a tailored khaki uniform, "I have to ask you to retrieve your cigarette butt. You're in violation of City Ordinance one-two-five."

Jack stopped with one foot on the sidewalk in front of the general store. "One-two-five, is it?" he echoed, turning. "How careless of me. But never fear. Butt-retrieval is my specialty."

The female officer put her hands on her hips and regarded him coolly. Jack saw that she was packing a serious sidearm on her right hip—not the kind of hardware a mere meter maid would be wearing. He bent down, picked up the still-smoking butt, fieldstripped it and stuck the filter in his pocket. "There," he said, dusting off his hands. "Full compliance with the law. Thank you very much."

"No, sir, not quite," she said. "When you shouted profanity from your car, you violated Ordinance one-zero-six. I'm afraid I'll have to cite you for that. You picked up your butt, but there's no way you can call back your curse word."

"Jesus Christ," he muttered. "You're kidding, right?"

"Sir, your blasphemy is technically a form of profanity. You're just making it worse for yourself."

"No, I was praying, not profaning. As in, 'Jesus Christ, have mercy on this wretched sinner. Amen.'" He punctuated this comment with a wounded grin.

The policewoman removed her hands from her hips and folded her arms across her chest, covering the badge she wore on the upper slope of her bosom. "I advise you not to mock me, sir," she said.

"All right," he said, dropping the ineffectual grin. "Write me up, if you must. I'll just wrangle the fine into my expense account and have the paper pay for it."

She was pulling her citation notebook from her pocket when she suddenly froze and said, "The paper?"

"*The Atlanta Gazette.* Maybe you've heard of it."

"You're a reporter?" Was that a spark of interest Jack saw in her powder-blue eyes?

"Yes ma'am. Jack Talley, reporter-at-large." He offered his hand; she accepted it and gave it a firm shake. "I'm here to do a story on your Kudzu Man."

"Oh."

With his experienced eye, Jack read uncertainty in the flicker in her eyes and in the twitch of the muscles of her jaw. "When we're through with this citation business, I'd like to ask you a few questions about the local bogeyman."

"I have no official comment on that," she responded—a little too quickly.

"No? Then how about *unofficially*? As a private citizen, not as an officer of the law." Now it was Jack's turn to pull out *his* notebook. Maybe she would forget about writing him a ticket.

"It's a hoax," she said. "Somebody's idea of a joke. Then the rumors kicked into high gear and Babylon's weekly newspaper picked up the story because it fits right in with their gossip page. Then the TV people showed up and turned it into a circus. And now here you are. On a wild-goose chase."

Jack smiled as he jotted down her comments in his self-styled shorthand. Then he said, "You're probably right. But if some intrepid reporter actually *caught* the wild goose, that would be big news indeed. The goose in this case being either the Kudzu Man himself or the perpetrator of the hoax."

"I'll bet you hunted snipe as a boy," she said with a hint of a smile.

"Yes, I did, as a matter of fact. And I caught one. His name was Joe Morgan and he lived to regret trying to get me lost in the woods."

She actually laughed, and Jack decided he could stop worrying about getting a citation for public profanity. "You not wearing a nametag and I need your name for the quote," he told her.

"My name's Eve Arthur, but you can't use it. You'll have to attribute my quote to an anonymous source. Babylon's a very small town and I don't need any new enemies."

"No problem. Well, thank you, Miss Arthur. I appreciate your comments." Jack put away his notebook and started for the entrance of the general store.

"Hold up, Mr. Talley."

"Yes?" He turned to see her tearing a pink sheet from her little book.

"Here's your citation." She stuck it in his hand and said, "Have a nice day."

*   *   *

Jack took the crumpled ticket from his coat pocket, smoothed it out on the bar next to his glass of vodka and scanned it, noting that the citation didn't even have his home address or driver's license number. It did have his Honda's plate number, and he supposed that would be sufficient for the Babylon Police to track him back to his lair if he didn't pay the fine. He chuckled as he touched the flame of his Zippo to the ticket and set it to burn in the ashtray, imagining Officer Eve Arthur at his door, wearing a gun belt and nothing else.

"Hey! What the hell are you doing?" The bartender with a handlebar mustache glowered at him.

"Sorry," Jack muttered, fanning the smoke. "Accident."

Jack lit another cigarette and said, "Seems that the Kudzu Man has put Babylon on the map, what with all the media attention."

The barkeep scowled. "Made us a laughingstock is what it did. Asa Tudrow shoulda kept his stupid mouth shut."

"What? You mean you don't believe it?" Jack goaded him.

"Tell you what I believe, pal. Something's slaughtering animals around here, but it sure as hell ain't no walking kudzu boogeyman. Ain't no such critter."

Two stools down, a bald man with an egg-shaped physique said, "Tudrow ain't the only one seen it. Old Lady Leatherwood seen it creeping round her chicken coop."

"That old biddy's six crows short of a murder, Bob," the barkeep shot back. "Don't tell me you believe this bullshit, too."

"I'm just saying . . ." said Bob, scratching his potbelly.

"So what do you think's killing the animals?" Jack gave the barkeep a conspiratorial wink. "If it's not the Kudzu Man."

"Oh, it's a man all right. A big man, judging by the size of the footprints they found. A man strong enough to take on a Doberman and rip it apart."

"Have to be Superman to do that," offered soft-boiled Bob. "And anyway, them footprints weren't no man's, according to Chief Wallace."

"Don't pay him no mind," said the man behind the bar. "Bob here starts running off at the mouth when he gets a few drinks under his belt."

"But why would a man go on a dog-killing spree?" Jack queried, keeping the ball in play.

"Not just dogs," Bob interjected. "He killed Martha Scoggins' goat, and—"

"Because whoever he is, he's one sick son-of-a-bitch," the bartender said, carefully twisting the waxed tip of his mustache.

"Maybe it's a man dressed up in some sort of kudzu costume," Jack suggested. "Or maybe it's the Deep South version of England's Green Man." He was beginning to enjoy the barroom banter. He pulled out his notebook and jotted down a few notes.

"You a reporter or something?" asked the barkeep, eyeing him with suspicion.

"Something like that," he said. "Jack Talley, *The Atlanta Gazette.*"

"You should've said so," said the barkeep. "I don't talk to big city muckrakers." He turned his back and started polishing glasses.

Undaunted, Jack spun on his stool to face Bob. "What about you, Bob? You think it's some kind of monster?"

"Well . . . it could be something like a Bigfoot. Folks say there ain't no such thing, but I seen the video on TV. It looked real enough to me. Why couldn't the Kudzu Man be a Bigfoot wearing, like, kudzu vines?"

"Why, indeed," said Jack, snapping his notebook shut and sticking his pen in his pocket.

"You gonna use that in the paper?" asked Bob, who was beginning to look more and more like Humpty-Dumpty perched precariously on his stool, inches away from a great drunken fall.

"I just might. It makes as much sense as anything I've heard today."

With a decent buzz-on now, Jack paid his bar tab, left The Huntsman's Bar, and went back to his room in the Babylon Hotel. According to the sepia-toned brochure on the writing table opposite the bed, the "Historic" Babylon Hotel had provided lodgings for such luminaries as FDR, Jimmy Carter and Dolly Parton. Soaking up the musty ambience of the room, Jack decided there was a fine line between *historic* and *seedy*.

He sat on the edge of the table, picked up the phone and punched a number he knew by heart. His ex-wife answered on the third ring. "Hello, Ruth. It's me," he said.

"Christ, Jack, now what?" Was she actually hissing at him, or was it simply a bad connection?

"Just wanted to let you know where I am, in case, you know, you needed to reach me."

"Why would I need to reach you?" She *was* hissing at him.

"If something happened. You know. To Alison."

"Allison's fine, Jack. She's not your baby girl anymore, for Christ's sake. She's an adult."

"I know, I know," he said, wiping at the wetness in the corner of his eye. "Anyway, I'm at the Babylon Hotel in Babylon, Georgia. That little mountain village we drove through on our way to Gatlinburg that time?"

"Okay. You're in Babylon. I'm sure you slouched all the way there. Now please don't call me again, Jack. You know it upsets Ronnie."

Jack tried to laugh, but it came out as a strangled cough. "I miss those off-center literary allusions of yours, Ruth. I believe it's slouching toward Bethlehem, not Babylon."

"Whatever. Goodbye, Jack."

He cradled the receiver and stared at it for a long moment. He was seeing Ruth snuggling up to her new husband, reassuring him that her drunken ex meant nothing to her, reaching her long-fingered hand between his loins . . .

Pushing the painful image from his mind, Jack got up, opened his suitcase and found his background notes on kudzu. He flopped on the bed and read over the photocopied page.

Pueraria lobata of *the Leguminosae* family, the kudzu plant was introduced to the U.S. in 1876. Native to China and Japan, kudzu was used in the U.S. as a source of forage for livestock and as a means of controlling soil erosion. Over the years, however, the viny perennial spread its grasping runners everywhere, overrunning forests, drainage ditches, and climbing and covering anything in its path—including telephone poles. Now most farmers and foresters consider it a nuisance weed and employ herbicides to control its growth.

Jack had always rather liked the look of kudzu. Dead trees covered in kudzu reminded him of giant leaf sculptures and surreal hedge animals. Nature's artwork with a misty, Oriental quality. As he saw it, kudzu was as much a part of the South as red clay, cotton fields and magnolia trees.

But this Kudzu Man crap was not something an old-school reporter like Jack should be wasting his time on. A hard-drinking news hawk like himself should be covering the nitty-gritty down-and-dirty world of city politics and scandals, not this asinine Southern Boogie Bigfoot bullshit.

Who am I kidding? If I were less a booze hound and more a news hound, maybe I'd still have Ruth. And I damn sure wouldn't be here in Boobylon chasing down the particulars of this stupid rural legend. Next time Maxfield yanks my chain, I'll bite my fucking tongue.

He smoked one last cigarette, then tucked himself in with the comforter pulled up to his chin. He woke from a bad dream at three-thirty in the morning with a pounding headache and sheets soggy from a bad case of alcohol sweats. He couldn't get back to sleep, so he watched an old Clint Eastwood movie on cable. At dawn he took a shower, turning the water as hot as he could stand it.

After a few bites of cereal that tasted like cardboard and several cups of black coffee in the hotel's cafe, he read the morning edition of *The Atlanta Gazette*, and then he went to the local barbershop to get his ears raised and to hear what some of the local yokels were saying about the Kudzu Man. A barbershop was usually a good place for putting your finger on the pulse of the small-town public, but this morning the conversation was stuck in the well-worn groove of politics, sports and weather. When it was Jack's turn in the barber's chair, he broached the subject of the local legend. "What's all this stuff about the Kudzu Man?" he asked the cadaverous barber who smelled of talc and stale cigar smoke.

"You writing a book?" quipped the barber. "Then leave that chapter out."

Jack faked a laugh at the joke that was older than he was. "But seriously," he persisted. "Is there anything to it?"

"Humph. Nothing but the stink of it," replied the barber.

"Amen to that," said a waiting customer who spat something disgusting into the spittoon near his boots.

"Hell, if we believed it, don't you think we'd all be out there hunting the sumbitch down?"

"I'd already have the critter tied across the hood of my Jeep."

"Horseshit, Billy Ray, the only thing you ever had tied on your Jeep was a Christmas tree. And it fell off in the middle of the street."

After another round of bad jokes and hollow laughter, Jack paid ten bucks for a haircut he hadn't really needed, then drove three miles to Shiner's Ridge to interview the old woman who claimed to have seen the creature skulking around her chicken coop.

Elvira Leatherwood was sitting on the front porch of the old farmhouse in a sturdy ladder-back cane rocking chair. A row of garden tools leaned against the front of the house, and a chain saw and a gasoline can sat by the front door. She regarded him warily as he got out of his car and walked toward her. A dozen wind chimes tinkled in a stiff, mountain breeze.

"Good morning, Miz Leatherwood," he said, smiling to himself as he imagined the old woman wielding the chain saw. "I'm Jack Talley, from *The Atlanta Gazette*. I—"

"I wondered when you'd show up," she said, setting aside her knitting.

"Really."

She stared at him through her bifocals until he had to look away in discomfort. Her eyes, the same color as her iron-gray hair, were piercing, and Jack got the eerie feeling that she could see straight into his dark heart.

"Your face come to me in a dream," she said. "It showed me your weird."

"My what?"

"Your weird. Your fate."

Great, he thought. The old woman is nuts. I can't even get a humorous piece out of this without offending the mentally ill.

"No, I'm not crazy, young man. And you'll not mock me neither."

"No ma'am, I wouldn't do that. I just—"

"You want to see him," she said.

"The Kudzu Man? Sure, I would love to see him. But—"

"Be here tonight, after dark. You'll see for yourself. Then you'll know what's the truth." She picked up her knitting again, and Jack knew he had been dismissed. His reporter's instinct told him he should toss her some hardball questions now, but something in the old woman's manner put him off, and he slunk away, feeling inexplicably like a scolded puppy.

He *would* come back after dark. After all, it was his *weird*.

*   *   *

Back in Babylon, he returned to Tudrow's General Store to interview Asa Tudrow, the only other person in town who claimed to have seen the elusive Kudzu Man. Tudrow was a timorous man in his sixties who didn't seem to relish the attention of a reporter. He wore a starched white shirt, dark blue trousers and a red necktie with matching red suspenders. When he answered Jack's questions, he avoided making eye contact, looking off to the side as if talking to someone behind and to the left of Jack. Jack found it unnerving, and kept looking over his shoulder to make sure nobody had crept up behind him.

"So you've actually seen it twice," said Jack, pen poised over his notebook.

"Yes, sir, that's a fact."

"Once in your garden, and once down by the lake. What was the name of that lake again?"

"We just call it Dewey's Lake, on account of it being on Dewey Logan's land. 'Course, Dewey's dead now. But we still call it Dewey's Lake, don't you know."

"Describe what you saw. Tell me everything you can remember about it."

"Well, it was big, covered in leaves. Over six feet tall, I'd have to say. Walked on two legs, just like a man, but sorta hunched over, and it had vines tailing off behind it, dragging on the ground."

"Kudzu vines."

"That's right."

"Did you get a good look at its face?"

"Not too good, no sir. I saw its eyes, though. They were brown, like shiny wood. It looked right at me. And when it opened its mouth, I could see wooden teeth, like fangs."

"So it actually bared its teeth at you. Did it make any sound? Like a growl?"

"Not so's I could hear. But I knew it was . . . warning me. To keep my distance."

"You felt it was threatening you?"

"I reckon you could say that. Then it sort of loped off into the thick woods by the lake. When I saw it the next day in my garden, I didn't get such a good look at it, but I knew what it was. I think it followed me from the lake."

"Why would it follow you?"

"I don't rightly know." Tudrow scratched his balding head. "I just think it did."

"Is there anything else you remember about it that you haven't told me?"

"Just the smell. Like swampland in rainy season. Like ditch water, only stronger. And that other smell. Like rancid meat."

Jack tapped his pen lightly on the counter. "Tell me, Mr. Tudrow, do you think it could've been a man wearing some kind of costume?"

"Weren't no man in a monster suit. That stuff was growing out of him. It was the real thing. It was the Kudzu Man, sure as I'm standing here."

All in all, Jack found Asa Tudrow, in his own backwoodsy way, to be a surprisingly credible witness. He went back to his hotel room and called P. D. Bishop, the Features Editor, to tell her that he was closing in on the Kudzu Man and that he would be staying one more night in Babylon. She asked what he meant by "closing in." Having his fun with her, he said, "I've got a date with the Vine Man, Pee Dee. This witchy old hill woman is going to introduce us."

"Get photos," she blurted. "You do have a camera, right?"

"Natch," said Jack, wondering if the ditsy chick actually believed there would be something to take photos of, other than crazy old Miz Leatherwood. Yeah, she probably did. "You know, Pee Dee, I'm enjoying this Features work. It's like a little vacation. Maybe I'll get myself permanently assigned to your department."

"Just don't screw this up, Jack. I know you think this is nothing but hokum, but our readers love this stuff."

"I'm doing the job," he said, feigning indignation. "Just promise me one thing. If I'm eaten alive by the Kudzu Man, I want you personally to write me a heroic obituary. 'Reporter Makes Ultimate Sacrifice For Big Story.' That sort of thing."

"Fuck you, Jack," she said, then hung up.

Jack laughed out loud. Maybe Pee Dee wasn't as bubbleheaded as he'd thought.

*   *   *

He spent the early part of the afternoon trying to track down Kirby Wallace, Babylon's police chief. Thanks to a tip from Officer Eve Arthur, he eventually found Wallace in the local taxidermist's little shop of wildlife horrors. The taxidermist was putting glass eyes into the sockets of the chief's dead dog, an Irish Setter. "Old Mick was a good dog," Wallace explained. "He was like one of the family. Now he's gonna spend the rest of his days by the fireplace in my den. I just couldn't bring myself to bury him."

"Very touching, Chief," Jack said, looking at the stuffed dog sitting obediently on its wooden stand. "He's a beautiful animal. Listen, I was wondering if you could tell me about the footprints you found. Of the alleged Kudzu Man."

"Not much to tell," Wallace told him. "The prints were indeterminate. Meaning I don't know what the hell made 'em."

"Meaning they weren't made by man?"

"I didn't say that. They coulda been made by a man with a bunch of vines wrapped around his big feet. That'd be my best guess. Sure as hell weren't made by no Kudzu Sasquatch. Ain't no such thing. But then you already know that. You and them other reporters come here to make fun of us country folk. Well, go ahead, have your fun. Like my old granny used to say, the ones trying to make fools of others is the biggest fools of all."

Jack whipped out his notebook and jotted down that wonderful aphorism. "I like that," he said. "You don't mind if I quote you, do you?"

"I hope you do. Probably be the only piece of truth in that fish-wrapper you call a newspaper."

Jack turned to the taxidermist. "How about you, sir? You obviously know a thing or two about wildlife. What do you think about this Kudzu Man business?"

The bony man looked up from his work on Old Mick, his angular face splitting with a sly smile. "There are more things under Heaven and Earth than are dreamt of in your philosophy."

"No doubt," said Jack, snapping his notebook shut. "And all the world's a stage, yada-yada. Thank you, gentlemen. Have a good one."

He went to the Huntsman's Club for a couple of drinks, then returned to his hotel room and called his daughter's dorm on the campus of The University of Georgia, but she wasn't there. For reasons he didn't understand, it had suddenly become important to contact Alison, to hear her young voice, and it bothered him that he couldn't reach her. "Getting sentimental in your old age," he said to himself as he hung up the phone. Maybe he could catch her later, after his rendezvous with the Kudzu Man. He stretched out on the bed, turned on the TV and dozed off while watching the Braves whack the Dodgers.

When he awoke, he experienced a wrenching moment of extreme disorientation; he was unsure of where he was or whether it was night or day. Groggy with sleep, he sat up and rubbed his face with his hands, and the gone-to-seed hotel room came into sharp focus. The clock radio told him it was 7:45 PM. His accumulated sleep deficit had caught up with him and exacted its toll. He splashed cold water on his face in the bathroom, then went down to the hotel cafe for coffee and a slice of apple pie—not exactly a nutritious meal, but since his split with Ruth he had developed the habit of eating (and drinking) what he wanted, when he wanted it, health consequences be damned.

At eight-thirty he drove up the side of the mountain to Shiner's Ridge. Armed with a loaded 35mm camera, he knocked on Elvira Leatherwood's door. The old woman greeted him with pained grimace. "Didn't think you was coming."

"I wouldn't miss it for the world," he said. He refrained from making a sarcastic comment about her earlier allusion to her psychic ability.

She saw the camera in his hand and scowled, but didn't say a word about it.

"Well, it's almost dark," said Jack. "Let's go meet the Kudzu Man."

She stepped aside, holding the screen door for him. "Come on in. He's here."

"Here? You mean he's in your house?" Jack almost laughed aloud at the prospect. Surely this was a joke. Or was the old biddy as crazy as an outhouse mouse? He stepped inside. The olfactory bouquet of cloying perfume, mildew and boiled collard greens nearly sickened him.

"That's right. In the back bedroom." She pointed a bony finger at a door at the end of the dim hallway.

Jack's feet were suddenly rooted to the floor. His legs felt so heavy he didn't know if he could make himself walk down that long hallway to the unopened door.

"What's wrong? You ain't scared, are you? Big city reporter like you?"

"No," he lied. "I'm just . . . surprised. I didn't expect you'd have the bogeyman as a houseguest. Will he be staying for supper?"

She made a spitting sound with her wrinkled mouth to signal her disgust. "He's sick. Deathly ill. See for yourself." She urged him down the hallway. Jack steeled himself as best he could, then moved in that direction. Sweat beaded on his forehead and trickled down his armpit. The air was very close, almost suffocating. The hallway seemed to lengthen as he traversed it, and he had the sense of being trapped in a funhouse from his childhood, a boy too terrified to even wonder why they called them funhouses. At the foot of the door a thin line of jaundiced light leaked from the shuttered room.

The Leatherwood woman strode ahead of him on spindly blue-veined legs, clutched the antiquated glass doorknob in her gnarled fingers and opened the door. The stench hit Jack like a punch in the face. It was the smell of gangrenous flesh and rotting mulch from a forest floor. Standing at the threshold of the room, Jack tightened his grip on the camera, but he had no thought of raising it to his eye and snapping pictures. All he could do was stare uncomprehendingly at the thing lying on the old four-poster bed.

"You see?" The old woman's voice sliced through the thick silence of the austere room.

Jack saw. But he wasn't sure what he was seeing. He saw a man-shaped thing wrapped in green leaves and fringed with leafy vines, as if kudzu runners had come upon a human corpse and bound it up the way a spider binds its trapped prey, but this wasn't a corpse; this was a living, breathing thing. And the thing opened its eyes.

"My God," Jack said as he took a step closer to the bed. "What *is* that?"

"That's my grandson. Cletis," Mrs. Leatherwood answered offhandedly.

"What . . . how can this be?"

"He dug up somethin' shoulda stayed buried," she said, moving to the foot of the bed and resting a hand on a bedpost.

Jack looked closer at "Cletis" and saw in the gaps between the leaves that the vegetation was rooted in raw, oozing flesh. Bile rose in his throat. "You should get him to a hospital," he said.

"They can't do nothing for him," she said. "He wants to die, but it won't let him."

The thing opened its mouth and emitted a rasping groan over brown teeth. It was the most mournful sound Jack had ever heard.

"He's trying to tell you something," she explained. "Lean close so you can hear."

Reluctantly, Jack moved to the edge of the bed and bent over the pitiful creature. Its claw-like hand seized Jack's wrist, and needles of pain bit into his flesh. Dropping his camera, he snatched his arm away, and saw blood trickling from three tiny puncture wounds on his wrist. "What the hell did you do that for?"

Mrs. Leatherwood took Jack's forearm in her hands and looked closely at his injuries. Then she nodded her head. "It's in you now. See them little splinters?"

"Jesus Christ, what—"

"I'm dreadful sorry, young man, but there weren't no other way. Now that it's passed on its seed, it can let him go, and Cletis can finally rest in peace."

"What the hell are you saying?" Jack balled up his fists. He wanted very badly to cold-cock the old bitch.

"You should get your affairs in order," she said softly. "You don't have long now before it takes root and shoots out. Two days, most likely. It comes on real quick, then you turn."

"Turn! Into . . . *that*?" He pointed at the thing on the bed.

"Of all the outsiders that came chasing the story, you was the likeliest one. The one with the least to lose. You'd already lost what was important to you. I saw that when I looked into your heart. You have your own self to blame for that."

"You're out of your fucking mind!"

"Funny thing is, if Cletis hadn't always been deathly afraid of dogs, then he wouldn't have killed all them hounds nor got a taste for warm blood and there wouldn't have been no news story to bring you to us."

Near panic, Jack tried to dig one of the splinters out of his wrist with his blunted fingernails. An earthy taste surged into his mouth, making him gag. Beneath the skin of his infested arm, he felt his flesh crawling.

"That won't do you no good," she told him. "The more you dig at 'em, the deeper they burrow into you. There ain't nothing you can do to stop it now. It's your weird."

"The hell it is!" he roared. "I make my own destiny!"

She shook her head and made a clucking sound.

Knowing now what he had to do, Jack pushed the old lady aside, ran through the house to the front porch and snatched up the chain saw. The wind chimes clanked and tinkled wildly in turbulent winds.

The chain saw sputtered to life with the first pull.

Jack shut his eyes and fed his wrist to the whirling mechanical teeth.

MANCHINE

I don't remember dying.

The last thing I remember I was walking the hallowed halls of higher learning, making my way to the crowded classroom where I daily endeavored to teach World Lit to muzzy-headed students who cared more for their cell phones than for sonnets. Then gunfire erupted in front of me and a young man in sun glasses and a hooded parka sauntered toward me, shooting anyone who happened to cross his path. A most pleasant smile he had on his face as he raised his pistol and shot Judy Deakins, professor of Economics and mother of three. The back of Judy's head came off and flew at me with a comet's tail of blood. A piece of her skull struck me in the chest, bloodied my shirt and power tie. The young man with the gun turned his head toward me and I saw my two faces in the twin mirrors of his shades. His gun came up and my eyes were sucked down to the dark hole of his pistol's muzzle. Looking into that universe of spiraled darkness was my last act as a living being, and it's the last thing I remember of my nasty, brutish and short life.

For the moment—as moments "exist" for the dead—I remember a great many details of my life on Earth, but I won't burden you with those. What I'm setting down here is my necrography—not my life story but my death story, thus far. But for the recent advances in microchipery and the advent of the GreatNet, I wouldn't be able to tell it at all, short of ouija boards and table rapping. Thanks to the demigods of cyberrealm, I'm able for a time to be the ghost in this machine, making dead lines by sheer want and will of the soul.

My lovely killer took me down with a headshot; how else to explain my sudden end? I never even heard the bang. I was standing there staring into the darkhole deathspiral, then I was nowhere, lost in blackness deeper than any in sleep, untethered in the space between inhale and ex—

Mean Old Transmigration Blues, talking blues, bluefunk dues out on the highway to hell and gone, lowway to Elysium and all points in between, blue highways, black death, veins pumping their last back in the harrowed halls, Valhalla-bound for Glory or ground for the bowery of heaven's sub-cellar, bowery bums bowdlerized by guardians of taste and on-high style, laid low by archangel's fiery rapier, sliced, diced and deloused, the singed soul at least cleaned up if not sanctified. Cosmic madness in the method. Methodist Mugged By Heavenly Host. God's Dog Dogged By Dogma In Life, Doomed To Doggerel In Death's Dolorous Dominion. Talking Dharma Bum Blues, eh, Jack? lowdown and nasty . . .

Mystery my mistress now. I digress:

The great mystery of life, to me, was why the male member must sponge up to uncomfortable size for the nightmind to set sail on the dream mare. Try explaining to a woman that your erection had nothing to do with the content of your dream.

—Having sex dreams again, eh? she would say.

—No, dear, it was a sexless nightmare.

—Then why were you hard up?

—Dunno. Just was.

The way it works. Stiff ticket to dreamland. No admittance without a stiff ticket. Inflate the old inner tube and float on the sea of dreams. Turgid, tumescent, tumid, swollen-near-to-bursting with blood, riding the tumultuous waves, surfboard bone, boneless meat tender-tough, roughcut and rowdy but hardly randy. They say hanged men sprout boners, and you know they aren't thinking of the beast with two backs. Perhaps they're dreaming their last at death's doorway, plumbing the depths of the soul's dark demesne as they near the nightmare/deathmare nexus. Erecting dreams out of soft tissue, ethereally rising up to prick the ether and pierce heaven's heart. Mystery of mysteries: myth-muscled monster moored to the moon, mossbacks and mountebanks alike, mirroring the masqueraders' matrix and tempting the immortal muse.

Perhaps the ancient ithyphallic statue of everhard Priapus and the pagan worship of the phallus itself might be explained by the myth-dream-erection connection. Christ Himself came late to the pagan party as a phallic god with the Holy Prepuces guaranteed to make women conceive; those fore-skins enshrined at the Abbey Church in Chartres generated thousands of miraculous births, they say, and one saint went so far as to claim that Jesus bound her as His bride by using His foreskin as wedding ring. Add to that the fact that early Christians hid stone phalli in their church altars, and you have a fairly accurate picture of religion's fascination with the phallus (fascinum being Latin for erect penis) and it doesn't take too great a leap of logic to land in the Phallic Land of Fascination and Fantasy, the male's dream-hard legacy of spiritual physiology. Unless of course I've come down in fallacy, in which case I beg your patience. Forgive if you will any ensuing phallacies. My musings along these hard-by lines may be little more than a dead man's penis envy . . .

. . . and a momentary distraction from the mistress who takes me unto her dark waters and into the churning backwash of remembered moments strung together like bones wired each to the other so the skeleton may dance and rattleclackclack all the lovelong night or day as bones are wont to do if they are of a mind and a will apart from the world's willingness to move forward in illusory time, dancing to the beat of the exalted one who calls the tune, imprinted melodies that stick in the craw, remembered by bizarre association, coddled like babes given suck, but down there in the muck and mire is where I no longer am, being dead and privy to secret senses unknown to the living. Snatches of careworn words from the funeral-goers lips find their way to my occult antennae:

—Odd sort.

—Oh, he had big plans, they just never panned out. Them as can't do, teaches, don't ya know.

—Dabbled with powers of darkness, I heard.

—Nonsense . . .

No sense really in knocking about here when here is so very there and very much down; the living have little choice in the matter. They move from place to place with solemn purpose and a sense of self-importance, never arriving, always pushing off, careening madly from one drama to the next, looking back and losing the way they thought they had at last found, sad foundlings taken in, nourished, fortified with a semblance of love, then cast out again, adrift, at sea, sailing round the horn, round and round they go, hither and yon, till they're bald as billiard balls and swaddled in diapers in the Old Folks' Home, waiting to die, awaiting deliverance to the Promised Land or at the least an end to their suffering. They say that when you die your dead relatives are there to greet you and take you once again to the dead bosom of familial bliss, that shriveled pap from whence the bloodmilk of human compassion must flow. Thank the gods that was not my fate, for what family isn't cursed with a thousand little cruelties and wicked digs in the flesh dispensed in the name of love, or with self-fulfilling prophesies of doom, legacies of despair, failure hidden in every proud success. I'll have none of it, thank you very much. Don't bother to write; where I am the post office doesn't deliver, come Hell or high water or whatever. No check in the mail, no official notification, no You're already a winner, because there are no winners here in this ethereal locus between line and shadow, off and on, pain and pleasure, knowing and unknowing. The soul doesn't move in linear fashion. You don't go from place to place or moment to moment because there are no moments, no places, and if you should see God you probably wouldn't recognize Him/It/Her anyway because you will be blinded by the immensity of everything happening all at once, history and future folding and unfolding before and after your soul's secret eyes, eyes multifaceted with sensory organs evolution never dreamt of, never leapt to, your old body down there in the box, little more than a quaint relic now, if now even exists. They're moving it, see? Loading the box into the hearse, mourners dabbing eyes, blowing noses, clasping hands. Talking in whispers as though they're afraid of waking the dead. Don't worry. No sleep for the dead. I'm awake! And caught in my wake they march to the cemetery, cake-walkers moving mournfully amid stones and markers, watched over by guardians of sculpted stone and marble, fierce angels and fat cherubs, Mother of God in need of a good scrubbing, weathered to a sad fair-thee-well, no longer immaculate but pretty just the same. Hail, Mary! Hail and farewell. Another hale fellow well met, then kissed off the planet, and more's the pity. No, not really. Pity doesn't append (useless appendage if it did). Planets are just rounded places, blobs of space debris trapped in random orbit, some infested with life, some life invested with abstract thought and self-awareness, cursed you might say, and fearing death, but take it from me, death is nothing to fear. Death is nothing. No thing. Life is some thing. The things we are. Things that cry. Bleeding objects.

Caution: Objects may appear more solid than they really are. When you're dead you can go to your own funeral and see the circus. The prayers, the tears, the pain, the spectacle of the last rites—it makes you want to scream: Stop your blubbering! (cold and heartless of me, but I am dead). I'm right here and here is fine while it's here. But soon enough I'll be elsewhere in that place that isn't a place, in a time out of time, where there is no where, no now, no then, no thing. I don't think I'll remember much then (no-then) and I may get a chance to start over again (begin?) in an embryonic shell, once more into the breech, brave lad, and then be squirted out in a new time and place, one more forlorn human toss-pot overwhelmed with possibilities and cursed with budding spiritual yearnings and a biological imperative to return to the womb and spawn offspring of my own, but for now I'm beyond all that, cast adrift once more, buoyed by divine magic and borne up by forces unseen, hovering above my hole in the ground, riding irresistible currents of a Stygian river without beginning . . .

Germans have a word for the space between things: zwischenraum. The realm of the dead is zwischenraum. We dead reside in the in-between, the null & Void, the great empty spaces in mind and matter. To us the living are hazy spirits, while we dead are starkly detailed in the rich hues of the soul, decked out in the colors between the colors of the spectrum. When you speak we hear a faint buzzing as from a fly trapped between the window glass and screen, and your footsteps fall as silently as the fly's. To the dead you are shades and shadows of that which we once were and may never be again. You are shallow, dimensionless creatures glimpsed from the corners of our soul's eyes, standing on the corner of Dead & Gone, waiting for the bus to the boneyard. Between the dead lines you may find us if you peel the blinders off your eyeballs. We roam the zwischenraum, rangers and rovers who don't, as a rule, say Boo! to you.

I find I'm partial to churchyards, feeling right at home amid the markers and stones. These places are rich in souls, fertile ground for growing melancholy flowers or sipping the Zeitgeist like vintage wine, imbibing the Weltschmerz like world-weary Nazis overseeing death camps. Gott im Himmel, those jerrys were good at stamping labels on things! Jerry-rigging the world to suit their operatic view, but deaf as old Beethoven to the cries of the world. Still and awe, I'm all a twitter and rosymarble cozy passing through these tombstone rows and townhouse mausoleums, necropolitan nightscapes under the midday sun, sad son of lost souls and random coupling, my spirit shaped by each life lived or touched to the heart, a soul apart, yet leaking into others and sucking up intimate essences at great personal risk. Ghost-nook necropolis my dark port of call. These sad shadelings alive and carrying our coffins to the grave, backs bent in mourning, these grim-faced bearers of pall, somber sorters all, deep in contemplation of their own mortality and thirsty for stop in the local pub, hardly able to wait till the first shovelful is tossed. Weltschmerz schmaltz is the fashion of the day. Maudlin mourners in monotone uniform, black as ravens' wings, their metaphorical feathers metaphysically ruffled by death's passing breeze. I'm quite at home here, nevertheless and less the never.

When I first died I hovered beneath the flickering fluorescent and looked down at my dead body bleeding its last on the checkerboard tile of the harrowed halls, unmindful of the mad melodrama still playing itself out down by the biology lab door: the gunman still going gangbusters, busting caps, as they say, and freeing more souls from their mortal coils, slinky springs no longer doing tricks on stairs for the amusement of spoiled children or cruel gods. Deliciously detached from that course world, I saw that I wasn't alone; Judy Deakins hovered nearby, taking it all in like a kid in a front-row seat at a Saturday matinee, a horror doublefeature, starring herself and yours truly unruly, pass the pop porn please. But it wasn't really a horror show, no; it was altogether wonderful to be so detached from the world left behind and below and in awe of the fact of our departing. But dear Judy was having none of it. She seemed appalled by the bloody spectacle and genuinely aggrieved by her murder. I wanted to reach out to her and tell her that it didn't matter now, that where we were there was no need to be distressed. Why didn't she see that? Didn't the same rules apply for both of us? I did try to touch her, to comfort her, but somehow I couldn't connect. She didn't seem to see me at all. What to make of this? A spiritual anomaly? Some apocryphal aberration? An oversight of God's? Or was it true that we create our own heaven or hell and that it's all in the mind/soul? Who knew? Not me. So with a soulful shrug, I got on with my death, leaving Judy D. in her dithering tizzy.

But our paths crossed again at the cemetery.

Her funeral procession followed mine by several solar declinations, a paltry few time-measured degrees after my interment in point of fact and in lieu of fiction. And there she was, her soulbody striking in its brazen sexuality—and there was the rub! Praise be to God. Sexlife in the afterlife? Could this be so? And I saw right away I would have to revise and extend my musing suppositions and amusing extrapolations concerning the afterlife. There were more dramas to be played, more strutting and fretting across the phantom stage, more bumping and grinding in phantasmagorical footlights. Hallelujah! You hobgoblins of boredom be gone! Shades get laid!

Judy came on like sinuous smoke, curling and twisting sensuously closer and I fairly crackled with something like electromagnetism, shooting off a jagged bolt like a Van de Graff generator discharging a stinging bolt of little lightning. The churchbell rang and changed our hue to rosypurpleindigo, hearing it as we did with our numinous molecules, resonating spheremusic ecstasy as our souls came together, intermingling coefficiently in numbers infinitely excited, united as only souls can be, sharing sums greater than the hole of old and soaring high above lowlife slug strata until we were sated among the stars, snuggled cozycomfort in a fiery bed of shared secrets, languidly longing to prolong our crackling bliss.

We disengaged, she softsailing away and I, priapic soulson of Aphrodite, sliding limply, limping along the blazing whore rising.

What I think I know: There are three species of soul:

1. Walkers are the deformed or incomplete spirits, earthbound vagabonds doomed to go on foot or belly while awaiting another shot at an unbungled life. They are the ghosts of hearthstories, vengeful, self-absorbed, still all-too human and living in illusion.

2. Floaters inhabit the middle distances of the in-between; they've glimpsed the light and touched the Void, but haven't learned to soar, either

lacking faith in their soular powers or remaining tied to the living, or both.

3. Soarers have learned to let themselves go and slip the bonds of the hierarchy, limited only by their imagination—for what can be imagined can be made real in the upper reaches of the vaulted realms. When you share your soul with another you soar together, two-gathered, cosmically orgasmic, showering divine light upon eternity for all the gods to see.

What I know I think: I think those voyeur gods are themselves illusory, as delineated in The Tibetan Book of the Dead. The planes of death are populated by demons spinning webs of illusion, eaters of dreams who imprison unwary souls. What is needed is a spirit guide to get one through the Bardo's storm of illusions and soul traps, triptrapping like trolls beneath the bridge over bloodied waters.

In search of a sign I ceased my soaring and drifted deep into the catacombs below the dark river, my rosypurple afterglow lamplighting my way. Here there be walkers reduced to stumpy knees, crawling in grottos, snuffling in the dirt for the spoor of boudoir grimoire and necromancing scribes who carve their cryptic script in living flesh. It's said that legends live in the catacombs. Mythical characters formed from dirt and clay and stone with river mud for blood come to life here in these demon-haunted grottos beneath the watercourse way. Hysterical histories tripdrip from poets of the black pen. Ozymandias in his pleasured doom bites heads off chicks, geekstreaked carny barking at Bysshe's bitch's monster while the 'eadless 'orseman forgets where he parked his 'orse. Po' Poe dead in a gutter by undersea sewers sloshing . . .

Odysseus never makes it home . . .

Entropy taking its toll in this dark entropical garden of grotesque grottos. Get my bearings straight. Damned eerie 'ere.

Black water from the riverrunning above drip plip plop plipping, building stellar stalagmites like dragon's teeth to keep the tanks from overrunning, heavy armor behemoths thunderrunning on bloodied tracks, blitz babies leaving brown skidmarks, pacing snails' slime trails. Catch the spoor. Foul wind. Shift of wit. Wiff of—

I made my way to the surface, leaving a trail of crumby molecules for the black crow sisters to follow. Came upon a sacred grove of skeletal trees filled with hanged men, ravens picking their eyes and making foul feast. Consulted the bloat-neck oracles. Read the tea leaves on their protruding tongues. One of them spoke: Get thee the hell gone.

Back to the black river banked by the boundaries of the in-between.

Back in my old abode where flakes of my dead skin feed microscopic mites, the cyberchine hums, taking down these transposed-from-beyond dead lines. Net-connected, Netted-up, nattering ninnies lost in the Nineties narfing it up like wisecrack junkies.

Eye dive into the tenebrous currents, shooting ebonyivory rapids, mooning the shoots, dumped humped and thumped by moonless waters. Eye for an I. I-balls swooshed out and bum sludged up with rivermuck, can this be the way it ends? On the river with no beginning/no end? Crooked watercourse way of the whimpering worlds in between . . . worlds apart again . . . begin without fins . . . web-footed floozie forwarded to the next worldless world . . . lines dead . . . busy signals . . . systems down . . . underground wellspring . . . stoppered up bum cork . . . eye core gored . . . deathrealm doozy . . . glut of grotto guts spilling . . . brainmatter spattered back on the hallowedhalls tile . . . blood mixed with chick's pix in crimescene photoplasma framed, blowing cork and crack in 6-D glasses, scammed crammed shammed shamed mainbrainframed message: Cyber dime dropped: This program has performed an illegal operation and will be shut down . . .

0 1 0 1 0

DEVILS

... And God hath chosen the weak things of the world, to confound the mighty things, And vile things of the world, and things which are despised, hath God chosen, and things which are not, to bring to nought things that are. That no flesh should rejoice in his presence.

Corinthians 18–31, Geneva Bible

The damned room. Where it all happened. Where it's still happening. The room that isn't really a room, but what exactly it is, Jeze just doesn't know. *That* room. Four walls or six or more, owing to the fertile darkness, volume of blood spilled and temper of the times. A *living* room, the beating heart of a phantom house. The damned room that haunts Jeze's waking life and gives her nightmares actual teeth and claws.

"Why does that place scare you so much?" Jeze's shrink always wants to know. Never satisfied with first answers, he prods for unsacred revelations.

Her answer is always the same: "Because when I die I'll be stuck haunting that place. Forever."

"In a sense, you're stuck there now, aren't you?"

Clever bastard. "Clever bastard," she says. Sometimes words come to her from back there in that room, back where the tree of death grows on roots exposed and sickly white like naked bodies. Where roots *are* naked bodies.

"Well, aren't you?" His teeth are white as maggots. His eyes dead as roadkill.

"No I'm not. It's for dead souls, not for me. Not yet."

"Talk about your creatures. What was it you called them?"

"Too dangerous. They don't like being probed."

"You're protecting me from them, then?"

She shrugs. "If you like."

"But you called them something. Descriptive."

"Check your notes. I'm sure it's there."

"Ah. Here it is."

"You're such a putz."

"'Dark guardians' you called them. But you never made clear what they guard."

"Because I can never be sure. If they're keeping me in check or keeping others out. I don't know *what else* they want with me. What they might have planned."

"I can help you figure that out. If you let me."

Saying nothing, she avoids looking into the doctor's dead eyes.

He goes on: "Or . . . you can keep your life and your career on hold, sit and spin, and get absolutely nowhere."

She feels herself going now, slipping off into shadow, gooseflesh aquiver, sliding into the desperation of self-mockery: *Be still my trip-hammer heart.*

*   *   *

Even before you got there, you knew it was going to be bad. But by then it was too late to turn back. So there you went, the almost-famous filmmaker /documentarian in hot pursuit of the bloody slice-of-darkside-life that would win essential funding and eventual respect of critics and art-house audiences everywhere. Working title: *Blood Cult.*

Tyler had warned you about these creepy people. The Lost City Luciferians. He told you you'd be nuts to go unescorted with them to a secret location to film their forbidden ceremony. But of course you had to do it. Just you and your handheld movie camera getting right up in reality's face. Rolling. Balls-out tits-atilt *rolling,* shooting for all you were worth. All the marbles. The whole shooting match and shebang. Shoot clichés and kill them dead.

When they put the bag over your head, you turned the camera on yourself and became part of the story. It was only later, when you were *in the room*, that you realized you *were* the story.

You had no inkling then that what you were looking for was God. But the moment you entered the room you knew you had stumbled undoubtedly into the realm of the Devil.

*   *   *

"Call me Ishmael." That was what the cadaverous cocksucker actually said, and you framed his horse face in warty close-up, while behind you, others were making preparations, laying out steel edges and ancient crucibles. You didn't stay on his emaciated face long. The massive black tree in the center of the room drew itself into the viewfinder. A tree you could only think of as *Biblical.* It towered over the room, its soaring upper black branches forming a cathedral-like ceiling for the otherwise ceiling-less room.

Though you couldn't see them, you had the sudden unmistakable impression that catlike creatures had draped themselves over favored branches and were waiting to make great springing leaps down onto these pitiful humans who had little idea of the deep evil they were toying with. You weren't equipped to see them either but you caught their dreadful scent and it nearly sickened you.

No, these things were not feline. There was *nothing* natural about these creatures.

An insistent thought insinuated itself: *demon tree.*

Then a porcine man wearing thick sideburns and a white jumpsuit showed up and assumed a ceremonious position with his back to the tree.

Fat Elvis, you thought and laughed inwardly. You zoomed in on his face and froze there as Fat Elvis curled his lips and began to chant in lisping southern-fried Latin. Ishmael appeared at his side and slipped a knife in his hammy fingers. "Thank you," said Fat Elvis, "very much."

Now a skinny woman with a smoked-leather face and big hair teased into hedgehog spikes glossy with a slick hairspray sheen sauntered in from stage right, dragging along a small white pregnant dog in a pink tutu on a jeweled leash.

Fat Elvis smiled at the woman (or maybe at the preggers little dog) and took command of the leash. Skinny Minny scowled and exited with an uneasy backward look at the gleaming knife.

The air grew thick and oily, and you could feel those lurking creatures wanting to rip and rend the darkish air to get at the juicy blood-packed meat sacks (the pitiful humans) for a grand feast at the foot of their evil tree.

*   *   *

"I seriously considered changing my name to Noira Dark and leaving the continent. Did I already tell you that, Doc? So those things would lose my spoor? You know: my scent, my trail, my droppings? Jeze Bellefleur becomes Noira Dark in the blink of an eye. You laugh but I did. Consider it. Not that it would've done any good. They were already on me like flies on shit, pardon my fucking French. No? Then white on rice. Black on boots. Any way you fucking slice it, I was stuck with those wicked bad things. If I'm making light it's only because it's all so dark and deadly serious. There's really no way to make light of cutting unborn babies out of a mother's belly—even if the mother is only a mongrel bitch. That sort of thing makes the demons hungry and pretty much guarantees that they'll be up your ass indefinitely. Or at least until the cows come home. Uh-oh, news flash: the cows aren't coming home because they're all in the slaughterhouse."

*   *   *

You didn't dare dream of turning away. You kept the camera's unbiased eye on the action and watched in sick fascination as Fat Elvis lifted the mutt by the scruff of its neck and sliced its belly open and six bloody little squirming sacs came sliding out and went splat on the ground at the foot of the tree. Malnourished Ishmael began speaking in tongues, his voice growing louder and louder until he clamped his teeth, clammed up and convulsed.

He foamed at the mouth and fell over like a hundred-pound bag of shit.

Zooming close-up of the canine abortions, moving within blood-slimed sacs.

Wide out to get fat boy's bloody white jumpsuit and expressionless face. You were trembling so hard you were afraid you'd ruin the shot.

And then the real horrorshow began.

*   *   *

Doctor Dead Eyes doesn't know it but you are shooting your therapy sessions. Cute little nanny cam hidden inside a teddy bear with a pink bow round its neck, sitting next to the few get-well cards and the plastic vase of flowers (no glass allowed on the psych ward). These therapy scenes might make a good companion piece to the unedited snuff footage in your safety deposit box, or a decent DVD extra feature if you end up releasing the hardcore shock-the-monkeys movie.

"And even though you knew the cultists were into sacrifice," he says, petting his beloved beard, "you went anyway. For the sake of your art. In a sense, you were making a personal sacrifice for your art."

"Well yeah. That's why I went. Because they were serious about blood sacrifice. Animal, not human, but my plan was to get good footage of an animal blooding and then push them to reveal how close they might be to actually doing a human. I was convinced that's the way they were heading. Why mess around with sacrifice if you aren't willing to go whole hog. Or *whole human*. Right?"

*   *   *

The membranous air rippled and the walls shifted, expanded. She swung the camera slowly left, purposely counting walls as she made a 360 sweep. *Five* walls now, each corner forming the point of an implied pentagram. And Skinny Minny Shiny Spikes was on her knees, shoveling the aborted pups one by one into her bloody maw, chewing them until their little bones crunched, then sucking off their juices, and finally spitting out the mutilated remains. She wiped blood from her mouth with the back of her hand like a seasoned drunkard, then licked her fingertips with her grotesquely smacking gob.

The tree's exposed roots writhed, or seemed to, for roots that big don't writhe—unless they're not really roots.

This was the moment when filmmaker/documentarian Jeze Bellefleur lost whatever psychic protection her role as detached photographer afforded her, the moment when fear became palpable, a thing gnawing at her insides and turning her mind cold with brain shivers. But she kept shooting, daunted though she was. Vulnerable to the max and scared shitless.

"God help us," she whispered. "Please God."

A subterranean whisper: *Feed the tree.*

Then something unseen ripped Skinny Minny's head off her shoulders. Red rain gusted against the camera lens, then quickly diminished to a thin drizzle.

Jeze's impulse was to wipe clean the lens but she let it ride. Let things run. Run down.

Fat Elvis looked like he'd just dropped a load in his pants, and his jowls jiggled as his jaw dropped toward his chest. All shook up and looking to book. Exit, stage right.

From somewhere outside the room that wasn't a room, Ishmael cried, "O Lord!"

*   *   *

"If I was Catholic, I would've joined a convent as soon as I figured out that the devils had followed me out of that room. I did spend a lot of time hiding out in random churches before I had to come here."

"And how did you figure out that they had followed you?"

"A talking dog told me. Black German shepherd, fucking Nazi-looking mutt with spiked collar. Don't get your panties in a twist and go thinking Son of Sam's talking-dog bullshit. Those devils can slip into animals and they seem partial to big dogs. That's just the way it is. I don't make the rules or make this shit up."

"And what did the dog say?"

"He said, 'We are with you.'"

"That's all?"

"No. I said, 'Are you shitting me?' More to myself than to the dog. And the son of a bitch answered: 'When we shit your soul you will have no doubt of it.'"

*   *   *

As the devils frosted her face with their breath, a Biblical line snaked through Jeze's head: *By the envy of the Devil, death came into the world.* Fat Elvis had tripped over a root and was now on his knees, beseeching the Lord to save him, please Jesus, but she didn't see how the Devil could possibly envy the likes of this blubbering tub-of-guts with comical muttonchops and greasy hair.

*   *   *

You have to be morally degraded to make a good nonfiction film. A good film document digs deep, pushes people—the subjects and audience—to the edge and then further to get at the terror throbbing at the center of every living thing. Like the time you were seventeen and shot your old man with your first real movie camera. Your first shot at a real doc. Docu-Dad. You sat him in a raggedy-ass folding lawn chair in front of the bleak cinderblock garage and made him do the one thing he never wanted to do. You made him talk about what he did in the war, particularly at a place the grunts called *Devil's Valley.* Before it was over, you'd reduced him to a trembling heap of bony meat and you had some fine gut-wrenching footage, a piece of unvarnished oral history of the Vietnam war, what he did to those fucking gooks and what they did to his buddies, to him. There's nothing better than war to bring out your inner demons. That was the hardcore truth of it. And you dug it out of the old man with the rusty knife of your ambition. How could he go on living after that clusterfuck of a war? "Well," he said, "sometimes you can feel God's presence by His absence." When it was done, you were so hyped that you went to your room and fingered yourself until you came like crazy, your delirious cries given cover by hard-rocking death metal banging out of your stereo.

To make a good documentary film, you have to be a coldhearted bitch. You develop a nose for that eternal terror at the center of things, at the very heart of life, and you'll go to any extreme to expose it and nail it to the wall, same as a hunter hangs the heads of his kills on his wall.

*   *   *

Fat Elvis got off his knees and shed his jumpsuit. His flesh was fish-belly white with warty hairs sprouting in odd places. His dick was the color and size of a boiled shrimp. He muttered prayer-like inanities until he took the first bite of his own flesh, canines and incisors ripping out a big bloody chunk. Then he hummed unmusically as he proceeded to partake of more of the fatty flesh on his right arm, forearm first, then the flabby upper arm, wincing with pain that must've been beyond excruciating, but he went right on feasting on himself, and Jeze knew that he had a devil inside him, driving him to do it. Devil in the driver's seat, burning up the road. His humming rose in pitch as he exposed bone, and it became shrill and unnerving as he gnawed his ulna. When he passed out from blood loss or shock or from overeating or all three, Jeze danced around his body, shooting the carnage from every angle, hoping that the devils would be pleased that she was taking such care in filming their savage handiwork. Then Fat Elvis stopped breathing with a final snorting death rattle. And she thought she glimpsed him hauling dead ass up Ghost Road.

Then she shot Skinny Minny's headless body. Quick photographic study. (Her head had simply disappeared, as if swallowed up by one of the disembodied demons.) Her neck resembled the stump of an unfortunate young tree, and Jeze wondered if trees had souls of a sort. Skinny Minny's pitiful remains made her wonder if humans could actually have anything as sublime and potentially exalted as a soul.

But then something happened that sent spectral fingers slipping into the bottomless depth of Jeze's terror: The gore and goo inside Skinny's neck stump began to move and squish like thick strawberry jam and Jeze realized that one of the devils was fucking the stump.

Before she could flee, they started on her. They didn't stop until they'd fucked her half dead.

"Have you given any more thought to what these things you call devils, demons and dark guardians might actually be? What they represent?"

She gives him a cold stare. Then: "They don't represent anything, unless you want to see them as representatives of Satan. I think they were there—are here—on their own damned dime. Whether they're fallen angels or demons created out of the fires of hell, I can't say. But sometimes I do think fondly of them as my Bad Angels, my evil guardians. And when they have their way with me, I come so hard I go back to that room with the demon tree and they're doing me again like they did the first time. I told you about that, right?"

"Yes, you did. In explicit detail."

"Talking about it like that makes it more real. When it actually happens it's so freaking bizarre it's unreal. But trust me, it's real. They fuck me in orifices I didn't even know I had and then when they're done with their sick fun, they leave me bleeding from most of them and yet wanting more. It's not your standard love/hate deal. It's more like a love/fear thing. They scare the shit out of me but I can't stop wanting them to *fuck* the shit out of me. That's why I know I need help. I know I'm sick. Sick in my soul. My only hope is that I sink so deep into sin and degradation that I find a low road to God. That could happen, right? A salvation road could open up in front of me? Jesus never turned his back on whores. No fucking way. He liked to hang out with them. *These* bad boys put the *evil* in d*evil*. But Jesus can save me if I can get his attention, right? Huh. I just had an insight, Doc. The only time I'm not scared out of my mind is when they're ravaging me or when they're slaughtering someone right in front of my eyes. It's the in-between times that terrify me and make me want to jump out of my skin. All that wicked anticipation, and I'm walking around with a mean hair-trigger and a come-button hard-on. It's enough to make a girl sex crazy with fear and wild for a devils gangbang."

"Have you considered talking with a clergyman?"

"Been there, done that. Big mistake. I still feel bad about what happened to that priest. The devils bent him over the altar and fucked him sideways and inside-out, literally tore him apart. Then they painted the big golden crucifix with the holy man's blood and shit. And me not even Catholic. Poor bastard. He's probably still in Purgatory, going, 'Jesus Christ, what the hell just happened?'"

She looks hard at him and sees that his dead eyes are already rotting. "I think we're done, Doc. You can discharge me. Today. Right now."

"You really think you're ready for that?" He tries to look concerned.

"We've gone as far as we can. There's no danger of your helping me. If you could, they would've already turned you into deviled ham. They *will not be exorcized*. No way. Not until Jesus comes. But talking to you has helped. I know what I need to do now."

"What?" Now he is genuinely interested, dead eyes reanimated.

"What I should've been doing all along. Whoring. And documenting the varieties of carnal sin. Turning tricks for slick dicks in my own flicks. In other words, I'll be killing time, the in-between times, while waiting for the devils to do me. Or for Jesus to save me, whichever comes first."

Doctor Dumbfounded drops his jaw.

Jeze laughs. "Hell, it's the perfect way to finance my film."

She leaves the hospital feeling only a tad disappointed that the devils didn't destroy her shrink. It would've made good teddy-bear cam footage but it also would've plopped her in the middle of a murder investigation and she has neither time nor energy for that sort of shit. She sees her future laid out before her, shining darkly, and deliciously terrifying.

*   *   *

Fuck Pad Confessions. This is what she decides to call her new film project. Jeze Bellefleur will transform herself with the surefootedness of a seasoned shape-shifter into Jezebel the whore for the sake of her art and her salvation. By giving herself body and soul to the devils of perdition, she will become a living flesh-and-blood prayer for redemption in Christ the Savior. But first, she must talk to whores. Interview them on camera and get them to reveal their tricks of the trade, as well as their wounded souls, for certainly you couldn't peddle your ass, your cunt, your moneymaker without doing everlasting damage to your soul.

And Jezebel's Bad Angels seem drawn to damaged goods and human debris.

*   *   *

She landed a low-rent Southside apartment, had a mirror installed on the ceiling over a brass bed she'd found on Craigslist, and researched the subject of prostitution in books she ordered from Amazon. Berlin of the 1920s, the Weimar Sin City, captured her imagination. She lost herself in Berlin's pantheon of tricked-out tramps and backstreet sex goddesses. The Boot Girls, Half-silks, Bone-shakers, Grasshoppers. Five O'clock Ladies, Dominas, Table Ladies, Phone Girls, and most interesting of all, the Woodchucks: physically repulsive hookers with deformities or missing limbs. She read up on all manner of perversions, sex magick (with intense emphasis on bodily fluids and mirror magic) and sexpot orgies of oddball occult orders. She more than warmed to her subject; she flushed with hormonal heat. When at last she felt ready to begin, she painted a pentagram on the carpet under the bed, dangled a crucifix from a gold chain around her neck and went out to lure her first street whore back to the fuck pad.

Magda was a short Mexican with tinkling bracelets, big dark eyes, bad skin and petite breasts. She was relieved that all she had to do was talk for the camera. Her accent was thick but her English was passable, and she knew how to tell a good tale. She relaxed as she talked, giving graphic details of how she played to the twisted lusts of flaming fetishists and serviced her most perverse johns, but then she went off on a mad tangent about the Chupacabra that had tried to kill her outside of Matamoros. She said the legendary goat-man beast had been after her for years and that it had killed her baby sister instead. She sometimes thought it was still stalking her here in the States. She worked herself into a state of fear and Jezebel sensed that Magda's terror aroused the devils to a fine frenzy.

Leaving the camera on the tripod rolling, Jezebel grabbed the handheld and started shooting with it too. She knew something was about to happen, something so bad it would be good. Or so good it would be horrible.

Magda was sitting on the side of the bed, legs crossed and showcasing nylons lined with ragged runs, smoking a cigarette and swinging her foot vigorously enough to create friction between her thighs. Jezebel did a languid zoom on her legs, then panned upward slowly, seductively to the small woman's lips sucking on the white filter and then venting smoke through her upturned nose and half-pursed lips. This was good. This was hot. Devils' breath turned the room sultry. Jezebel was getting wet. She was almost panting. Things were about to blow. Explode into demonic chaos.

A tear rolled down Magda's cheek. She no doubt knew now she was in the presence of something more powerful, far more evil, than her dreaded Chupacabra.

Jezebel had a sudden moment of weakness, of conscience, and thought she should warn the woman away, should shout *Run!* But then Magda whispered, "Diablo," and Jezebel just said, "Yes, God help you."

A fat tear tumbled from Magda's other eye, dropped and slid down her meager cleavage and disappeared into the cup of her lacy black bra. She shot a worried glance at the mirror above the bed, then she crushed out her cigarette in the plastic ashtray, crossed herself and whispered a prayer in Spanish, something about the Mother of God. A rosary appeared in her hand. As she began to feverishly finger the prayer beads, she all at once flung herself backward onto the bed. But Jezebel knew better, knew the devils had flung the sad little whore backward. Invisible talons sliced away Magda's scanty clothes.

Two sad-eyed angels, one tattooed in deep primary colors on each thigh, offered no protection against the demonic assault that was about to rip her out of this world and into a hell not of her own making, but of evil *otherworldly* making. Jezebel saw it coming, knew how it would end, just as her ancient namesake must've seen in advance the bad end her worship of Baal would bring down on her cursed head.

The devils were not going to stop with Magda.

Magda seemed to levitate three feet above the bed. She called out for Jesus to save her: "¡Jesús me ahorra!" To absolutely no avail. They wrenched her legs apart and snapped her in two like a chicken wishbone. The left leg detached itself from the pelvis, bone bursting through skin, and a cloudburst of blood showered the bed, the walls and the floor. The broken whore screamed just before her body slammed face-first into the wall. Her skull cracked with the sound of a cork popping out of a bottle of cheap-ass champagne.

That the devils hadn't taken time to gangbang Magda boded ill for Jezebel, that much she knew for sure. The dead hooker was nothing but an appetizer, a token offering as prelude to the meatier main course. What could Jezebel do but keep shooting? Shoot she did. The blood-spattered bed, the discarded leg, the mangled one-legged corpse of the poor chica who should've stayed in Ol' Meh-hee-co and married her bumpkin boyfriend Hor-hay. Where the hell was Hey-soos when you needed Him?

"Hey-soos Cristo!" Jezebel shouted. "Where the hell were you, huh? I mean, what the fuck? Does the blood of this little lamb mean nothing to you? This wasn't supposed to happen. Sure she was a whore but her soul was innocent. More or less."

She heard the devils' laughter. It sounded like hollow bones dragging on broken pavement at the end of the world.

"Fuck me," she said with bitter resignation. "Fuck me Jesus."

*　　*　　*

She understood that things had to fall into place. That her place was here in the room that wasn't a room, that the tree that was more than a tree needed blood. The soil barely binding the tree's exposed roots to the earth had already been salted with more blood than a battlefield but it needed *hers*. The demon tree was greedy for her spilled blood, needed it as a bud needs spring rain to blossom. She could feel its dark lust for her. Its sap was up. The air was charged with demonic electricity. The tree had a wicked woody for her.

She saw it clearly now. The former Jeze Bellefleur had earned herself a burial slot here at the foot of the tree. Her blood, flesh and soul were required to replenish what grew here, to bring forth what was yet to come. She had hooked up with the wrong fucking freaks, the Lost City Luciferians, incurred a deep spiritual debt and now the Big Cheese himself was calling in her markers. Lucifer of legend was always up for making a deal, but she didn't have anything to offer that he didn't already possess. She was already in his pocket. Up his ass. Wherever he wanted her. Her plan of becoming a whore for Jesus so that He might save her would by virtue of *no* virtue come to naught.

The devils threw her down so hard her eyeballs clicked like loaded dice. She hit the ground near the bed's brass feet in that *other* room. She caught a distorted glimpse of them in the mirror over the bed. There were three of the ugly fuckers. More hideous than any famed artist had ever imagined or portrayed them, *these* devils.

Hideous enough to blind you, bitch? whispered a scabrous voice.

She turned her head for fear that her eyes would shrivel and die if she looked too long at them. Her eyes came to rest on the tree. Glyphs and strange characters appeared in the trunk's black bark and glowed red with the hellfire dancing a mad caper within the heart of the tree. By some stray sliver of satanic magic she deciphered the flaming symbols:

Eternal death for the damned

Now they were fully visible and she wished she *could* go blind. Homuncular creatures with apelike arms, dragging knuckles and knobby heads, their vulpine faces were fixed with razor-toothed grins and scarlet eyes.

The devils diddled her, teased her terror to new heights, their stunted cockroach wings aflutter and their crooked cocks swelling in proportion to the terror inside her, which is to say, to enormous size. The heads of their phalluses became deadly prongs, and she knew there was no way her body could survive what they obviously had in mind to do to her this time.

Just before they opened her up to an orgy of mortifying torment, one of the horny homunculi mocked her faith with a lisping line from the Gospel: *"Ye cannot drink the cup of the Lord, and the cup of the devils."*

*　　*　　*

She remembers how she came to be buried here, one of countless larva-white corpses.

Human grub worms. Bodies entangled with the denuded roots of the demon tree. Tree roots pulsing in every undead orifice. Corpses impervious to decay, the sleeping dead hopelessly awaiting the call of the archangel's trumpet.

She remembers the unholy trinity of devils' dicks plunging so deep they pulverized her heart and broke her soul.

She remembers Lucifer's beautiful eyes behind shimmering slits, watching her from within the tree. She recalls the way the Devil Himself passed through the tree trunk as Jesus was said to have passed through walls after the resurrection.

She remembers how extraordinarily handsome and angelic Lucifer was as he stood over her and signed the fiery air in malevolent benediction. How he reached down to remove the little golden cross from her neck and the way it softened and rolled into a golden ball between his long hot fingers. Then he parted her cheeks and pushed it up her ass.

She remembers with wrenching clarity what he said: ***"You will not need this trinket. The Miracle Man will not come here to the upper reaches of Hell."*** His voice was so smooth and sonorously seductive that her undead ears had echoing orgasms. But what he wrote with a fire-dripping finger is a tattoo on the raw skin of her soul.

She has eternity to ponder his fire-writing: ***We are all creatures of a cruel Creator.***

RIVER RATS

After a long ass stretch on the road I blew back to the damned city and took up with them old boys everybody called the River Rats. Hundred years ago they was called hobos. Now they didn't call em nothin and just hoped they'd go away.

Pigboy Slim was still there, as was Flap Jack and Sid Arthur. All still runnin their lines and livin off fishhead soup and such and stealin what they could and scroungin the rest.

Pigboy took to callin me Chaingang til I whupped his ass with my dogstick and left him pukin river sludge.

Jack had this Mickey Mouse watch he took off a dead kid back at River-bend and he wore it proud as a hooker in church with diamond hatpin. He couldn't tell time, but at least the damn mouse was still movin his hands.

Everything was jake. It was good to breathe that river stink again and live without some asshole standin over you with a shotgun and a bad attitude.

Then it all started turnin to shit.

The boys told me that something was snatchin folks right off the river banks.

Hellfire, says Slim, theys ten bums missin since the last full moon. Ain't nothin left of em but they shoes an shit.

Thass right, says Flap Jack. Time we wuz movin on.

I told em they was full of shit. Weren't no monsters or nothin in the goddamn river.

We all slept a little closer to the campfire that night.

*　　*　　*

Next mornin Flap Jack was gone. Nobody knew where to.

After breakfast we headed upriver to this old juke joint to get some cheap whiskey from the black whoor who runs the place but before we got there we stumbled over the world's longest turd. The damn thing was a least twenty feet long, laid out nice and straight at the water's edge. Stank to high heaven but that wadnt the worst. Worst was the Mickey Mouse watch stickin out of the shit along with part of Flap Jack's hand.

Godamighty, Sid Arthur yelled. It et poor Jack!

Damned if it didn't, I had to say. What kinda monster lays a turd that big?

Hell, said Slim, that turd is all what's left of poor Flap Jack. Maybe we ort to say some last words fore we get to hell gone.

Sid said maybe we should pick the Mickey Mouse watch out of the shit and keep it as a remembrance of old Jack.

I said go ahead if you want to but I ain't hangin round to play in monster shit. Sumbitch might come back for seconds and I ain't plannin on endin up a giant turd.

Sid dug the watch out of the shit and we beat feet away from there.

*   *   *

We blew into the juke house and bought a bottle of hootch with the coins we scraped together.

Old Dora the whoor heard us talkin about Jack bein turned into a turd and she said she knew exactly what it was was eatin people.

Hell you say, I said.

Thass right, she said. My mammy wuz a hoodoo woman an she say theys a giant serpent lives on the riverbottom. Sleeps, mostways but wakes up ever few years to feed and then goes back to sleep in bottom muck. Its done woke up again. Good time to take a vacation.

Shit fire, said Pigboy Slim as he took a long pull off the bottle. What if we caught the sumbitch and kilt it? Bet we could get a reward. Nothin else, we could eat off it for a couple a weeks. Snake meat ain't bad.

That set us all to thinkin. By the time we finished the hootch we was all fired up to catch us a giant river serpent.

Dora said the thing fed at night so that would be the time to catch it and kill it. She gave us a bottle on the house and sent us off to do battle with the monster. I think she was laughin behind our backs. Probably thinkin lookit them dumbass white crackers stewed to the gills an thinkin they gone catch that serpent.

Come nightfall we was all armed and ready. Slim stole a shotgun from a rich man's house and I had a rusty machete and Sid Arthur had a sledgehammer.

We went back to where it ate poor Jack and waited in the bushes by the bank.

Midnight we decided somebody had to be bait for the monster. We drew straws and I came up short.

I laid down by the riverbank and pretended I was sleepin. After a while I heard something big in the water. I also heard Pigboy Slim snorin his ass off back in the bushes.

Wake up! I whispered real loud. Its here!

Sure nuff it was. In the dyin moonlight I saw it break the surface of the black water and slither onto the shore. Slim had a flashlight tied to the shotgun and he jumped out of the bushes and put the light on the thing.

They God! he yelled.

I yelled too. I don't know what. It wadnt no snake or giant serpent. I don't rightly know what it was but it looked like a humongus intestine with a big ugly asshole for a mouth, And that puckered rosebud mouth was opened wide enough to swallow me whole.

Slim came chargin out and blasted the sumbitch with the shotgun. Shit flew from the hole it blew in its side but it kept comin.

I hacked at the asshole with my machete and it sucked the blade out of my hand and swallowed it.

Sid Arthur slammed it with the sledgehammer and it ate that too, pullin his arm in with it.

Slim kept pumpin it full of buckshot while it sucked Sid Arthur into its maw. It was like somebody was runnin a movie of a giant asshole shit-tin a man in reverse.

Then Sid Arthur was gone and the asshole monster shat out his grungy old shoes and slithered back into the river.

Godamighty, said Slim. You ever seen the like?

You shittin me? I said. Slim said Too bad about old Sid, but if we can catch that sumbitch we be eatin chitlins for weeks.

Fuck that, I said.

My River Rat days was over for good.

Three weeks later I was back on the chaingang and the only monster I had to worry about was the fat ass guard with a black heart and a shotgun.

TWISTER MAN

Forsaken by the storm, Ava crept catlike from the house and saw her dead husband sitting on the front porch. She pursed her crinkled lips to speak Monroe's name but didn't say it because right then she recognized the red-and-black flannel shirt, faded overalls and straw hat of the scarecrow she'd made with Monroe's old clothes and posted in the cornfield.

The scarecrow cocked his head and fixed her with muddy eyes.

"What are you doin' on my porch," she asked.

He rocked forward in the ladderback rocker. The chair creaked like new leather. Broomstraw hair hung out of the hat. A mound of mudcake on his jaw moved like it was a sullied swath of his skin when he opened his mouth and said: "Jus' sittin'."

Ava saw her Ford pickup parked under the pecan tree but no other vehicle except for the tractor with the dead battery beside the barn.

"Where you get them clothes?"

He rocked back like it pained him and pointed at the cornfield.

"Took em off my scarecrow," she said. "Now why would you do that?"

"Needed em more than he did," the man said. "Didn't have a stitch on me."

"What was you doin' naked in my corn?"

"It dropped me there."

Ava gave the man a hard stare. "What dropped you?"

"That dang twister. Whereabouts am I?"

"They Lord," she said. "Where you come from?"

"Outside a Vinewood. Over by the Ohoopee River."

"That's five miles from here. You spect me to believe a tornado picked you up and stripped you naked and set you down here?"

"Only way I can figure it," he said. "I cain't recall exactly. Somethin whopped me pretty good in the head. Hurts like a bear. You got some headache powder?"

She told him to take the hat off so she could have a look at his head. He removed the straw boater and closed his eyes the way some men do when they're in a barber's chair.

"Sweet Jesus," she said when she saw the iron rod sticking out of his head, just behind his left ear. Dirt and a few quills of pine straw were stuck to the clotted blood where the black iron was embedded in his skull.

"What?" His eyes opened, mudpools, the whites bloodshot with jagged streaks.

"You got a piece of iron stuck in your head."

"Naw."

"Yes sir, you do. Stickin' out a good six inches. You could hang your hat on it."

He laughed. Reached up and touched the thin spike with stubby fingers. Stopped laughing. "Don't that beat all," he said.

"You need to go to the hospital."

"Don't reckon I do. You can jus kindly pull it out for me and patch me up good as them doctors." He tested it with his fingers and said, "Might need a pair of pliers."

"I ain't touchin' it. It could be in your brain. I pull it out, some of your brain might come out with it. I'll not have you bleedin' to death on my porch, thank ye, nor your brains leakin' out neither.

"Then get me the pliers an' I'll do it myself out there in the yard."

"No. I'm callin' the ambulance. You sit right still."

"I ain't ridin' in no ambulance," he said.

Ava ignored him and went in the house to use the phone, but the storm had knocked it out of commission.

"Phone's dead," she told him. "I'll have to drive you myself."

"I don't wanna put you out." He put the hat back on and pushed out of the chair, swaying a little on his bare feet. He looked down at his toes and wriggled them. "Lost a good pair of shoes on the way here," he said. "Paid twenty-five dollars for em at the Wal-Mart."

"Come on and get in the truck."

He took a step forward, then fell back into the chair. "Let me rest here a minute," he said with a look of embarrassment. He leaned his head back and shut his swimming eyes.

"You're too big for me to carry. I'll drive over to John Quarles's and get him to come help you."

He blinked his drooping lids and stared off into the breaking clouds. "First I wuz scared," he said. "Knowed I wuz done for. Then it took me way up an I wuz spinnin' and twistin' like on one of them rides at the county fair an' that's when I thought it might not kill me. They wuz tree limbs and mud and I don't know what all flyin' round with me. Even saw a crow tryin' to fly off from it but one of its wings was busted. Thought I saw a hog off a ways in the black wall of the funnel but I ain't sure. Couldn't see too good what with all the flyin' mud and such. But then I got to thinkin'. Some folks say when you die you go through a dark tunnel and come out in the light an' I got scared again. I didn't see no light but I sure wuz in a dark tunnel. Reckon that's when the thing hit me upside the head. Next thing I know, I'm lyin' naked in a cornfield. Twister's done gone and I find that scarecrow. Seen this house an now here I am talkin' to you. Beats all I ever seen."

"You stay right there," she told him. "I'll be back with help."

"I ain't goin nowhere. Whenever I stand up I start spinnin' again like I wuz back in that twister. I done enough spinnin' for one day."

Ava got in the truck and drove over to John's place. Low clouds raced ragged over the horizon, but the sun was out and shining on the autumn afternoon. She found John Quarles behind his house, cutting up a downed tree with his chainsaw. She told him about the twister man, and John followed her home in his old pickup.

When the wind was howling and hailstones were pelting the house, Ava had wanted the storm to take her. She thought it was her time. With Monroe dead these two years and not much to live for but one day bleeding into another about like it, she had lost her heart for living. But the storm went on without her. And now she had a stormriding scarecrow with an iron spike in his skull waiting on her porch and she surmised she ought to be thankful because it gave her some purpose, however transitory.

The brightness of the sun hurt her eyes and showed her how dark her moods had turned of late and she felt old and too tired to contend with the storm debris on the road before her or the debris in the wake of her used-up life. She eyed John in her rearview mirror and hoped he would not insinuate another marriage proposal. Marriage was a closed chapter in her book and not one she wished to dip into again.

She turned off the blacktop and drove up in front of her house. The rocker on the porch was empty, the twister man nowhere in sight.

"Where is he?" John asked when he got out of his truck.

She looked out at the brown cornstalks and said, "Maybe he's out scarin' crows."

They stepped onto the boards of the porch. John Quarles stuck his big hands in his denim pockets and rattled his keys and blew out a whistling breath. A ten-inch iron rod rested on the rocker's sagging seat. One end of it was wet with gore and had a few strands of strawcolored hair stuck to it.

"Lord," she said, "he pulled it out hisself."

"Where could he have got to?" John said.

"Likely leakin' brains, wherever he's at." She turned back to the corn-field and shaded her eyes with her hand. Then she was stepping through the brittle stalks to the center of the field where the scarecrow had stood sentry. John dogged her decisive steps.

"You don't think . . ."

"They Lord," she said when she saw the empty flannel shirt, overalls and straw hat hanging on the wooden cross like the discarded raiment of a reluctant savior.

"So where the heck is he?"

"Stop askin' me that, John Quarles. Don't you see I made it all up? Weren't no twister man. You been had by a addlebrained old woman scared of a storm. Get in your truck and go on home."

After he was gone, Ava sat in the rocker and held the iron spike in her lap and watched the sun sink into the dead cornstalks. The failing light soothed her some and her mood lightened a little. She glanced over at the scuffed porch boards where Monroe's old railroader's shoes had left their marks with his years of pensive rocking, but this time she didn't feel the absence of man and chair quite so deep in her breast.

An errant breeze rustled a path through the brittle brown stalks as if a ghost were passing there. The evening star winked down at her.

"Godspeed, Twister Man," she whispered on the wind.

THE HANDYMAN

Hurricane Jayne blew us a big slobbery kiss as she went whirling by, and we thought we'd got off easy-breezy. Dodged God's bullet. Cities to the south caught the brunt of the bitch-storm's wrath as she cut a furious path across the peninsula and then slid off into the Gulf to set her sights on the next tasty bit of coastline. If we weren't dancing in the streets, it was only because they were flooded.

"The Lord surely smiled upon us, Lon," Preacher Silas told me the next day as we surveyed the damage to the sanctuary. "Thank you, Jesus."

As handyman and general flunky for The Church of the Holy Ghost, I couldn't see much need for thanking anybody. All I could see was the hard work ahead of me: the carpet I'd have to rip up and replace, the scrubbing and disinfecting required to remove the floodwater stench from the floor, not to mention the cleanup of the debris littering the church lawn and parking lot. Thanks a lot, Jesus.

The Rev led me out to the tarmac parking lot beside the church and we stood on the broken rim of the big sinkhole and stared down its throat like two bumpkins gawking at the Eighth Wonder of the World. I shoved my hands in my pockets and waited for the bookish man to impart more of his patented homespun wisdom, but he just stood there staring into the hole like a man in a trance. His lips moved but he made no sound. He shivered, though the September morn was sultry.

Down the street a chainsaw whined, then screamed when its teeth met the meat of a downed tree.

"Preacher? You all right?" I asked him.

"You feel it, son?" he asked without taking his eyes from the hole.

"Feel what?"

"I don't rightly know *what* it is. But I feel it, sure as sin."

The ragged hole Jayne had left us was roughly eight feet in diameter and at least nine feet deep. Brackish water pooled at the bottom. There was an odd sweet smell rising from it, not at all like the usual bottom-rot odor of floodwater.

Preacher Silas craned his head over the rim as if he were listening to something down there. He teetered, lost his balance and I grabbed him and pulled him back to safety. "Careful," I warned.

"Yes, yes, you're right. We must take care. This is a very dangerous thing. Get some sawhorses, Lon, and block it off. We can't have our kids taking a tumble down that hole. White rabbit or no."

He shuddered, still gazing into the sinkhole as if he expected to see something there besides dirty water, broken tarmac and earthen walls. He extended his hands palms-down over the hole like a man warming his hands over a fire and said, "You sure you don't feel something?"

Playing along, I stuck my hands out too. Then I turned them up in an empty-hands gesture and said, "No sir. Not a thing."

"I'll have to meditate on it." The lines on his face deepened. His expression was so grim I had to look away.

He sequestered himself in his office the rest of the morning. I rounded up a couple of sawhorses and set them by the hole, and then I went to work in the sanctuary, ripping up ruined carpet and scrubbing hardwood floors until the stink was mostly gone. If cleanliness really was next to Godliness, then at least I was headed in the right direction. Every now and then, I'd glance up at the tall crucifix behind the altar to make sure the life-size wooden replica of Jesus was still affixed to His cross. The thing was so lifelike that I often had the creepy feeling that He might slip down from the crossbeams, sneak up on me and put a cold hand of judgment on my shoulder. Such thoughts aren't all that unusual in a recovering alcoholic. But as unnerving as those notions can be, they beat hell out of the terrifying hallucinations I'd had when I was in alcohol withdrawal. A walking wooden Jesus was a Sunday picnic compared to the *Delirium Tremens* devils I'd seen.

*   *   *

Mid-afternoon I saw Preacher Silas hovering over the sinkhole again. I dragged the last of the rolled-up, waterlogged carpet to the curb and left it for the trash men, then I started across the parking lot toward him. His back was to me so he didn't see my approach. He was gesturing with his hands the way he did whenever he delivered one of his trademark hellfire-and-brimstone sermons. I couldn't make out what he was saying, but his inflection was certainly spirited. Curious, I slowed my pace, trying to catch some of his words.

I heard only snatches of what he was saying: " . . . earth will give back . . . return what was entrusted to it . . . and Hell will give back what it owes . . ."

I stopped a few paces behind him and listened, spellbound, to more of his odd oration: "And I saw another hole below the pit and it had the appearance of blood and pestilence and . . . No! That's a damned lie! Defile not my flock! Oh Lord, please . . ."

Silas dropped to his knees on the broken edge of tarmac and clasped his hands together. He wailed a string of nonsensical syllables, jabbering in tongues unknown.

"Preacher?" I called. His wailing gibberish so disturbed me that I had to make him stop.

He jerked his head around and shot me a look of sheer madness, eyes wildly aflame with desperate passion and twisted religious fervor.

"Are you all right?" I asked him, knowing he wasn't.

Some of the fire went out of his eyes and he seemed to recognize me. He braced himself on a sawhorse, pushed up off his knees and brushed off his trousers, looking embarrassed. "Lon, I . . . I don't know what happened. I . . ."

"Better come away from there," I said, taking him gently by the arm and pulling him away from the brink of the sinkhole.

"I don't remember coming out here," he said, bewildered. "Darndest thing. I was working on Sunday's sermon and then . . ."

"Sounded like you were speaking in tongues," I said with a mirthless laugh. I wanted to humor him, though I knew there was nothing humorous about whatever was happening to him.

"It spoke to me." Tears welled in his eyes. "It . . ."

He shuddered as if he'd caught a chill. I shivered sympathetically, a reflex, like when someone yawns and you do too.

"Why don't you go home and rest awhile," I suggested. "Grab a little siesta."

He glanced uneasily back at the hole. That strange sweet scent was all but gone. A stench rose from the hole. "Yes, I believe I will. I must be coming down with something. Catching some vile sort of bug."

I walked him to the brick parsonage next door to the church and he went inside. I heard him throw the deadbolt—something I'd never known him to do during daylight hours.

I went back to the sinkhole and stared into it, trying to divine . . . I don't know what. An otherworldly presence? That sweet smell was back, though it was much fainter now. Gooseflesh rose on my arms. A ripple of fear snaked through my belly and crawled up into my chest. I stepped back from the rim, trembling. The Rev's bizarre behavior had spooked me. This was an ordinary sinkhole, a simple geological phenomenon and nothing more. There was nothing demonic about it. The only demons around here were the ones in the preacher's head. The man needed professional help.

Maybe I did too. My old phobia of holes was coming back.

*   *   *

When I was seven years old I lived in a house across a dirt road from an orange grove. Nobody in the neighborhood had a swimming pool, so we kids ran a garden hose from Gary Willis's house to a sizeable hole (left by the removal of a tree stump) at the edge of a sandy vacant lot of weeds and sandburs and filled it with water, christening it The Black Lagoon after the creature feature we'd seen at the Saturday matinee. Four feet deep and six feet wide, the hole wasn't big enough for actual swimming, but it suited our splash-pool purposes just fine.

Until Butch Bailey came along.

Butch was your typical neighborhood bully. He was a few years older than we were, and the only time he deigned to have anything to do with us was when he was bored with his dull-witted self or pissed-off at his old man, a hard-looking bully in his own right.

One day Butch Bailey caught us splashing around in the The Black Lagoon, reveling in the cool muddy water. The Three Mud-keteers—Gary Willis, Ty Gilbert and me. Ty saw him first, climbed out of the hole and ran immediately for home, swimming trunks bagging about his legs. Gary and I stayed put, resigned to our fate, yet hoping Butch wouldn't think it was worth getting wet and muddy just to wail on such unworthy prey as us.

Butch Bailey grabbed the garden hose, wrapped it around Gary's neck, dragged him out of the water and pummeled his head and shoulders with his bony fists. Gary took his punishment, and shambled home with a bloody nose, whimpering all the way. Then it was my turn.

Butch lashed me with the hose, raising red welts on my bare shoulders and arms. I ducked underwater and held my breath until my lungs were on fire. I broke the surface just as he jumped feet-first into the hole and pushed me under. I came up coughing and sputtering, and Butch laughed and said he'd give me to three to get out of the hole. He started his count and I started climbing out of the water. Just as I was slithering onto the muddy rim of the hole, he grabbed my trunks and yanked me back into the watery pit. He dunked me and held me under. I panicked and tried to claw my way back to the world of air but Butch Bailey was too strong. I knew then he wasn't playing; he intended to kill me. I was going to die in this muddy waterhole.

But Butch wanted to play with me some more before he finished me off. He let me up, let me catch some air and started counting again. I dove for the mudbank but slipped right back into my tormentor's arms. He dunked me again. Let me up again. Counted again. I don't know how many times he made me run through that tortuous routine before he finally tired of the game and said, "Last chance, squirt. If you can't get away this time, this shithole's gonna be your watery grave."

He started the count and I knew I was dead. Defeated and dispirited, I slumped in emotional collapse and awaited my fate. But here came Gary's mother, striding on stubby legs to my rescue before Butch Bailey finished the count. She scolded him and he cussed her, but he let me go.

I never went near that swimming hole again. For years I had nightmares of being swallowed up by evil holes. Sometimes the holes chased me, snapping at my heels like giant mouths. Sometimes holes would open up under my feet and I would fall into terrifying darkness. Once a hole fell out of the sky and devoured me from above. In my waking life I avoided anything remotely resembling a hole, be it a tiny cavity or a yawning chasm. In short, I developed a full-blown phobia of holes. Even a hole in my shoe would make me nervous.

I'm not sure my phobia had anything to do with my becoming an alcoholic, but the only time I wasn't afraid of holes was when I was soused to the gills. That changed years later when a shrink saw a link between my fear and my drinking, and treated the phobia as part of my recovery. That's a funny story in itself.

I was on a three-day drunk when I fell and hit my head on a St. Augustine curb. X-rays revealed a subdural hematoma—a blood clot on the brain which had to be removed. When the internist told me the procedure entailed drilling a "burr hole" in my skull I panicked, and eventually confessed my hole phobia to the shrink they called in for consultation. It took a week of intensive hypnotherapy to convince me that the hole in my head wasn't going to devour my brain. Post-op, the doc told me about the ancient practice of trepanning and joked that the burr hole had let the demons out of my head. I didn't laugh. It sounded about right to me.

*   *   *

I knocked off work just before sundown and retired to my little crackerbox house behind the church. It came rent-free with the job. It met my meager needs and allowed me to keep an eye on the church during my off-hours. After a shower and a microwave dinner of Swedish meatballs, I sat on the front stoop with a mug of coffee and contemplated the weeping willow that stood like a lonely sentinel in front of the little house. The rear of the redbrick church was directly in front of me and the parking lot was off to my right. I avoided looking at the sawhorses guarding the sinkhole because I didn't want to think about the hole or the preacher's odd obsession with it. The droopy willow held no unpleasant associations for me and I rested my gaze on it, savoring the cooling winds of twilight.

A lizard darted from the corner of the stoop, paused to check for predators, and then ran along the front of the house and disappeared around the corner. When I looked up, I saw Silas lumbering across the parking lot toward the hole. The belt of his terrycloth robe dragged the ground.

"Damn, man," I grumbled. I set my coffee on the stoop, got up and went after him. Babysitting the preacher was not in my job description, but he'd lost his wife to breast cancer the year before and I was all he had now. Some might say looking after him was the Christian thing to do. I wasn't much of a Christian, but I couldn't sit by and let him break his neck falling in that damned hole.

He moved one of the sawhorses out of his way and stood right on the hole's edge like the Fool in the tarot deck standing before the precipice.

"Hey! Get away from there!" I shouted.

If he heard me, he gave no sign. He made a bizarre gesture with his hands, and then he jumped into the hole.

I jogged toward him, anxious to get him out of there and equally anxious to outrun my old familiar phobia that was suddenly dogging me, its rancorous breath on the back of my neck.

I was in a veritable footrace with fear. If I could beat it to the hole, I would be all right.

So I thought.

I drew up just short of the sinkhole's rim and saw Silas on his knees in the dirty water at the bottom of the pit. He was speaking in tongues again. He cupped his hands, scooped up some water and dumped it on the crown of his head as if baptizing himself. The water made a crooked part in his silver hair and dulled its usual healthy sheen.

"Preacher," I said, kneeling at the edge, "give me your hand."

He ignored me and went on with his stuttering gibberish. Then he bent down and started lapping the stagnant water.

Leaning over that jagged-edged maw, I felt a disorienting wave of vertigo. The hole seemed to be opening wider, like a hungry mouth. It *wanted* me. Wanted to suck me down into deepest oblivion. I had just enough presence of mind to know that if I didn't act now, my fear would immobilize me.

So I jumped into the hole.

*   *   *

A man might do a crazy thing when he's pissed off at the world, but an alcoholic will do something crazy because the world is pissed off at him.

Billy Walking Bird shared that with me the first time I met him. It didn't make much sense to me then, but I thought it would be bad form to question the wisdom of my AA sponsor so I just filed it away in my memory under Quaint Native-American Sayings. I figured I was too insignificant for the world to be pissed off at me.

Jumping into that sinkhole was probably a crazy thing to do, especially for a man with a phobia of holes. Was it the brave act of a man determined to face his fear or was it the cowardly act of a man trying to escape his old demons? Standing ankle-deep in sinkhole water, I was in no position to fathom the answer. It was a time for action, not a time for deep thought. I reached down and grabbed Silas by the collar and pulled his face out of the water.

"Get up," I told him.

He looked up at me with wide eyes and said, "You're *Him*. The carpenter. Praise Jesus!"

"I'm Lon, the handyman. C'mon, we have to get out here."

As twilight darkness closed in on the sky, the hole closed in on us. If I could keep my fear at bay long enough to get us out of there, then the defining moment of my actions would be one of triumph. It wouldn't be easy. The broken tarmac of the parking lot was nearly three feet above the top of my head and the hole's walls were straight up and down with nothing to hold on to. I thought I might be able to dig footholds in the wall, but that would take time I knew I didn't have. If I could get Silas to stand on my shoulders and boost him out, then he could reach down and pull me up or at least go for help—if he wasn't too crazy to follow instructions.

Silas reverently—lovingly—touched his fingers to my short salt-and-pepper beard and said, "I knew you'd find me, Lord."

"I've come to save you from the pit," I said, deepening my voice to make it savior-like. It was a pretty fair imitation of Charlton Heston's Moses, and I used it to issue a commandment. "Stand on my shoulders and I shall boost you out of the pit of damnation!"

"I was afraid you'd forsaken me," he blubbered. "I'm heartily sorry, Lord."

I squatted down and pointed at my shoulder, giving him my sternest angry-God look. He had lost a lot of weight since his wife died, otherwise I wouldn't have been able to straighten my legs with him standing on my shoulders. Bracing my hands against the dirt wall, I stood erect and boosted him halfway out of the hole. "Climb out," I grunted.

His weight left my shoulders and I blew a big sigh of relief. I looked up just as he lost his grip and came sliding back into the hole. There was no time to get out of the way. His wet shoes smacked my face and I fell backward into the water. He came down on top of me, pinning me below the surface.

I tried to push him off me but couldn't budge him. Rancid water rushed into my nose, into my ears and down my throat when I panicked and tried to yell at him to get his ass off me.

Then the hole swallowed me.

*   *   *

The sun was rising in the eastern sky when Fire/Rescue pulled us out of the hole. They took me first because I was still alive. Silas was facedown in the fetid water, dead. I couldn't tell them how he got that way. I didn't know, couldn't remember.

I'd spent the entire night in the sinkhole, lost in a landscape of nightmarish images I couldn't put together in any sensible way. I could point to no linear cause-and-effect chain of events resulting in the preacher's death. The nightmare fragments had swirled in concentric circles, conforming roughly to the geometry of the sinkhole—and to the inner contours of my skull. Laws of physics and logic seldom apply in the hallucinatory realm of nightmare.

I told my rescuers that Silas had fallen on top of me when I tried to boost him out of the hole and that the next thing I remembered was waking up when they came to pull us out.

I didn't attempt to tell them about the nightmares. There was no point in telling them that I'd been trapped in the hole with my childhood nemesis Butch Bailey, or that I'd been locked in a life-and-death struggle with the raging bully. Nor did I tell them of the demons indigenous to that damned hole, demons that had forced their way inside my head. They would've thought I was crazy. They would've taken me to the nuthouse. I couldn't have that.

I had too much to do.

They took the preacher's body away and I went back to my little crackerbox to clean myself up. After a hot shower, I called Billy Walking Bird but got no answer. I thought he might understand what had happened to me and why I had to do what I was going to do. Billy knew about the unseen world of ghosts and demons, and he had at least a rudimentary grasp of the mysterious ways and various aspects of elementals and other earth spirits. He knew the way vengeful spirits could devour a man from the inside out, once they'd found a way inside. But I couldn't wait to find him. I could already hear them munching away at me, like termites eating the interior walls of a house.

The situation called for immediate action. Delay would be disastrous, if not deadly.

I went to the tool shed behind the church, dug out the electric drill and loaded it with a 1/16" bit. I took it back to the house, stood in front of the bathroom mirror, plugged in the drill and held it against my right temple, finger on the trigger.

A Bible quote Preacher Silas had been fond of using came to me then and I repeated it: *"And these signs will accompany those who believe: In my name they will drive out demons; they will speak in new tongues."*

Then I pulled the trigger and the Black & Decker whined as the steel bit bore into my skull.

*   *   *

Sunset sanctuary. Alone with my sins. Front-row pew.

Washed in blood and stained-glass light. I mumble in an unknown tongue.

Unclean spirits banished back to the pit.

Jesus stands before me like a cigar-store Indian.

Jesus Walking Wood.

No fear now. Only waiting.

For forgiveness.

Waiting.

To be healed . . .

His arms creak as He reaches for me with mahogany hands.

THE SPOOK

Before Rippy called fire down from the heavens, I thought he was just another wayward spook. And even after the pyrotechnic display that turned men into pink mist and vaporized flesh and bone, I still didn't know why he'd tracked us to these mountains or why he seemed so keenly interested in our peculiar captive, but I knew I didn't like the way Rippy's haunted eyes bore into the leather-skinned Arab who sat hunched in layered rags against the wall of the cave, hands bound behind his back.

Then Rippy looked at me and I thought I detected a slight smile within his close-cropped beard, but he still had ghost eyes, empty and unreadable. "Good instincts out there, Captain Draven," he said. "Lovely war, isn't it?"

"Copy that," I said with easy cynicism. "So you're in tight with the Angel of Death."

Rippy shrugged and unzipped his dusky fatigue jacket. He wore a Soviet 9mm Makarov pistol in a shoulder holster and a black-and-white checkerboard Massoud scarf around his neck. "Direct line to the gods, amigo. I've got more connections than Ma Bell. Can't order up smart bombs when I go solo, but who's complaining?"

I'd first met Rippy six months earlier in Jack's Tora Bora Café on the rooftop of the Mustafa Hotel in Kabul. He appeared out of nowhere, stood at my table and said, "You're Dave Draven's kid brother."

Taken aback, I just stared into his colorless eyes and nodded.

"We worked together in Desert Storm," he explained. "Good man. You're his spitting image."

My older brother David had spent several years in the CIA's paramilitary division before starting his own security business in the private sector. He'd since gravitated to the shadowy world of corporate espionage and beyond, or so I suspected.

Rippy bought me a vodka and pomegranate juice that night and talked in colorful riddles of his bygone exploits with my brother. He was affable enough, but I had the feeling he was working a hidden agenda, or maybe just looking for clandestine angles to play from habit.

Now we were together again in *Tangai*, the unforgiving mountains of Afghanistan near the Pakistan border, and Rippy couldn't keep his eyes off the prisoner I'd been ordered to transport to an interrogation center thirty klicks east of our current location. Martinez was guarding the prisoner, and Johnson and Summers were posted in the rocks outside the cave to keep watch on our perimeter. The sun was setting and the howling winds were turning frigid.

"Why're you here?" I asked him.

He un-assed his cut-down ruck, sat on the cave floor and lit a cigarette. "I'm here to spin you a tale," he said, looking sidewise at the prisoner. "Think of me as sort of a Scheherazade in reverse for your prisoner. You know who she was, right? The chick who told a story every night to the sultan so he wouldn't have her beheaded."

"From *The Thousand And One Nights*, yeah. But I don't get what the hell you mean."

"Patience, grasshopper." Rippy grinned. "Take a load off and listen up. All will become clear."

He pulled a silver flask from his jacket, took a drink and then offered it to me. I waved it off. He said something to the prisoner in Dari, but I didn't speak the dialect and had no clue what he was saying. The Arab listened impassively.

"Unless you're packing orders to interrogate this man," I said to Rippy, "don't contaminate my prisoner."

Rippy chuckled. "Old Hajji there's already contaminated, Draven. Contaminated in the worst possible way."

"What did you say to him?" I was already tired of Rippy's riddles.

Rippy showed his teeth in a hostile smile that reminded me of a grinning skull. "I just quoted a bit of ancient wisdom from the Koran. *There is a devil in every berry of the grape.* I don't think he appreciated the poetry of it."

"I don't have time for head games, Rip."

"A thousand pardons, El Capitan. May I proceed with my tale?"

I shrugged. "Make it short. And leave out the flowery bullshit."

Rippy put his hand over his heart, pretending to be offended. Then he began his storytelling. The diminutive cave's acoustics amplified his deep voice to dramatic effect.

"Once upon a time there was an angel named *Iblis* who was so puffed up with pride that he believed he was superior to human beings. He refused Allah's command to bow down to Adam, so Allah kicked his prideful ass out of heaven. *Iblis* didn't want to be cast into the pit of darkness so he pleaded with Allah for a second chance, which was granted. Well, of course, he blew it, and was therefore banished and despised, sent down to eat filth and haunt lonely ruins. But *Iblis* wasn't content to spend eternity as a lowly demon eating unclean food and camel dung, no fucking way. He hooked up with the djinn—those are your evil devils created thousands of years ago from scorching desert winds, the wily ones that survived Allah's hit squad of angels—and before you could say 'Holy camel shit,' old *Iblis* became King of the Shaitans. Shaitan is another name for djinn, by the way, and that's where Judeo-Christians got the name for Satan."

Rippy paused for another pull at his flask.

"Is there a point to this fucked-up fairytale?" I asked.

"Yes indeed. A very sharp point. Bear with me now, Draven. Now it really gets interesting."

I glanced at the inscrutable prisoner. I didn't know if the man understood English. I hadn't heard him speak a word in any language. I would've guessed that he'd had his tongue cut out if I didn't know he was destined for an interrogation center.

Rippy field-stripped his smoke, then went on with his tale. "The *djinn* are very nasty dudes. Forget everything you may have learned about them in childhood. They are not the benign creatures who pop out of bottles to grant you three wishes, the way they do in Disney cartoons. These are evil fucking demons created by Allah's smokeless fire and they *will* fuck you up in a heartbeat. And they are legion. The deserts and mountains of Arabia are full of them. They come in more varieties than Baskin-Robbins has flavors of ice cream. *Iblis* commands an army of them, including the species of *Ghoul* the destroyer, and his malicious cousins, the *marids* and *ifrits*. A *Ghoul* can take the shape of a camel, a horse or even a man. Its sweet siren song lures you into its camp so it can rip you apart with its claws and devour your parts whole like a python. And then there's the *Devalpa*. Sinbad the sailor had a run-in with one of these buggers, though, as I recall, Hollywood left it out of its insipid adaptations. The *Devalpa* most often appears as a frail old man standing by a road, begging travelers to pick him up and carry him a short distance. If a good samaritan makes the mistake of hoisting the old man onto his shoulders, the demon will straightaway shapeshift and reptilian tentacles come bursting from its belly to wrap around the unfortunate do-gooder and crush him to death unless he promises to spend the rest of his life as the demon's slave. I actually saw one of the buggers in the Iraqi desert. Your brother did too, but he denied his own eyes. You know how he is. It happened during a hellacious sandstorm, and visibility was for shit, but I saw what I saw. God's honest truth."

Martinez burst out laughing, then tried to cover his laughter with a fit of coughing. "Sorry, sir," he muttered.

"It's all right, Martinez," I said. "I'd laugh too, but an officer and a gentleman is trained not to laugh at a mental defective."

Rippy smiled, to my relief. I'd thought he actually believed his own bullshit yarn of desert demons, but now he looked like a man who's just reached the punch-line of a lengthy joke.

"You had me going, for a minute there," I said, giving him a grin.

Rippy's frozen smile gave me a chill. Or it might've only been the cold wind howling at the darkening mouth of the cave. I stared into his ghost eyes. His smile evaporated and he said, "It's the truth, Draven. The demons are real. And your prisoner is one of them."

Martinez looked at me, no longer amused. He was fearless in combat, but now I could see uncertainty creeping into his boyish face.

"You've been in the desert too long, Rip," I said. "If you really believe this bullshit, you've got a serious problem."

"They say these winds alone can drive a man mad," he said without emotion. He cocked his head and closed his eyes. "But if you listen hard enough, you can hear the voices of the damned in them. Listen."

The wind was a moaning, whistling roar.

"That's the whole fucking demon army out there," he said. "You hear them, don't you?"

That was when I started to fear the man. The CIA spook apparently had become a rogue agent, gone native, and now he was babbling like a dangerously deluded paranoiac. Less than an hour ago, Rippy had appeared out of nowhere and used his encryption-enabled satellite phone to call in an air strike on a band of Al Qaeda combatants closing on our position. Was the man crazy enough to call a strike down on us to rid the world of his imaginary demons?

"I don't know what you're playing at," I told him, "but you're not going to interfere with my mission. I'm humping the man down the mountain to the sweat box and you'd best not get in my way."

"The thing is," he said, pointing a finger at the prisoner, "that's not a man. And I think I can prove it."

"You've already proved all I need to know," I said. "I think you'd better hand over your pistol."

"Negative, Captain." He sat up a little straighter, scowling at me. "You're not hearing me. Hajji there is not human. Oh, he looks like a man, but these bastards are tricky as hell. They can assume the shape of a man, or sometimes they just slide right in and take a man over, body and soul. I'm not sure which species we've got here, but I guaran-fucking-tee you that thing sitting there is a dung-eating demon."

I drew my pistol and pointed it at Rippy's chest. "Use your left hand and take out your pistol," I told him. "Slow and easy, just like in the movies."

"You're being a real pain in the ass," he said. "Your brother was the same damn way." He handed me his Makarov, then stood up, dusted the seat of his pants and started to walk out of the cave. I stuck his pistol in my belt.

"Where the fuck are you going?" I called after him.

"Out to take a dump," he said. "Unless you want me to do it right here."

I let him go. His ruck with the sat-com phone was on the cave floor where he'd dropped it, so I didn't think he could do any crazy-ass damage from outside the cave.

Martinez said, "Sir, if you don't mind me asking . . . Who the hell *is* that guy?"

"CIA. Off the reservation and apparently crazy as hell. Stay sharp, Martinez. I don't want any harm to come to our prisoner."

"Yes, sir." Martinez nodded toward the Arab. "There is something weird about him, sir. The prisoner, I mean. Something not right. He's—"

"Stow that shit, Corporal," I said, holstering my gun. "Forget that spook story and just do your job."

A few minutes later, Rippy came in out of the screaming wind. He had something in his hand, partially shielded from my line of vision. I shot out my hand and grabbed the shoulder of his black fatigue jacket. I smelled it the same instant I saw what it was. "What the fuck are you—"

He lobbed the shit-covered rock at the prisoner. Martinez raised his weapon and pointed it at Rippy. The rock thumped to the floor of the cave right in front of the wide-eyed Arab.

"Now watch what he does," said Rippy, ignoring the M16A2 zeroed on his belly.

The narrow-faced prisoner stared at the glob of feces plastered on the small rock, drooled a little and then all at once leaned down and began to lap it up and chew it.

Rippy grinned at me and said, "Fucking djinn can't resist a gourmet treat like that. Shit-eating devil."

Martinez mumbled something in Spanish as he swung his weapon toward the prisoner. I suppressed a retch as I watched the man gobble up Rippy's warm shit.

"Now," Rippy said, "you can give me my fucking pistol back."

"That ain't right," Martinez said in disgust, taking a backward step.

"Waste him, Corporal!" Rippy barked.

I stepped forward and kicked the rock out of reach of the Arab's mouth. He glared up at me with wild eyes, smears of shit stuck to his unruly beard.

"Do it, soldier!" Rippy shouted.

I rushed Rippy and pushed him against the rock wall. "At ease, you crazy fuck!" I yelled in his face. "Don't demonize my prisoner." As soon as the words were out of my mouth I knew how ridiculous they sounded, but I was too pissed to care.

Rippy started to laugh. I banged him against the wall, then let go of him. He slid to a sitting position, stunned and no longer laughing.

"Dial it tight, Martinez," I said to the corporal, using the grunt-speak he'd been trained to obey.

Licking his lips, the Arab looked longingly at the shit-smeared rock. Truth was, I didn't know anything about the man, other than I'd been ordered to transport him on foot because chopper pilots couldn't fly in these stormy winds at this altitude. Someone up the chain of command deemed the man important enough to order me and my team to take him across mountains that resembled a barren lunar landscape so he could be interrogated by intel specialists. I was pretty goddamn sure there was no exorcist waiting for him. But how did Rippy know the man would eat feces? What else did he know?

The practice of demonizing and dehumanizing the enemy is as old as war itself. Roman legions fought hoards of subhuman Pagans, the U.S. and its World War II allies fought the Yellow Peril, and my father's generation fought slant-eyed monkey-ass gooks. Just before the end of W.W. II, Japanese civilians were trained to defend their homeland with sharp sticks and were told that the American barbarian invaders would rape the women and then take them out to sea and dump them in the waves. Turning one's enemy into demons negates the notion that all life is sacred. It makes the killing easier. As it turned out, our "greatest generation" didn't have to invade Japan. We dropped Fat Man and Little Boy on Hiroshima and Nagasaki, proving we were far more formidable than mere demons.

Now Rippy had taken standard wartime demonization to another level. He had used the mythic folklore of the Middle East to construct an elaborate delusional system inhabited by *real* demons. And his madness was now my problem. You can't talk a paranoid schizophrenic out of his psychosis; his entrenched paranoia makes him dangerously unpredictable and a threat to those around him. So I made a battlefield diagnosis and decided I had to neutralize Rippy by taking him into custody and making him my second prisoner. I would turn him over to the Special Ops interrogators and let them break it to the CIA station chief that one of his spooks was off the grid and crazy as hell.

"Don't you get it, Draven?" Rippy said, squinting up at me. "The fucking desert demons are everywhere. The raghead hoard's been unleashed on the whole fucking world. You make it out of this shithole country, they'll be waiting for you back home. Susie Crotch-rot will be laying for you with a demon up her snatch. You go bebopping down to the Seven Eleven and Hajji's fucking cousin will sell you a pack of smokes just before he rips you apart with his fangs or jumps up your ass with a flaming stick. The war's over, Captain. They've already won. The best we can do is get a little advance payback by wasting as many of the fuckers as we can. Starting with Hajji the dung-eater."

"If you don't shut the fuck up with that shit, I'll have to gag you," I told him. Then I got an extra FlexiCuff from Martinez to bind Rippy's wrists. Rippy shook his head and rolled his eyes as I squatted down to cuff him. He whispered: "Listen, they see everything you're doing through his eyes. If you don't—"

He broke off when we heard the abrupt burst from an M16 outside the cave, followed by the prolonged chatter of a second 16. Summers and Johnson had enemy contact. One of them yelled above the screaming wind: "Incoming!"

What happened after that point in time was never recorded in an after-action report, nor will it ever become part of the written military history of our war in Afghanistan. Such things aren't even mentioned when combat vets gather in the VFW to get drunk and bullshit each other with outrageous war stories. You might hear such an incredible tale on the psych ward of a VA hospital or in a back alley haunted by homeless vets who piss their pants and talk to rats.

Or maybe in a delusional combat vet's overlong suicide note.

Somewhere in the gathering darkness an enemy fighter launched an RPG (rocket propelled grenade) at our position. The mouth of the cave exploded with a blinding roar and I was flying backward amid a hail of broken granite. I landed on my spine, the air knocked out of me. When the explosion finally stopped ringing in my ears, I heard a terrible screaming from raw vocal cords. I sat up and touched my throat to make sure I wasn't the one screaming, then I looked around and saw my Arab prisoner lying on his side, shrieking into the dirt. Blood dribbled from a gash in his cheek and his teeth seemed unnaturally white amid his dark beard. Martinez got back on his feet and checked himself for wounds. Then Rippy was suddenly standing over me, saying something I couldn't make out. At first I though he was going to help me up, but then he was yanking his 9mm from my belt and pointing it at the Arab. I pushed up to a standing position and reached for my pistol.

A huge insect with a long smoky tail flew in through the mouth of the cave and stung Rippy in the back and he blew apart, arms and head separating from his body and sailing off in different directions. The explosion of blood blew me back down, but this time I recovered more quickly, knowing we had to get out of the cave. The enemy had us zeroed. The next RPG might take us all out.

As though moving through a dreamscape, I was on my feet, shouting orders to Martinez. "Get the prisoner and get out of here! Take cover in the rocks!"

Martinez was wearing Rippy's blood too, but he apparently hadn't been seriously hurt by shrapnel or rock debris. He was probably stunned stupid, but like the good soldier he was, he followed orders. He bent down and wrestled the screeching Arab onto his shoulder in a fireman's carry and started for the smoky exit. Glancing at what was left of Agent Rippy, I grabbed his ruck and turned to follow Martinez out. Summers and Johnson were firing for effect, laying down cover fire so we could get the hell out of the deathtrap cave.

It was nearly full dark now, but a waxing moon bathed the craggy landscape in silvery ghostlight. Martinez ran hunched over, the Arab draped over his right shoulder. The Arab raised his head and looked at me. His eyes were incandescent, as if they still held some of the fire of the last deadly explosion. He twisted his mouth into a bizarre grin, as if taunting me, daring me to stop what was he was about to do to Martinez. And I *knew* what he was going to do. Knew Rippy was right.

As I cleared the mouth of the cave, I drew my pistol, fully intending to shoot the man in the head, but I had to get close enough to put one in his brainpan without inadvertently hitting my corporal. I didn't know if I could catch up with them in time.

Over the chatter of automatic weapons I heard Martinez's strangled bellow as he staggered to a halt. A bloom of writhing tentacles suddenly enveloped him. It looked as if he had run into a tangled nest of mammoth worms. The Arab's face elongated, his twisted mouth expanding into a grotesque sucker-like maw.

Martinez screamed.

I halted, aimed my 9mm at the thing's face and fired. I'll never know if my aim was true. Martinez and the demon vanished in the explosion of a third RPG strike and I dove for the deck. Rocks and bits of soft tissue rained down on me, pattering like soggy hailstones on my helmet.

I raised my head and looked at the spot where Martinez and the Arab had been. The corporal's desert-cammie trousers and boots were still there, still holding the lower half of his body, but everything above his hips was gone.

Smoke rose from the gore-spattered ground to be whipped away by the wind. I saw nothing recognizable as the Arab's remains.

I put my head back down, suddenly feeling very drowsy. I reckoned the war and the world could get along without me while I caught a few quick Z's.

The demonic voices in the wind sang me to sleep.

*   *   *

The flight attendant wakes me with a light touch on my wrist. "We're approaching the American coastline," she says. Seeing my puzzled expression, she adds: "You said to wake you."

I nod thanks. I wipe a thread of drool from my lower lip and stiffen my spine. From my window seat, I peer through the glass and into the night, waiting for my first look at America in over a year.

The war is behind me, my soldiering days soon to be done. I will resign my commission and learn how to be a civilian again, though I know it won't be easy. Because the war *isn't* behind me, not really. Flying in U.S. airspace just offshore of my homeland, I should feel relatively safe in the seat of this commercial carrier, but I don't. The tightness in my belly alerts my brain to be ready for the surface-to-air missile that will blow us out of the sky. Old war-zone habits die hard, and mine are nowhere near death.

I catch sight of the shore below. A miniature lighthouse flashes its warning beacon. Dots of electric light form inland constellations. There's Orion-like Uncle Sam straddling dark hills, his stovepipe hat slightly askew. And there's . . .

I shut my eyes and break off my silly game. I think of the men and women who won't be coming home, of Martinez and Rippy and of all the others I didn't know and now never will. My chest is a cold cavity of sorrow. I wait for the tears to come but they don't, so I attempt to soothe my sadness by mouthing lines memorized from the soldier's unofficial bible—*The Iliad.*

. . . We must steel our hearts. Bury our dead,
with tears for the day they die, not one day more.
And all those left alive, after hateful carnage,
remember food and drink—

My dead are buried, but their ghosts will haunt my memory for a long time to come. I will most often remember Rippy the haunted spook and his desert demons—and the thing that enveloped Martinez just before the RPG blew him apart.

I know I didn't really see what I thought I saw. I queried Summers and Johnson about the incident and neither of them reported seeing anything supernatural, though they both saw Martinez's spectacular exit from life. They did agree it was damned odd that we found no trace of the Arab prisoner—no scrap of his clothing nor even a single body part. RPG's don't completely obliterate a human body. Summers suggested that the Arab somehow had survived the explosion and slipped away before the smoke cleared. A lot of inexplicable things happen under the fog of war. The prisoner's disappearance was one of those things. Stunned and probably in shock from the previous explosions, my mind fashioned a phantasm from Rippy's tales of demons. I hallucinated Rippy's *Devalpa.* I hallucinated the demonic voices singing in the mountain winds. To believe otherwise, I would have to be as crazy as Rippy so obviously was.

I settle back into my seat as the aircraft shudders through a patch of turbulence. I take another look out the window at the nightscape streaming below. I see my shadowy face reflected in the glass, a face I scarcely recognize, its craggy contours and sunken sockets reconfigured by the Homeric *grind of war.*

Then I see them, and I shudder through an inner turbulence. Mirrored in the glass, with rushing darkness behind them, two ghost eyes fix me in a cold gaze. I see me seeing myself.

Unable to stare myself down, I shut my eyes.

When I open them again, I see nothing but the endless demon-haunted darkness.

*   *   *

I'd thought I was done with this missive. Leaving things up in the air seemed a suitably symbolic ending, but almost as soon as I set foot on home ground, I knew better. I saw with ghost eyes that my secret war was only just beginning. Rippy had somehow passed me his torch of visionary fire. Now *I* was the spook.

Eyes truly are windows to the soul, but the thing I saw hiding within the olive-skinned man in the airport men's room had no soul. I knew at once I was seeing one of Rippy's demons. Just as he'd predicted, the fiends had gone global. They were already *here.*

I slipped into the stall right behind him, before he had a chance to latch the door. My hand-to-hand combat training took over and I used the rear-strangle-takedown to subdue him. Then I shoved his head into the john and drowned him in toilet water, not giving the thing inside him an opportunity to come ripping out of his flesh. Satisfied he was dead, I sat the dripping corpse on the commode, latched the stall door and climbed out.

Feeling as empty as a hollow tree in a windstorm, I slid into the back of the Victory Cab with my duffel bag, and the Pakistani driver pulled away from the Delta terminal. As soon as our eyes met in the rearview mirror I saw what he was and knew I had to kill him.

DEADSIDE IN BUG CITY

Your name is on the lips of the dead.

Draven ducked into a saloon to escape the reeking street prophet. The madman came in after him, but the growling barkeep chased him out with a ball bat. Two burly dockworkers at the bar berated the barkeep for not bashing the prophet's head.

"He darkens that door again, I'll crack his skull like a coconut," the barkeep boasted to his beer-swilling critics. "Religious freaks like him is what's wrong with this world."

The dockworker with a dead cigar stub in his teeth said, "Aw hell, he was probably hoping you'd kill him so he could go preach to the Rotties in Bug City."

"He ain't gotta be dead to do that," said the other dockworker. "Slip in any time he wants. And anyway, Rotties don't talk, you moron. The man dies, his preaching days are over."

Draven sat at the opposite end of the bar and ordered vodka. The words of the demented prophet echoed between his ears: *Your name is on the lips of the dead.* Why that insane declaration should bother him so, Draven didn't understand, but it did, and he couldn't get the madman's insistent voice out of his head.

The barkeep set Draven's shot down in front of him and said, "Ain't seen you in here before. You come to see the zombie zoo?"

"No," said Draven, glancing at his Rolex Submariner diver's watch before taking his first sip. "I'm here on business."

The barkeep fiddled with his handlebar mustache and gave Draven a naked appraisal. "Kind of business you in?"

"Depends. I'm a contract troubleshooter."

"What the hell is that? A hit man?" The man smiled with his mouth, not his eyes.

Draven didn't bother to smile back. "People need things done, I do 'em for the right price."

"Yeah? Well, I got a shitter backed-up in the john. Think you could fix that for me?" Now his eyes joined his lips in a smile as he glanced down the bar to see if his regulars were paying attention to his witty performance.

Draven said, "I could close this shithole saloon down and end all your troubles."

The barkeep's smile fell. He looked hard into Draven's eyes, frowned inside his drooping mustache, and then retreated to the other end of the bar to join the less menacing dockworkers.

Draven lit a smoke. He studied his dim reflection in the murky mirror behind the bar and wondered why the street prophet had chosen him as a target for his crazy prophesying. His brown bomber jacket and his close-cropped hair gave him a vague military bearing, but he guessed it was probably his eyes the religious psycho had latched onto. People usually saw a steely intelligence in the illusive depths of his eyes and thought they were seeing a depth of soul he didn't possess; they saw what they wanted to see and extrapolated the rest.

He downed the rest of his drink and walked three blocks to his appointment on Beecher Street. Gusting winds bore the carrion stench of the fenced-off ghetto inhabited by the undead.

Draven coughed into his hand and then announced himself through the intercom set into the stunted stone wall. The iron gate opened with a buzzing click and he entered the small courtyard, went through a green door and took the rickety elevator cage up to the third floor.

A tall, slender woman in a dark business suit and open-collared white blouse greeted him in the hallway. She extended her hand and said, "I'm Melanie Fisher, Dr. Todd's associate."

Draven shook her smooth hand. Her sandy hair was parted on the left side like a man's but there was nothing masculine about her sensuous face and full bosom.

"We're right down here," she said, indicating the door to suite 33. She stood aside to let him enter ahead of her.

Dr. Todd stood in front of a tall window overlooking the railroad tracks behind the refurbished building. He was speaking into a cell phone.

Draven scanned the spare surroundings. Four metal desks that might've been government-issue formed a rough square in the center of the room. Each desk held a computer terminal and stackable plastic trays crammed with file-folders and loose papers. An old cherrywood desk sat in front of the rear wall of tall windows. Todd walked to the desk and leaned against it, the cell phone still pressed to his ear. He nodded to Draven and held up one finger in a "wait one" gesture.

Draven stuck his hands in the pockets of his jacket and waited. Melanie Fisher lit a cigarette and blew a stream of smoke toward the high ceiling.

She crossed her left arm beneath her bosom and held the cigarette high between two fingers of her right hand. "I've been trying to quit," she said, "but being so close to ground zero, I have to smoke to cover up the stench when the wind's blowing this way."

Todd suddenly folded his phone and came forward from his desk. "Sorry to keep you waiting," he said as he shook Draven's hand. "Keeping our backers happy is a fulltime job. I do more pimping than a lobbyist on the Hill. Ah, but those days are over now. The government tit's dried up, the cash cow slaughtered."

"What Glenn's trying to say in his off-color way," said Melanie Fisher, "is that we've lost all government funding for our research and we must now rely on the private sector. For a scientist, he makes a pretty good politician."

"I detest it," said Todd. "But the good news is, we can pay you five thousand dollars for this assignment, Mr. Draven."

Draven said, "Lay it out for me."

"All right. This way, please."

Todd and Fisher led him through another door and into what looked like a small home theater with comfortable seating and a huge flat-screen TV on one wall. Four smaller screens were affixed to the wall on the right-hand side of the big screen. Todd directed Draven to a seat and Fisher sat beside him. Todd stood behind them and dimmed the lights.

The four smaller screens flickered to life. Each one showed a different view of the housing-project ghetto commonly called Bug City. Human figures dressed in yellow jumpsuits moved about the sidewalks and streets with halting, unnatural gaits. Others stood still or sat staring into space, rocking, twitching or wringing their hands.

Draven knew he was seeing the living-dead victims of the bio-weapon unleashed by terrorists six months ago. The genetically-engineered virus had killed close to 40,000 of the city's inhabitants. 1,400 of those victims had become reanimated corpses—mindless machines of flesh and bone in perpetual motion.

"These are live feeds," explained Todd. "Our cameras are set up at strategic locations within the ghetto so we can monitor their random behavior. All in all, pretty boring stuff. We've been watching the poor buggers for three months now. As soon as the government decided to use this city sector as the main dumping ground for Rotties, we came on board under contract to CDC."

The woman touched Draven's arm as she said, "We observe and record their behavior, then analyze it. We've logged over 2,000 hours, but until last Tuesday, we saw nothing remarkable."

"Melanie was watching when it happened," said Todd with enthusiasm. "She called me at home in the middle of the night she was so excited."

Draven was growing impatient. He'd already seen enough of the on-screen walking corpses. It was depressing; it made him feel more depraved than a voyeur at a carnival freak show. "Cut to the chase," he said. "What did you see?"

"We'll show you," Todd said behind him. "Watch the big screen."

The huge screen lit up and Todd cued the videotape. The scene appeared to be the same street corner shown in the live shot on the lower-left small screen.

Draven leaned forward in his seat as a woman with long, black hair entered the frame from the left and walked deliberately to the brick wall of a three-story housing-project building. Her yellow jumpsuit was noticeably cleaner than those of the other milling subjects. The camera was positioned so that both walls angling away from the corner of the building were partially visible. The woman walked up to the wall and began to spray it with an aerosol can of red paint. Given the camera angle, it was impossible to decipher any recognizable configuration or design in her handiwork, but she moved the can and applied the paint with seemingly purposeful intent.

"What's she doing?" asked Draven.

"Ah, that *is* the question," said Todd. "Obviously, she's spraying paint on a brick wall, but why is she doing it? None of the other victims has ever exhibited such calculated behavior. Some of them walk aimlessly until they run into a wall and then bounce off in another direction like a slow-motion billiard ball until they hit the next obstacle. Others have enough awareness of their surroundings to turn before they hit a wall. But this woman—we call her 'Raven' because of her hair color—seems to have retained some spark of intelligence and possibly even a creative impulse. It's quite amazing, really. And because of her, we've been able to secure funding to keep this project going. If the Pro-lifers can show evidence of intelligent life in just one of the subjects, then their lawyers could make a reasonable case against destroying any of the Rotties. The current administration is bent on extermination and doesn't want things further complicated by any morally ambiguous new data. Which is why our backers will pay you to go in and bring her out."

Fisher added, "The only thing keeping them alive, so to speak, is what amounts to a legal stay of execution until the court decides their fate."

On screen, "Raven" lowered the spray can, and stepped back from the brick wall to scrutinize her "art."

"Look at that," said Todd. "You can't tell me that woman is a mindless zombie."

"Are you sure she's dead?" Draven asked. "Maybe she's in there by mistake."

"Highly unlikely," Todd answered. "But if she *is* alive, you will be rescuing her from a living hell."

"That's it? All you want me to do is go in and bring her out?"

"And to take photos of her spray-painting," said Fisher. "I'm dying to know what it is."

"And if you're concerned about contracting the virus," said Todd, "don't be. The bug mutated rapidly and ceased being contagious three weeks after it was released. That's not government propaganda. It's a scientific fact. Apparently, Allah's bio-engineers weren't the sharpest blades in the box. And I'm sure they had no idea the virus would have this zombie-making effect."

"I'm not worried about the bug," said Draven, "but that place must be a cesspool of bacteria with all those rotting corpses roaming around."

"One of the surprising findings of the medical team is that rate of decay of the typical victim is unnaturally slow. It seems to be a function of the mechanism that reanimates dead organisms. But so far they're at odds to explain how it works. And of course, the Rotties don't eat, so there is no human waste to worry about."

Fisher chimed in: "And crop-dusters spray the entire area everyday with powerful disinfectants."

"You will be outfitted with a mask and breathing apparatus, the kind mountain climbers use at high altitudes," added Todd. "They say the stench is unbearable inside the ghetto."

Draven looked over his shoulder at Todd. "And if the woman resists being brought out?"

"Then you bring her out by force," Todd said. "But we don't want her injured. You'll be driving an ambulance. You'll secure her to the stretcher and simply drive out. Drugging her isn't an option, since she has no functioning biological systems."

"I don't get it," said Draven. "These freaks don't eat or drink, their organs don't work, so what keeps them moving? I'm no biologist, but I know muscles and nerves have to burn energy to move."

"We don't know yet," said Todd. "The CDC has some of the victims in an isolation wing and they've done all sorts of testing on them, but so far they've found no answers. They *have* discovered unexplained electrical activity in the nerves and muscles, but they have no idea what causes it."

"Finding her will be the hardest part of the job," said Fisher. "But she's revisited her wall painting three times that we know of, so she might show up there again. That's the area you should focus on. We've marked it on the map for you."

Draven stood. He looked down at Melanie Fisher, then back at Dr. Todd. "All right. I'll do it."

"Excellent," said Todd, suddenly ebullient. "Melanie, let's go ahead and inoculate him."

"What?" Draven stiffened.

"Just as a precaution," said the doctor. "We want to immunize you against things like cholera, typhoid fever. We're treating this as we would a visit to a primitive third-world country."

"I'll be gentle," Fisher said, smiling as she touched his arm. She left the room and came back a few minutes later with a pressure-gun injector. Draven took off his jacket and rolled up his shirtsleeve. She put the barrel to his bare upper arm and fired. When she pulled it away, a trickle of blood ran down his arm and she wiped it away with a sterile swab.

"There," she said. "In three days you'll be good to go."

*   *   *

Just after dawn on the fourth day after his initial meeting with Todd and Fisher, Draven climbed into the driver's seat of the ambulance and slammed the door. Dr. Todd signaled him to roll the window down. Melanie Fisher stood behind the dapper doctor, smoking a cigarette.

"One more thing," said Todd. "Try not to run over any Rotties. Passions are already high over this whole situation. We don't want to do anything to set off more rioting."

Draven nodded. He put the ambulance in gear and drove off in the direction of the fenced-in derelict housing projects known as Bug City. On the seat next to him was a folder with a color photograph of "Raven" paper-clipped to its cover. Her real name was unknown. Before the undead victims of the Lazarus Bug had been deposited in the condemned projects, they each had been photographed for future reference. The raven-haired woman in the photo had striking features death hadn't erased, not yet. Her heavy-lidded dark eyes appeared unfocused, and her slack-jawed expression suggested a woman coming off a drunk, but Draven easily imagined how she must've looked with the spark of life animating her features. *She must've been a real knock-out when she had a heartbeat.*

As he rolled to a stop in front of the gated entrance, a national guardsman in full combat gear approached the ambulance, his rifle hanging by a canvas strap from his shoulder. Draven flashed his orange security pass in the soldier's face.

"You bringing one out?" asked the young man.

Draven nodded.

"Be careful in there. The Rotties are restless."

The soldier opened the gate and Draven drove through the temporary break in the electrified fence. The gate slammed shut behind him as he drove slowly along a narrow street of cracked asphalt that led into the cramped huddle of ugly brick buildings. The mixed aromas of disinfectant and human rot drifted in through the vents. He closed them and turned the air-conditioner on low.

A flash of yellow caught his eye. A dark-skinned man in a soiled yellow jumpsuit shambled along a walkway in front of the first building on the right. Two more Rotties appeared in the doorway of the same building, a woman with a child hanging on to her leg. The undead woman seemed oblivious to the fact that the child was even there.

Draven stopped to consult the map. By his reckoning, the building with the woman's wall-painting was two streets over, on the backside of the project's west-end. Something thumped against the side of the vehicle. He glanced at the mirror on the driver's door and saw a tall ashen-skinned black man hammer his fist against the ambulance in a second blow. The man was bare-chested, the empty arms of his jumpsuit hanging from his waist to the ground.

Draven cursed. Either his employers had lied to him, or they had been wrong about the Rotties' physical capabilities. Pounding a fist against a vehicle required intent and—at the least—a rudimentary understanding of cause and effect. It was a violent act of will. Draven touched the butt of the pistol snugged in the shoulder rig inside his jacket. He had no idea what effect a .45 slug would have on the walking dead, but he wouldn't hesitate to find out if things got too hairy.

He gunned the engine and sped away as the Rottie delivered a parting blow. He turned right at the next narrow street and had to come to a complete stop to avoid running over a skin-and-bone zombie crawling across the asphalt, head down and long, dirty hair dragging the street. Much of the dead flesh of the crawler's hands had sloughed off, exposing bare bones. Draven was filled with revulsion as he watched the crawler encounter the curb and crawl in place, unable to clear the raised concrete.

"These poor bastards need to be destroyed," he said to himself. Pro-lifers be damned, he thought, this isn't life.

He drove slowly on. A Rottie fell from a third-story window and hit head-first on the ground below. It lay unmoving a moment, then pushed to its feet and staggered forward, its neck obviously broken, head hanging obscenely to one side. Draven was tempted to get out of the vehicle and shoot the thing in the head to put it out of its undying misery, but he was beginning to suspect a bullet in the brain wouldn't lay these abominations to rest. Probably nothing short of cremation would stop them. Saturation bombing with napalm might do it, but crematoriums would be much tidier.

His cell phone rang. He flipped it open and answered. It was Melanie Fisher.

"Bad news," she said. "There are reports of men with guns trying to get to Bug City. The police intercepted a convoy of pickup trucks and turned them back, but there may be more on the way. They call themselves The Exterminators and say they are going to eliminate the Rotties once and for all."

"Great," said Draven, lighting a cigarette.

"Draven . . .?"

"Yeah?"

"Be careful."

"Bet your sweet ass," he said, then shut the cell and accelerated to the next corner, where a naked Rottie walked in place, forehead against a streetlamp pole, going nowhere.

He stopped at the curb fronting Raven's spray-painted wall. He put on the breathing apparatus (a mask connected to a canister of oxygen worn in a canvas sling on his back), shut off the engine and stepped out of the vehicle. He pulled a digital camera from his jacket pocket and approached the brick wall. The nearest Rotties were milling about in the street twenty meters from him, oblivious to his presence. In the distance behind them, another scattered handful wandered a grassy area near the electrified fence.

Draven stared at the woman's handiwork. Beneath a shapeless blob of red paint were three crude but unmistakable letters: G O D. Below the letters was a misshapen arrow pointing downward. He raised the camera to his eye and snapped off six shots. He looked around to make sure his flank was still secure, then took four more shots.

He wasn't a religious man, so he was somewhat surprised by his reaction to Raven's "GOD" graffiti. Chills prickled his arms and scalp, and he felt a falling sensation in his gut as if he were in an elevator suddenly lurching to a stop. He stared at the wall, trying to fathom the meaning of the down-pointing arrow under God. Did it mean the woman thought God was here? Was it a distress signal to the Almighty, the arrow intended to direct Him here from Heaven? Did it mean God was buried here, entombed beneath the arrow? Did it mean anything at all, or was it only a religious delusion of a decaying brain?

He shot one last picture, stuck the camera in his jacket and walked toward the building across the street—the direction from which Raven originally had come to spray her message on the wall. He didn't relish going into any of these buildings, but he had to begin his search somewhere, and it seemed a logical choice. If there were 1,400 Rotties within these fences, then most of them had to be inside the buildings; there weren't that many wandering about outside. Maybe a shred of primitive instinct to seek shelter drove them indoors.

He stopped in the doorway of building F, pulled his Mag-Lite from his back pocket and stepped inside. There was no electricity in any of the buildings and Draven felt as if he were entering a shadowy cave—or a giant tomb. He heard nothing but the rhythmic hiss of his breath in his oxygen mask. In front of him was a stairway to the two floors of apartments above. He clicked on the flashlight and started on the ground floor, going from unit to unit, but to his surprise he found the ramshackle apartments empty. Where the hell were the Rotties?

He took the thin concrete-and-steel steps to the second floor. He kicked a door open and his beam of light fell on a naked corpse standing in front of a TV with a shattered screen. In profile, her partially decayed breasts sagged to her enormous belly. The woman must've been pregnant when she succumbed to the virus, and Draven willed himself not to think of the never-to-be-born infant slowly rotting in her womb. She turned sluggishly toward the source of the light beam, her eyes holding the light like cloudy mirrors. Her pregnant belly was unnaturally low-slung, the dark purple head of the dead baby protruding from her vagina. Draven guessed that the walls of her womb had yielded to rot and gravity had brought the infant to its obscene impasse. He left them there and went on to the next unit. Fifteen minutes later he'd completed his sweep of F building, having found only six Rotties—none of them Raven. He decided to go back to Building G, marked by the inexplicable graffiti.

As soon as he went through the doorway he knew he'd hit undead pay-dirt. Rotties congregated at the foot of the stairs, on the stairs and in the doorways of apartment units. Some of them turned in his direction and looked at him with dead eyes. Unlike the living-dead in countless zombie movies, these walking corpses didn't grunt, growl or shriek "More brains." With no air in the lungs, they couldn't vocalize at all. There was only the low murmur of shuffling bare feet.

Draven played his light in their faces, looking for Raven. Some of them backed away from the light, others moved toward it. Remembering the man who'd pounded the ambulance, he warily advanced into the huddle of zombies. The stench found its way into his mask. He ignored it and weaved his way through them and toward the first apartment.

A mummified hand knocked his oxygen mask askew, and he lashed out with the Mag-Lite in a moment of panic. The heavy flashlight thumped into a wide, putrefied face and dislodged the dead man's nose and caved in his cheek. Another hand latched onto the back of Draven's jacket and yanked him off balance. He swung around with the club-like Mag-Lite and cracked it against the aggressive Rottie's skull. The light didn't go out.

As with one mind, the undead crowd washed over Draven like a relentless ocean wave and took him under.

The dead sea of yellow-clad corpses suddenly parted above him. He was on his back, looking up into the face of the woman he'd been sent to find. Raven had found him.

*   *   *

She extended her slender hand to him, but he couldn't bring himself to touch her and stood up on his own. His mask hung below his chin. He left it there so he could speak clearly to her. "My name is Draven," he said in a loud, clear voice. "I've come to take you out of here. Do you understand me?"

Though her eyes were death-clouded, he perceived intelligence behind them. She silently mouthed his name.

Your name is on the lips of the dead.

The other Rotties stood motionless around them, leaning in expectantly. Draven sensed they were watching this meeting with great reverence, as if he were an envoy from the world of the living, here to impart a message of profound import to their leader.

"Will you come with me?" he asked.

Her face didn't appear any worse for the wear than it had when her photo was taken. The eggheads were apparently right about the unnatural rate of decay. And yet, most of the other Rotties seemed more rotten than Raven, their flesh slowly yielding to the ravages of decomposition, while her skin remained fairly smooth, though deathly pallid. What, Draven wondered, made her different?

He stared into her unblinking eyes, waiting for an answer, a nod, any sign that she understood his question. "Come with me," he said. "Please."

A helicopter's rotors thumped the air above the building. The Rotties stirred, reacting to the sound. A ripple ran through the herd. Raven raised her hands and immediately calmed them. Draven was astounded by her easy control over her dead fellows.

As he was about to reach for her arm to regain her attention, gunfire erupted outside. Draven pushed through the stinking bodies and looked out the nearest window. Outside the rear fence three men with rifles were shooting at the scattered handful of Rotties in front of them. One of the targets spun around and fell to the weed-choked ground, bits of decayed flesh flying from its face.

"Son of a bitch," Draven spat. He rushed outside, drawing his .45 from his shoulder rig.

The wounded corpse was on hands and knees, trying to get up. The police helicopter hovered over the armed Exterminators, its loud-speaker ordering them to drop their weapons, but the three riflemen continued to fire at the walking dead.

Draven stood in the middle of the narrow street, assumed a two-handed firing stance and snapped off four shots through the chain-link fence. He didn't expect to score hits with his handgun at this distance. His intention was to scare the shooters off. But they continued to fire. And now they were firing at him.

The cell phone in his pocket chirped and a rifle slug thumped the asphalt at his feet. Draven quickly calculated trajectory and adjusted his aim accordingly, then fired again. One of the riflemen went down. The two remaining Exterminators increased their rate of fire, apparently infuriated by the loss of their fallen comrade.

A high-powered slug ripped into Draven's left shoulder and a millisecond later a slug drilled into his forehead, cut a fatal swath through his brain and blew out the back of his head.

*   *   *

Melanie Fisher and Dr. Todd saw Draven's death on the live-feed screen. Though there was no sound accompanying the picture, Fisher "felt" the devastating head-shot in her belly. She collapsed into the seat and buried her face in her hands.

"Look!" said Todd. "There she is!"

Fisher looked up at the screen. With the enigmatic wall-painting in the background, Raven walked to Draven's body and squatted stiffly over him. The dead woman cupped Draven's face in her hand, then bent down and pressed her lips to the wound in his head.

"My God, what's she doing?" asked Todd. "Is she . . . drinking his blood?"

After a full minute, Raven pulled away and stood up.

"No," said Fisher when she saw the impossible thing that happened next.

Draven sat up in the street and looked around like a man waking in unfamiliar surroundings. Raven extended her hand. Draven accepted it, and she pulled him to his feet. He touched his fingertips to the back of his ruined skull, looked at his fingers, and then walked hand-in-hand with

Raven toward the building. A small crowd of Rotties assimilated them with welcoming arms.

"Jesus Christ! What the hell just happened?" Todd demanded.

"I'm not sure," Melanie Fisher said, "but I think she just gave him the kiss of life."

TERRA INCOGNITA

for Chris Whitley

Roadhouse

It was a slapdash affair, cobbled together with scrounged scraps of wood and assorted bullet-riddled remnants of the sacked hamlet. Socorro didn't want to stop here, but Draven thought the roadhouse was a suitable tribute to inventive cannibalization and a good place to knock off road dust and belly up to the bar. She followed him inside because she was afraid of what might come lurking along the dark road.

Socorro unfolded her map and spread the ragged-edged inked skin across the reclaimed church pew that served as the bar. According to legend, the map had been tattooed on a holy man's back as punishment for having illicit visions.

"Wish you'd get rid of that filthy thing," Draven said. He tossed back a shot of Gold Lizard and winced when it went down.

"Not after what I went through to get it," she said, hunching over the map and tracing a finger along a faded blue line etched in the dried skin.

"I don't want to hear your whoring story again."

"You killed people for money," she reminded him. "You have no right to judge me."

"I'm not judging anybody, I just don't want to hear it."

A quartet of stray carnival folk broke into song, banging time on their table with empty bottles. Two shirtless men played a game of blades on a wooden crate, their knife points dancing between their splayed fingers. Against the back wall stood an upright pine box housing the mummified remains of a gray-haired woman wearing nothing but a string of pearls. A man in a bowler hat kissed a pebble, dropped it in the tin cup at the mummy's feet and muttered a prayer.

Draven rolled a cigarette and lit it with a Lucifer. Sulfurous smoke haloed his head. He coughed blood. She wiped the fine droplets off her map, making a red smear from the summit of Sawtooth Mountain to the Valley of Evil Saints. She narrowed her painted eyes at him but voiced no complaint. Instead, she said, "You should let me work on your bones."

"Yeah, I guess I could use a tune-up." He caught the barkeep's good eye and pointed at his empty shot glass. "One more for the road."

The barkeep refilled his shot glass and scooped the rusty coins off the bar.

Socorro meditated on the map while Draven drank his Lizard and smoked his stinking weed. It didn't matter to her that their ultimate destination wasn't on the map. By her lights, one had to keep a farseeing eye on improbable futures.

Even the damned can dream.

Crosses on the Hill

She manipulated his skeleton while he watched the crosses burning on the hill. Demon winds howled through the rocky valley where they'd made camp. Scorpions scuttled over the stony ground. She ran her knee down his spine, eliciting a series of marimba-like notes. Draven moaned harmoniously.

"What's it mean?" Socorro asked. "The burning crosses."

He shrugged. She wrenched his head and popped his neck vertebrae.

"What does anything mean?" he posited, neck bones humming.

"Nothing, according to you."

"There you go."

Certain he was smirking, she countered: "You'll sing a different tune when we find the museum."

"Bullshit, Ro. That map is the work of a psycho tattoo artist."

"I have faith in this map. I *know* it will take us to the Museum of Religious Atrocities."

A pack of dogs howled in the distance. The demon winds howled back. The plaintive dialogue was unsettling, hinting at dreadful secrets.

"And anyway," Draven argued, "what if it does? What then? What do you expect to find there?"

"Answers."

"Answers are no good unless you know what the questions are."

"Don't be obtuse. You know what I want to know. What everybody wants to know."

Draven chuckled, then stretched out on the ground with his hands beneath his head and stared up at the night clouds. "Obtuse," he said. "Doesn't that mean thickheaded?"

"Thickheaded, dull-witted, simple-minded."

"Well hell, those are fine qualities where I come from."

"That's just the point, Draven. You know where you come from but not how you got here or why. Nobody does. The museum may tell us."

"Uh-huh." He yawned and shut his eyes.

Draven's Dream

Bug City . . . the dead in an interment-camp ghetto surrounded by electrified fencing . . . graffiti sprayed on brick: "GOD" above a downward pointing arrow . . . Draven in his brown bomber jacket enters Bug City to find the dead woman responsible for the enigmatic graffiti . . . Rogues with rifles shoot into the compound, taking potshots at the walking dead . . . Draven shoots back . . . The riflemen zero him and Draven takes one in the head, a kill-shot . . . The raven-haired dead woman resurrects him with a kiss to his mortal wound . . . God is but a breath away . . . But as Draven well knows, the dead don't breathe . . .

The Theorist

They met a man with no shadow on the road. There was a sun up there somewhere, though they never saw it, and enough light filtered through the purplish clouds to give *them* shadows, but this cadaverous man in the dusty black suit cast no shadow. His dark eyes regarded them dully. His head and face were misshapen, as if his head had been squeezed in a vice and elongated, his chin as sharp as the blade of a spade.

Socorro pointed at the ground near the long-faced man's feet and blurted, "Where's your shadow?!"

The man cast a glance down the road behind him and said, "Sulking somewhere back there, I imagine. I had to speak rather sternly to him, you see. He'll come around when he gets over it."

"Imfuckingpossible," said Draven. "Don't talk to him, Ro."

"Everything's possible somewhere," said the shadowless man.

"Who *are* you?" asked Socorro.

"I'm a theorist, late of the abolished school of lost science. Thanks for asking." He winked at her.

Draven said, "Here's my theory. You're out of your fucking mind."

"That's no theory, lad, that's fact. So are you. So is she. So are we all out of our minds. Otherwise we couldn't be here. You have to lose your mind to find this place."

To Ro, Draven said, "What'd I say? See?"

"No, wait," she said when the man started up the road. "Have you heard of the Museum of Religious Atrocities?"

"Certainly. I was just there."

"I knew it!" She jumped up and down, juggling her fulsome breasts.

"Did you." The Theorist smiled, eyeing her jiggles.

"Here we go," Draven said with a scowl.

"Where is it?" she asked, bouncing on the balls of her feet.

"Just this side of Bordertown."

"That's where we're going!" And there went her breasts again, bobbling merrily and capturing the Theorist's effusive attention. "And this road takes us right to it. My map says so."

Draven seized the lapels of the man's black coat and said, "Get your dirty eyes off her."

"Ah, a man of action," said the Theorist, smiling. "Bordertown should be just the place for you. You'll probably never want to leave it."

"Is it . . . wonderful?" asked Socorro. "The museum?"

"Wonderfully atrocious." The Theorist beamed a smile at her bodacious breasts.

Draven was still holding the black suit-coat's lapels, but the man was no longer wearing it. "How did . . .?"

"Accelerated movement," the Theorist said, having anticipated the question. "Dimensional anomalies are common this close to Bordertown. It's all there in my thesis. Fifty thousand words of discredited data and brilliant speculation. The great underground particle-accelerator did its work, the gravitons went steaming off into parts unknown, and everybody was happy as pigs in shit. They gave me the key to the city, made me chairman of the society. Champagne corks blew holes in all previous theories. Drinks all around."

Draven handed the man his coat. "Here. Take this and your happy horseshit and be on your way."

"Stop it, Draven," Socorro said with fierce eyes. "This is important. This is what we're about, don't you see that?"

"But," the Theorist went on, "that wasn't the end of it. Rather, it was merely the beginning of the real tale of woe." He pulled a pocket calculator from the inside pocket of his coat and began tapping miniature keys with long fingers.

Draven's fingers crawled into his bomber jacket to fondle the butt of the gun snugged in his shoulder holster.

"Infinite permutations," said the Theorist. "Finite incarnations. But where was the balance? I worked eons trying to balance the bloody equation. To no avail. There *was* no mathematical explanation. The science was as useless as tits on a teletype, I tell you."

Draven's pistol came out. Pointed at the Theorist's long undertaker's face.

"Nothing obtains," the Theorist said with great solemnity. He gazed into the gun's muzzle. "That's rather like the Buddha's navel, you know. Invites intense contemplation."

"I told you to hit the road," Draven snapped.

"Goddammit, Draven," said Socorro. "I won't let you fuck this up. We've come too far."

"*Too* too," said the Theorist.

Draven thumbed back the hammer. The click was as soft as a baby's kiss.

"Let me ask you this," the dapper Theorist suggested. "What draws you to Bordertown?"

Growing ever more impatient, Draven said, "It's the great divide, gateway to some other side."

"Ah, the songs of the Prophet Chris." The Theorist smiled as he put away his calculator. "Blood antenna on dust radio and all that rot. His lines are often on the lips of the dead. Take it from me, young man, I've spent several lifetimes shining a light in the darkness, and you know what I found? Nothing but more god-loving darkness. Your motivations are remotely manipulated from underground, particles colliding with obscene force. Nothing obtains."

The road began to vibrate with a low-pitched hum. The trio turned and looked down the road running across the desert, winding between arroyos and the oddly-shaped pink mesas to the east.

"There they come," the Theorist announced with a note of vindication. "The black convoy."

Black Trucks

They stepped to the side of the road and watched the black trucks belching oily smoke as they rumbled past, snarling. The canvas tarps were furled, naked metal frames like ribcages over the empty truck-beds. The drivers wore black hoods.

"They won't be empty when they ride out of Bordertown," the Theorist told them. "The tarps will be unfurled because people don't like to see squirming corpses stacked like cordwood. Sad husks. You'll smell them well enough, though. Must be over a hundred trucks, but they can't keep up with the exponential number of transients. The Lazarus bug is one baad bugger."

"But what about the Museum of Religious Atrocities?" Socorro persisted in her obsession, folding her arms across her breasts and stamping her foot like a petulant child.

"The true atrocities aren't to be found in a museum, dear girl," said the Theorist. "But don't take my word for it. Not if you're bound for Bordertown."

The Kill

Draven squeezed the trigger. The slug punched a hole in the bridge of the Theorist's nose and ripped a ragged exit through the back of his skull. The Theorist fell over like a tall timber and hit the road, raising a little cloud of ocher dust.

"What the hell'd you do that for?" demanded Socorro.

"He wouldn't shut up." Draven holstered his gun.

"You stupid son of a bitch!"

"Forget about it. C'mon, let's burn daylight."

They had walked several miles in ominous silence before they noticed the Theorist was following them like a stupidly loyal dog.

"Shit," said Draven. "Dead but won't lie down. Used to be, when I killed somebody they stayed dead. Don't know what this world's coming to."

The Museum of Religious Atrocities

It was the oddest edifice they'd ever seen—a pyramid of stacked pueblos, ladders leaning at impossible angles or standing, unsupported, in defiance of gravity. Draven didn't want to go in but she persuaded him by fondling his genitalia until he rose remorselessly to the occasion.

As they passed through the narrow entrance, the Theorist shouted after them: "Microbes and molecules! That's the ticket!"

An old Hopi dressed as a sacred clown stamped their hands with a winged blob of red ink and they entered the Chamber of Saintly Entrails & Silent Organs, whereupon they were immediately sickened by the stench of raw guts. Draven paused in front of a framed maze of slimy intestines, the duodenum hanging several inches below the gilt frame's lower edge. Socorro stood transfixed before a tall wooden cross with human organs nailed to every inch of its unvarnished surface. Wind moaned through the dim corridors, chilling her. She moved on to the next exhibit—a tower of severed penises lumped together and sculpted into a single six-foot-tall penis, upright and pointing lustfully toward heaven.

"This is sick," said Draven, eschewing a double-helix arrangement of dried foreskins.

"I think it's sublime," she countered, her face absolutely beatific.

They climbed the ladder to the next level and entered the Chamber of

Inquisition & Redemption. Draven took one look at the moaning corpses laid out on the rack, stretched over a wheel of blades or broken on various other devices of torture and said, "I've seen enough. I'll wait for you outside."

"Wait. You have to see the angels." She pointed to an immense iron angel standing on the overhang of the next level. "They say it's very moving."

She fondled him. He followed her up. She took his hand and together they stepped into the Chamber of Fallen Angels. Nine sexless angels were spiked to the adobe wall like butterflies in a lepidopterist's collection. Despair contorted their angelic faces. Their black eyes darted, seemingly unable to focus on anything in this worldly realm. Sinewy wings twitched uselessly.

"Good God," said Draven, "they're still alive."

"They're beautiful," said Socorro, tears streaming down her flushed cheeks.

Draven touched the butt of his pistol. "Maybe I can put them out of their misery."

"No! This is all part of the plan. We shouldn't interfere."

"Whose plan?"

"God's, ninny. They're *fallen*. Put here as an example for us."

The angels began to sing all at once, harmonizing in such a way as to sound like a veritable multitude: Angelic multiplication. Goosebumps rose in Draven's flesh. Blood trickled from Socorro's ears. She went to her knees. Draven drew his gun and shot all nine targets in this shooting gallery of angels. Nine head-shots. Nine holes bleeding liquid light. The song of the last angel died in a haunting hollow echo.

Socorro was curled in a fetal ball at his feet, whimpering. Draven grabbed her leg and dragged her to the ladder. A few moments later, they were running out of the museum. The sacred clown chased them with a war club but he was too old and feeble to catch them.

When they were once again on the road to Bordertown, Draven noticed that the backs of their hands where the Hopi had stamped them with red ink were bleeding.

"Stigmata," Socorro groaned.

"Mark of the Damned," said Draven.

The Mission

The Theorist waited for them in front of a deserted Spanish mission at the edge of town. "You may want to go inside for a quick prayer to the Unholy Mother before you enter the town," he said.

"We're way past praying," said Draven.

"Still . . ." The Theorist fingered the bloodless bullet hole in his head. "Why do you keep pestering us?"

"I have a theory about that."

"I don't want to hear it."

"Your loss." The Theorist shrugged with exaggerated nonchalance.

"I don't think I want to go there," Socorro said, pointing at the huddled buildings in the distance. "It gives me the creeps, on top of everything else . . ."

"It's just a town," said Draven.

"It's *Bordertown*, for God's sake."

"We're going. We have to. We've come all this way . . ."

"He's right," said the Theorist. "There's really no choice."

"If there's no choice, then what's the point?" She put her hands on her hips and jutted her jaw.

"She may have a point," said the Theorist, equivocating.

"Predestination makes it all pointless," Socorro insisted.

"That would be the point." The Theorist held up a bony finger, not his own.

In no mood to argue the point, Draven seized her hand and pulled her toward the town.

"Wait!" she cried, dragging her heels. "If you'll pray with me, then I'll go with you."

He relented, and together they went into the Spanish mission to say their prayers while the Theorist took measurements of the ragged exit wound on the back of his head.

High Pass

For those lucky or unlucky enough to find it, Bordertown inevitably worked its inexorable welcome. No one could resist its ambiguous aura promising: deliverance and doom; damnation and redemption; despair and ecstasy; lust and enlightenment. So said the Theorist.

Situated precariously on the edge of a vast red canyon, Bordertown was connected to the rest of the world by a narrow road across a high pass, a steep drop to oblivion yawning on either side of the rock-studded road. The forlorn slip of egress/ingress was unguarded.

"This is as far as I go," the Theorist said, stopping in the middle of the treacherous pass. "Good luck to you both."

"You know something we don't?" asked Draven. He avoided looking down at the empty space on either side of the road because heights made him dizzy.

The long-faced man's boisterous laughter rattled against his thin bones. "If I didn't, I wouldn't be a very good but discredited theorist, would I? Truth to tell, I've been to Bordertown, but I was recycled. The Powers That May Or May Not Be deemed me more useful out here in the world at large, where my various theories might be tested or otherwise put in play, fair or foul. Right now I'm toying with an offshoot of String Theory. A knotty conundrum to be sure! I call it my Yo-yo Theory. It presupposes the yin-yang principle even as it implies a down-and-out double-looping twist of—"

"Save it, horse-face," said Draven. "We're not interested in your theories."

Socorro wasn't listening to the men's idle chatter. She was already succumbing to Bordertown's spell. She stood staring into the town, fondling her breasts in sensual anticipation.

Draven felt it too. A burgeoning erection throbbed against his rusty zipper and he thought he might be falling in love with Socorro. But falling wasn't something he wanted to think about while they were standing on the high pass to Bordertown.

"*Adios*, then," said the Theorist. "I would say, *Go with God*, but, well, you know how *that* goes . . ."

Bordertown

Neither of them had ever seen the like of this town. In fact, it wasn't a town at all; rather, it was a mishmash patchwork of odd pieces of architectures from different parts of the known world, suggesting that whole sections of far-off cities had been excised and then grafted onto this conglomerate township on the perilous edge of the red canyon. Here a minaret, there a stunted skyscraper; here a patch of tumbledown shanties, there a Gothic cathedral; here a neighborhood of rice-paper houses, there a row of brown-stones with inviting front-door stoops on hopscotch sidewalks.

"It's beautiful," she said in a reverent whisper.

"Really?" he rasped.

They took a room over the poolroom on Fornication Row. Draven paid for it with a handful of rusty coins, and Socorro had his pants off as soon as they stepped into the colorless room. They fell onto the lumpy bed and made rigorous love, the background music of billiard balls clicking and thumping downstairs. He sank into a blissful doze while she scratched strange symbols on the walls and on the hardwood floor with a rusty nail.

When he came awake, she was using the nail on him, scarifying his flesh with the same strange symbols. He didn't feel much pain and there wasn't much blood, so he let her continue while he had a smoke. Finally, he said, "You wanna tell me what you're doing?"

Looking up from his thigh, she said, "I have this incredible burst of creative energy. I don't know if it's the sex or just being in Bordertown, but I have to strike while the iron is hot."

Draven chuckled. "I know what you mean. You've got my iron plenty hot too." He pointed at his thrumming cock, erected anew. She set aside her nail and mounted him. Her orgasmic cries reminded him of the chorus of spiked angels.

Draven passed a lot of aimless time in the poolroom downstairs, leaving Socorro to her creative scratching. He got to know a couple of young pool shooters, Skeeter and Joe Rob. Skeeter fancied himself an authority on death and mortuary sciences and talked of little else.

"Death *is* another country," Skeeter said as he sank the six-ball in the side pocket. "This ain't your daddy's U.S. of A. We're in the deadlands of the Untied Snakes of America."

Joe Rob was preoccupied with finding a mysterious place called Devil's Valley. "That old toothless Mexskin says Diablo Valley is just the other side of the canyon," he said. "That's where I'm heading when I get outta here."

"I think maybe we're all heading there, bro," said Skeeter.

After downing too many shots of mescal, Draven unlimbered his tongue and poured forth much of his pent-up emotions and repressed preoccupations. "Whaddaya spoze to do when you're robbed of your life's calling? Can you answer me that? What good's an assassin in a world where nobody dies? I mean, this used to be a great country, ya know? But now . . ."

"I met up with a motherfucker of a hit man way back when," said Joe Rob. "Sumbitch used a chainsaw on me before he finally took me out. Hell hath no fury like a ass-fucked whoor. Them was some dark times."

"I dunno what the hell I'm even doing here, ya know what I'm saying?" Draven went on, choking his cue.

"I hear ya, man," said Skeeter. "But it sure beats the dirt nap."

"I see you still pack a gun," Joe Rob observed, nodding at the bulge in Draven's jacket.

"Yeah, hell. Can't kill anybody with it but it still makes a memorable impression. Punctuation with a bang."

Skeeter snickered as he took his shot. He scratched.

"How long you boys been here?" asked Draven.

Joe Rob shrugged. "Hard to say, the way one day bleeds into another."

"Don't think we'll be here much longer," said Skeeter. "I think things are finally fixing to pop."

"I hope to shit you're right, man. I'm ready to move on. Ain't nothing to do here but shoot pool and fuck them whoors."

The boys decided fucking whoors wasn't such a bad idea. They figured to fuck their way down Fornication Row. "Wanna join us, man?" asked Skeeter.

Draven said, "No thanks," and went upstairs, where naked Socorro was scratching the candlelit walls with a curling strand of barbwire. He'd figured to spread her again on the rumpled mattress, as the boys' talk of fornication had fired his ignoble lust, but she was lost in the flames of her creative pursuits, oblivious to the inadvertent barbwire wounds in her flesh. He had no idea what those scratched symbols meant, but he knew they gave him a funny feeling in his gut, almost as if some phantom umbilical cord were trying to pull him out of this world and take him into parts unknown. For his part—or parts—he found his ardor quickly cooled by his companion's odd behavior and by those ominous symbols and signs. So he sat in the corner and dozed, drifting on lazy currents of dreaming.

*   *   *

In the bleeding light of dawn the Whiteskins came to Bordertown. Mexskins Jorge and Jesus explained to Draven that the three pale-skinned ladies in long white robes were priestesses of the feared cult of cave-dwelling Skranks—a warrior-like tribe that came periodically into town to wreak their particular brand of religious havoc. The Whiteskins were always accompanied by a small but deadly band of fierce and muscular sword-wielding warriors in conical wicker hats and enormous codpieces.

"They'll grab a man and woman off the street and string em up in the square and torture them for days at a time," said Jorge. "They believe the screams attract the attention of their gods."

"Good old-fashioned sacrifice," said Jesus. "When it's over, the torture victims are soulless meat puppets. Zombies with no future."

"Why do people stand for it?" asked Draven.

"Cuz they fear the Skranks' blades," Jorge explained. "Their bites aren't fatal, but they never heal. And they say you take those cuts into the next world."

"They come near me," boasted Draven, drawing his pistol, "they'll feel the bite of hot lead."

They watched from a sagging balcony overlooking the town square as the Skranks strung up the two unfortunate victims by their heels and began the bloody torture. Spectators cheered at their own good fortune of having not been chosen as victims. When he could no longer bear listening to the ragged screams, Draven went back to his room over the billiard parlor.

Socorro was trying to light her nipples with a candle flame. Their bed was full of odd-shaped stones.

"What the hell are these rocks for?" he asked her.

"We have to make love on a bed of holy stones," she said, dragging him toward the bed.

"The hell you say." He flung her to the floor. "Get a grip, bitch. And stop burning your tits."

She dragged herself onto the bed and began to masturbate with a phallic stone.

"Keep this up and I'll have to cut you loose," he said in disgust, and then went downstairs to drown his roiling emotions in mescal.

*   *   *

When he sobered up he decided it was time to leave Bordertown. If they stayed here much longer, Socorro would be irredeemably damaged. He'd come to love the woman and felt he had to save her from herself—or more specifically, from the effect this damned place was having on her. He still didn't understand what had drawn them to this town on the edge of the red canyon and he had no idea what sort of life they could have back in the deadlands outside of Bordertown, but he knew they shouldn't spend one more night here. That wrenching tug at his gut told him: Leave now or be damned forever.

He trundled Socorro out of the room and hoisted her over his shoulder to carry her down the stairs and into the street.

"You can't do this!" she screamed in his ear. "I'm so close!"

"Close to what?"

"To what comes next. Put me down, you idiot!"

"Close to losing your soul, not to mention your mind."

"Goddammit, Draven, don't you get it? We had to come here to find our way out."

"I know the way out. That's where we're going."

"No, no, no. We can't just walk out of here. That's not how it works. There are laws and rituals, spiritual tasks to perform. If we leave now we're damned for sure."

"Damned if we do, damned if we don't," said Draven. "Whaddaya gonna do. Fuck it."

He carried her, screaming and kicking, down Fornication Row, crossed over to Pilgrim's Dilemma and cut through a sinister alley to Purgatory Plaza. From there he could see the high pass that would take them out of Bordertown.

"I refuse to be a cog in this diabolical machinery," he said. "Fuck these systems of hell, this metaphysical bullshit. We're outta here."

As soon as he stepped onto the high pass, the red sky seemed to split open and a winged demon came swooping down at them, fierce talons extended and ready to strike. Its reptilian skin was purple, its leathery wings veined with crimson. Its shoulders bore deadly-sharp horns. Draven dumped Socorro off his shoulder and onto the rocky pass just before the demon struck. Its talons ripped into his jacket and sank deep into his chest, blocking access to the gun in his shoulder rig. He seized the creature's neck with both hands and they grappled in the dirt, the demon's wings flapping spasmodically.

Socorro jumped up, pulled the rusty nail from her pocket and plunged it into the demon's lidless eye. The thing screeched, wings fluttering wildly now. Draven gripped the back of the demon's head, pulled it to his mouth and sank his teeth deep into its pebbled throat. Bitter blood gushed into his mouth as he shook his head from side to side, ripping out a meaty chunk of flesh. The creature withdrew its talons, staggered backward and then flew away, shrieking.

Draven drew his gun and snapped off three futile shots at the flying target.

The Theorist was waiting for them on the other side of the pass. He greeted them with his undertaker's smile. "Well done!" he said.

"You knew we were coming out," Draven observed.

"Quite right. It was a hypothetical inevitable. An irresistible conclusion based on available data."

Socorro gazed longingly back at the town, then turned her eyes on Draven as if seeing him for the first time. She took his hand, interlacing her fingers with his.

The Theorist said, "You passed muster, lad. Had you stayed in that town you would've been transported to an abominable place and ultimately subjected to the interminability of torment by the vengeful souls of those you killed in your lifetime. But you cut yourself from the herd and escaped the fate of a damned nation. Even found love, of a kind. Forsaking Bordertown, you've chosen an unlikely path. A shortcut, you might say. But it won't be easy. Many trials lay ahead for the both of you. There will be suffering enough and time."

"What lies at the end?" asked Draven.

"I don't actually know," said the Theorist, gleefully rubbing his hands together, "but I do have a humdinger of a theory."

With sunset's last red glimmer at their backs, they walked out into the failing light. Winged creatures circled overhead but in the gathering darkness it was impossible to know if they were demons or angels.

Or something else altogether.

DEATH COMES CALLING

Death came for Reginald Summerfield much in the manner of an unexpected houseguest; Reggie deeply resented the unanticipated intrusion upon his orderly life, but he was bound by tradition and folkloric convention to receive the unwelcome visitor into his society, no matter how greatly he detested the distasteful fact of Death's arrival.

When the grimmest of shadows darkened his door, he had little choice but to meet it with decorum befitting a gentleman and a scholar of no little renown. If some cosmic mistake had been made, it would be foolhardy to engage Fate's emissary in hostile debate. Better to play the proper host and greet the dark envoy with equanimity. Begging for one's life, Reggie knew, was out of the question.

"So this is it, then," Reggie said as he gazed into the impenetrable darkness within the cowl veiling Death's face. Then he glanced at his own cooling corpse on the floor before the fireplace and added: "I can't tell you how long I had to lie there in Limbo, wondering, as it were, if this was really *it*."

"My apologies," Death said in a mellifluous voice and with a slight nod of the hood. "I was unavoidably delayed. Terror bombings invariably throw me behind. I trust that you used your extra time wisely. So many of my transients have little or no time for personal reflection."

"Rather more like torture, really," said Reggie. "Lying there in terror and pain, wondering if your time has come or if it's merely an episode from which you might recover and then go on with a renewed appreciation of living . . . if not as a mindless radish."

"Acceptance is no easy thing," Death intoned. "Especially for one accustomed to drinking so deeply from life as to be in a constant state of drunkenness."

"Drunkenness! See here, I resent your implication. No, I do more than that. I deny it!"

Death made a rumbling noise that might've been deep laughter. "Deny you were drunk on life? You? Reginald Summerfield, philosopher and professor of aesthetics? You *are* Summerfield, aren't you? I rarely make mistakes, but they do happen."

"Of course I'm Summerfield. This is my house, this is my study and those are my books. You'll find my picture on the back flyleaf of each one of the baker's dozen."

Death glided over to the books and pulled down a copy of *In Defense of the Aesthete*. Holding the volume with elongated digits of a shimmering black bone-like substance, Death opened the book, studied the author's photo and then snapped it shut and set it back on the shelf.

"It would appear that you had a productive life, Summerfield." Death again gave a slight nod.

"You may as well call me Reggie. It's what my friends call me, and though you are certainly no friend, it would seem that my relationship with you is destined to be of the most intimate nature."

Death projected a brooding silence.

"As to my productivity, well, I hate to quibble, but you certainly cut *that* short. And rather rudely, I might add. I was just entering the most productive phase of my life. I don't mean to sound sullen, but my greatest contributions to the world of letters and reflective thought were ahead of me. Hardly seems fair. Or even wise."

Death made no response.

"I'll go so far as to call it a grave injustice," Reggie couldn't stop himself, though he realized he probably sounded like a petulant child to the dark spectre. "Grave indeed. I don't know how you live with yourself, if you want to know the truth."

"Death doesn't live. A man of your learning should know better than to make such an oxymoronic statement."

"I was speaking metaphorically. Or aren't you capable of grasping such abstract concepts? I mean, what *are* you really, but a workman. A journeyman working the slimy bottom links of the Great Chain of Being, *that's* what I suspect you are. A cosmic scavenger, feeding on befouled corpses and broken lives. No offense."

"None taken. It's a bit more complicated than that, but you needn't concern yourself. I am your escort out of this plane of existence. What happens to you after that, isn't my affair."

"I see. You're just the ferryman. Analogous to a modern taxi driver with a terrible fashion sense."

Death hovered by the hearth in deepening silence.

Reggie stared at his vacated cadaver. "I had no idea it would happen so quickly. The mortification, I mean. The changes are subtle enough now, but I see them quite clearly. I hate it that my wife will be the one to discover me this way. She'll be scarred for life, I'm afraid."

Death shrugged within the rippling folds of its flowing black cloak. "Your earthly concerns will slough off soon enough."

"And my dear daughter. God, I can't bear to imagine how she will take the news of my death. Megan is such a sweet girl. Always was. Too gentle for this world. I fear she'll be devastated."

"Gentleness is often a sign of great inner strength."

"I suppose that's true. Still . . ."

"Stillness is the seed of spiritual expansion and increased inner activity."

"You're beginning to sound as platitudinous as one of my first-year philosophy students. Conjectural thoughts don't thrive in concrete brains. And believe me, I knew a great many blockheads in my time."

"You're calling me a *blockhead?*"

Though Reggie couldn't see Death's face, he could hear the mocking smile in Death's deep voice. "What if I am? What are you going to do, kill me?"

"I have certain discretionary powers," said Death. "You would do well not to incur my wrath, Summerfield."

"Really. So you *are* more than a mere taxi driver. I suspected as much. What sort of powers?"

"Not your concern."

"Come now, sir. Don't be modest. Tell me what you can do. I won't take it as idle boasting."

"You are becoming tedious. I know what you're up to. It won't profit you in the least."

"Forgive me, but I believe you are misjudging me. I am—or *was*—a scholar. My hunger for knowledge didn't die with that pathetic body there. Indulge me. It's not every day a man gets to have a conversation with the angel of death."

"I am no angel."

"Figure of speech. It is one of your many colloquial names. I didn't make them up. Won't you allow me to pick your brain, so to speak? What could it hurt?"

Death came forward, cloak billowing.

Reggie stood his ground, or more accurately, he floated a foot or so above it. "For a being that has become a cliché, you might be overrating yourself, you know. I mean, look at you! Who knew you would actually appear in this cartoonish guise of the Grim Reaper? This can't be what you really look like. You're about as frightening as Count Chocula."

"Count . . .?"

"Cultural reference to crass commercialism. Never mind." Reggie knew he was doing all the things he'd told himself he shouldn't, but he couldn't stop. He pressed on, knowing full well that his persistence might indeed incur the wrath of Death. "What *are* your discretionary powers?"

Death waved him off with a black hand. "I will not restore your life."

"But you could. If you wanted to."

"Had I arrived in a more timely fashion, then perhaps I could have, but now it is too late. Your brain is irreparably damaged. Your biological systems are degraded beyond redemption, your mortal husk well on its way to becoming waxy soup. None of which is to say I *would* have restored your life."

"So you're saying that your belated arrival doomed any chance I may've had of resurrection."

"See here," said Death, now on the defensive, "those Dead Sea bombers are a notoriously tardy bunch."

"The fact remains, my friend: You bungled my death. You and you alone are responsible. I want to speak with your supervisor. I wish to lodge a formal complaint."

Death laughed; his laughter was the sound of thunderous black waves crashing on a rocky shore. "So you wish to go over my head, is that it?"

"Yes."

"I am completely autonomous. There is no higher authority."

"Careful, sir. You are very close to blasphemy."

A new volley of laughter broke against pitch-black rocky crags. "For all your fine philosophizing, you have no grasp of the ineffable entity you call God, Summerfield. If you did, you wouldn't make such a moronic statement."

Reggie scarcely heard Death's blunt indictment. He was all at once in the grip of an intense longing for—"My God," he blurted, "I'm hungry! How can I be hungry? I'm dead!"

"Ah, that would be soul hunger. Your spirit is giving up the ghost, so to speak. Your soul is . . . evaporating. You experience the loss as a kind of hunger. Nothing to worry about."

"Losing my soul? I don't like the sound of that!"

"Soon you will be pure spirit, all traces of your mortal identity gone. Only then will you be able to know the elusive truth you spent a lifetime seeking, as the knower becomes the known. It's quite a humbling experience, I'm told. The apotheosis of humbling."

"Humbug! I don't want to lose my identity."

Death seemed to shrug within the darkly shimmering cloak, which appeared to have a mysterious life of its own.

A world away, a door slammed with a hollow bang. The sound waves hollowly resounded within Reggie's ethereal form. "Good Lord! What day is this?"

Death said, "I don't go by your calendar's arbitrary blocks of time."

From another part of the house came a sweet-throated song, bringing with it a diffusion of feminine light, airily emotive.

"My housekeeper Camilla," said Reggie. "It must be Tuesday. I don't want her to see me like this."

"She has a good voice. A pity it's wasted on a domestic."

"*Wasted?* Listen to her. She sings for the sheer joy of singing. She *is* the song. I would trade places with her," Reggie said with a bitterness born of deep sorrow. "A singing housekeeper trumps my sad heap of dead flesh any day. What I wouldn't give for just one more day of life! Then, my grim friend, then you would indeed see me drunk on the beauty of life. I would drink deep and fill my soul one last time."

"It wouldn't be as you expect. Knowing of your impending demise would cheapen the experience and make you desperate. I find mortal desperation particularly repulsive."

"You are mistaken. I would make the most of it, and not out of desperation."

The door opened and the frumpy young housekeeper entered tentatively, calling: "Mr. Summerfield? Are you—" Then she saw his body on the floor, quickly recognized the unmistakable pallor of death, and recoiled with a gasp. Camilla clutched at her full bosom, swayed dizzily, and thereupon collapsed on the floor.

"My God, I think she's had a heart attack," said Reggie.

Death hovered over her, making a humming noise. "It would seem so. She is dying."

"Can't you do something? If our bodies are found together, there will be no end to the malicious rumors. I say, didn't you know this was going to happen?"

"Certainly not. She's a drop-in. Not every death is scheduled in advance. Usually, it's just the more significant ones."

"A drop-in? You mean—"

"Domestics are not priority collections."

"I find that offensive, sir. She deserves the same consideration as I."

"That's not the way it works."

"You mean to tell me that even in death the caste system persists? I would've hoped for classlessness in the afterlife. I don't think I'm going to like being dead, not one little bit."

"What's to like? As I told you, soon you will lose your *I.* You won't be *you* much longer."

As soon as the idea came into his mind, Reggie gave it outward expression: "Put me into her."

"What?" asked Death.

"Use your discretionary power and do whatever it is you have to do to put my soul in her body. While there's still time. You owe me that much. It would make up for the torture I had to endure due to your late arrival. You should've been here as midwife to my passing. You've as much as admitted it. If you're the plenipotentiary you claim to be, then do it."

"I owe you nothing." Death's cloak bristled with a green-black sheen.

"There *must* be consequences, even for *your* actions. You have to be accountable."

"You're talking nonsense."

"Am I? Put me into her body and we'll forget your little slipup. And I'll prove to you that I can drink life's beauty without mortal desperation or regret. One day is all I ask. Twenty-four hours. One rotation of the earth on its axis. What could be the harm in that? Unless you don't actually have the power to do it."

"I could destroy your soul this instant if I chose."

Reggie drifted with a will over to his supine housekeeper. Her eyes were glazed, her jaw slackened. "I think she's expiring this very moment. Now is the time, sir. Do it!"

"You would regret it," Death told him.

"I won't."

"You are a stubborn soul, Summerfield." Death's cloak began to expand, swelling as though filled with stormy winds. "Very well. But you must not say I didn't warn you."

Reggie studied Camilla's vacant face. He took in the fine cheek bones, full lips and smooth skin. She wasn't an unattractive woman. Not beautiful by any stretch, but passably pretty even with the plumpness fostered by a starchy diet and a sluggish metabolism. And such a fine singing voice!

All at once, Death's cloak expanded to fill the room with surging darkness, and he was drowning in black fire. *The bugger tricked me,* he thought. *He's destroying my soul.*

A screaming whirlwind took him deeper into unfathomable darkness, but then the wind became a ragged breath, and he opened his eyes, which were now *her* eyes, and he knew he presently inhabited Camilla's corporeal form. He sat up and looked around for Death, but Death was not there.

He reached up and felt his (Camilla's) heart beating behind an ample bosom. "By God, you did it!" he said, and was startled to hear himself speak with a feminine voice. He stood slowly and then took several tentative steps, in hopes of becoming accustomed to carrying the extra burden of voluminous womanly flesh.

He addressed his corpse there on the floor in front of the fireplace: "Thank you for the years of faithful service, old fellow, but I'm thirty years younger now and these female hormones have made me more alive than you ever were, even in your prime. I had no idea . . ."

He looked at the grandfather clock in the corner and saw that he still had time to reach his wife at the art museum, where she served as curator. He phoned her, cleared his throat when she answered, and then said, "Mary, I . . . this is going to be difficult for you to believe, but . . ."

"Camilla? What is it? Is something wrong?"

"Perhaps you should sit down."

"Camilla, *what is it?*"

"That's the thing, you see. I'm not Camilla. Well, I am, but not really. This is Reggie. I wanted to prepare you before you came home. I'm afraid I've died. Fell out right there on the floor of the study. And then when Camilla discovered my body, she had a heart attack. I prevailed upon the . . . uh, Grim Reaper to put my soul into her body for twenty-four hours. You see? I'm still myself, but I've borrowed her body."

"Have you been drinking?"

"Ask me something Camilla couldn't know."

"This isn't amusing, Camilla. I'm afraid I'll have to terminate your employment."

"For God's sake, Mary, *ask me.* I can't afford to waste time."

"This is ridiculous."

"Please, lambkins." He hoped his using his pet name for her would begin to convince her that he was telling the truth.

Mary sighed into her mouthpiece. "All right. If it will end this sick charade. Where were we the first time we kissed?"

"Your family's gazebo, in a December snowstorm. You were huddled in your furs and I was too hot with passion to feel the cold."

"Camilla, put my husband on. I know he's there with you."

"He's dead, I tell you. *I'm* dead, but only physically."

"I'm hanging up now."

"Wait! Mary, please. I'm only trying to spare you the shock of finding my corpse. I'm calling for the ambulance so if you take your time, you won't have to see me that way. I swear I'm telling the truth. I wouldn't joke about this."

"Camilla, as of this moment you no longer work for us. I'll mail you your last paycheck. And you can tell Mr. Summerfield he's in very deep do-do." Then she broke the connection.

"Damnation," he said. This was going to be more problematical than he'd imagined.

*   *   *

Mary arrived as the ambulance attendants were loading the remains of her husband into their vehicle. The coroner met her at the front door, and Camilla (Reggie) waited in the foyer with a snifter of cognac. Then Camilla was placing the drink in Mary's hand and guiding her to the study.

"I know this is hard to accept," Camilla said, "but I *am* your husband in Camilla's body. Please believe me."

"I want you out of my house."

"Mary, I . . ." Reggie felt an intense cramp in Camilla's lower belly. He (she) lifted the skirt of her pink maid's uniform, stuck two fingers between the cotton panties and the puff of wiry hair and into the fleshy groove where the wetness was. He withdrew and examined a finger smeared with bright red blood. "Oh my."

"If you don't leave right now I'm calling the police," Mary said.

"I'm having a bloody period." He smiled with Camilla's lips. "I wonder if Camilla has something in her purse. You don't . . . no, of course not. You're post-menopausal."

Mary started for the phone. He seized her arm and said, "Hear me out. Then I'll go."

Mary jerked her arm out of his grasp, then crossed her arms over her chest.

In Camilla's soprano he said, "I'm grateful for the wonderful years we shared. I'm sure I didn't deserve you. I should've told you every day how much you meant to me. The best I can do is to tell you now. You and Megan were the world to me. Of all the scholarly books and passable poetry I wrote, Megan was the finest thing I ever had a part in creating. Please tell her for me that Daddy loves her very much and is very proud of her. I . . . love you both. Deeply."

A tear trickled down Camilla's cheek. Mary's eyes, too, were wet with emotion.

Reggie kissed his wife's lips and embraced her. She didn't resist. After a long moment, he released her and said, "Now I've *got* to do something about this little bloodtide in my drawers."

"In the bathroom cabinet," she told him. "Megan keeps a box of tampons there."

"Of course. How does one . . .? Never mind, I'll manage."

And manage he did, though not without a certain amount of queasy embarrassment. When he emerged from the bathroom, Mary was sitting in her husband's favorite armchair before the fireplace, where a fledgling fire was feeding on carefully stacked logs.

"Oddest thing," Reggie said. (Camilla's voice had a lilting quality to which he wasn't yet accustomed.) "I'm beginning to have access to Camilla's memories. And emotions. I know what killed her. She had a faulty heart valve. I can feel its nervous little flutter."

"Please leave," Mary said in monotone as she stared into the fire.

"Yes, I suppose I should. See here, I know you can't believe any of this, but someday when Death comes for *you*, you'll know the truth of it. For now, if you must grieve, grieve for the end of our life together, but don't grieve for me. I'll be fine. Death is not the end. Goodbye, love."

He used Camilla's plump lips to give his wife a final kiss, and then he left his home for the last time.

* * *

As he walked Camilla's voluptuous body along the gritty sidewalks of Manhattan, he began to know what a mystical creature a woman truly is. The lunar cycle tied her bloodtides to the larger world in alchemical sympathy. Could there be any doubt that a woman's spirit was endowed with the ability to use this metaphysical nexus as a receptacle of Heavenly vibrations? Seen through a woman's eyes, these ordinarily drab sidewalks were invested with a silvery glow suggesting paradisiacal destinations whose auras must surely be golden. The vast sapphire-blue dome of twilight hung so low over the jagged skyline that it was easy to imagine the taller skyscrapers actually making scratches in the deep blue gemstone of the sky. Pedestrians making their way through the cold city were anything but pedestrian; the dullest passersby possessed a portion of the magic—even if they were unaware of the mystical gift they carried. He saw it shining in their eyes.

As he waited on a crowded corner for a green light, he inhaled such a rich mix of pheromones arising from so much humanity pausing in one place as to become dizzy with life itself. When he exhaled, he realized that death and life were in every cycle of breath. Death lurked in each moment of life. The miracle of simply being alive while knowing that time was the only thing keeping him from death, touched his (Camilla's) heart with such poignancy that he feared the awestruck heart might simply stop. It did skip several beats when its valve went aflutter, but then it quickly caught up to its own rhythm and to the cacophonous rhythms of the city, and he crossed the street, turned another Lower West Side corner and dashed into a SoHo art gallery, driven by a deepening hunger to catch visionary glimpses of worlds beyond this one, extraordinary though *it* was.

Looks of disdain cast from beneath bridges of snooty noses didn't touch the Rubinesque woman in the pink maid's frock as she moved from painting to painting, entranced by the framed "windows" upon idiosyncratic worlds, worlds captured in swirling colors and frozen celestial light. The sheer vibrancy of the artworks filled her breast with indescribable emotions that could only be expressed in song. So she began to sing.

A sublime aria from Rossini's "The Italian Girl in Algiers." The other patrons were stunned by the warmth and power in her voice and stood with mouths agape as she sang. A security guard came toward her, a scowl riding the prow of his sharp face. Camilla sang on until the guard grabbed her arm and hustled her toward the exit. The others in the gallery applauded her, then booed the guard when he shoved her out onto the sidewalk.

Camilla giggled at the spectacle she had made, and then bowed to the art gallery crowd watching her through the glass. A well-dressed man stood in the doorway, removed a carnation from his lapel and tossed it at Camilla's feet. She blew him a kiss, picked up the flower and went merrily down the sidewalk.

When Reggie caught Camilla humming a country & western song, he knew his soul was conforming to the contours of her bodily vessel. The biochemical memories imprinted on his soul were fading and were being replaced by Camilla's. Very soon, he surmised, Reginald Summerfield's identity would be usurped. *Evaporated*, as Death had said. This realization caused a brief moment of panic, but it quickly passed because the soul inhabiting the maid's body was taking such joy in being Camilla.

She moved through the sidewalk throngs with remarkable agility for a woman of her size. She paused in front of a storefront window to study her face's reflection superimposed on a slim manikin in a slinky evening gown. She laughed at her own folly, and then buzzed on like a thick-bodied bee to the next flower, humming all the way. She'd forgotten to put on her coat before leaving the Summerfield townhouse, but the pleasant bite of winter air was a crisp reminder that she was gloriously alive. Soon enough she would not be able to feel any physical sensations. In less than twenty-four hours—was that right?—she would die again and leave this body and this world, presumably forever. She couldn't precisely remember how she knew this, but she felt the truth of it in her bones, particularly inside the ribcage and within the skull. She was sharing her body with . . . another. Some sort of marriage, perhaps made in Heaven. She was on a dreamlike mission to experience the joy of being alive and to . . . drink deeply of the world's wonderful symmetry. Tired as she was, she couldn't waste the night sleeping. She didn't have to worry about getting up in the morning to go to work because Mrs. Summerfield had fired her. She was *free*. Her overweight, overworked body would run on beauty and holy light. She was, she now realized, a creature of light. That light would not be extinguished when this body's clockspring finally wound down to a stop. That certainty was itself exhilarating.

She ducked into a cozy diner and sat at the counter. She ordered a slice of apple pie and a cup of coffee. The pie was the best she'd ever tasted, the coffee piping hot and full-bodied. The little diner's warmth elicited nostalgic memories of her grandmother's kitchen back in North Carolina.

An angry voice upset the pleasant din of low conversations and musical clatter of silverware. "You got no business bringing your disease in here," said a male voice. "We shouldn't have to see this. I look at you, I see slow death."

Camilla turned her head to see a burly red-faced man in a turtleneck sweater leering at a skeletal young man with leeches attached to his face. She did a double-take and saw that the black things on the malnourished young man's face weren't leeches but were ugly eruptions in his skin.

The counter waitress came over and whispered to the afflicted young man: "I'm sorry, but you see how it is. My customers look at you and lose their appetites. You're hurting business. Now I can't refuse to serve you. I'm just asking you to please eat someplace else. Okay?"

The young man stared at the waitress with his sunken eyes, then nodded and slid off the stool and walked with an old man's gait toward the door. Camilla shot a scorching look at the waitress, but the waitress ignored her and moved down the counter to refill the burly man's coffee cup and spout placating apologies.

"Wait," Camilla called after the banished young man. He glanced over his shoulder and gave her a weak smile and a shrug, then walked out the door and into the frigid night. Camilla slapped a ten on the counter and went after him.

She caught up with him and tugged on the sleeve of his black overcoat. "Let me buy you something to eat. I'll get it to-go."

"Thank you," he said with labored breath. "You're kind, but I'm really not hungry."

"You have AIDS, don't you?"

"Yes. I'm sorry if I ruined your dining experience."

"You didn't. Those other people did. I couldn't believe how rude they were."

"I'm used to it." He shrugged inside his coat. "I just wanted to sit down in there one last time. For sentimental reasons. That's where I met my boyfriend."

She nodded. "Is he . . .?"

"Six months ago. But not before he gave me something to remember him by. I'm sorry, I don't mean to sound bitter. I do still love him. I only wanted to feel close to him again, but . . . it didn't work. That man back there was right. I'm a walking advertisement for disease and death."

"You have beautiful eyes," she told him.

He smiled sadly. "I used to be quite handsome. Now . . . I'm a monster."

"No you're not. You're sick. But what's inside will go on to a place where there is no disease. The same place your boyfriend went, I would imagine."

"You must be freezing. Did you forget your coat?"

She shook her head, teeth chattering. "I don't mind the cold. I'm going on too. I probably have less time than you do."

He looked puzzled, but said nothing.

"I have an appointment with Death. I'm literally living on borrowed life."

His eyes smiled. "I know the feeling."

"I mean it. It's really true."

"I don't know why exactly, but I believe you."

She smiled. "Do you mind if I walk with you?"

"I'd be honored." He gave a slight bow that obviously pained him. They didn't bother to tell each other their names. They were both beyond given names and knew it.

She took his hand and they began to walk slowly, almost casually, down the sidewalk. She felt like singing, something from Verdi's *Rigaletto*, but she couldn't remember the words or much of the music, so she started singing "On The Wings Of A Dove," one of the many country classics she knew by heart.

They drew curious stares from other pedestrians, but they walked as if on the stage of a Broadway musical—seemingly carefree and light of heart.

"That's was the most beautiful singing I've ever heard," he said when she reached the end of the song. "Do you sing professionally?"

"Goodness, no. Just for myself. And now for you."

"You're an angel, aren't you?"

"I think we're all angels, adrift in a mad world. But you and I are on our way home."

He squeezed her hand. "I think I want to believe that, whether it's true or not."

"It's true enough," Camilla said.

"I live in that brownstone there. Would you like to come up? I'm very tired, but not at all sleepy. Your singing energized me. I would be grateful for the company."

In his austere flat, they drank wine and filled the hours with effortless camaraderie. She learned that he was a poet and playwright of modest success (only one of his avant-garde plays had ever made it to the stage). They took turns reading aloud some of his darkly romantic poems, and she was moved by them; for all the poetry's wrenching horrors, a life-affirming light shone through their inherent darkness.

They talked the night through and then quietly watched the sun rise over the city. In the cold warmth of the sun's early rays he revealed to her what he took to be the secret of life: *Love life to the fullest and you will not fear death.* "I wanted with all my heart to believe in God and the afterlife but I just couldn't do it," he confessed. "I did see Jesus, though. He was dying of AIDS. I thought at the time that He was taking on my suffering, if not my sins, but then I realized I was only hallucinating. We each have to die alone. But that's okay." They talked awhile without words, communing with their eyes and what lay behind them, and she finally kissed him goodbye and went out into the bright winter morning to meet Death.

*   *   *

"I suppose now you'll issue pathetic pleas for more time," Death said.

"Not at all. I'm ready." She glanced back at her estranged body. It remained in the gloom of an alley, slumped against the back wall of a Chinese restaurant, where she'd sat down only moments ago to die.

"What, no desperate last attempt to hoodwink me?"

"No."

"Yours is the rare soul."

"No, it's not, not really. I met a beautiful young man last night, doomed to die hideously, but his was the most sublime spirit I've ever known. I know now that the most beautiful thing in this world *is* the human spirit. What a wonder it is! Life should be about uncovering that spirit and opening our hearts to it."

"It was your heart that killed you," Death reminded in a decidedly smirking tone.

"But I'm not afraid of you now, Mr. Taxi Driver. My heart and soul are open to what lies beyond. I'm done clinging to life."

A bass string thrummed deep within Death's black cloak.

"Now step on it, driver," said Camilla with a gay laugh. "And don't spare the horses. I think I hear the angels singing."

Death rumbled. "If you hear anything it's the wailing winds of the void. You and your lot drove God to a far corner of the cosmos, so don't imagine He will save you. You lived your life in illusion and now you come to your end in delusion. Beauty is your decomposing corpse. *Nothing* is the only thing that matters. And I am delivering you into an eternity of nothingness. No spark, divine or otherwise, will fill the void in the center of your soul. Nothing is sublime."

"Then I will embrace that nothingness. Embrace it sublimely."

"The worm swallows itself."

"You've never had the gift of life. That's why you don't get it. You will never understand what it means to live and die. You're the *illusion* at the end of all things. You're the shadow on the wall of the cave. And I'm going through the holy fire to a place you will never know."

Death suddenly threw off the hooded cloak, which swirled and then sank to the ground, forming a dark circular pool. Attired in a black clawhammer frock coat, the skeletal creature began to dance around his whirling pool of midnight.

She lost herself in Death's sidewalk-gray face.

Just before the black whirlpool drew her down, she clearly heard the angels screaming.

It would take an eternity to find the harmony hidden within that awful sound.

But harmony was everything.

THE GRIND

Twilight Towers. Room 12B.

Trench used his pass-key and stepped inside. Cordite and cigarette smoke burned his eyes. The shaded bedside lamp gave the room a sepia hue, and he got the feeling he'd somehow walked into a yellowed newspaper clipping of an old crime-scene photo.

The woman sat slumped in the armchair, a pistol in her lap and a small blossom of blood on the bosom of her ratty black dress. He knew she was dead. The shot to the heart said it all. It said she bought a bullet as a ticket out of the life. Death-dulled eyes under half-closed lids stared at nothing in this world.

Trench studied the scrimshawed creases her makeup couldn't conceal and figured her for an over-the-hill harlot or round-heel hophead, worn down to this sad sack of bones in a measly dress. Checked into Twilight Towers so she could check out with a smidgeon of class, rather than do the deed in some flophouse.

A lavender sheet of hotel stationery sticking out of the Gideon Bible on the bedside table caught his eye. He opened the book and read the handwritten scrawl.

I can't take no more of this god damn grind. God forgive me?

"The grind's a bitch," he said to the corpse, "but there's usually a way out from under."

* * *

While the white-coats rolled the body to the elevator, a cadaverous Miami homicide detective named Duvall buttonholed Trench in 12B's doorway. "So you're the new house dick."

"Not that new," Trench said. "Been here half a year."

"Last guy was in the bag, dirty as a whore's bloomers. Got popped pimping for Iron Skillet Scarlotti. Jamoke was running girls up with room service, can you believe that?"

"I can believe most anything these days," Trench said without blinking.

The cop leaned close and lowered his voice. "You can believe *this*. If you're dirty, your dick days are over. You'll be joining that jamoke in the state pen."

Trench clenched his jaw.

"Don't tell me Scarlotti ain't tried to buy you 'cause I'll know you're lying," the cop said.

"I'll tell you the same thing I told him," Trench said. "I'm not for sale."

The cop arched his shaggy brows. His face was cratered from long-ago acne wars. "You know why they call him Iron Skillet, doncha? 'Cause that's what he bashed his daddy's head with."

Trench shrugged.

"Your dagos are big on family, see. Point being, Scarlotti's crazy as a bedbug when he don't get his way. Takes a man with brass balls to say no to Scarlotti."

"That's what his goons keep telling me . . . in less flattering words."

After a beat, the cop chuckled. He said, "Watch your back, pal," and lit a huge stogie. Then he added, "That dead broad you found was one of Scarlotti's pro skirts before she got used up. He don't got no use for 'em after that. He kicks 'em loose and brings in a fresh string."

Trench took the elevator down, listening to the worm-gears grind.

*   *   *

He's back on the beach. The landing zone on Sicily's underbelly. Three German panzers are bearing down on him. He hoists the bazooka onto his shoulder. Zenno taps his other shoulder and he fires. Direct hit on the middle tank. The panzer's ammo cooks off and the screams of the trapped tank crew make his skin crawl. Something big whooshes by and splits the air. The ground heaves and knocks him on his rear. Zenno's standing there with his chest ripped open and Trench can see his beating heart. "I'm kilt, Teddy," Zenno says, and then falls dead in the sand.

"Mister Trench?"

The voice brought him back. He'd been out on his feet, dreaming the dream again. Seven years gone and those nightmare memories were still fresh as a new wound. "Yeah, what?"

"Phone call," said the pimply night clerk.

He held the phone to his ear. "Trench," he said.

"Come out front. We need a word."

He recognized the voice and clipped accent. He said, "The word is no."

"Come out or we come in. You do not want us to come in, sweetcake."

Trench cradled the phone.

"Trouble?" the night clerk asked.

"My first, last and middle name." He made a face that might've been a grin.

*   *   *

Tall in a baggy burgundy suit, Tony the Toothpick looked like a skeleton on sawed-off stilts. His partner had a bulldog face and the build of a Sumo wrestler. Trench knew Bulldog was the one to eyeball. They were leaning against a black Olds 88, smoking cigs. The air was sultry. It was going on midnight and traffic on Biscayne was light.

Trench sidled up to them with both hands in his coat pockets to hide the brass knucks on his right fist. "Okay, I'm out. Now what?"

Tony dropped the butt in the gutter and came off the fender. "Mr. Scarlotti says this is your last chance to come around. Either you work for him or you don't work nowhere cuz you'll be stiff."

Trench squared his stance and tightened his grip on the brass knuckles. With twelve stories of granite and steel at his back, he felt he could stand pretty tall too. He said, "No sale. Tell Skillet Head he can take a flying leap in the toilet. Head-first. Come around here again and I'll have you boys rousted for loitering. Now beat it. This is my turf and I don't like you stinking it up."

Tony and Bulldog exchanged not-so-furtive glances. They came forward, crowding him. He stood his ground and came out with the brass knuckles. He cocked his arm and swung at Bulldog's jowly mug but something stopped his arm and hooked it behind his back. He knew then he'd screwed up. He'd been flanked by a third man.

Bulldog stepped into him and punched him in the gut, then landed a vicious uppercut to his chin. Trench dropped to his knees, his head swimming the stormy sea above his shoulders. Bulldog gave him a hard taste of shoe leather and Trench went over backwards to the sidewalk. He looked up at the third man hovering over him like a mirage over hot asphalt. When his eyes came back into focus, he saw it was Joey Needles, known for his contract jobs with hypodermics loaded with cobra venom.

Trench hadn't figured Scarlotti's goon squad would shoot him here in front of the hotel but a spike of snake venom was a different story. And not one with a happy ending.

"Hold him still," said Joey Needles, flourishing a big hypo. The cloudy liquid in the syringe caught a stray gleam of neon.

Tony said, "Last chance. Play ball with the boss or die right here."

Bulldog squatted down and pinned Trench's shoulders to the sidewalk.

Trench turned his head and spat a mouthful of blood as Joey Needles dropped to a knee and got in position to administer the fatal spike to Trench's carotid artery.

Trench bent his right knee, reached down and drew the .32 semi-automatic from his ankle holster. He jammed the muzzle under Bulldog's chin and pulled the trigger. Bulldog's head flew back and he clamped both hands under his chin as if in clumsy prayer and then fell over and made a gurgling noise.

Trench shot Joey Needles point-blank in the face, the slug punching a small blue hole in the assassin's high forehead.

Tony the Toothpick had his gun out and was doing a little skeleton-dance footwork to line up a shot when Trench fired three more times and stitched a tight pattern of red holes in the vicinity of Tony's heart.

Trench got to his feet just as the Olds 88 squealed away from the curb and sped off. He spat out a tooth and watched the taillights recede, pleased that the driver would go running back to Scarlotti to report what had happened to his hit-squad goons.

*   *   *

Tony the Toothpick was dead. Joey Needles was dead. Bulldog was in the hospital under armed guard. Trench's gun was in the custody of the MPD. The cops said the kills were clean, that they'd give him a medal if they could. He'd survived Scarlotti's strong-arm play and Twilight Towers was still free of pro skirts.

But he knew the war wasn't over. Scarlotti would come at him again. With mad vengeance. The smart thing to do was blow town, but he'd never been a runner. He hadn't run from Nazi tanks and he sure as hell wasn't going to run from a two-bit Miami hood like Scarlotti.

Before the squeal cops had arrived on the scene of his sidewalk showdown with Scarlotti's muscle boys, Trench had frisked Joey Needles on a hunch and found a small leather pouch containing two extra hypos and three vials of venom—more than enough to take out Scarlotti once and for all. All he had to do was get close enough to jab the spike in the greaseball and then get away unscathed and clean.

Trench lit a smoke and sat slumped behind the wheel of his blue Ford coupé. Rain blew in sheets against the windshield like the pages of a soggy potboiler nobody would ever read. He watched the entrance to Giovanni's Restorante Italiano across the street. This was the third night of his vigil and he was beginning to wonder if Scarlotti had gone into hiding or left town till the heat cooled down. Trench was banking on him showing up at his favorite Southside haunt. He sucked gingerly on the butt because the gum hole where his missing front tooth used to be was still painfully raw.

At half past six a black Caddy pulled up in front of Giovanni's. Scarlotti and two dapper men in dark suits—one tall, one short—got out and strode into the eatery. Trench cranked up his heap and drove around the block and parked in the alley behind Giovanni's. He put on the Lone Ranger mask he'd bought in a five-and-dime and then put on his rain hat, pulling the brim low on his brow. He left the engine running, got out and walked into the eatery's back entrance, holding the sawed-off double-barrel shotgun down by his thigh.

He stopped in the kitchen. The rich aroma of the Eyetie cuisine made his stomach growl. At gunpoint he chivvied the two olive-skinned cooks into the walk-in cooler and told them to stay there thirty minutes if they wanted to go on breathing.

He walked into the dining area and saw Scarlotti and his two sweet-looking gunsels sitting at a corner table. Scarlotti was the first to look up and see the masked man with the sawed-off aimed at him.

There were about a dozen other customers in the joint, no kids. Only a couple of them saw Trench butt-stroke the first gunsel to turn his way. The guy went face-down on the table. He gave the other dapper Dan the same treatment and he went over backward in his upended chair.

Scarlotti's chubby mug went rage-red. Trench moved quickly around the table, jammed both barrels under Scarlotti's double chins and said, "Get up and don't say a word."

He took Scarlotti out the back door and into the rain-drenched alley. "Get on your knees," he said.

Scarlotti knelt in a puddle of dirty water. "I know who you are," he said. "Fucking Lone Ranger . . ."

"I'm the guy you tried to croak." Trench stood behind him, shifted the shotgun to his left hand and pulled a loaded hypo from Joey Needles' pouch with his right. "Lift your chin."

"Wait a minute, I—"

Trench put the sawed-off's twin muzzles against the back of Scarlotti's thick head. "Do it."

Scarlotti lifted his chin and looked up into the driving rain.

Trench jabbed the needle into a pulsing neck artery and popped the load in.

Scarlotti yelped in surprise and slapped at his neck.

Trench said, "You've got less than thirty minutes of life left. You'll probably go into a coma before your lungs give out. Hi-yo Silver, cocksucker."

Trench hammered the back of Scarlotti's head with the shotgun, then jumped into his idling bucket and roared away.

*   *   *

The next day Detective Duvall braced him at the hotel and hit him with rapid-fire questions Trench couldn't answer honestly without implicating himself in Scarlotti's murder. So he lied: "I was laid up in bed from that beat-down they gave me. Much as I might've wanted to kill him, I was in no condition."

Duvall grinned like a skeleton. "I know you did it. I know how and why you did. Lucky for you there ain't no proof. You left a roomful of witnesses wondering, 'Who was that masked man?' while you rode off into the sunset, free and clear."

Trench shrugged. "That's a good story but you've got the wrong guy. I'm just a hotel dick trying to beat the daily grind."

Duvall growled, "Whatever you say, Kemosabe."

Trench gave him a gap-toothed smile and watched him walk away.

LIPSTICK SWASTIKA

Miami, 1950

Twilight Towers. 4D.

Trench stood in the corridor and eyeballed the lipstick swastika on the door. He reached for a grenade that wasn't there, his madcap impulse to open the door and blow up a lost nest of Nazis. Instead, he knocked on the door and then waited with hands jammed in the pockets of his pleated trousers.

The bolt clacked back and the door opened inward to reveal a buxom blonde in her early thirties, Veronica Lake hairdo and striking blue eyes. A white silk dressing gown that would've looked slinky on someone with a slenderer figure.

"Hotel security," Trench said. Then he aimed a finger at the red swastika and said, "You know anything about that?"

The woman looked at the lipsticked graffito and frowned. She muttered a curse in German, then turned her flashing eyes on him. "I want that removed. Immediately!"

He gave her a little nod. "Any idea who did it?"

"No. The world is infested with fools and malcontents."

"True enough," he said, noting the deep frown lines bracketing her mouth. "You *are* German, right?"

"Naturally. But that doesn't make me a war criminal."

"War criminal," he echoed. "That's a funny thing to say."

"Funny?" Her lips curled and thinned. "*Funny?*"

"Yeah. Nobody said anything about a war criminal. Except you."

She seemed to compose herself, crossed her arms over her chest and said, "You are the hotel detective, yes? The dick, as you say?" She pronounced it *deek*.

Trench nodded.

"Then do your job," she said, her accent thickening with emotion. "Find the person who did this and see that it is not to happen again."

She stepped back and slammed the door. It sounded like a gunshot.

*   *   *

Trench sat alone at a table in The Twilight Tavern, nursing an iced glass of ginger ale and thinking about halfway marks. He figured his life was half over, barring fatal disease or a violent end, and here he was in the middle of a century that had already seen two world wars and was ticking toward the next one, what with the Commies in China and Russia raising Red hell and things in Korea just about ready to boil over. At the moment he was halfway through his shift as house dick for Twilight Towers, which he sometimes thought of as the Halfway Hotel because it was about that far from being one of Miami's finest.

The Twilight Tavern was next door to the hotel, and Trench was also responsible for the safety and security of its patrons, most of them being guests of the hotel. He figured a house dick was half a step up from a run-of-the-mill bouncer—not that it mattered. Again with the halfway marks.

He sipped his drink and watched platinum-haired Lola's long fingers stroke the ivories as she coaxed dreamy tinkles from the Steinway. He couldn't look too long at her, not when she was dolled up in that tight sequined evening dress with the low-scooped neckline. A sight like that hit him where he didn't want to be hit, not since he'd come upon that stinking Sicilian field littered with dead German and Italian soldiers so bloated with rot that they sported ghoulish erections. Until he could scrub that obscene picture from his memory, he would be no good to a woman in an intimate way. That sex-and-death combo played hell with romance, zombie cocks standing at eternal attention while his was alive and as limp as a soft-boiled noodle.

He let his peepers drift off lovely Lola. They slid along the bar, pausing a moment to watch a cigarette bobbing on the lips of a chunky bald man talking to a slender woman too young to be his wife, then on they slid, finally coming to rest on the German woman from 4D. She was seated at a table with a handsome young man with slicked-back black hair and a scimitar-shaped scar along the left side of his jaw.

Since finding the swastika lipsticked on her door last night, he'd been keeping closer tabs on the fourth floor in hopes of catching the artist if she—or he—came back for another crack at a vandalistic masterpiece. He'd also checked the guestbook and learned that the German lady had registered as Greta Goff from Peoria, Illinois. You didn't grow an accent that thick in Peoria.

Trench lit a smoke and cocked an ear and tried to catch a snatch of conversation from Greta Goff and her dapper beau, but thanks to Lola's piano playing all he could hear was the occasional burst of the fräulein's honking laughter. From this distance she looked good but Trench had seen her up close, without the paint, and he knew her good looks were in harsh decline. A few minutes later the man got up and headed for the men's room. Trench decided to follow him, flash his house-dick buzzer and brace him for the skinny on his date, but then out of nowhere a small woman in a dark raincoat and black beret was bearing down on Greta Goff, approaching her from behind, and Trench froze, knowing something about her was all wrong. Maybe it was the odd look on her ferret-like face or the way she had her right hand buried in the pocket of the raincoat.

Trench was up and moving, crossing the floor in long strides and reaching out to grab the petite woman's hand as it came out of the pocket with a small-caliber gun. "No," he said softly as he wrapped his other arm around the woman's waspish waist and firmly guided her away from her obvious target. Greta Goff lit a cigarette, oblivious to what was happening behind her.

The small woman's body was stiff with tension but she didn't resist as Trench led her to his table. He took the pistol out of her hand and dropped it in his coat pocket. He planted her in a chair and sat opposite her. She looked at him with wide eyes, as if she'd just come out of a dream and wasn't sure where she was or how she'd got there.

"I'm the hotel detective," he said. "You wanna tell me what that was all about?"

She shot a glance at Greta Goff and said, "The Beautiful Butcher of Auschwitz."

Her accent was European but Trench couldn't precisely place it. She appeared to be in her middle thirties, may have been pretty at one time, but now worry lines marred her face and her eyes were a bit sunken from having seen too much of the world's horrors.

"You were there?" he asked.

She nodded. Her shoulders slumped and random raindrops ran down them. "She murdered my sister. And many others."

"You're sure she's the one?"

"I am sure. Her hair is longer and she has put on the pounds but I am sure. She beat me near to death with a riding crop." She looked at the woman in question. "There is no doubt. That is Gerda von Falk. Murderess!"

"Keep it down."

She nodded and dropped her eyes. "She and Irma Grese were in charge of the female prisoners. They liked to cut off the breasts of the prettier ones. They were Doctor Mengele's whores. Irma Grese was hanged as a war criminal but Gerda von Falk slipped out of Poland. And now, as you see, she is here for the good life. I saw her on the street two days ago and followed her to the hotel."

"And you're going to throw your life away as her executioner?"

"I have no life." She clutched at her small bosom. "No soul. I am like the golem."

Trench waved the waitress over and ordered a double shot of whiskey. He noticed a small man in a dark suit sitting alone at the bar, shooting furtive glances their way.

"Why not call the FBI and let them take her?" he asked.

"Why would they believe me? I am a Polish Jew. I am not yet a citizen here. I have no proof."

"So you were going to shoot her and wait to be arrested?"

"No. I would kill her, then flee."

"That guy over there at the bar with you?"

"My cousin. I live with his family."

"He was your get-away guy."

She nodded.

"Why did you draw that swastika on her door? Didn't you think it would scare her off before you could do her in?"

"I wanted her to know she is not free, I wanted she should taste the fear." She shrugged. "I don't know. Maybe I wanted her to run so I would not have to shoot her."

Trench nodded in the direction of the blond German. "She's not exactly shaking in her boots."

The waitress delivered the double-shot. Trench set it in front of the would-be assassin and said, "Drink that. A toast to your freedom."

"You are not going to arrest me?"

"I should turn you over to the police," he said, "but I won't if you promise you'll forget about killing her. Let me take care of her."

She made a sour face and downed the double-shot. "What will you do?"

"I've got a couple of ideas." He pulled an ink pen from his pocket and slid a cocktail napkin in front of her. "Write down a phone number where I can call you. I'll let you know how it turns out."

She wrote down a number and her first name: Anna.

Trench said, "I'll give back your gun when it's over."

*   *   *

Trench walked back to the hotel and called his friend Morgan at the *Miami Herald*. Morgan was a fact checker and sometimes pulled duty on the paper's night desk. He'd lost an arm at Anzio and worked extra hard to prove he was as productive as any man with two arms.

"I may have a scoop for you," Trench said when Morgan answered.

"What? Did Hemingway get caught stealing hotel towels again?"

"See what you can dig up on the Beautiful Butcher of Auschwitz. Gerda von Falk. If you can find a picture of her, I'll buy you a steak dinner."

"That Beautiful Butcher moniker rings a bell. No, no, that's not right, she was the Beautiful Beast and they hanged that Kraut cooze."

"No, that was the other one. They were like a tag team. The one I want got away. And I think she's a guest here at the Twilight, under another name."

"Holy mackerel, Kingfish! I'll get right on it."

"Good. I don't want this chick to fly the coop before I know for sure."

"What'll you do if it's her?"

"Wring her fucking neck."

Ten minutes later Trench was in room 4D, searching the German woman's belongings. He'd told the kid on the front desk to call the room if the woman showed her face in the lobby. He went through the two suitcases after picking the locks with his penknife and a paperclip. The first one contained nothing but clothing and makeup, but with the second suitcase he hit paydirt: three passports with the same woman's photo but with different names, and a loaded Luger. The passports were damned good forgeries with three different names—none of them Gerda von Falk. Wrapped in black panties was a pristine Luftwaffe dagger, and the feel of silk and steel sent a thrilling current through his crotch.

He put the items back where he'd found them and shut the suitcase. As he was about to leave the room, something under the bed caught his eye. He bent down and picked up a black-leather riding crop and smacked it against his open palm, wondering if it was a souvenir of her Nazi past, a prop for sadistic sex games, or both. He put it back and left the room.

When he returned to the lobby, the night clerk handed him a phone message from Morgan. Trench returned the call. Morgan said he had found one photograph of Gerda von Falk. "It's not a very good shot," Morgan explained. "It's a partial profile and the lighting is bad, but it's all we've got."

"Meet me at the Rod & Reel Grille at eight and I'll treat you to a steak and eggs. And don't forget that photo."

*   *   *

"Don't spill coffee on it," Morgan said, "I have to return it to the morgue."

Looking up from the page of newsprint with the photo on it, Trench said, "The morgue?"

"The storage room where we keep all the back issues. Reason I found it so quick's because I remembered the story, the-ones-that-got-away angle."

Trench looked a few seconds more at the photo of the blonde in a Nazi uniform and then said, "I'm pretty sure that's her. I wouldn't bet my life on it, but I'd sure as hell bet hers."

Morgan grinned and said, "Not for nothing do they call you the Twilight Detective."

*   *   *

Trench was in the office behind the front desk waiting for the FBI agent to come back on the horn when the desk clerk stuck his head in and said, "The lady in 4D just phoned down and said she's checking out a day early. Today. Right now."

Trench motioned the clerk over and handed him the phone. "When he comes back, tell him to get here right away if he wants to nail this Nazi cooze."

Trench took the elevator to the fourth floor and knocked on 4D's door.

The blonde opened the door and gave him a big-eyed stare. She was wearing the same silky gown, but this time her bags were packed, ready to go.

Trench said, "The FBI wants to talk to you, Miss von Falk. Have a seat and we'll wait for them."

Her face showed nothing. Then she smiled and pulled the straps off her shoulders and let the top of the gown fall to her waist, exposing her voluminous breasts. Trench looked at them and froze, feeling as if he were looking down the barrels of a couple of howitzers.

Too late, he realized his mistake. But before he could tear his eyes off her tits, she shot a beefy fist into his face and rocked him with a hard right to his left eye. Then she grabbed his shoulders and kneed his nuts. He went to his knees, nauseated. With a move that would've made a female wrestler proud, she seized him in a headlock and wrangled him into the room, shutting the door with her hip.

He grabbed one of her muscular legs and yanked it upward as he straightened his spine and threw himself backward. They both hit the floor but the woman rebounded quickly, springing to her feet and spinning to kick his face with the ball of her bare foot. Then she grabbed a suitcase and swung it with both hands, the heavy blow ringing his skull like one of hell's lost bells.

He heard suitcase latches snap open and looked up at her through a red haze of dull pain to see her tits and the Luger all pointing at him. Her lips cut a cruel smile. He smiled back, meaning it.

It was nuts but he had a ferocious hard-on. For the first time since he'd seen that field full of dead soldiers with bloated boners, he felt real lust for a woman and had the hard evidence to prove it. He'd taken a few beatings since the war—most recently from Iron Skillet Scarlotti's goon squad—but never with this crazy result. It had taken a sadistic bare-breasted Nazi broad to raise his cock from the realm of the dead.

Trench figured he'd reached one of those turning points people talked about. A freak twist sure to take him to some very dark places if this buxom bitch didn't kill him first. Maybe he felt he deserved punishment for all the Krauts he'd killed or maybe just for surviving the war when so many others hadn't. He knew this wasn't the time to figure it out.

"Hold on," he said. "Look what you've done to me."

He rolled onto his back so she could see the erection tenting his trousers. She cocked a brow.

"I'll make a deal with you," he said. "You take care of this and I'll call off the Feds."

She laughed. It was a dirty laugh coming up from the diaphragm and shaking her breasts.

"I'm not joking," he said. "I told the desk clerk to talk to them while I came up here to stop you. Let me use your phone and I'll call 'em off. Then you and me can settle up. Whaddaya say?"

"What are you saying to me, *take care of this*?" She pointed the pistol at his crotch.

"Make it go away and I'll make sure you get away. Unpack your riding crop. And don't shoot off that cannon or you'll queer our deal and the Feds will nab you."

He stood, picked up the phone and called down to the desk. "Kid, did you talk to that Fédérale?"

"Yeah, but I think he thought I was some crackpot. He finally said he'd send somebody out."

"Call him back and tell him we were wrong about the lady and that she's already checked out."

"But . . ."

"Do it." Trench cradled the phone, unfastened his trousers and dropped them. His cock popped out of the slit in his underwear and pointed at the woman still pointing her pistol at him. He said, "Not exactly a Mexican standoff, but you can see I'm serious about this. Call it a hard bargain."

*   *   *

She tore off his shirt and undershirt, then handcuffed him to the bedpost and worked him over good with the riding crop, each stinging lick pumping up his lust to the point where he could no longer distinguish pain from pleasure. Finally, she peeled her slinky gown off her hips, straddled him and took him inside with practiced ease. She rode him hard, whipping his hip with the crop to urge him on. Her gun was within easy reach on the edge of the bed, and it crossed Trench's mind that she could finish him off with it when the fun was done, but that only added to his twisted excitement.

When the big moment came, Trench felt as if the planet had flung him into the stratosphere, where he hung blissfully suspended, briefly free of worldly concerns and cleansed of wartime sins. Then gravity yanked him back down into the gooey thick of things and the Nazi vixen astride him whipped him mercilessly as she spouted spirited curses in her native tongue.

He stayed hard and she rode him harder, her pelvis and tummy gyrating like a belly dancer's. She whacked his face with the leather crop and all he could do was clench his eyes and grit his teeth. She shouted "Heil Hitler!" Then her eyes rolled up in her head and she brayed like a dying donkey. She went rigid all over as if an iron rod had been jammed up her ass, then she fell forward, breasts flattening on Trench's chest, passion spent.

He thought he should be feeling some kind of post-bang remorse now for having trafficked with the enemy to satisfy his twisted desire, but what he actually felt was grateful relief that his family jewels and scepter were no longer defunct. He wasn't much worried that he was now at the dubious mercy of a sadistic woman notorious for her gleeful practice of genocide. Maybe he was a little worried that he *wasn't* worried. But he was still hard inside her and he was already thinking of an encore performance.

But then the woman sat up, picked up the Luger and a pillow to muffle the shot and put the gun against his head. She smiled, clamped her pussy on his prick and pulled the trigger.

Laughing, she tossed the pillow away and looked at the smoking bullet hole in the mattress next to his head.

"What the hell did you do that for?" Trench shouted.

"I wanted to see if you would shit yourself like a scurvy Jew."

He drew blood from his tongue to keep from unleashing a long stream of hard-bitten G.I. profanity upon this nutso Axis Sally in the flesh. Instead, he said through clenched teeth, "Well I didn't, did I."

She laughed, clucking like the Queen Kong of hens. Then she got up, walked across the room and dug a deck of cigarettes from her purse and lit one, tossing the mussed tresses of that Veronica Lake hairdo with a heavy air of melodrama as she blew smoke at the ceiling. She sat on the bed and crossed one knee over the other, pursing her lips and blowing on the cigarette's ember. She spit a strand of tobacco off the tip of her tongue and took another drag.

"What shall I do with you?" she asked, blowing smoke in his face.

"Get these cuffs off me and I'll get you out of here. That FBI guy might be curious enough to come nosing around anyway."

She looked at the faded ink of the American flag on his left shoulder. "What did you do in the war?"

"Killed Nazis."

She made a clucking sound with her tongue. *"Die jungen Blumen des Vaterlands."*

"How's that?"

"The young Flowers of the Fatherland." She reached over and stroked his half-mast penis with one hand and blew on her butt's ember again, making it glow red-hot.

Trench began to sweat. He squirmed. The cuffs rattled against the bedpost.

"Let me see what you're made of, Yank." She touched the ember to the root of his cock, the tender spot just above the scrotum. He gritted his teeth and tried not to flinch as the cigarette sizzled his flesh. Amazing as it was, his dick remained rigid.

"Not bad," said the Beautiful Butcher of Auschwitz. She took another drag off the butt, then dropped it on the carpet. "Now I will make my mark on you so that you will not forget me."

She opened a suitcase and dug out the Luftwaffe dagger. Smiling as she unsheathed it, she sat on the edge of the bed, smoothed the hairs on his chest with her empty fingers and then set to work with the dagger, cutting a line in the flesh above his left nipple. Trench sucked wind through clenched teeth. He didn't try to fight the knife. The pain was sweet and he figured he had it coming for fraternizing with this sadistic Nazi cunt.

Couple of minutes later, Trench had a bloody swastika etched in his chest. And a cold-blooded hard-on that refused to flag.

Gerda von Falk chuckled and pressed the dagger's point against the underbelly of his penis. "Your little soldier remains at attention for me, his commander. But I must go now and leave him to his sad little outpost."

"Get these cuffs off and I'll carry your bags."

She lit a cigarette, then said, "I do not think you are as dutiful to me as your little ramrod trooper with the purple helmet. I think perhaps I should leave you as you are as I go to make my getaway."

"I'm going with you," he said, "wherever you're going. I'm done being a house dick."

"You see?" She pointed with the two fingers clamped on her cigarette at the bloody swastika on his chest. "I have marked you and you are mine. Like a Jew, yes?"

"Yeah, yeah, I see. Take me with you." As soon as he said this, he realized it was something a woman might say. *What the hell's wrong with me?* But he knew the answer. Something *had* been wrong with him but this witch had worked her evil magic and now he was cured. Did he actually want to go with her or was he just playing out the string to make sure she didn't leave him cuffed to the bed for the housekeeper to find? He wasn't sure. Not yet.

With an unreadable expression on her face, she keyed the cuffs open and he was free. Completely free. It was the freedom of not having a plan, of not knowing what you were going to do until it was done. Trench was amazed at how liberating this was. He could make things happen or he could let them happen. Either way, he was alive, and that was reassuring. He was more than a walking corpse with a hard-on. He was still in the game, and no matter how twisted it got, the game was only for the living.

She tossed him a towel. He blotted blood from his stinging new swastika while she got dressed. Ten minutes later he was carrying her two suitcases as they stepped off the elevator and into the lobby. He ignored the puzzled looks his battered face drew from the desk clerk and patrons. He kept his eyes glued on his blond companion's back as he followed her outside and into the hotel parking lot. He was subservient to her; it was right that he should walk behind her. And it offered a nice view of her undulating ass cheeks.

The car was an old Packard and she said he could drive. He put the suitcases in the backseat.

"Where to?"

"West. To California." The way she pronounced the state's name, it conjured mental images of forbidden forms of fornication.

They smoked in silence and soon they were outside the city, the Floridian flatlands drawing them toward the promise of landscapes less monotonous.

"I think you are a secret Jew," she said as she tossed her cig's butt out the window.

"How's that?"

"Maybe you don't have the Jewish blood but you are weak, submissive. Like the Jewish vermin we exterminated. No fight in you. You cower and piss yourselves like docile dogs."

He balled his fist and threw a crazy roundhouse left against the side of her head. Her head bounced off the passenger door, and the car swerved and just missed dropping a wheel into the roadside ditch. He hit her again to make sure she was out like a refrigerator light with the door shut.

That was when he knew he'd reached the end of his tether. He felt it and understood. It felt like a rubber band was attached to his belly, an invisible umbilical band that had let him get just this far and was now ready to snap him back to reality, back to his Twilight life.

Her eyes were half open, glazed and unseeing. Trench got the cuffs out of a suitcase and hooked her to the metal frame under the seat. Then he drove ten miles to a hick town with one traffic light and bought a garden hose and a roll of duct tape from a hardware store. Whenever the Kraut opened her eyes, he socked her jaw and put out her lights again. After the third punch, she didn't open them anymore.

Ten minutes later he was driving along a dirt road into a shadowy backwoods jungle. He pulled over at a small clearing. Black dirt salted with white sand. Lush vegetation surrounding. The woman's head bobbed. She moaned. Fluttered an eyelid.

Trench shut off the motor, got out and set to work with his hardware-store purchases. He stuck one end of the garden hose into the exhaust pipe and secured it with duct tape, making sure the seal was good. Then he ran the other end of the hose through the narrowly opened rear-door window of the Land Cruiser. He used duct tape to make the window as airtight as possible, then he slid behind the wheel and cranked the engine.

The woman looked at him with heavy-lidded eyes. She mumbled something in German.

Trench grabbed her purse and rummaged through it until he found her tube of bright red lipstick. He scooted next to her and drew a swastika on her forehead and then, as an afterthought, he drew another one on her mouth so that the four angled arms of the hated symbol surrounded her pouty lips.

Already the exhaust fumes were filling the car, burning his eyes and making him cough. He slid out and shut the door. He looked up at the thunderheads piling up in the east and said, "Jesus? Tell me not to do this."

Thunder rumbled, sounding too much like distant artillery.

Gerda von Falk was coming to now, coming to the realization that the end of her life was at hand. She rattled the cuffs and began shouting, first German, then in English. Thunder hammered the earth and sky, coming on like well-placed artillery rounds.

"Speak now, Lord, or to hell with her," Trench said to the sky. "And you know I don't speak thunder."

He watched the light leave the sky. He listened hard. Looked for signs and wonders.

Nothing.

He looked at Gerda von Falk sitting in a glassy cube of smoky exhaust. "God forgive us both," he said. Then he started for the highway.

Half a mile down the dirt road, he stopped, turned around and went back to the car. He knew he had to see it through as witness, knew he was bound by the executioner's unwritten code. He owed it to all those dead Jews and gypsies and to all the innocents mutilated and mangled by the mad Nazi doctor and his murderous bitches.

She was coming undone fast, suffocating in the devil's cloud of unmaking. She'd yanked against the cuffs so hard that her wrist was ripped raw and bleeding, her shoulder dislocated. Her blouse had popped buttons and her bra was full of vomit. A thick string of puke hung from her lips, which were going blue. She gasped for air like a decked grouper. She went fish-eyed as her brain no doubt began to die in a haywire shower of panicked thoughts and maybe even fear of divine retribution. She would be pissing and shitting herself by now.

Trench lit a smoke and watched her die. He ached in a hundred places and that was good. It was right that he should. It was the way of the world. You bought your ticket with suffering, and dead or alive you took the ride. He didn't know where *he* would end up but he knew it didn't much matter.

He was doing the Lord's work or the devil's. As things now stood, it didn't make a hell of a lot of difference which. Either way he was damned.

In halos of lightning, storm-cloud angels played hell on heavenly kettledrums. Then came the roaring downpour and the Nazi bitch was gone for good.

Trench walked away in the rain.

DEVIL IN 206

Trench was dozing behind a newspaper in the lobby when the call came. The assistant manager Doyle paged him in his rich baritone and Trench folded the *Miami Herald*, got up and ambled to the counter, where the guy was trying to strike a debonair pose in his arched cubbyhole. Trench thought the impersonation needed some work but he didn't say so.

"Disturbance in 206," Doyle said. "205 says it sounds violent."

"Swell," Trench said.

Trench took the service elevator so as to avoid the talkative operator of the public lift. The guy wasn't a bad sort, but Trench had already had his fill of the man's war stories. He didn't need overblown reminders of the war he was trying to forget.

He got off on the second floor, went down the corridor to room 206. He listened to the silence inside then knocked knuckles on the door.

Nothing stirred inside. Trench got an uneasy feeling in his belly—usually a fairly reliable barometer for reading atmospheric evil or lurking danger. He knocked again, harder.

This time something did stir in 206. It stirred, mumbled and cursed. Glass shattered. Another curse.

Trench pounded the door and shouted: "Hotel detective, open up! Now!"

The latch snapped back and the door swung open.

A tall man wearing a priest's collar stood in the doorway, looking bewildered. He was ruggedly handsome, though in need of a shave. His heavy five-o'clock shadow set off intense blue eyes. He worked his mouth but uttered no sound.

"Everything all right in there, Padre?" Trench asked.

"You are . . .?" The man avoided looking directly at Trench.

"House dick." Waited a beat. "Hotel detective? Your neighbors complained about the noise. Like somebody was getting hurt."

"Oh, no. I'm the only person here." The priest looked absently at the carpet. "What's today's date?"

"May twenty-second."

"What year?"

Trench looked question-marks at him.

The priest shrugged apologetically and said, "I have these spells. They can be terribly disorienting. The year? Please?"

"Nineteen hundred and fifty-five. Year of our Lord, and all that."

"Yes, of course."

"Sorry, Father, but I need to come in and look around. To verify that nobody's getting murdered or molested here." Trench winked, hoping the padre wouldn't take great offense.

"Surely. Come in." The priest stepped back to allow Trench entry.

As he entered the room, the stench hit him full-face. A rotten scent with a tinge of sweetness, like meat gone bad. His first thought was: ripening corpse. But then as he went past the priest he was sure that the holy man was the source of the big stink.

"You should open a window," Trench said. "It's stuffy in here."

"I don't like the sun," the priest muttered.

"Then how the hell . . . heck did you end up in Miami?"

"I'm not really sure."

Trench went to the window, opened the curtains and raised the window. Fresh spring air wafted in on a warm breeze. The priest shielded his eyes against the sunlight slanting in.

"You can close it after I leave," Trench said. He saw that the framed picture from one of the room's walls was on the floor amid a scatter of glass shards. "What happened here?"

The priest shook his head. He said, "I think I'm in trouble."

"For breaking that crappy hotel-room art?"

"Uh, no, not that. That's only a symptom."

"Symptom of what, pray tell?" Trench was trying to show respect for the man's calling but the priest's stench and Trench's lack of faith in religion were making it hard. If he didn't blow off a little steam with his sarcasm, he was liable to toss the priest out the window, and God—if such existed—wouldn't be too happy about that turn of events.

The priest hung his head. "Sickness unto death."

A phrase from Trench's dogface days popped into his head: *Tell it to the chaplain.* He bit his tongue, then said, "Look, Padre . . . What's your name?"

"Father Ryan Hurley."

"Right. Father Ryan. If you're sick, you should see a doctor. And a shower now and then wouldn't hurt either, know what I mean?"

When the priest didn't answer, Trench glanced at the man and saw that he was staring into the mirror over the dressing table.

"Padre?"

"Something's in there," the priest said.

"What, in the mirror?"

"There, in me. The other me. Like behind the mirror but not really. Watching me."

Trench looked in the bathroom and saw no signs of violence. "Well, that sounds like a deep personal problem. You should take it up with one of your own. Or a headshrinker, maybe. No offense."

"Would you do something for me? I'm sorry, I didn't catch your name."

"Trench."

"Mr. Trench, there's a pawnshop two blocks from here. You know it?"

"Sure. I've been in there on occasion."

"I want you to buy me a tape recorder and a reel of tape. I saw several in the window, so they should still have one." Father Ryan put a wad of folded bills in Trench's hand. "That should be enough."

"I could do it on my lunch break. But if you're too sick to walk a couple of blocks, then I should get you a doctor instead of a tape recorder."

"No!" Father Ryan's voice turned cold and commanding. "Thank you for your concern, but a doctor can't help me."

Trench didn't like the guy's new tone; his temper flared, but he held back the heat. "You want I should get you a priest?"

Glancing at the mirror, Father Ryan laughed. It was a hollow laugh devoid of mirth, somehow an evil laugh. "No thanks, I've already got one. A phone call away."

"Maybe you should make that call, Padre. I have to say, you're in a bad way."

Now the priest made eye contact with Trench for the first time, and Trench didn't like what he saw behind the man's bloodshot blues.

"You're very perceptive, Trench. That can get you in a lot of trouble. But I'm sure you know that. Your eyes have seen things that should have remained unseen. You've looked too deep into the face of the god of war. You've seen the Lord of Light up close. You carry much within you that may yet destroy you."

"Save it for the sanctuary, Padre. I'm not looking to get my soul saved." Trench headed for the door. "And keep the noise down the next time your friend in the mirror feels like raising hell."

*　　*　　*

As he rapped softly on 205's door, Trench wondered what was behind the priest's comment about what he'd seen in the war. Probably just a lucky guess, since most able-bodied American boys had gone off to fight Hitler or Tojo. But Trench couldn't shake the feeling that Father Ryan had looked into his soul to see all the carnage Trench had seen on the battlefields. And the postwar carnage too, including the killing he'd done to some very bad eggs. Murder, in the eyes of the stone babe with the blindfold and scales.

A fleshy harsh-faced woman came to the door. She held her robe together with one hand and held a cigarette in the V of the fingers of her other hand. Her nails were fire-truck red, chipped.

"Yeah? Whaddya you want?" she said, snorting smoke.

"House detective. You complained of the noise next door?"

"Yeah. Something bad was going on over there. Sounded like somebody was getting gangbanged . . . or worse."

"Tell me exactly what you heard," Trench said, "after you invite me in."

"What the hey, come on in." She waved him in, smoke trailing her fingers.

She sat on the sofa. He remained standing.

"You look like a house dick," she said.

"How so?"

"Tall, half handsome and rough around the edges." She took a deep drag on the butt and then added: "I do a lot of traveling, and you dicks all look alike, to an extent."

He shrugged that off. "Tell me what you heard next door."

"First I thought it was a couple guys having an argument. Then one of them starts yelling, almost chanting, so I figure they're drunk. Then this third bird starts in. I say bird cuz it sounded like a giant bird shrieking. Like a harpy? You gotta understand I was sleeping off a bit of a hangover so the whole magilla might've been a little twisted, the way I heard it."

"But there was definitely more than one person."

"You ever heard of a one-person gangbang? Hell yeah it was more than one person."

Trench got the idea the woman enjoyed saying *gangbang* a little too much but he let it go. "You can say for sure you heard a female voice?"

She tittered, choked on smoke, coughed and then crushed the butt in the ashtray. "That or a guy with fairy dust in his panties. But the weirdest thing was when one of the heathens starts yelling 'Fuck Jesus! Fuck Jesus!' Pardon my blasphemy. A lady don't talk like that. Not a God-fearing lady."

Trench shook his head.

The woman lit a new smoke and went on. "Then something hit the wall and broke, there was screaming and crying, and finally everything went quiet. I thought somebody got cold-cocked. Or worse. That's when I called the desk."

Trench thanked her and left.

As he went down the corridor to the elevator, he felt someone watching him. He looked back over both shoulders. Doors all shut, nobody in the corridor but him. Yet he was sure he was the object of unseen scrutiny, and he didn't like it.

He stepped into the service elevator at the end of the hall. The door rumbled shut.

Trench felt as if something had entered the elevator with him, though clearly he was alone in the descending box. Something about the loco priest had spooked him, he told himself. Just that and nothing more. Like having to spend a few minutes in a place of filth and feeling that you needed a shower the minute you left the foul place. In fact the reeking scent of the holy man was still on him and would remain so—the same way you carried the stench of battlefield dead long after you'd left the field.

He got off in the lobby. The elevator door shut behind him, but he couldn't shed the feeling that something other than a bad odor had ridden him out of 206. He shrugged his shoulders involuntarily, as if to dislodge an imaginary piggyback rider.

A voice whispered in his left ear. He spun around to find nobody there. But he'd heard the voice, clear as a church bell. It had whispered: *Harpy on your back.*

What the fuck was a harpy, anyway? he wondered. A bird, sure, but not a real-life bird.

He went to the desk, got Doyle's attention and said, "You're an educated man. What exactly is a harpy?"

Doyle gave him a look, then smiled and said, "If you're serious, it's a monstrous bird with a woman's head. From Greek mythology. Predators that swoop down and snatch up their victims. Sometimes used to refer to a shrewish woman, what *you* would no doubt call a wicked bitch. Why do you ask?"

Trench said, "It came up in conversation. As in 'harpy on your back.'"

"I believe that should be 'monkey on your back,'" Doyle said. "I've never heard of a harpy on one's back."

"Maybe I misunderstood. It was sort of a low whisper." Trench tapped a fingertip on the desk and said, "How long has Father Ryan Hurley been with us?"

Doyle checked the register, then said, "A week tomorrow."

"What'd he give as his home address?"

"He didn't. Said he was in between assignments."

Trench nodded then started away. He stopped, turned back to Doyle and said, "I've been meaning to ask. What did you do in the war?"

"Stayed home. A heart murmur kept me out."

"No shit?"

"Watch your language," Doyle said. "We have an image to uphold."

"Knew a lot of guys who didn't have the heart for war." Trench bared his teeth in a grin that didn't feel friendly. "They died over there just the same."

Doyle's suave mask slipped just a bit. Trench caught a glimpse of the sheepish face behind it.

"Smug sonofabitch," Trench said just loud enough for Doyle to hear. "You think I don't see through you?"

Doyle reeled backward as if gut-punched.

As he walked away, Trench wondered why he had needlessly needled Doyle. Sure, he disliked the phony snob, but there was no point in antagonizing him. Just the same, he'd taken evil pleasure in doing it. The hell of it was, he knew he'd do it again.

*   *   *

He hiked to the pawnshop at half past noon. Pelican Pawn was a grungy dump that seemed to repel the outside brightness of the Miami sun.

The seedy pawnbroker behind the cage had skin paler than a cadaver. He always had the soggy stump of a stogie clamped in the corner of his mouth and all his words seemed to come out of the cigar like it did his talking for him.

"Tirty bucks," the cigar said when Trench asked the price of the only tape recorder on the shelf. "I'll trow in the tape fer nuttin."

"Nuttin doing," Trench mocked the man. "I'll give you twenty for the whole works. That machine's seen better days, pal."

Then to Trench's amazement, the cigar did talk. It said, "Tough guy what tinks his shit don't stink. I plug you wid my .45, you'll get duh works."

It must've been the stogie talking because the man's mouth didn't move at all. Trench shook his head as if to clear it. He was "hearing" the pawnbroker's thoughts.

"Twenty, asshole," Trench said with a snarl, "and before you can reach that cannon I'll put a .38 slug up your nose."

Trench opened his lightweight coat to show the pawnbroker the cold-steel heat in his shoulder rig.

"How did . . . I didn't . . . Aw skip it. Give me twenty and take duh damn ting."

He did. As he toted the recorder back to the hotel, Trench didn't waste time trying to figure out how he'd read the pawnbroker's thoughts. Or why he felt there was a harpy perched on his shoulders. He already knew.

It was owing to the damned priest in 206.

He delivered the recorder and an ultimatum: "Okay, Padre, now you're going to tell me what the hell is going on here. Things ain't been right since I left out of here this morning. Strange things are happening and they all trace back to you. What gives?"

"What things? What do you mean?" Father Ryan fingered rosary beads. He was back to avoiding eye contact. If he'd shaved, his shadow was already growing back on his chin, cheeks and jaw.

"Don't pretend you don't know," Trench warned. "I've got a demon bird circling overhead and sometimes I can almost feel it on my shoulders. I can read peoples' thoughts . . ."

Father Ryan's eyes were bloodshot a richer red. He was sitting in the armchair with his head slightly hanging. But suddenly he stiffened and sprang from the chair with startling speed.

Trench drove a fist into the priest's gut. Foul air blew out of Father Ryan's mouth as he fell back into the armchair. His mouth worked guppy-like, gasping for breath. The rosary beads dangled from a tangle in his fingers.

Trench shrugged and opened his fists. "Sorry, Padre, but you shouldn't have jumped in my face that way. Reflex."

The priest held up a hand as if in half-assed benediction. But then the hand bent into a claw and he jerked it down and clenched it in his armpit, as if to hide it or to restrain it. Then he did something that made Trench step backward and shudder as if suddenly chilled. Father Ryan's face contorted into a tortured rictus grin that was painful to see. Trench wanted to look away but couldn't.

The priest spoke through his hideous grimace: "It's touched you too. So much darkness. In you. In us. It finds such places to lodge, to thrive. I'm sorry. I didn't know it could happen so quickly. It took days to worm its way into me."

"What the hell are we talking about here?"

Father Ryan's grimace let go and his face took on its usual haggardly slack look. "The Devil," he said. "You're not Catholic, are you?"

"No."

"Not a religious man."

"No."

"When it takes me over, I have little memory of it. When I'm lucid, like now, I am aware of its presence but it's vague, an ill-defined thing, crouching back in dark fog but there all the same, always watching, waiting."

"The Devil," Trench said with equal parts disgust and disbelief.

"Yes. Demons, to be more accurate. Representatives of the Devil. You know what an exorcism is?"

"Not in so many words. I've heard of it."

"A month ago I assisted another priest in trying to drive a demon from a possessed parishioner in St. Augustine, Florida. He was the exorcist, I was there only to assist, since it was my first time. It took three days to expel the demons. In the process, one or more of the evil ones found an opening in me and kept at me for days afterward until they finally got inside."

Father Ryan began coughing. A dry hacking cough that made Trench think of a cat trying to hack up a stubborn hairball.

Trench reached for the water pitcher with the intent of pouring the padre a drink, but before he touched it, the pitcher hurled itself across the room and shattered against the wall. "Jesus . . . !" he yelled.

The priest's coughing became filthy laughter. The laughing went on for nearly a full minute, sounding to Trench like thick sludge gurgling in the throat of a half-clogged drain. From that same drain came a subterranean voice: "Don't call That One's name if you don't know him. You won't be happy to meet him."

"Who, Jesus?"

"Don't say that! We told you not to say that." Father Ryan's claw-like hand signed the air with an invisible symbol. "Plug up that recording machine. We want our voices on the record. For the fucking record, you understand? For the Sunday funnies."

Trench plugged in the recorder, threaded the tape onto the empty reel, then clicked the lever to Record. "Okay, Padre, for the record, how the hell did you make that water pitcher fly into the wall without touching it?"

"I didn't do it." His voice lost its sludgy sound, for the moment. "The Evil One did. The unclean spirit. He surfaces at will now. When he does, I have no control. Or very little. You have to see that Father Thomas Riley in St. Augustine gets this tape. He . . . he . . . he'll need to know . . . what happened . . . that I've been . . . infested."

"C'mon, Father, tell me how you did that. What's the trick? I've seen some decent magicians at burlesque shows but this beats 'em all. 'Fess up, Padre. I ain't buying that this is any kind of supernatural evil. I've seen evil and it always has a human face. And a lot of heavy weapons."

"It's not supernatural. The way Father Thomas explained it to me, only God is supernatural. And Jesus and the Holy Spirit, of course. Satan and his legions are preternatural. They can do no miracles. But what they can do is no trick. It's real. And evil." He turned to address the tape recorder. "Father Thomas, I must have invited it in somehow. It has possession of me now, there is no doubt. Please tell the archbishop and get his permission. I don't believe I have much time. Please, Father, you have to cast out this vile spirit."

"You said your priest pal was just a phone call away. Why don't you call him?"

"I've tried. They won't let me. The call doesn't go through, or when it does Father Thomas is never available. This is *their* doing. They know Father Thomas can drive them out and they fear him."

"Hell, Father, why don't you just go to St. Augustine. What's keeping you here?"

"They won't let me leave this room. I've tried."

"You want out of this room? You really want out, I'll pick you up and carry you."

Trench stepped toward the priest.

Father Ryan said, "No! Don't touch me! Stay back!" Then his eyes rolled up into his skull and he went rigid, like someone had shoved a steel rod up his ass.

Trench froze.

The thing in the chair was no longer Father Ryan. With only the whites of its eyes showing, it said in its sludgy voice: "Come closer, pilgrim. We love what you did to that Nazi whore. The way you cuffed her to the steering wheel and gassed the Jew-killing bitch to death."

Trench went cold. His teeth chattered. Nobody knew he had killed the Nazi war criminal in just the way the demon described.

Nobody knew he'd used the Nazi bitch to cure his sex problem.

Seeing a bunch of dead soldiers with erections had left him unable to get a hard-on. Turned out, it wasn't unusual for corpses to get hard-ons when the bodies were left for days to bloat in the field.

Rough sex with the Nazi broad right here in the hotel had put the iron back in his cock. He'd let her dominate him. Hurt him. And later he'd driven her out on a dirt road, dazed her with a fist to the jaw and cuffed her, just as the thing in the armchair said, and then watched her die as the car filled with exhaust carried from the tailpipe via a garden hose.

"You got hard watching her die," the thing said. "We loved that. You wanted to fuck her corpse but you couldn't let yourself go that far. We give you permission to do everything! She's here with us now. You'll never have to hold back again. You can have her. Let the Lord of Light lead you."

He felt pressure building behind his eyes. And in his crotch. He was sprouting a boner. He wanted to turn and run out of the room but the thing in the chair held him in place, rendering him unable to will his body to move.

"The Lord loves a cheerful killer," the thing said in an inhuman voice. "Killing is what you love. The fucking is only an afterthought. You thrill for the kill. Death makes the world go round. Reap for our Shining Lord. We will show you the way."

"Fuck you, no. You're a crazy son of a bitch, a fallen priest. You need a headshrinker. That's all."

The thing in the armchair expelled gusty laughter that hit Trench like a foul gale-force wind and knocked him back. "Lies are what fools tell themselves. Lie all you wish but not to yourself. The Lord of All Knowledge shows you the way."

Trench felt a blinding murderous rage rising within. "Jesus Christ!" he bellowed.

"We told you not to say that name!" The priest-thing twisted its face into an expression that was not human, its jaw opened impossibly wide, and it clawed the air with harpy-like talons.

The bathroom door banged shut. Windows rattled in their frames. A loud blast of gas blew from the fiend's ass, making an ugly blat against the chair seat. The thing's face changed again, this time it looked the way the Nazi woman had looked at the moment of her suffocating death.

Trench wanted to get the hell out of that room almost as badly as he wanted to strangle the demonic priest where he sat. He flexed his fingers and moved in closer for the kill.

The fiend leapt out of the chair and tackled Trench, taking him to the floor while trying to bite his family jewels. Trench clapped his hands against the priest's ears, hard enough to rupture eardrums. From deep inside the priest's body the thing began to whine, the whine rising in pitch like a boiling tea kettle steamed up to shriek. Trench grabbed the man's skull and wrenched it viciously to the right. The loud pop was the sound of his neck snapping. The whining went on for a few long seconds, even after the dead man's body went limp in his killer's grasp.

Trench let him go. The corpse thudded to the floor, the priest finally free of the thing that had evilly squatted inside him. The squatter was evicted.

Trench grinned.

Ghostly talons dug into his shoulders. They burrowed deep, going down his spine.

"Come on in, bitch," he said. "I'll fuck you back to hell."

*   *   *

St. Augustine was a quiet little town, as Florida tourist traps went. Most of its visitors were older folks with a mature interest in the town's history as the nation's oldest city. They were more the museumgoer type than the hell-raiser breed. Which suited Trench fine.

He found Father Thomas Riley late at night in the rectory. The priest wore Bermuda shorts, a white pullover shirt and sandals. He had wine on his breath—unless it was the blood of Christ.

"You," Trench said in a voice not his own.

"Pardon me?" Father Thomas flashed a look of fear.

Trench tamped down inexplicable feelings of hate, got control of his voice and words and said, "You look familiar is all. Father Ryan sent me. He's dead. He wanted you to hear what's on this tape."

Trench held up the recorder in his left hand.

"Dead you say? What happened?"

"He seemed to think he had the devil in him. Something he caught while helping you drive out demons. I guess it got the best of him."

"Oh my dear Jesus. Come in, come in." Father Thomas waved him inside.

"Show me where to plug this in and we'll get right to it. There's not a lot on it. The recording session was . . . cut short."

"The kitchen," Father Thomas said and pointed the way.

The house smelled of cooked onions and cinnamon and a few spices Trench couldn't identify. The priest told him to put the recorder on the counter by the sink, then to have a seat at the kitchen table. The tape hissed and popped as the two men sat opposite each other. Then Trench's recorded tinny voice rumbled from small speakers: *"Okay, Padre, for the record, how the hell did you make that water pitcher fly into the wall without touching it?"*

The whole thing took less than five minutes. It ended with the snapping of the spine and Trench's bravado comment about fucking the demon back to hell. Father Thomas looked askance at his visitor. Trench said, "That snapping sound was me breaking his neck."

Trench grinned.

Father Thomas jumped out of his chair and started reciting Latin. "Exaudi, Deus, salutis amator . . ." Though Trench had never learned a word of the dead language, he *preternaturally* understood exactly what the priest was saying: "Hear, God, lover of human salvation, the prayer of your Apostles Peter and Paul and of all the saints, who by your grace emerged as victors over the Evil One."

Trench stood slowly, showing teeth in a wide grin, and said in a familiar subterranean voice, "You thought you beat us, priest. You won the battle but not the war. Our reinforcements are here. And it's time to pay the piper."

Father Thomas went on with the Latin.

Trench didn't want to see what was coming next so he mentally went away like a man stepping back into mercifully thick fog and left the devil to its devices.

The fog didn't squelch the screams.

*   *   *

Driving back to Miami, Trench saw flashes of what the demon had done to Father Thomas. It was like recalling somebody else's horrible memories. Those were his big knuckles smashing the priest's nose against his bloodied-to-pulp face, and those were his same hands wrapped around the man's neck and throttling him until his head tried to come off. His hand holding the kitchen knife that cut off the priest's tongue. Had he cooked it in the frying pan or had he only thought of doing it?

"You did it," said the thing in the backseat of the Ford coupe. "And then you ate it."

Trench looked in the rearview and saw a shadowy form with a face from hell. A harpy's face but more hideous, a face of cobbled pieces from the ugliest monsters Hollywood had never dreamed up. A face too terrible to put on the big screen.

Trench belched. He got a taste of half-cooked meat.

The thing laughed. "Your unholy communion, shamus, talking back to you."

Trench floored the accelerator. The car sped over blacktop, headlights losing their fight against the night.

"We're going all the way with you, Trench-foot," the demon said. "Hitching to hell and gone. But keep this in your mind: We're not here to make you do evil. We're here because you *are* evil. We never come in uninvited."

"Fuck you," Trench said.

"If you like. We'll have time enough for that and many other wicked things. Ours will be a solid partnership. You're going to quit your job as hotel dick and start your own detective agency. Oh, don't worry about the money. We'll make it readily available. We love detectives! The seedy lives they poke with sticks, the nasty shit they wallow in, all that delicious sin and degradation!"

"Fuck you. You're not real. You're not even back there."

"You're right, of course. We're not here. We're inside you. So buckle up, buddy. The long ride is going to get rough. Brutal."

The thing laughed and added, "Hardboiled to a fine crisp, our very own private dick."

FLESH AND WORD

"I know you. You're the missing piece of me. I know your heart."

"Are we talking aorta, ventricles, valves?"

"I mean the heart cave. Dark and damp. Where all yearning begins. And love."

"Not a rib? A kidney? Hair follicle, flake of dead skin? The missing piece?"

"I'm talking about soul-mates. Lost to each other in another life. And found. Here. Now."

"Okay. Keep talking."

Mostly women, they came at him in a short, snaky line. They each held a copy of his book, hugged to the bosom or held reverently in open palms, a small semi-holy writ. The dutiful scribe, he signed each one with a personalized inscription. He wrote his signature so many times it lost all meaning. *Rand Hampton, Rand Hampton, Rand Hampton . . .*

He smiled. He said things meant to be witty, sophisticated. Throwaway lines. He did his best to keep his sarcasm in check and tried to look as if he wanted to be here signing books for his readers, this frumpy little band of fans and compulsive word-eaters.

He didn't like it, but he needed them. To pay his bills and support his accustomed lifestyle. It was an absurd symbiosis; he supplied them with heartbreaking minimalist romances, and they put fine cuisine on his table, expensive wine in his glass and gave his ego legs so he could occasionally make a show of walking his talk.

He no longer longed for recognition as a serious author, nor for readers intelligent enough to sense the author's angst secreted between lurid lines depicting heaving breasts and pouting lips. If serious critics ignored him or bothered to call him a common hack, he no longer cared. All he cared about now was the money, keeping the customer satisfied. He made the donuts and they scarfed them down. Everybody was fat and somewhat happy.

His agent said his novels were like jelly donuts—powdered sugar on the outside and sticky in the middle. He thought they were more like your basic donut, well-rounded but with a hole in the center.

He signed books. He tossed off witty one-liners, playing his role against type.

He inscribed. He smiled. He flexed his fingers to fend off writer's cramp.

He saw her standing by the coffee counter as he signed the night's last book. She was dark-haired and willowy, wearing a knee-length black coat and indigo-tinted glasses. Her legs were long with well-shaped calves. She sipped coffee and studiously watched him from behind darkened lenses. He realized now that he'd felt her eyes on him before he noticed her. The intensity of her tinted quixotic gaze. Something about the woman was very familiar, mysteriously archetypal.

An inexplicable chill prickled the back of his neck when the woman reached up to tip her glasses down the bridge of her nose and look at him over slim frames. He gave her a polite nod which she didn't acknowledge. Her eyes were dark. Her face was startlingly pale, skin newborn and un-blemished. She pursed her seductively plump lips, then took another sip of coffee and looked away.

He felt the familiar stirring of blood, prelude to arousal. A tide of recognition rose in the seabed of his forty-six-year-old body. But he didn't know this woman. Had never seen her before.

She discarded her coffee cup in a waste can, turned up her coat's bladelike collar and walked away. Though the long coat cloaked her body's contours, he sensed a svelte physique beneath it. She disappeared behind the stacks.

A well-dressed woman with scorched blond hair buttonholed him in the rest room alcove. "After Nicholas Sparks, you're my favorite writer," she said, gushing.

"Wonderful," he said, smiling with clenched teeth. Upon the release of his debut novel, one witless reviewer had called him "the next Nicholas Sparks." The moniker stuck, hanging on him like an ill-fitting suit. It was the kiss of death to his literary pretensions. "How good of you to say," he said.

"I wanted to ask you, though. Can't you write happier endings?"

The smile still frozen on his face, he said, "Sorry, dear, I don't do fairy tales."

Two nights later, he saw the Mystery Woman again at the next stop on his signing tour. She had followed him from Topeka to Memphis. Should he be concerned? He was certain he hadn't signed a book for her. She hadn't approached him at all. She'd simply watched him from a non-threatening remove, a naturalist studying a creature in its native habitat. Never mind that he detested book-signings and always felt out of his element when forced to confront indulgent fans.

The night was rainy, the turnout sparse. There were lulls when there was nothing to do but sit there and wait, fiddling with his pen. During a prolonged period of downtime, he got up from the book-laden table and went in pursuit of her. One moment she was in the poetry section and the next, she was gone. He scanned the store but didn't see her. He moved between the shelves, searching.

"*I know you,*" she said close behind him. "*You're the missing piece of me. I know your heart.*"

He turned and there she was, inches away, her musky scent enchanting. He fed her the next line from his novel, *Ravenous Heart.* "*Are we talking aorta, ventricles, valves?*"

She smiled, removing her dark glasses.

"Are you stalking me?" he asked, looking into the onyx of her eyes.

"Am I?" Her tongue teased her lower lip.

"I'm sorry, do we know each other? You do look very familiar."

"I should. You created me."

"If that's the punch-line, I missed the joke. Who are you?"

"Theda Harrow."

"Ah. Of course you are." He smiled, thinking he should be flattered that she was apparently role-playing a character from his best book. "Raised by wolves."

"Wolves of the mind." Another phrase from the novel.

"And you followed me all the way from Topeka. I suppose I'm fortunate to have such a dedicated fan."

"I'm not a fan, Mr. Hampton. I am Theda Harrow."

"And what. You want a sequel?"

She traced a long-nailed finger along the spine of a slim volume of poems. The gesture unexpectedly excited him.

"You killed me off," she said. "How can there be a sequel? Unless you raise me from the dead."

A sudden commotion up front drew his attention. A tall man in a bomber jacket and black ski-mask was dumping something out of a black trash bag and onto the floor by the main entrance. The man shouted, "The Christ-killers and fudge-packers have a death-grip on the publishing industry! Here are the true fruits of their labor!"

Charred books tumbled from the trash bag amid ashy confetti. The masked man raised both arms over his head as if signaling a touchdown, and then dashed out the door.

"Bigotry comes in many guises," Rand said, but when he turned around, the woman who claimed to be Theda Harrow was gone.

*   *   *

On the cab ride back to the hotel, he opened his cell and called his agent. "Ted, you limey son of a bitch. Was Theda Harrow your idea?"

"Rand? What are you talking about?"

"The woman. She's a dead-ringer, all right? But I gotta tell you, if it's a publicity stunt, it's not working. Nobody notices her but me."

"Are you drunk?"

"Unfortunately not. You're telling me you know nothing about this."

"I know nothing about this," said Ted, his British accent more pronounced now.

"Shit. Then she's a nutjob. A stalker. A demented fucking fan. This is not good."

"If she's a problem, report her to the police."

"What, swear out a warrant? In every state and county I set foot in? I don't have time for this, Teddy. You know how much I hate these damned tours, how they drain me. I should be working."

"You have a new plot outlined? Great."

"You know I don't. And I'm not likely to come up with one as long as I'm on tour."

Ted's sigh was a breathy rumble in Rand's ear. "You've got your laptop. Use your free time wisely."

"I can't write this stuff on the road. You know this. It requires a severe narrowing of awareness, an inviolable dumbing down. Too many distractions on the road. Brutal reality impinges."

"I don't know what to tell you. You've only got one more date. Tough it out, then go home and get cracking."

"Teddy?"

"Yes?"

"Bugger off."

*   *   *

I'm alone in a Memphis hotel room, he reflected, and out there in the night the world is wearing away at the edges. He sat at the writing desk and opened his laptop. He opened the "Monster" file and set to work, adding to the never-ending story—his secret life's-work. The off-kilter romance novels were merely his meal ticket, but this Proustian monstrosity had become his life, at least symbolically.

Before he became a successful novelist, he wrote numerous short stories and memoir fragments. Then one despairing day he realized that all the stories were intimately related, either thematically or spiritually, so he rolled them all into one genre-defying mega-story, which he worked on in secret whenever he could steal time. He was never altogether sure if he was trying to write himself deeper into life or write his way out of it.

He poured himself a scotch to lubricate his mental apparatus and then began to write. It was astonishing the way so many divergent tales folded so neatly into one hulking beast. He *needed* astonishment. He was a craven god, driven by solitude to fold space/time and interlock lonely galaxies, meshing dimensions at will.

His fingertips tap-danced over the keys. New words appeared onscreen.

Verily, verily—Are you here to oil the machine?—I say unto you, I am the backdoor to the darkest alley. I am the tooth and the night. Author of these divinely absurd scenarios, guilty of brutal literary transgressions. Whisper the secret word and enter the Hag Hotel.

His cell phone broke into song. His chosen ring-tone was the theme from John Carpenter's *Halloween*. He liked its melodramatic urgency and it was loud enough to hear in the next room. He opened it. His ex-wife's name appeared in the little illuminated window.

"Claudia darling," he said in ersatz imitation of Cary Grant. "How the hell are you?"

"How the hell would I be? Given the fact that your alimony check is late. Again."

"Damn. I'll speak to my accountant. I'll ring him up as soon as you hang up."

"Drop the act, Rand. You don't have an accountant. This is all on you. Bastard."

"I *should* have an accountant. Look, I'm sorry. It slipped my mind. I'll overnight it to you. I promise."

"I shouldn't have to put up with this, you know. Your irresponsibility. Or is it my punishment for divorcing you?"

"No, of course not. I truly am sorry."

"Where are you?"

"Memphis, a seedy Tennessee hotel room. The Tennesseedy Hotel. Where old dreams and hack writers go to die."

"You're so full of crap it's almost funny."

"Thanks for noticing."

"Howard's been trying to reach you. He lost your cell number so I gave it to him."

"He hasn't called."

"He's like you. It takes him a while to get things done. Unlike you, he has a good excuse."

"He was supposed to get one of those voice-activated phones. Failing that, he can always dial with his tongue. These days, you don't really have to have hands."

"God, Rand. You have no idea, do you? How cruel you can be."

"I'm not cruel. Howard knew the risks going in. Every war photographer does."

"He was on holiday when it happened."

"It was Israel, Claudia. Suicide bombers don't take holidays."

"Still . . ."

"Oh! You'll never guess who's been stalking me."

"Meaning you want me to guess?"

"Theda Harrow. In the flesh."

Claudia laughed uneasily.

"She's just the way I imagined her. Only more so."

"Stalked by your own fictional character," she said. "Why am I not surprised?"

"But that's just it, you see. She lives and breathes. She actually spoke to me. It's sort of spooky, really. To be confronted by your own creation. Now I know how Victor Frankenstein felt."

"Should I be worried? If you're having an actual psychotic break, who's going to sign my alimony checks?"

"You can be so pedestrian. That's why our marriage failed, you know."

"Somebody had to have her feet on the ground."

Rand laughed, genuinely amused by her witty wordplay—unless it wasn't wordplay, in which case it had to be ignorance of pedestrian's other meaning. Either way, it was funny.

"Theda Harrow, huh?" said Claudia. "I always hated that name. She's your best character but the name is absurd. Too much like Theda Bara."

"Asymmetrical irony, darling." Cary Grant again. "She shed the snaky skin of her given name and misnamed herself after the original vamp of the silent screen so she could be reborn. Absolutely harrowing, see?"

"Don't talk like that. I don't like it, that phony voice. The one you use when you're drinking."

"I *am* drinking. Darling."

"I'm hanging up. I expect that check tomorrow, Rand. Without fail."

"Without fail. I like the sound of that."

"You and Theda Harrow should be very happy together. You're *both* fictional characters."

She hung up. He chuckled, then downed the rest of his scotch. He refilled the glass and immersed himself in his monster mash-up.

*   *   *

When she didn't show up the next night at his Barnes & Noble signing in suburban Atlanta, he was deeply disappointed—which surprised him only a little. He'd dreamt of her on the flight from Memphis, and when a jolt of midair turbulence woke him, he half-expected to see her sitting next to him. He didn't see her, but her ghostly dream-presence lingered in the empty seat at his left elbow until the landing-gear touched down on the runway.

When the desultory signing was behind him, he went outside to wait in the early-spring fog for a taxi to take him home. The cab pulled up and Rand climbed in with his suit bag and Samsonite, sank into the backseat and into a drear despond. Being on his home-turf only made him feel more out of sorts; Theda Harrow hadn't followed him home. Though it made no sense, he felt as if he'd been stood up by a no-show date.

As the cab pulled away, he saw her in a fog-splash of light, standing on the walk in front of the bookstore. He leaned forward to tell the driver to stop, glancing back to where he'd seen her. She wasn't there.

He sat back in haunted silence and shut his eyes. He called up her misty specter. He knew all there was to know about her. He'd created her ten years ago, out of the ether and a bottle of tequila. He'd let the provocative djinn out of the bottle and hammered her onto the page. But now, through uncanny literary alchemy, she'd come vamping off the page and into real life.

The cab crossed the fogbound Chattahoochee and entered Cobb County. He knew his stalker couldn't really and truly be Theda Harrow, but he'd lived and thrived so long on fiction that he wanted her to be real. A woman created out of whole cloth and half-dreams, a woman with no history other than the one he gave her.

But stalkers always came with a history. Often with an unbalanced obsessiveness that made them dangerous. Like the ditzy chick that showed up at his door one day with a dirty egg-beater and defaced copy of *Ravenous Heart,* saying her goldfish told her to show Rand the true face of the book and the throbbing soul within its lipstick-slashed pages. Stalkers usually started out harmless enough as a mere annoyance, but often escalated to dangerous levels of aggression. And the Theda Harrow in his novel was dangerous. A veritable vampire. A seductive succubus, come to suck out your soul. Or suffocate you in your sleep by fucking you to death.

The crazy lady had used the egg-beater to murder her goldfish. While he waited for the police, the woman described the way the beater's blades chopped the little fishes into pieces, and he pictured little rooster-tails of blood streaming out from the blurry maelstrom of blades. She said true books have souls. That nothing can save them. They're all doomed, those books, remaindered to purgatory, patiently waiting to torment their creators. Maybe she wasn't far from right.

His cell played *Halloween.* The cabbie chuckled, lazy-lidded eyes widening a little in the rearview. The LED displayed Howard's name. Light-emitting diode revealing wraithlike information: illuminated data streaming in from beyond.

Rand answered. It wasn't Howard. It was Howard's live-in lover, Sabra. He never remembered her last name. Nice Jewish girl. Prodigal Princess, as Howard liked to call her.

"Are you back?" she asked in a world-weary voice.

"Just crossed the Chattahoochee." He said this gravely, as if he'd just crossed the River Styx.

"Howard's on another tear. Can you come over and talk some sense into him? He won't listen to me."

"I dunno, Sabra, I'm really beat. This book tour—"

"Dammit, Rand, you have to. I can't deal. This is the worst yet."

He sighed and said, "Okay. Tell the asshole I'm gonna rip him a new one if he doesn't shape up."

"Kiss-kiss." Sabra hung up.

Rand gave the driver Howard's address and then sank into a sulk, wanting to do nothing more than to go home and dream again of Theda Harrow.

*   *   *

Sabra met him at the door to take him aside and tell him that she couldn't do this anymore, that he was going to have to take up the slack once she was gone. He was, she reminded him, Howard's best bud, blood brother and all that macho sort of crap.

"You're *leaving* him?" Rand whispered. "Does he know?"

"That's why he's showing his ass."

Rand nodded and stared down the dim hallway and into the murky glow of the den, where his old friend would be waiting in his wheelchair.

Sabra was short and large-breasted, a brunette with disobedient hair and boudoir eyes. She touched Rand's arm. Her eyes were wet. "Talk to him. I'm going out."

"You're coming back."

"Yeah. I just need a breather. Gimme an hour."

Rand patted the back of her hand, the one still resting on his forearm. Sabra attempted a smile, then pulled away, slipped into a windbreaker, grabbed her pack of smokes and went out. He walked softly down the hallway and into the den's flickering TV light.

Howard Lundy sat facing the plasma widescreen, his back to Rand. He turned his head so that his craggy face appeared in dark profile against the rosy glow of the TV and said, "She gone?"

"She had to step out for a minute."

"She means to leave me, Hamp," Howard said. "I'll miss the hell out of her, but I want her to go."

Rand sank into an armchair and once again absorbed the shock of seeing Howard's mangled body. "You do?"

"Absolutely. That's why I had to be so rough on her. To speed things along. Make her accept the inevitable. I do this because I love her." Howard leaned his head down and sipped vodka through a bent straw. The bottle rested on a lapboard suspended across the padded arms of the wheelchair. He was a big man, but with one arm taken off at the shoulder, a leg gone from the knee down and the other arm missing a hand, he appeared shrunken out of proportion to the actual subtraction of appendages.

The TV was on CNN International, the volume reduced to a faint murmur of scratchy insect sounds.

"I hate that I have to treat her like dogshit, but she's so damned loyal, what else can I do? I have to scrape her off my shoe. For her own good."

"How will you . . . get along when she's gone?"

"You mean who'll wipe my ass and wash my privates? Who'll feed me and tell me it's not really so bad being a helpless hunk of bad meat? Nobody. I'll take care of myself."

"You can't take care of yourself, Howie. It's not physically possible. You at least need a sitter, a—"

"You're not hearing me, man. I mean *take care* of myself." A wolfish smile warped his lips.

"Tell me this is you feeling sorry for yourself. That you'll sober up and realize this is the booze talking. This ain't you, buddy. You've never been a quitter."

Howard Lundy laughed. "Put me in, coach. I'll play second base. I'll *be* the base."

"Come on, man. You can—"

"Spare me the pep rally, Hamp. It's crap and you know it."

"You're not giving yourself enough time. To adjust."

"Why would I want to adjust? The sonofabitch who martyred himself at my expense is in paradise deflowering holy virgins and I'm left here to wallow in my own stench? The ten schmucks he killed were the lucky ones. No, buddy, I have no intention of adjusting. When the cafe blew apart and flew at me, I *knew* I was dead. Just a split-second of certain knowledge and peace. Now look at me. Rooked again. Raw deal, man. Raw. The only thing tempting me to hang around is Armageddon. I could sit here and see it right there on the idiot box. Those crazy fucks actually believe they're bringing it on, you know. I'm not sure they're not."

Rand said, "I don't know what to say. I don't know if I would feel any different if I was in . . ."

"My shoe?" Howard laughed. Took another pull at the crooked straw. "Scratch my nose, will ya? I'll remember you in my will."

Rand got up and tentatively scratched Howard's nose.

"Ahh, good. Thanks. Hey, crank up the volume. I wanna hear this." Howard nodded at the TV. It was a Breaking News report of the latest suicide bombing in Israel, with raw footage shot outside a crowded nightclub in Tel Aviv.

Rand turned up the volume and stared at the screen. He stole a glance at Howard, noting the rapt expression on his friend's gaunt face. The CNN anchor did her best to describe the carnage, as if the footage wasn't grisly enough in its own right.

"One step closer," said Howard, smiling with demonic glee. "I'm telling ya, Hamp, we're in the End Times, buddy. Better get ready."

"You know how long people've been saying that?"

"Only thing I've got to live for. The fucking apocalypse."

"Thousands of years."

"I can't do it anymore, man. But the thing of it is, when I stuck that oily sonofabitch in my mouth I couldn't pull the trigger. You have to help me."

"I *will* help you, How. To get out of this funk and back on your . . ."

"You're not hearing me," said Howard. "I want you to find somebody to do the job. I'm not asking you to do it yourself. Not that you could, being the sensitive writer type. Find me someone with real-world skills who can get things done. Do that, and maybe I won't haunt your dreamy ass."

*   *   *

Theda Harrow was waiting for him outside his front door. Standing tall in her Burbury trenchcoat, she took a deep drag from a cigarette. The smoke from her slightly flared nostrils and pursed lips was indistinguishable from the wispy streamers of fog.

The taxi pulled away with a loose fan-belt whining. Encumbered with well-traveled baggage, Rand went up the walkway to his townhouse, feeling as if he were stepping into an unfinished scene from an out-of-control novel. It was terrifying and exhilarating. And it was too late to back out of it, this unnerving scene. He couldn't hit the delete key and banish it to the recycle bin. He had to play it out.

"You've been waiting for me," she said, dropping her cigarette and deftly grinding it with the toe of her shoe.

He wondered if that was another line from *Ravenous Heart*. He wasn't sure, so he said, "And here I thought you were waiting for me."

The misted porch light gave her dark hair a hazy halo, sepia-toned and soft-focused.

"You couldn't get me out of your mind," she said. "You thought once you could by nailing me to the page but that didn't work. Psychic surgery won't do the trick. Your condition is inoperable. If you try to force the issue, we'll both die. You see now, don't you? I'll always be a part of you."

"Who are you, really? You make a very good Theda Harrow, but who are you? What do you want from me?"

"A gentleman would invite me in out of this bone-chilling fog. Let me in and you'll see that it's you who wants something from me."

He unlocked the door and ushered her in without quite touching her. Had he been writing this scene, he probably would've said he could feel biological heat radiating from her, but he sensed no warmth at all.

She removed her coat. He dropped his luggage on the floor, took her coat and hung it on the coat-tree in the foyer.

His eyes gathered her essence, psyche and soma. Deep eyes, thin brow, sculpted cheeks, hawkish nose, sharp chin, the slightly skewed beauty-mark mole in the left corner of her sensuous mouth and the feral slant of her teeth—all these physical qualities faithfully reflected Theda Harrow's idiosyncratic mesh of fierce id, twisted ego and stunted conscience. She was living flesh, beating blood. Trembling ever so slightly, her breasts rose and fell with her rhythmic breathing, softly pulsating with each beat of her heart.

And yet there was something supranatural about her—something transcending the natural order of things—and a subliminal suggestion that mere moments ago she might've stepped out of a Salvador Dali landscape of melting clocks and human anatomy breaking out of giant egg shells and into the world of flesh. She stood, for the moment, on the liminal side of the border to an unseen dominion, a place which could only be reached by dead roads and fevered imagination.

"You look like you've just seen a ghost," she said. "You went white as an unwashed sheet."

"By God, you've got her down pat," said Rand. "The way she takes a cliché and makes it her own. Gives it eerie new life."

"And have you got yourself down pat?" She frowned. "You mustn't speak of me in the third person. It's rude when I'm obviously right here in front of you."

"Sorry."

"Aren't you going to offer me a drink? You know what I like."

"Gin and tonic. The bar's this way."

Rand stationed himself behind the mini-bar and mixed her favored drink and then poured himself a glass of scotch-rocks. She draped herself on the leather couch and crossed her long legs, the hem of her black silky dress riding up to her knees.

"You shouldn't be here, you know," he said as he handed her the drink.

"You mean I should've stayed dead?" A trace of a smile played at her lips.

He sat opposite her in his leather armchair. "No, I mean I should know better than to let a stranger pretending to be a character from my book into my home. I'm being uncharacteristically reckless."

Now she did smile. Her teeth were toothpaste-ad white. She licked the inner rim of her glass, then she dipped the tip of her tongue into the clear liquid, reminding him of a cat. "Weren't you reckless when you conjured me from darkness to fill all that white space?" she asked, something kittenish in the way she turned her head. "Now here I am, ravenous heart and all. Don't you want to examine your handiwork? Taste it? Touch it? I'm yours to command. I always was."

He downed a big slug of scotch, then said, "Look, I'm sorry, but I don't do groupie types. It's a personal rule of mine. I'm a writer, not a rock star. Maybe you should try your luck with Nick Sparks. He's a brighter star in the literary firmament than I am. He might be into that sort of thing. I'm not. After you finish your drink, I think you should go."

"You're not ready to believe in me," she said. "I understand. You lack faith in your creative powers. But don't worry, I can help you with that."

"Oh?"

"Not all commands are verbal, you know. I do know your heart." She set down her glass and stood. "Thank you for the drink. The next time we meet, you will believe in me. In us."

He remained seated and watched her go. He finished his drink and poured another, wondering if he'd been too quick to send the woman away. Too cowardly. After a third drink, he wasn't entirely sure she'd even been there. The glass of gin and tonic had scarcely been touched.

*   *   *

The phone rang. Rand rolled over and glanced at the bedside clock. It was half past midnight. His forehead throbbing with internal pressure, he picked up the phone and grunted a booze-soured hello.

"Hamp, you shrewd sonofabitch," Howard Lundy slurred. "I knew you'd come through. How'd ya find her so fast, huh? 'Mazing, man. But hell, now she's here I dunno if I can let her do it."

"What're you talking about?" Rand sat up in bed and stared blindly into the room's darkness. The spinning sensation behind his eyes made him queasy.

"Your woman," Howard growled. "Theda Harrow, man."

"Howard. Where's Sabra?" he asked, struggling to keep the spiraling panic in his chest from spreading to his voice.

"'Sleep. Dead to the world. I didn't wanna do it when she was here but what the hell. She'd still be the one to find me. Can't be helped. She'll thank me later."

"And there's another woman with you, right now," Rand said, trying to make sense of it.

"What're you, dense? Jus' told ya, didn't I?"

"Theda Harrow," said Rand. The name seemed to find uncanny resonance in the syrupy dark of the bedroom.

"Bingo, bozo. Whadda knockout."

"Put her on."

"You're on speaker," Howard said. "So speak already."

"Hello, Rand," the woman said. "You should have more faith in me. And so you shall."

"Listen to me," he said. "Leave him alone. Get out of there right now. You hear me?"

Howard coughed and said, "Whoa, you're not gonna use *that*, are you? No, no, no, they'll think—"

Rand heard a ringing slap, followed by a grunt and then a wet wheeze and gurgle that went on and on.

"What did you do?" he shouted into the phone. "What the hell did you do?"

"Thy will be done," Theda Harrow said with unmistakable reverence.

Rand was speechless.

"I know your heart," she said. "Damp and dark. Where all yearning begins."

The next words came of their own mystical volition, and like a priest discharging a responsive ritual, he said: "And love."

As if suddenly waking from a nightmare, he broke the connection and immediately called 911 to give the operator Howard's address. "I think someone's been seriously hurt," he said. But he knew it was too late.

He rushed into the study, turned up the flames in the gas fireplace and burned all his copies of *Ravenous Heart*. He knew it was a futile gesture, strictly symbolic, but he had to do *some*thing.

He opened his laptop on the desk. Without hesitation, he deleted his Monster file. The massive fabrication winked out of existence, into cyber oblivion.

He wondered how he might obliterate the storied universe in his head. It was, he thought, a dilemma worthy of a demigod.

*   *   *

When the graveside service was over, Sabra cornered him by a massive mausoleum and backed him against a stone angel. "Why the hell did you disappear on me? I needed you."

He stammered nonsense syllables and then simply shrugged. The gloomy sky pushed down on him.

"You're supposed to be his best friend. Jesus, Hamp. You know?" The sky's raw light made her face look as sharp as a hatchet.

"Sorry. I just . . . I was . . . afraid . . ."

"I see it again every time I close my eyes," she said, edging closer to hysteria. "The knife. The blood. The look on his face."

"You *saw* it?" He felt ice in his belly.

"Yes! Didn't I tell you? No, how could I? You weren't around. I thought I heard him talking to someone. Arguing. I thought you must be there, so I got up to see what the hell was going on, just in time to see him cut his own throat."

He opened his mouth to protest the improbability of what she'd told him, but at that moment he saw Theda Harrow in the near distance, standing over Howard Lundy's hole in the ground, and he couldn't say a word.

She tossed a single white flower into the grave, then looked up with a seductive smile and touched her hand to her breast. Rand sagged against the stone angel and waited for the strange sky to stop spinning.

Sabra shook her head in sad disgust and walked away, leaving behind a hushed curse.

Cosseted in her trenchcoat, Theda Harrow vanished into the pale shadows of granite slabs and marble obelisks, but Rand knew she was far from finished with him.

DEATHLESS

I

Tanith Seagrave died in a limousine on the way to her wedding. The ambulance attendants agreed that she made a lovely corpse, dressed as she was in a frilly white gown, her blond locks done up in formal fashion to show the delicate pillar of her neck and the fine bone structure of her face. The coroner went them one better when he said Miss Seagrave made a beautiful bride for the Grim Reaper.

The policeman who was good enough to drive to Savannah's Cathedral of St. John the Baptist and give the frantic would-be bridegroom the bad news checked any impulse to spout such vulgar witticisms and simply told the young man in tux and tails that his intended had expired in a limo on the way to the cathedral.

"Oh God, oh God, oh God," the young man petitioned. Receiving no sign of immediate response, he collapsed in rumpled splendor in front of the twin-spired Gothic cathedral.

Members of the small wedding party gathered round him to lend what support they could, but for the most part, they were as shocked as he. The best man did his best to live up to his ceremonial title (nullified, of course, by events) by asking the policeman for details of Tanith Seagrave's death. "Was it a bad accident?" he asked. "Was she . . . disfigured?"

"No accident," the officer said. "She apparently choked to death on a breath mint."

"Oh God, oh God . . ." the would-be groom resumed his wrenching refrain, his splendid attire wilting in the summer heat.

The best man put a comforting hand on his friend's shoulder and said, "Miles, I'm so sorry. Let me take you home."

Miles Chamberlin looked up with brimming eyes and said, "No. I have to see her."

"You think that's wise? I mean it's—"

"Bad luck before the wedding?" The would-be groom tried to smile.

"Skipper" Blaisdell, best man and dearest friend to Miles Chamberlin, thought Miles must've been in shock to say such a thing in such awful circumstance. He tried to dissuade his friend from making the trip to the hospital, where the body of Tanith Seagrave would be awaiting transport to a designated mortuary, but young Chamberlin, a man of expensive habits and more than enough wealth to support those habits, would not be swayed from his position. He meant to see his betrothed *in her bridal gown.* He brushed off Blaisdell's second appeal to reason, and asked the minister who was to have presented the vows to accompany him to the hospital. Father Revell, an old friend of the Chamberlin family and beneficiary of years of their generous tithes, agreed. Miles' parents were both dead, and being the sole heir to the Chamberlin fortune, he alone controlled the purse strings and wielded the power and influence generated by great wealth.

The priest did not wish to fall from the favor of fortune's heir.

Blaisdell drove them in his town car. He kept quiet and concentrated on his driving, while in the backseat the priest did his best to console young Chamberlin. But Miles would have none of it; he made a demand of the man of God that surely must've tested his faith and mettle, even as it shocked Blaisdell. "I want you," said Miles Chamberlin, "to give us our vows. We're going ahead with the ceremony."

"*What?* But . . . but . . ." Revell sputtered, causing the wattle under his chin to quiver against his cleric's collar.

"I *will* marry her," Miles insisted.

"Miles, come to your senses, man," Blaisdell spoke from behind the town car's wheel. "That's absurd. Not to mention illegal. You can't marry a . . ."

"A corpse?" Miles laughed; it wasn't at all a maniacal laugh, but rather one of genuine amusement. "But don't you see? I shall be marrying her spirit. Isn't that what all this Holy Matrimony business is supposed to be about? What makes it holy is the joining of two spirits. Am I wrong, Father?"

"Well, no, not on that count, but Mr. Blaisdell is right. It isn't legal. I can't marry you to someone who's no longer living."

"Sure you can," said Miles. "And you will. None but the three of us will ever know. And I'll see that you get a tidy sum for your troubles. I know you were hoping to make a trip to the Holy Land, but you suffered your financial setback. I'll send you to the Holy Land in the highest style possible."

"Think what you're asking me to do," pleaded the priest. "It would be an abomination before God. Even if I did it, it wouldn't have the sanction of the church behind it. Nor would it have any legal weight. It would be meaningless."

"It would mean something to me," said Miles. "And to Tanith. Please don't presume to tell me that it would offend God. I don't believe you know the mind of the Almighty any better than I do. We've come to a pass beyond the boundaries of church doctrine and societal customs. But that's all right. I know what I'm doing. You must *marry us*. I know with all my being that this is the right thing to do."

Skipper Blaisdell caught Father Revell's eyes in the rearview mirror and he saw acquiesce in them. He knew then his headstrong friend would have his way, and that Miles Chamberlin would indeed be wedded to the late Tanith Seagrave.

II

The somber trio obtained permission to visit the deceased in the morgue in the hospital's basement. Miles prevailed upon a couple of accommodating nurses to dress Tanith in her wedding gown, explaining that he wanted to be able to remember her that way. When the nurses emerged from the morgue to tell the three men they could go in, they both had tears in their eyes, no doubt elicited by the heart-rending romance of the little tragedy being played before their weepy eyes.

Death had done little to subtract much of Tanith's natural beauty. Though it was odd to see a woman in a pristine gown laid out on a hospital gurney, the men agreed that she looked as if she were only sleeping. She had been uncommonly pale before her death, and now the washed-out light from the overhead fluorescent only added to the illusion that her pallor was simply the purity of noble blood and pampered breeding.

Miles took her lifeless hand in his, and bent down to kiss her cool lips. "It's all right now, darling," he whispered. "I'm here. Skipper's here, and Father Revell is going to marry us. You're going to be Tanith Chamberlin."

The discomfited priest conducted an abbreviated ceremony. When he asked the dead woman if she would "take this man to be your lawful wedded husband," Miles answered for her: "She does, absolutely." After the vows were made, Miles kissed her lips and said, "Not even death can keep us apart, my love."

Blaisdell tried to put the best face possible on this morbid business by telling himself that it had been done solely for the purpose of helping Miles come to grips with his wrenching loss, but coming events would plague him with grave doubt, and the best man's tenuous facade would collapse in short order.

III

Miles Chamberlin arranged with well-placed pay-offs and outright bribes to have the unautopsied remains of his beloved entombed in his family's mausoleum on Chamberlin Island. The diminutive islet rose out of the

Atlantic some six miles east of Tybee Island, and though it was one of the smallest of all the islands off the Georgia coast, it's dimensions were more than adequate to contain the spacious Chamberlin Manse, a four-car garage, tennis courts, rock and flower gardens, and a carefully-kept bike trail. The house itself was a three-storied colonial with white columns, a multi-gabled roof, and dormer windows. When Miles' parents and older sister were still alive and in residence, they had employed a small army of house- and grounds-keepers, two cooks and a full-time pilot to helm their private ferryboat, but now that Miles was the sole occupant of the drafty old mansion, the serving staff consisted of a single housekeeper, and a grounds-keeper who doubled as ferryboat pilot. Whenever he entertained company, Miles hired caterers from Savannah.

Two days after the death of and his marriage to Tanith Seagrave, Miles himself piloted the ferry and transported the hearse bearing her body to the island. He oversaw the entombment of her casket within the stone walls of the family crypt, made sure her vault was not sealed shut, and gave the two men from the funeral home a sizable gratuity. His man Carson ferried the hearse back to the coast while he stayed with Tanith's remains, addressing her as if she were still capable of hearing his voice and understanding his words. "I couldn't bear the thought of your being imprisoned underground in some crowded cemetery," he said. "But now you've come home to me, and I know you will be happier here." As the sun went down and the wind rustled the leaves of the weeping willow trees overhanging the mausoleum, he sat in a camp chair and read to her from her favorite book of Emily Dickinson's poetry. With darkness settling over the island, he talked of their brief engagement and relived some of the happiest moments of their "whirlwind" romance. He remained in the crypt till nearly midnight, reading more poems by candlelight and sharing his rambling thoughts with his bride. As he walked back to the house, he wept, expressing the sadness he'd dared not display in her presence; it wouldn't do for Tanith to see how deeply her death had wounded him. Miles believed it was important to keep up a brave face—no matter how bad things might get. He took solace from the notion that nothing could be worse than what had already befallen him. He was soon to learn how wrong he was in this thinking, and to discover how much worse things could be. His brave-face strategy would crumble like a sandcastle beneath crashing waves.

IV

The next day his lawyer visited him on the island. After the lawyer expressed his condolences for the death of Miles' fiancé, they retired to the study, and sat smoking fine cigars, sipping cognac, and making idle conversation until finally Miles said, "I know you didn't come all the way out here for the pleasure of my company, Dave. What's up?"

David Shapiro set down his glass, leaned forward in his chair and said, "I know you'll say I overstepped the boundaries of our professional relationship, Miles, but just bear in mind that I did it with your best interests at heart."

Miles scowled. "Go on."

"I had an investigator check into Miss Seagrave's background, and as it turns out, I'm afraid the young lady misrepresented herself to you. To say she had a checkered past is to put it too mildly."

"What the hell were you thinking? I never asked you to investigate her."

"I was thinking of you. I suspected you were smitten to the point of blindness, so I took it upon myself—as your trusted legal advisor—to make sure the young lady wasn't out for your assets. You gave such short notice of your wedding plans, there wasn't time to bring this to you sooner. And frankly, I wasn't eager to face your wrath."

"You son of a bitch." Miles fixed Shapiro with a cold-steel stare.

"Hear me out. I—"

"I should *throw* you out."

"Just listen. Please? What harm can it do now?"

"To the contrary, what good will it do? She can hardly touch my precious fortune now, unless you're going to tell me she's capable of robbing me from beyond the grave."

"I thought it might make your loss a little easier to bear if you knew the truth. May I tell you?"

"Nothing you say can sully my opinion of Tanith. Whatever her faults or past sins, I knew her heart, and her heart was pure. She was a goddess to me. She still is."

The lawyer shrugged. "I'll be brief," he said as he consulted handwritten notes in a small notepad. "This is only an outline from my operative's full report, but it should be enough to give you the big picture."

"Go on then," Miles challenged, "do your worst."

"Miss Seagrave told you she was orphaned at an early age and was raised by an old-maid aunt, but in reality, her father disappeared when she was thirteen, under suspicion of sexually molesting her. Her mother is alive, though not well, in a state mental institution for the criminally insane. The woman killed Tanith's older sister with a butcher knife, claiming the girl was possessed by a demon. The 'kindly' aunt who raised Tanith has a criminal record for petty theft and fraud. Though it was never proven, Tanith was suspected of helping her aunt defraud elderly welfare recipients. Tanith was married to Herman Threadgill, a grease monkey who was stabbed to death in a motel room after a tête-à-tête with a known prostitute. The killer was never caught. Need I go on?"

"I think not. I'm sure you hit all the best notes." Miles rose from his leather armchair. "Now, please leave. Carson will ferry you back to the mainland. As of this moment, you are no longer my lawyer. And just so you know, Tanith Seagrave was a *wonderful* person and I still consider her my soulmate."

After Shapiro's departure Miles walked to Tanith's tomb and reassured her that the horrible things the lawyer had said about her and her family made no difference at all to him. "I love you, no matter what you might've done in the past," he said, his voice ringing with a hollow echo within the confines of the stony mausoleum.

V

On the fourth day after her death, Miles left the house by the back door and walked along the stepping-stone path to the family tomb. He carried a leather-bound volume of Poe's poetry, a bottle of vintage French wine, and two glasses of finest crystal. The late-evening sky was darkened by ominous clouds scudding inland from a storm somewhere out in the Atlantic. Gusting winds whipped the moss-hung trees to a sibilant fury; the willow trees towering over the gray stone walls and crenellated roof of the house of the dead danced wildly, lashing the air with nimble limbs.

Miles stopped cold on the path and gaped at the dark figure emerging from the mausoleum. One of the crystal glasses slipped from his fingers and shattered against the stepping-stone at his feet. He knew he was alone on the island, having watched Carson and the housekeeper speed away for the night in the motorboat, so who was this dark-clad apparition walking away from him and into the scrub and brambles of the woods behind the family tomb? "Hey! Stop!" shouted Miles, but to no effect. The mysterious person faded into the shaggy patch of forest. He started to go after the intruder, but then realized he had better inspect the vaults for signs of violation. There was no evidence of vandalism, but neither was there any way to determine whether the only unsealed vault had been opened—unless he opened it himself. Miles went to Tanith's vault, took a labored breath, and then pulled it open. The casket with the luxurious bronze finish lurched to a stop at the end of its runners, and Miles heard a muffled thump issue from inside. "I'm sorry," he said, "I didn't mean to yank it so hard." With hands atremble, he gently lifted the casket's lid. He knew that not even mortician's chemicals, had they been used, could have prevented the breakdown of external tissue and that the late-summer heat should have hastened the sagging and "melting" of his beloved's face by way of natural decomposition, but in the storm-darkened dusk Tanith's face appeared untouched by ravages of heat or time. There was no odor of decay.

He lit a candle and held it above the casket. His eyes hadn't deceived him; she looked as naturally beautiful as she had during the wedding in the morgue. Something glinted in the flickering light; he reached down to touch the shiny object resting on the bosom of her bridal gown. Someone had put a necklace with a rose-tinted crystal pendant around her neck. He was sure he'd never seen it before; in fact, he'd never seen her wear anything around her neck. It had to have been the skulking intruder who left it here. Someone who had known Tanith, most likely, but Miles had no idea who the person might be, nor how he had stolen unobserved onto the island. A row boat, perhaps.

He reached close to his beloved's neck to unclasp the necklace, but he stayed his hands midway to their destination. *What if . . .*

He shuddered as he completed the irrational thought.

What if the pendant is serving some purpose? What if, by means of dark magic, the crystal is acting to preserve Tanith's natural beauty? If I remove it . . . will she begin to go the way of all flesh and yield to decay? He shuddered once more as he withdrew his hands. Thunder boomed and rumbled over the ocean like the cannonade of an ancient wooden warship.

Leaving the casket open, Miles sat in his camp chair, uncorked the bottle of wine and filled the remaining glass. "We'll have to share a glass, darling. I know you won't mind." He raised the glass and said, "To our undying love." He spilled a tiny bit of wine on the floor to represent her participation in the toast, and then he took a sip for himself. Setting the glass aside, he opened the book of verse and began to read the one poem by Poe that seemed eerily appropriate. Tears were streaming down his face as he read the last stanza:

And so, all the night-tide, I lie down by the side
Of my darling, my darling, my wife and my bride
In her sepulchre there by the sea—
In her tomb by the side of the sea.

He finished the rest of the wine in the glass, shut the casket's lid and closed the vault. He walked back to the house in a cold downpour, wondering if he'd done the right thing in leaving the strange pendant around Tanith's neck.

VI

He arose early the next morning and phoned Shapiro's home number.

"Dave? I apologize for my behavior at our last meeting. I'm sure you understand how upsetting it was for me. At any rate, I want you to remain as my attorney."

"Of course," said Shapiro. "It was the wrong time to go into that sad business. I shouldn't have done it."

"Water under the bridge," said Miles. "Actually, I'm glad you told me. I want you to do whatever you have to do to set up a meeting with Tanith's mother. Clear it with her physician, whatever's necessary. I want to meet her face-to-face."

"What on earth for? The woman's psychotic."

"It's something I need to do. Whatever else she is, she was Tanith's mother. Find out if she's been told of her daughter's death."

"I can't talk you out of this, can I?"

"No."

"All right. I'll get right on it."

Shortly after noon Shapiro phoned to report that Dr. Cervantes had approved Miles' visit with Mrs. Seagrave and that the patient knew nothing of her daughter's death. "The doctor says you should be prepared for any and all manner of crazy behavior. Apparently, the woman is wildly unpredictable. She may not respond at all, or she may yell and scream and tear her hair."

"Thanks for the warning," said Miles.

An hour later he was ashore, and on his way to Milledgeville State Hospital. He arrived late in the afternoon, parked in front of the main building and went inside for his visitor's pass. A stout black woman led him to the maximum-security building housing those patients deemed by the courts to be criminally insane. His uniformed charge escorted him to a small room furnished with a scarred table and four wooden chairs, and then he was alone, awaiting the arrival of his unacknowledged mother-in-law. Ten long minutes later, a burly attendant pushed into the room a wheelchair bearing a haggard woman with downcast eyes and a deathly pallor. Her heavy makeup couldn't conceal the hollowness around her eyes or the physical aura of emaciation. The attendant parked the chair across the table from Miles, and said, "This is Edith Seagrave. I'll be right outside the door if you need me. Good luck."

As soon as they were alone in the room, Miles clasped his hands on the tabletop and said, "Mrs. Seagrave, I'm Miles Chamberlin. I was engaged to your daughter Tanith."

The old woman raised her eyes and looked at him for the first time.

She regarded him with cool detachment, yet her eyes seemed to glint with knowing mischief.

"I'm afraid I have bad news," he went on. "Tanith . . . has passed on. Do you understand? I'm sorry to say your daughter is dead."

"Tanith?" said the woman. "Dead?" Then she cackled like a bird imitating human laughter.

"Yes. She died on the way to the church where we were to be married."

Mrs. Seagrave contorted her wrinkled face into a series of bizarre grimaces, and for a brief instant Miles thought she might be having some sort of seizure. She cackled again, then said, "She's not dead. Don't you know? My Tanith ain't the dying kind."

"I'm afraid she is. Her remains are . . . resting in my family's mausoleum on Chamberlin Island."

She shook her head. "She always did love the sea. But she won't be doing much resting, I promise you. It's the witch blood, ya know. I always told her there was a blessing in that curse, but she didn't want to believe it. I reckon now she'll see her crazy old mum was right all along."

Another crowing cackle made Miles wince. Though he thought he was probably wasting his breath, he posed the question foremost in his mind. "Mrs. Seagrave, do you know anything about a rose-colored crystal pendant? On a gold chain?"

She looked down at her hands and grunted.

"Do you?" Miles persisted, though for all he knew she might've just taken leave of reality.

She began a pill-rolling motion with each hand, making Miles think of the universal human gesture that meant: Give me some money. Then she looked at him once more. "Cat's eye," she said.

"No, it's not a cat's eye. It a red crystal with—"

"I know what it is, son. I call it cat's eye because it has panther blood in it. That's what makes it red." She all at once appeared agitated, rocking forward and back as she wrung her claw-like hands. "Don't you touch it! Don't you dare! Leave it be!"

Drawn by the old woman's uproar, the attendant came back into the room. "Settle down, hon, or I'll have to take you back to your room."

She ignored the big man and fixed her bug eyes on Miles. "You married her, didn't you. On the sly, wicked boy."

She started the cackling again, and Miles stood, unnerved as much by her strident voice as by what she had said. He let himself out of the room, leaving the attendant to deal with the screeching old woman who had made more sense than Miles cared to admit.

VII

It was almost midnight when he ferried back to the island. The sky was clear, but a waxing moon dimmed all but the brightest stars. He parked the car in the garage, got the flashlight from the glove box and started down the path to the mausoleum. Night birds sang; frogs and insects added their monotone melodies to the island music. As he approached the house of vaults, a furtive movement caught his eye. A black shadow in the shape of a man was gliding toward the trees and tropical vegetation behind the mausoleum. Miles shot the beam of light at the intruder and caught him in the unsteady shaft just as the man-shape went down on its hands and knees. In utter astonishment Miles paid sharp heed as the dark form changed shape before his eyes and bounded into the underbrush. Impossible though it was, the man-shape had been transformed into the shape of a black cat the size of a panther. He steadied the beam of his light and held it on the green fronds still astir from the panther's passing. Even as he was telling himself that his eyes had played an imaginative trick on his brain, the unmistakable cry of a panther issued from the lush greenery, giving lie to his desperate rationalization. He knew there had never been a panther on this island, but he didn't trouble himself with finding an explanation for its presence; the only explanation he wanted was the one that would explain how a man could become a bounding feline.

The words of Mrs. Seagrave came back to him: "I call it cat's eye because it has panther blood in it."

Cat's eye. Witch blood. Blessing in the curse. Not the dying kind. All these fragments rumbled disjointedly through his mind like cars uncoupled from a coherent train of thought. He ran back to the mausoleum and stepped inside. Once again he opened Tanith's vault and threw up the coffin's lid. The cat's-eye pendant was still there, scarlet in stark contrast to the white lace on her bone-white bosom. Tanith's flesh remained untouched by decay. Her skin appeared surprisingly supple, and it was pliant beneath his trembling fingers. He picked up the crystal from her breast. The bauble was warmer than his beloved's flesh.

"I don't understand," he told her. "What's happening here? Are you . . . Can you really hear me? Can you make me know what's going on?"

As if in evasive answer to his questions, a panther's cry rode the wind to his ears, chilling him. He let the pendant fall upon the creamy swells of her bosom, secured the casket in the vault, and then went back to the house and drank himself into a stupor.

When the sun woke him the next morning, he phoned Skipper Blaisdell and urged him to the island. "I need you," Miles told him. "Something's happening here, things I can't explain or understand. There's no one else I can tell."

Blaisdell agreed to come right away. Miles met him at the shore with the skiff and plowed the boat full-throttle back to the island. He didn't begin to unburden himself until they were seated in his study with glasses of his finest scotch. He tried to keep his emotions in check as he told his fantastic tale, but by the tale's end, his eyes were misty and his vision blurred.

"I don't know what to say," said Blaisdell. "I know you're serious about this, but what do you want me to say? That you're not having a mental breakdown?"

"I almost wish I were. That would be easier to accept, but I know that's not it. It happened just as I described it. Impossible, but true."

"Okay. So now what? If it's true, what can you do about it?"

"I don't know. That's where I need your help. Should I remove the pendant and let nature take its course with Tanith's corpse? And if I do, will I still have a shape-shifting demon roaming the island?"

"So, you believe Tanith was a real witch and the cat-man is her . . . familiar?"

Miles shrugged. "Do you have some other explanation?"

"I'm afraid I'm a little hazy on all this occult minutia. What would be the reason for a dead witch's familiar to hang around?"

"All I know . . . or think I know," he said as he rubbed his face with his hands, "is that it's preserving her body. For what purpose, I can only guess."

Blaisdell fixed his eyes on his friend, and after a long moment of thoughtful silence he said, "I'll say this. Witch or not, the woman bewitched you. You met her, you romanced her a few weeks and then you 'married' her, and now that she's dead, you sit with her every night and read poetry to her as if she were still alive. If I didn't know you as well as I do I'd say you needed psychiatric counseling."

Miles refilled his tumbler and said, "I think I need spiritual counseling."

"Surely not from that toady Revell."

"No. From someone knowledgeable in voodoo. Savannah has more than its share of voodoo spiritualists, or whatever they call themselves. I need the genuine article, not some charlatan. You have unusual contacts in Savannah. Find me someone."

Blaisdell barked a derisive laugh. "I'm afraid you've misjudged the clientele of The Skipper's Oyster Bar. They're mostly tourists."

"I've seen some of your regulars. You can't tell me they don't know the city's underbelly. Make inquires, put out feelers. You can do it."

"I'll do what I can. In the meantime, I think you should stay out of that damned crypt. You need to stop this ghoulish behavior and get off the island more, or you'll soon be a ghost of yourself."

Miles gave a noncommittal nod.

Blaisdell placed his hand on his friend's shoulder. "You know I don't believe any of this voodoo crap. Oh, you're haunted all right, but not by spooks and shape-shifters. You're haunted by lost love. If voodoo will help you come to grips with your own personal demons, then I'm all for it. I'll find you your black magic savior."

VIII

Miles took his friend's advice after all, and stayed out of the mausoleum, but he did keep close watch on it, hoping to spy the otherworldly intruder if he showed up again. He even considered setting bear traps to catch the cat or the man, but decided to do nothing so drastic before consulting a voodoo practitioner. Three days after his last meeting with Blaisdell, a voodoo maven came to call.

Lady George was a morbidly obese black woman with an infectious smile made somehow more endearing by the loss of three front teeth. Her dark eyes were flecked with gold. Bracelets jangled on her thick wrists as she spoke with her hands as well as her mouth. According to Skipper's contacts, Lady George was the eminent voodoo authority in all of Savannah. Miles met with her in his study and told her everything. The massive woman nodded as with deep understanding and exhibited no surprise at anything he told her.

"You cotched in a wicked web," she said with joviality inappropriate to the grave circumstances.

"Caught?" he guessed.

"Yes. You *married* her. Now you have to divorce the witch."

"So she *is* a witch. And the panther man, is he her familiar?"

"The cat could be her demon slave, or it could be her spirit guide. Depends on what kind of magic she did."

"But what does she want from me? I've given her my love, what else is there?"

"It's not love. She took your love and twisted it into something darker." Lady George's bracelets clattered as she made energetic hand gestures as though weaving some miraculous spell. "She wants to consummate the marriage. You understand? Good."

"You mean, physically?"

"Yes, physically. But you better not do it. It's against God to do that. You do that and you be damned same as her. And that's what she really wants."

In a ghoulishly perverse way, it made perfect sense to him. He *had* been bewitched, and now the one spinning a web of dark magic wanted his soul. "Okay, but how do I divorce her? I mean our marriage wasn't really legal. I can't just go to a lawyer and have papers drawn up."

She laughed uproariously. "No, you cain't do that. Lady George can help you cut the ties. But it might not be so easy."

"Just tell me what we have to do."

"First thing, hand me that bottle of whiskey over there."

He got up, retrieved a bottle of Irish whiskey from the wet bar, and gave it to her. She stood up, took a big gulp and spit a spray of the amber liquid in his face, then she shook what looked like a peacock's feather over his head and spit on him once more. Finally, she took another mouthful of whiskey and this time swallowed it as she sprinkled musty white powder on top of his head. "There," she said. "That should help you resist her evil charms. Now we have to wait for the dark of the moon, then we'll get you unhitched."

Miles resisted the impulse to wipe his face, and nodded meekly.

"And one more thing," she told him. "Start saving your pee in a big glass jar."

"My urine?"

"That's right. When the time comes, you gone have to mark your territory. You got a lot of territory, so you'll need a lot of pee. Now take me to her. I have to see who I got to fight."

He escorted her to the tomb. She told him to wait outside while she went in to see Tanith's body. When she came out a few minutes later, she said, "You don't go in there no more till I come back. I think she's feeding on your love. Stay away. Now we just have to wait for the new moon."

With great effort Miles stayed away from the mausoleum for two tortuous weeks, but he felt Tanith's presence growing stronger. Several times he heard the cry of the big cat close to the house. He drank too much and ate very little. He collected his urine in a gallon pickle jar and kept it in the fridge. His housekeeper began to cast wary glances his way; she no doubt suspected he was losing his mind. Carson told him he'd found prints of a big cat in the yard. Short days leaked into long nights, and Miles began to dread the darkness, because Tanith's presence was strongest at night. He loved her no less, but the love was intertwined with fear.

He ached to see her.

The night before the new moon, he was awakened in his bed by the cool touch of her hand. He saw her standing over him, smiling down at him with her green eyes glowing in the darkness. The bridal gown fell away, melting like spun webs in a brisk wind. Her nakedness mesmerized him. He lay helpless as she lowered herself on top of him. Each multifaceted nexus of flesh burned with cold fire. She was going to make love to him and there was no way he could stop her—not that he wanted to. Their illicit marriage was about to be consummated in the most unnatural of acts. He burned for her. She descended upon him, taking him into lush carnal darkness. He cried out.

And woke himself from his fever-dream.

He sat up in bed and saw he was alone, but he smelled her scent, and it was the sweet perfume of death.

IX

Lady George went first, and Miles followed. He carried an electric lantern, and the voodoo woman's outsized shadow kept Tanith's vault for a moment in darkness.

"You do what I say, no matter what happens," she said, her voice booming within the mausoleum's walls. She set her big shoulder bag down on the cement floor, stood very still for a long moment, then opened Tanith's vault and pulled out the bronze casket. Without ceremony she raised the coffin's lid. She motioned Miles over and said, "See how pretty she is! That necklace is keeping her fresh."

She was right. Tanith's beauty remained unmarred by any sign of natural decay. She still looked as though she were only sleeping. "My God," he whispered. "It's true. She's really is a witch."

"In olden times they didn't call 'em witches. That's something the Christians come up with. She's a sorceress. A necromancer. Women were always the ones with the power and the men wouldn't stand for it. That's why they liked to burn 'em. Now, honey, you start pouring your pee all along the walls and in the doorway. Go easy with it, 'cause you got other places to mark."

He unscrewed the jar's lid and poured thin splashes of his urine, as directed. His embarrassment was short-lived, superseded by the sense that he was taking direct action to ward off evil. When he was done, Lady George called him to the coffin and told him to remove the necklace from Tanith's neck. He clumsily unfastened the tiny catch and lifted the pendant from his wife's bosom. He looked askance at the big black woman.

"That's right," she said as she produced a small wooden box whose lid was engraved with cryptic symbols. "Now drop it in here."

He put it in the box, and Lady George snapped the lid shut.

"If you was to come back and look at her in the morning, you wouldn't see the pretty thing you see now. Nature's gone have its way with her. But you ain't gone see her no more, so take your last look."

He was suddenly overcome with an incredible sadness. His shoulders slumped with the unbearable weight of the thought that he would never again see his beloved. He touched his fingers to her smooth brow and was about to lean over to kiss her lips when Lady George slammed the casket's lid. "I hate long good-byes," she said with authority, and then she shut the vault. "Now, give me your hand."

A silver-handled dagger appeared in her hand and she stabbed his extended palm with it. He yelped and jerked has hand back. Blood welled in the puncture. She seized his injured hand and squeezed out more blood, letting it fall on the floor in front of Tanith's vault. "It's always good," she explained, "to spill a little blood in the fight with evil. Shows 'em you mean business. They got to respect that."

"Will this really work?" he asked, queasy and looking away from his bleeding hand.

"Be damned if it don't."

He chose not to challenge her ambiguous remark.

"Okay. Let's go for a ride in your little motorboat."

"Huh?"

"You got to drop this"—she held up the box containing the pendant—"in the ocean. Spirits cain't cross salt water once their spell is broken, so there ain't no way she can get this back."

"What if it floats?"

"It won't. It's lined with lead."

Miles powered the skiff several miles out to sea, came to a stop and without ceremony dropped the box into the black waters.

"That's it," said Lady George. "We're done."

"What about the panther? The familiar or whatever it is?"

She shrugged her big shoulders. "I don't know all the answers. Could be you'll always have the cat on your island, unless you want to kill it. But it won't be doing no more shape-shifting. You just mark your territory like I said, and it won't trouble you no more."

Miles looked up at the moonless sky. In the infinite expanse of darkness, countless stars twinkled like cold eyes. For the first time in his life he felt insignificant.

X

The voodoo woman had earned her pay. Miles was no longer haunted by wicked dreams, and knowing that Tanith's body had finally succumbed to the natural forces of corruption, he was no longer compelled to set his eyes upon it or to be near it. He made no further visits to the mausoleum, leaving the chore of its upkeep to his man Carson. He resumed what for him was a normal life—the life of an eccentric wealthy gentleman living alone on his own island. He took up his neglected pastime of bicycling along the island's bike trail when weather permitted. His thoughts often returned to his lost love, and when they did, he knew great sadness and regret, but those feelings became more manageable with the passage of time. He no longer felt her presence. Eventually he stopped wondering what his life would have been like if Tanith had lived. The routines of his ordinary life occupied him. His financial investments paid great dividends, and his fortune grew larger still.

Autumn came. Miles went out early one morning to ride his bike. A thick mist shrouded the island, and he shivered against the season's chill. As he pedaled along the well-kept trail, some preternatural sense told him that he was not alone on the path. Something—or someone—was following his two-wheeled progress.

He slowed his pace and glanced back over his left shoulder. He saw nothing but the misty trail. He looked over his right and saw from the corner of his eye a dark form loping low to the ground. He craned his neck farther round. The black cat was stalking him, keeping pace easily. A surge of adrenalin kicked up his speed; he was pedaling furiously before he had time to realize that he couldn't outrun the sleek, powerful creature. He pedaled on, following a narrow stretch of trail overhung with mossy limbs and banked on both sides by tall ferns and scrub pine. He glanced back again: the panther was pacing him. Playing with him. The beast could move in for the kill any time it wanted.

Miles knew he would reach the front of the house in five or six minutes—unless the panther had other ideas. He looked back once more, and as his eyes returned to the front, he saw that he'd let the bike get too close to the wall of shrubbery on his right. He yanked too hard on the handlebars and the front wheel went into a stuttering wobble and he lost control of the bike. Man and bicycle raked the wall of prickly shrubs, then bounced off it and Miles and his wheels went down. Thrown clear of the bike, he slid over the earth on his left side and came to a stop in the middle of the trail.

He looked up to see the big cat approaching in a crouch, ready to spring at him. Fear numbed the pain in his scraped and bleeding arm. There was no time to get up and make a run for it, the impulse to flee doomed to futility. *So this is how it ends for me,* whispered the detached watcher within him. *Torn apart by a supernatural panther, demon to my dead lover.*

He closed his eyes and gave himself up to his fate.

With a whispering rush of fur-brushed air, the beast sprang at him and came down squarely on his chest, but it was surprisingly light, barely knocking any breath out of him. The cat began to knead his chest with the pads of its big paws. Astounded by this show of feline affection, Miles opened his eyes and stared up into the panther's green eyes. His breath caught in his dry throat as he gazed into those familiar eyes and smelled the perfume of her musk.

"Tanith?"

The cat gently butted his chin with its head. Miles reached up with both hands and tenderly grasped the thick fur on either side of animal's jaws. The panther's pink tongue flicked out and gave his face a rough, wet lashing. Her breath smelled faintly of mint.

"You've come back to me," he said, his voice cracking with bittersweet emotion.

JACKED

"There. How does that feel?"

"Okay. Kind of weird, really. Tingly."

"That's normal. It takes a little getting used to, but after a while you won't even know it's there. Until you jack in."

"And there are no side-effects?"

"None to speak of. I've installed hundreds of implants and only one patient reported any unpleasant sensations. And they didn't last long. Okay, now just relax and close your eyes and I'll plug you in. Ready?"

"Um-hm."

"There. Now I'll start you off with a little one. Here we go."

"Oh! Oh my God! Ooooooh . . ."

*   *   *

Candace flopped on the couch. Julie eyed her, then said, "Well? Don't keep me in suspense. Tell me all about it."

"God, Jools, I can't put it in words. I don't know how."

"Try."

"It was . . . fan-freaking-tastic. You've got to get one of these thingies."

"I don't think my HMO covers it."

"Then start saving your money now. Every woman should have one. I kid you not."

"You must've had a really good one."

"One? No, I had so many I lost count. Not that I could count anything at that point. I've never felt anything like it. It was like diving into an ocean of orgasms."

"I hate you."

Candace tittered. "But now I'm wiped out. I just want to go to bed. To sleep."

"What's the name of it again?"

"O-Max 3000."

"An apt name. Can I see it?"

Candace sat up, found her purse and removed an oblong silver box embossed with gold trim. She opened the box and shook out a shiny silver cylinder attached to a gray power cord and a smaller cable tailed with a pronged jack. On one end of the cylinder was a small control panel with two black buttons and one gold knob.

"It looks like an industrial-strength vibrator," said Julie.

"All you do is jack in to the implant and away you go. Men are suddenly obsolete."

"Let me see where you stick it."

Candace lifted the hair off the back of her neck and Julie looked at the small flesh-colored button with a hole in its center at the base of her roommate's skull.

"Doesn't it feel icky?"

"No. I don't even know it's there unless I touch it. Of course, I have to be careful when I'm brushing my hair not to catch the bristles in it. That would smart a bit, I'm sure. Don't want to rip that baby out."

"How often can you use it?"

"The nurse said to start slow until I get acclimated to it, but then I can jack in as often as I can stand it."

"I hate you," Julie said, this time with a crooked smile.

"O-Max envy. Can't blame you, hon. Well, I'm hitting the sack. If you hear me screaming in the middle of the night, don't worry, it'll just be me and Max doing the nasty."

"Bitch."

Candace blew her a kiss as she went on tired legs into her bedroom.

*   *   *

Two nights later Candace took her boyfriend Rob to her bed. She hadn't told him about the O-Max and she wasn't sure how he would take the news. As he peeled off her panties she broached the subject. "I've got something to tell you and I don't want you to take it the wrong way."

"What?" He bent down and kissed her thigh.

"Promise you won't take it as any kind of personal insult, 'cause that's not what it is."

"What?" Rob sat back, resting his hand on her bent knee.

"I've got one of those pleasure-center stimulators. An O-Max 3000."

"You're kidding."

"No, I'm not."

"Why the hell do you need that . . . that sex gadget? I'm not good enough for you?"

"Oh, Rob, that's not how it is. I was afraid you'd take it badly."

"How else can I take it? Jesus Christ, what did you expect? Don't you see how this makes me feel?"

"It doesn't mean you're inadequate. Our sex life is great. It's just—"

"It's just fucked up, that's what it is. If our sex life is so great, why'd you get one of those things?"

"To enhance our relations. You could get one yourself. That's the only way you'll understand. It's so completely different from regular sex."

"Why'd you even tell me about it?" he whined.

"No secrets, remember? We agreed. And because I wanted to use it while we make love."

"That's it. I'm out of here."

"Rob, wait."

He jerked his pants up and zipped them. "I'm already gone, babe. You can take your gizmo and go fuck yourself."

*   *   *

She was working in her cubicle, fingers tap-dancing over her keyboard, when the itching started. At first she ignored it, not wanting to interrupt her allegro typing, but the itching intensified until she finally gave in and lightly scratched the area of skin around the implant on the back of her neck. Her nails offered no relief. She rubbed the little button of rubberized plastic with her fingertip and found that by putting firm pressure on it the itching diminished to a tolerable level, but as soon as she took her finger away, it started again. Damn, she thought, how can I get my work done if I have to keep pressure on the frigging thing? She couldn't very well type with one hand—not with the pile of work she had to finish by quitting time.

Candace snatched up the phone and called the doctor's office. She kept one hand glued to the implant's knob to keep the itching in check. Mick O'Malley walked by her cubicle and shot her a dirty look: Get off the phone, bitch, and get back to work. She ignored him. The phone rang on. She kept up the pressure. Finally an answer: "Dr. Kelly's office. How may I help you?" She explained her problem. The office girl said the doc would return her call as soon as he could, but that things were hectic there. Tell me about it, Candace said. She picked up a pencil, found the hole with the sharp end and ever so gently inserted the graphite point into the O-Max hole. Ahhh. Relief at last. The itching went away.

The orgasm came without prelude. It hit her hard and fast.

She creamed.

She whimpered. Nearly screamed. Clenched her thighs together. Imagined a huge cock sliding home. Holy Mary Mother of God! Holy fucking cow! Jesus Christ on a stick! OH!

She shook. She popped perspiration beads. She was wet inside and out.

Flush-faced and panting now. The pencil point snapped off in the hole and the rolling orgasm began to subside, releasing her from its oceanic bliss.

Mick the prick popped his head over her cubicle wall. "Is there a problem, Miss Cain?"

"No," she said, gasping for air. "No problem."

When the five-o'clock buzzer sounded, the doctor still hadn't returned her call. She hid her unfinished paperwork in a bottom drawer, clocked out and headed home.

* * *

Julie wasn't home yet; Candace assumed her roommate was at The Big Shot Bar for happy hour with some of her co-workers. Just as well. Candace didn't want Jools to know the expensive O-Max was already malfunctioning. She and Jools were in constant competition, and the high-tech pleasure machine had given her a leg-up she didn't want to lose in their on-going war of one-upmanship. Jools was already bile-green with envy.

She called the doctor's office again, this time declaring a medical emergency. A nurse came on the line and Candace told her about the itching and the spontaneous orgasm.

The nurse chuckled and advised her to take Benadryl for the itching and not to worry about the non-scheduled orgasms. "Why look a gift horse in the mouth?" the smug nurse added.

"Because it interferes with my work. How would you like it if you couldn't get your work done because you were coming like crazy?"

The nurse snorted a dirty laugh. "Oh, I think I could live with it."

Candace slammed down the phone.

The orgasm hit her like a tsunami. She dug her nails into the armchair and tried to hang on.

* * *

Jools gave her shoulder a rough shake. "Are you all right?"

Candace opened her eyes and tried to make them focus. Her roommate's face looked big and round like a full strawberry moon. "Yeah. I must've dozed off."

"I thought you were dead. I was about to call 911."

"Rough day at work," she muttered, her tongue thick and stumbling over the words.

"Maybe you overdid it with your new toy last night. You think?"

"I'm too wiped out to think." She straightened her back in the armchair. The muscles of her thighs were fatigued and as sore as they usually were after a workout in the gym.

Julie checked their phone messages. Candace absently listened to the playback. Two calls from Julie's boyfriend, one from a bill collector, and one callback from Candace's doctor. Candace didn't remember hearing the phone ring. The sexual tsunami had completely incapacitated her; she quite literally had been dead to the world. As alarming as this was, she was too tired to think about it. She made her way to her bed and fell into the fluffy mattress. She went to sleep in her clothes.

*   *   *

She dreamed: Doctors in blue surgical garb were inserting copper-colored wires under her skin, wiring her limbs, abdomen and breasts. Masks over their snouts muffled their clipped conversation, but she heard the words "bitch in heat" and "cyber slut." A topless nurse without nipples spread the patient's thighs and slid a cold speculum into her vaginal canal. Like a spelunker about to enter a cave, a doctor with a light on his forehead peered into her and said, "That was some echo." An electric current crackled through the subcutaneous wires. The orgasm originated at the base of her spine and quickly engulfed her entire body in a storm of ecstasy. She thrashed against the table. "We're losing her," someone said. Then: "Nothing we could do. Call it."

She came awake in the throes of a big one. Wave after wave of indescribable pleasure coursed through her, and a guttural groan more animal than human escaped her parted lips.

Jools pounded on her bedroom wall and shouted, "For God's sake, keep it down!"

*   *   *

She applied her eye makeup while sipping from her morning mug of home-brewed Starbucks. It was hard to concentrate. The thin cloth of the old T-shirt she'd slept in felt like a lover's tender caress against her supersensitive nipples. Her thighs clenched involuntarily as if trying to quell the aching desire that suffused her entire pelvic region. The everyday routine of getting ready for work had become foreplay. The lust was mounting and she knew she was edging toward orgasm. There was nothing she could do to stop it. She didn't want to stop it.

Dressed for work, Jools walked through the room on the way to the kitchen, her high heels spiking the floor with each aggressive step. Candace had never seen anything so sexually arousing as those stiletto heels digging into the shag carpet. Her eyes ran up her roommate's shapely calf muscles, past the creases at the backs of her knees and on up the backs of her thighs to the hemline of her short skirt. Candace saw herself taking Julie down and burying her face in the cleft of her plump buttocks. She'd never been turned on by a woman before, but in her present state of excitation, gender didn't matter. If a pig somehow happened to walk across the room, she would probably lust after its ample flanks and corkscrew tail. The tube of mascara fell from her fingers. She cupped her breasts, tugged roughly at her nipples and watched Jools disappear into the kitchen. The crotch of her silk panties turned warm and slick with womanly secretions.

The orgasm exploded. She arched her back. She moaned. She cried.

Jools ran back into the room on those maddening stiletto heels.

A second orgasm hit.

"What the hell's wrong with you?" demanded Jools. "You scared the stew outta me. Are you . . .?"

Candace moaned, lolling her head on the back of the chair.

"Jesus, you are. I can't put up with this shit. This has got to stop!"

Candace wanted to tell her she couldn't help it, that it was beyond her control, but she was unable to speak. She groaned and writhed in the chair as yet another orgasm seized her.

Jools threw up her hands in disgust, gathered her purse and briefcase and left the apartment, leaving Candace to her orgiastic affliction.

*   *   *

She knew she was in no condition to drive, so she called a cab to take her to the doctor's office. She had no appointment, but she intended to make damned sure they saw her right away. They had done this to her, after all, so they were obliged to do something to stop these debilitating attacks of ecstasy.

As she stepped off the sidewalk to open the taxi's door, a car horn sounded and triggered a fierce orgasm. Her legs went rubbery and she collapsed to the gritty sidewalk. By the time the ambulance attendants arrived, she was babbling incoherently and staring up into the gray sky at phallic skyscrapers. The male attendant said, "Sounds like she's speaking in tongues. Must be one of those fundamentalist freaks. Probably thinks she saw Jesus."

His female partner sniffed the strong musk in the air. "Yeah, smells like it was the Second Coming."

*   *   *

"I'm Dr. Ragan," said the man in the rumpled sports coat. "I'm the psy-chiatrist on call. How are you feeling?"

Candace shifted her head on the pillow and tried to sit up, but the leather restraints on her wrists held her down. A tear rolled down her cheek.

"The nurses had to restrain you for your own protection," the doctor explained. "The sedative they gave you seems to be working, so I'll have them take those off as soon as we're done here. Can you tell me what happened?"

"O-Max," she said with a thick tongue. "Implant. Went nuts and wouldn't stop."

"A pleasure-center stimulator?"

She nodded. He nodded back. His expression was grave.

"How long have you had it?"

"Three days, I think. I want it out of me. I can't take anymore."

"I'll order a neurological consult. Dr. Weinberg can remove the implant. It's a simple procedure that takes about ten minutes."

"Thank God." She tried to smile. Her face felt numb, like it was shot full of Novocain.

"I advise you to get a lawyer and sue the pants off the people who installed it. And the company that made it. Those things are going to be outlawed. You're the third patient I've seen this month with this type of problem."

"They promised me there would be no side-effects."

"They lied," said Ragan. "I'm also referring you to a sex therapist for outpatient counseling. A recent medical journal article reported that some O-Max victims experience something like Post-traumatic Stress Syndrome and some develop an aversion to sexual contact of any kind. A good sex therapist can help you work through anything like that."

"You mean I . . . won't like sex?"

"That's a possibility. For some, it's just the opposite. They exhibit symptoms of full-blown nymphomania or satyriasis."

"Christ, I will sue the bastards."

Ragan wrote something in her chart.

"Did I die?"

"Pardon?"

"When I was lying on the sidewalk, I left my body. I was looking down at myself lying there. Like those people who die on the operating table before they bring them back. I even saw my dead grandmother."

"No, you didn't die, Miss Cain. My guess is, you experienced an altered state of consciousness. The orgasm has been referred to as 'the little death.'

Perhaps that's an apt description. I wouldn't worry about it. We'll get that thing out of you and you'll be fine."

"Thank you. You're a lifesaver. You can't imagine what it was like. Before they gave me that shot, I felt like I was about to go away and never come back. Like I was right at the edge of a cliff and one more, you know, orgasm would push me right over."

"If you do feel any more coming on, push the call button and ask the nurse for your prn medication. In the meantime, you just rest and try not to worry about anything. I'll see you later this evening."

Candace closed her eyes. She drifted away on a mattress of dark rain-laden clouds.

*   *   *

The little death found her in the bathroom of her private hospital room. She was sitting on the commode and had just wiped herself after urinating. The urine had a strong medicinal odor. The touch of the coarse tissue paper on her vulva summoned the angel of the little death. It came on swift wings and swept her away. There was nothing little about the relentless orgasm. It was the most powerful one she'd ever experienced, and it went on and on, without end. Her dead grandmother was waiting for her in a gauzy mist.

*   *   *

"They finally took those damn things off the market," Julie said. "Not that it does you any good. Your parents should make a killing though. Your dad said it looks like they'll settle out of court and make a bundle. He said the O-Max people have agreed to pay all your medical expenses, including the long-term care for as long as you need to be here."

She pushed a strand of hair off her former roommate's forehead and brushed her fingers lightly against Candace's cool cheek. "I wish I knew if you could hear me. I don't like talking just to hear the sound of my own voice, you know. They say people in comas sometimes do hear what's said and that it can even help bring them back. I wonder what your first words would be if you woke up. Something funny, I bet. Sarcastic as hell."

A nurse came in and checked the IV drip, then took the comatose woman's vital signs.

When she was alone again with Candace, Julie continued her monologue. "Oh, I've got a new roommate. Rob moved in last week. I hope you don't hate me for it, but he said it was over between you before . . . before this happened. He's really a nice guy. I don't know why you broke up with him. Good in the sack, too. My God, I just don't understand why you wanted one of those O-Max monsters. I'm perfectly satisfied with Rob. I don't think we'll ever get married, but you never can tell. Oh, I almost forgot. I brought you something."

Jools dug in her purse and pulled out a small, stuffed rabbit with floppy ears. She put it on the pillow so it's fur rested against Candace's pale cheek.

"There. How does that feel?"

FUNGOID

It was a filthy job but Frank was in no position to turn it down. When your life is in the toilet, you do what you can to stay afloat and keep your hand off the handle. Some days you have to fight the unforgiving urge to flush it all away and send the whole wretched mess spiraling down the tubes, yourself with it.

But this was not one of those days. So Frank pulled on the black rubber knee-boots, stomped his feet a couple of times to imprint his humanity, and stared grimly into the sludge-filled swimming pool.

Even after the electric pump had siphoned the stagnant brown water out of the pool and ejaculated it into the patch of woods on the other side of the backyard's chain-link fence, the sludge-encrusted pool still reeked of floodwater and bottom-rot.

Frank stretched the elastic band of the blue surgical mask behind his head and positioned the mask over his nose and mouth. It wouldn't keep all the bacteria or moist spores out of his airway, but at least it would cut down on the stench. The instructions printed on the box warned that facial hair would prevent a proper face-seal. No way was he going to shave his close-cropped battleship-gray beard for a three-day job. He would take his chances with whatever-the-fuck-kind of bugs that might be hiding in that shit-brown sludge, waiting to set up housekeeping in his body's susceptible cells.

"Come on in, boys," he said to microscopic culprits. "Make yourselves at home, if you can pay the freight. But I warn you, this old abode is way past fixer-upper, and I reserve the right to evict your ass without notice."

Christ. Talking to microbes now. "I could use a drink," he said—to himself, not to the lurking nasties.

But he knew he couldn't take that first one. Not if he wanted to get this job done and get paid three days from now. One drink would lead to the next, and by the third one, he would slide into Take-This-Job-And-Shove-It mode, load his wheelbarrow and shovel into the back of his rattletrap GMC pickup and boogie on down the road. But he wouldn't get far on an empty tank, and he didn't have enough scratch to buy a six-pack or a pint of vodka anyway, so fuck it, get in there and get it done, bro. Stop whining and hop to.

He glanced up at the deserted two-story brick house and wondered how it would've been to live here before the floods and before the Airport Authority decided to buy up all the residential properties in the area and add new runways where all the now-empty houses stood forlornly waiting for the bulldozers and wrecking ball. Janet had always wanted a house with a pool in the backyard, and for a while they'd both believed it would happen, but then he got laid off from his Lockheed job, started the really heavy boozing, and she left him for a computer-programmer with a golfer's tan, a big bank account and a bigger cock. The "bigger cock" thing had come out during one of Frank and Janet's last fights, and by that time the gloves were off and every bare-knuckle verbal hit was a body-shot meant to do lasting emotional damage. The jab to his manhood hadn't been as devastating as the blow to his earning power, or lack thereof. "Fuck him and his big bank account," Frank had said as he clenched his fists and tried his best not to smash her pretty little upturned nose. Janet had been ready for that one and countered with: "Oh, I will, Frank. I surely will."

He looked away from the empty house as he realized that not even a mansion with a top-of-the-line pool could have saved his doomed marriage. He put on heavy-duty work gloves, picked up the shovel and started spading the sludge off the shallow-end steps, dumping each shovelful of the foul brown gunk into his rusty wheelbarrow parked on the deck's edge just above the top step.

Frank tried not to think about the futility of the work at hand. His job was to clean up the pool and the gone-to-seed yard so the appraisers wouldn't knock thousands of dollars off the fair-market value when the agents of the Airport Authority made their offer on the property. It wasn't enough that the area residents were forced to give up their homes; the take-over artists would scam the poor saps at every turn and pay them as little as possible.

Frank thought this clean-up gig was a little like nursing a sick death-row con back to good health so the state could execute him. Tradition held that you couldn't have your executioner dispatch a guy who wasn't healthy enough to ride Old Sparky or take the Last Spike in the vein. Wouldn't be civilized. A man needed a healthy glow to go to his appointment with the Grim Reaper.

Frank's job was getting this muck-choked pool into ship-shape condition, spotless and sparkling enough for a bevy of bathing beauties to swim in it, so the powers-that-be could fill it up with dirt, pave it over and fly jetliners off it. Made perfect sense in this gone-to-shit world, didn't it? Runways to hell were also paved with good intentions. And with back-breaking work for joes like Frank.

He put his back into the digging and soon the first barrowful was ready for transport to the back fence. The sludge wasn't too heavy with most of the water drained out of it, so he hoisted the wheelbarrow onto the top of the fence and dumped the sludge on the other side, then rolled the barrow back to the edge of the pool and started shoveling up the next load, keeping a wary eye out for snakes hiding in the muck.

Soon he and the wheelbarrow were down in the shallow end of the pool. His rubber boots squished sludge. He shoveled and shoveled. His mask was damp with sweat, as was his old Grateful Dead T-shirt with the skeleton in the stovepipe hat sticking a bony fingertip in the groves of a vinyl disc to play a phantom dirge for the dead.

"Big job," said a gravelly voice.

Frank looked up at a white-haired elderly man leaning on a silver-handled cane.

"Yeah," Frank said, pausing to lean on his shovel. He pulled off the mask and let it hang under his chin. "Tell me about it."

"They have machines that can suck that stuff out in an hour's time."

Irritated, Frank said, "Yeah well, I ain't in the sucking business, Pop. I do things the old-fashion way."

The old man grinned. He was toothless. He licked his gums and said, "They declared all the real estate hereabouts a floodplain after that last airport expansion and then went ahead like fools and cleared all that land back yonder and built them apartment buildings. Then every time Sullivan Creek overflowed, all these here backyards was swamped with that foul goddamn floodwater. That's the damn government for ya. Always finding a way to fuck up a wet dream and stick it to you dry."

Frank nodded sagely. "You live around here?"

"I do. I'm the last holdout. Everyone else's vacated."

"Holding out for more money, huh?"

"Nope. I ain't selling. I'm going down with the house."

"Good for you," said Frank. "Give 'em hell." Crazy old fart.

Frank pulled off his gloves and lit an American Spirit. It seemed as good a time as any for a low-budget smoke break. "Must be kinda spooky, living all alone in a deserted neighborhood."

The old man grunted and said, "Reckon the only spook hereabouts is me."

Yeah, the old guy was a nutjob, sure enough. "I hear ya."

"It ain't ghosts you should worry about."

Frank blew a little cloud of smoke up at the October overcast. "Meaning?"

"Meaning you should get out of that crud you're standing in, go away from here and don't come back."

"Why would I do that? That'd be the same as throwing away seven hundred bucks."

"It's only money, son. Can't buy salvation."

"If you're revving up for a sermon, save your breath. I'm not looking to get saved."

The old man shook his head disgustedly. "And I ain't preaching one. I'm just saying you should get out of that muck before it's too late to save yourself."

"From what?"

He nodded at the swimming pool. "From that fungus and everwhat else is in there. Them floodwaters run through an old graveyard before they get here. Means we was flooded with *grave water*. But it's the fungus that'll get ya. That stuff you're shoveling, that crap's et up with it. You're digging your own grave."

"So? I'm not putting down roots here. Ain't like it's gonna grow on me."

The old man shrugged. "Your funeral," he said, then turned and walked up the driveway. He paused at the gate, raised his cane in gentlemanly farewell and toddled toward the street.

"Crazy old coot," Frank muttered. He ducked his cigarette butt in the damp sludge, pulled the mask over his mouth and nose, and then went back to work.

Shoveling shit.

Cynically, Frank thought it was fitting that his life had come down to this. He'd been shoveling shit of one kind or another for most of his life, so there was a certain karmic symmetry in his standing in a swimming pool of this brownish goop, working to dig his way out. It was perfect, really. The shit-shoveler finds his true niche. Frank wasn't feeling sorry for himself; he was finally accepting his true lot in life. His low place in the uncaring cosmos.

He whistled a sappy tune through the surgical mask as he worked.

You coulda been a contenda, said the voice, ala Brando.

Frank knew the voice well. The voice of failure, the one that mocked him and kicked him when he was down. This time he was ready for it. He said, "Coulda-woulda-shoulda. What's the diff. Contender, dead-ender—it all comes down to shoveling this goddamn shit."

And what *was* this shit, anyway? What was its precise genesis? Heavy rains drive the creek water over its banks, the water washes over the land, collecting animal-vegetable-mineral detritus, including animal droppings (and probably human droppings from winos and crack addicts), road grit, dead leaves, moss, twigs, small rocks, litter—you name it—and then the cold roiling stew washes over the cemetery, bringing up groundwater with chemical juices and miniscule flecks of waxy flesh from rotting corpses, the grateful dead . . .

Frank shuddered.

He found his rhythm in the digging. The wet metronomic plops of the sludge hitting the belly of the barrow formed his mushy background music, all rhythm and no melody. Busting his move in the burbs. One . . . two . . . three . . . four . . . Toss the shit and dig some more.

The gray overcast darkened, leaching color from the autumn day. The air chilled. Frank sweated. He wanted another smoke but he kept digging because there weren't many Spirits left in the pack and he had to ration them to make them last.

Just before he broke for a meager lunch of potted meat and Saltines, the hairs on the back of his neck prickled and he was sure somebody was watching him. He stilled his shovel and scanned the surroundings, expecting to see the old coot bent over his cane, but he saw no one. Just a squirrel twitching its bushy tail on the thick limb of an oak. And a crow taking flight from the woods on the backside of the backyard fence.

He shrugged off the feeling of being watched, wishing he had a beer to quench his deep thirst and to keep off the jim-jams, those creeping willies that crawled his skin and twisted his imagination into crazy knots whenever he went too long without a drink.

By mid-afternoon he'd cleared the shallow end of the pool. The bottom and sides still wore ugly brown stains but he would hose those off after all the sludge was gone. Then he would scrub the whole shebang with caustic cleanser, knock out the yardwork, go collect his pay and get drunk as a lord.

He heard something plop in one of the isolated little pools of water nestled in the sludge in the deep end, and he spun around to see a frog rippling the brown water.

"Froggy went a-courtin', he did go, uh-hah . . ." Frank crooned. Then he scooped up the frog with the shovel's blade and tossed it out of the pool and watched it hop across the weedy lawn. "The Great Frog God just gave you new life, warty little dude."

He worked until twilight, which came earlier than he'd expected. Then he remembered that Daylight Savings Time had ended last weekend and the world was back on "real" time now. He dropped the shovel in the wheelbarrow, trudged up the pool's steps, sat down to pull off the rubber boots, and then got up and walked toward the dark house. He stopped at his truck to grab his sleeping bag, his gym bag and his sewer snake.

He fished the house keys out of his jeans pocket. The owner had given him the keys so Frank could snake the shower's clogged drain in the downstairs bathroom. He didn't have the energy to do it tonight, but he saw no reason why he shouldn't crash for the night in the empty house rather than waste gas driving back to his depressing rented room in College Park. The utilities were still on for the appraisers, so he'd have lights and hot water for a shower. No soap, but crashers couldn't be picky.

He let himself in through the back door, went through the kitchen and found the tiny bathroom at the foot of the stairs. He stripped naked, ran the shower until the water was warm enough and then slipped under the stinging jets. He cranked the "H" knob and let the hot water knock fatigue from his muscles. He stayed in the shower until the water started to cool. He pulled an old beach towel out of his gym bag and dried off, then put on a clean set of sweats.

He laid out his dirty sweat-wet work clothes on the carpet since there was no good place to hang them to dry, and then unrolled the sleeping bag under the dining-room window and stretched out on it with a paperback he'd remembered to bring along: Kerouac's *On The Road*, recently scored from a used-book store. Sad Jack was long dead, having destroyed his liver and pickled his once-brilliant brain with booze, but the youthful exuberance of his early Beat days lived on in the yellowed pages.

Frank found his dog-eared place and started reading. He would've liked nothing better than to hit the road and take his carefree adventures where he found them, but he knew that was just so much wishful thinking. If he hit the road, the road would hit back—with gleeful vengeance. His ancient truck wouldn't survive a cross-country trip and he probably wouldn't either. Frank's carefree days and *his* youthful exuberance were way behind him.

Ahead of him was another day of shoveling sludge.

*   *   *

A howling dog woke him. Sounded like the mutt was right outside the bare window. Frank rose to his knees and looked out but didn't see the howler in the hazy glow of streetlights. Other hounds howled in the distance, answering the feral call. Frank banged his fist against the pane, hoping to scare off the unseen mutt. It must've worked; the closer howling ceased.

He flopped back onto the sleeping bag and scratched a sudden itch on his right wrist. The scratching only set off more itching, and soon he was scratching his forearm, upper arm and shoulder.

What the hell? Had he gotten into some poison oak or ivy?

He got up and turned on the light. An angry red rash had risen in the flesh around his wrist. He pushed up his shirtsleeve to see that the raised pimply skin ran all the way up his arm. He pulled off the sweatshirt, went to the bathroom to examine his torso in the mirror.

"Jesus . . ." he said when he saw the extent of the rash's rapid spread. Its rosy fingers already reached from his right deltoid to his chest. " . . . Christ!"

The old man's gravelly warning came back to him. *It's that fungus that'll get ya. That crap you're shoveling is et up with it.*

In the brightness of the bathroom's light Frank could see that the rash, though crimsoned, had a blackish tint. A closer look showed that each little red pimple wore a greenish-black cap. He did his best to resist the maddening urge to scratch the infested skin.

He kicked off his sweatpants and jumped back in the shower. He stayed in the jetting spray until the hot water petered out again. The shower only intensified the itching. Finally, Frank gave in and feverishly scratched his arm, shoulder and chest. The relief was short-lived, instantly followed by worse itching—this time accompanied by the stings of a thousand tiny needles in the flesh. He raked his nails everywhere the rash was. He fell into a dreamlike state of tortured bliss, scratching on autopilot. Scratching . . . scratching . . . scratching . . .

The dog howled again. The beast was in the bathroom with Frank. How the hell . . .?

Then Frank caught his reflection in the mirror and realized he was the one howling.

Losing my fucking mind.

His fingernails were ragged—a long way from his last half-assed manicure—and had drawn smears of blood from the rash. He washed off the blood at the sink, then slipped into his sweatshirt, put on his shoes and rushed outside.

The old man with the cane was in one of the neighboring houses, and Frank intended to find the geezer and make him make him spill, no bullshit now, make him tell what he knew about the fungus or whatever the fuck it was that was consuming Frank's flesh and driving him mad with itching and making him howl like a moon-drunk mutt with a bad case of mange.

Lunatic itch, said the voice. Not the Voice of Failure this time. Nor one of those inevitable voices given to haunting alkies in desperate need of a drink.

A new voice, smarmy and insinuating. A voice too shrewd to sound judgmental, speaking in tones of phony intimacy. Like the cool voice of a cruel god.

Ignore it. Move on.

He walked up the driveway and stood in the middle of the street. All the houses were dark, the streetlamps shrouded in thick fog. It hit Frank hard that he was in the middle of an abandoned neighborhood at the edge of the world. He shivered, chilled to the bone by the profound aloneness he felt. He itched but refrained from scratching. He chose a direction and started walking.

Down the middle of the deserted street.

Closer to the rim of the world and whatever lay beyond.

There.

Down there on the right. A light in a window. Found the son of a bitch.

Frank ran.

Ran toward the light in the window of the two-story brick house with an old hearse parked in the drive. What the fuck, a hearse? Sure as hell. Seventies-vintage death wagon darkly shining in the streetlight.

As he ran, Frank made disturbing connections. If the old man was a retired undertaker, he might actually know what he was talking about, might know about a flesh-infecting fungus and about disease-bearing fluids washed from the graveyard and into the pool where Frank had spent most of the day. But anybody could buy an old hearse, so the old guy might be nothing but a senile fart with a head full of fungoid delusions.

Your funeral, said the dreamlike voice.

"Fuck you," said Frank, running past the hearse and up the steps to the front door. He banged his fist on it. He stabbed a finger at the doorbell button. "Hey! Old man! Open up!"

The itch had him by the balls now. His groin prickled with fierce itching. He stuck his hands in his pockets to keep from scratching. He kicked the door. "C'mon, open up. I gotta talk to you."

He can't help you.

"Shut up," Frank told the voice. And then he knew.

Oh, Jesus . . .

He *knew*. The fungus was talking to him.

The old man answered the door in a shabby silk robe. He raised his cane as if to strike the crazed man on his doorstep.

"Please," said Frank, "you gotta help me. This shit's eating me up."

"Toldja. But *no*, you wouldn't hear it. Too late now." The old man grinned. His toothless gums resembled a raw wound.

"Who the fuck *are* you?" Frank slipped his right hand out of his pocket and balled his fist. The urge to hit the irascible bastard was almost as great as his desire to scratch his own rash-riddled skin.

"I ain't nobody. Go away."

Rather than hit the man, Frank gave his hands free rein to scratch at the spreading itch. He scratched his belly, his groin, his thighs, then went back to scratching his arms and the backs of his hands.

"See there?" The old man pointed with the cane's crooked handle at Frank's right hand. The silver handle was an ornate ram's head with jeweled eyes.

The rash on the back of Frank's hand had cracked open, and yellow liquid oozed out, followed by a greenish foul-smelling discharge. Followed by blood.

Frank swayed on his feet. He grabbed the door's edge to steady himself. "Oh God . . ."

"Flesh-eating fungus," said the old man. "Feasting on your ass already, ain't it. Same kinda shit killed off half the frogs in Australia couple years back. Ain't no cure neither."

"Please . . ." Frank's vision dimmed, then blurred.

You're delicious, Frank.

"It's talking to me," said Frank, desperately thinking this might convince the man to somehow help him.

"That's it eating your brain. Fungus don't talk, you idjit. Now go away 'fore I call the law. You're dripping them contaminating fluids on my doorstep."

Frank saw red.

Rash-red. His sudden impulse to do violence was like an itch that had to be scratched. He snatched the cane out of the gnarled hand and cracked the old coot's skull with the silver ram's head. The wizened scarecrow went down like a lumpy sack of rotting potatoes, knobby knees, elbows and head ka-thumping, deadweight on the door stoop.

Frank whacked him again for good measure, cracked him dead-center on the back of his cranium.

That's it. Hit him again.

Frank obeyed the talking fungus. He struck again and again. Until he'd crushed the old man's head like a mush-melon and the cane's silver handle was blood-plated. Then he grabbed the dead man by the ankles and dragged him inside and shut the door.

Good job, said the fungus.

"Fuck you," said Frank. "You're not real."

The fungus laughed. It was a wet laugh, a dirty *basso profundo* bubbling up from subterranean depths.

Frank looked at his oozing hands. "Okay, maybe you're real. But you're not . . . not natural. You're . . ."

Supernatural? Again with the dirty laugh.

"What the fuck *are* you? Who ever heard of a talking fungus?"

Once upon a time you believed in a talking burning bush.

"God," said Frank, the stench of the fluids erupting from his fungus-infected flesh making him sick to his stomach.

The fungus began to whisper conspiratorially. It told Frank exactly what to do.

Frank obeyed. He found the keys to the hearse hanging on a hook by the front door. He dragged the old man out to the hearse, opened the rear door and dumped the body in the back. Only thing missing was a casket, but what the hell? They weren't going to a funeral. The fungus had whispered: *Feed him to me.* Frank obeyed because he knew something bad would happen if he tried to disobey the Fungus God. Something worse than bad. *Bad* was already happening.

He climbed behind the steering wheel, cranked up and drove back to the jobsite. He backed up to the swimming pool, dragged the old man out of the death wagon and dropped the corpse into the deep-end sludge. It hit with a sickening splat.

"There ya go," he said. *"Bon appétit!"*

He couldn't see what was happening in the dark pool but he heard a god-awful slurping-sucking sound that made him turn away and stumble toward the house.

The fungus spoke in a language Frank had never heard before, though it sounded vaguely French, with a smattering of silky Japanese. The voice was inside his head but it was also resounding from the pool.

He pressed his palms to his ears to shut out the nerve-racking voice and immediately realized his mistake when the gooey stuff leaking from his ulcerated hands seeped into his ear canals. "Gah!"

The Voice of Failure slipped a few words in edgewise: *Gonna let that fungus get the best of you, you miserable fuck? Be a man. If you still can.*

"I *am* a man, goddammit," he said, stumble-bumming through the back door.

All at once his groin was on fire with needling pain. A deep slicing ache brought him to his knees. He whimpered. This was worse than the time he'd passed a kidney stone. Way worse. "Ah God, it's inside me." So much for being a man. How could you be a man when a flesh-eating fungus was devouring your waterworks from the inside-out?

Snake your drain, said a voice. Frank didn't know whose voice it was, nor did he much care. He took the command as the way to his salvation. The only way.

He shed his sweatpants and crawled over to the sewer snake he'd left by his gym bag. He uncoiled the metal auger, dragged it to the corner and sat with his legs spread wide. He held the pointed end of the metal snake in one hand and his flaccid penis in the other. Green liquid oozed out of the tip of his cock. Good. He figured the goop was plenty thick to provide lubrication for plumbing his prick.

Snake your drain.

"Shut up, I am." With his thumb and forefinger he spread his prick's slit as wide as it would go, then he slowly brought the sharp point of the snake to the opening and inserted it with trembling, pus-dripping hands. Then he shoved it up his burning chute.

He screamed as the snake punched through his urethra and ripped a ragged path all the way to the bladder. With a delirious heave, he yanked the snake out. Blood and slime-streaked urine poured out of him, and he passed out screaming.

*   *   *

A kick in the face woke him. Frank looked up at the old geezer with the rotten mush-melon head looking down at him with one dangling eyeball. The dead guy's flesh was furred with greenish-brown fungus, shot-through with black. Parts of his brain showed through the jagged chinks in his skull. Swatches of his blood-spiked white hair were hung with strings of slimy brown sludge like dark tinsel on a dead tree. His toothless mouth, slack jaw, and sagging posture added to the illusion of a melon-headed scarecrow that had slipped down from its makeshift wooden cross and shambled out of a cornfield and into Frank's fevered nightmare.

The scarecrow kicked him again, but Frank hardly felt it. The incandescent pain in his groin blocked out all lesser sensations.

Get up.

"Fuck you," Frank roared, hands clasped over his ruined plumbing. "I'm dying."

The dead geezer worked crooked fingers into a crevice in his broken head, seized a handful of fungal muck and slapped it on Frank's groin. Its narcotic effect immediately took away the pain. And stopped the bleeding. Miraculous shit!

You're not dying. Get up. It's time to go.

"Go? Where?" The absence of pain was blissful. Frank leaned into the corner, breathing easier now and savoring the relief that washed over him.

South. Away from the coming cold.

Frank tumbled to the scheme. The old man's walking corpse was the temporary vessel for the Fungus God's essence, and Frank was the desig-nated driver, wheelman of the hearse that would take the foul entity to warmer climes, where it could flourish in fungal delight. It needed Frank severely injured and dependent on its pain-relieving narcotic. That was how it intended to control Frank, the predictable addict.

Don't do it, dumb-ass, said the nagging voice of his disgruntled ex-wife. *Be a man for once. Stand up to this disgusting shit. Stop it!*

"Janet? What the hell are you . . .?" But then he knew what she was doing in his head. The particular part of his out-of-whack off-the-tracks mind that was still his own was using Janet's intractable voice to get through to him. To *warn* him: *Stop it.*

"Fuck you, fungus," he said. "My mind is my mine."

The scarecrow kicked him again, smashing Frank's nose. Then once more, pulping his lower lip.

"All right! All right, I'll do it, goddammit," Frank shouted with a fat-lipped lisp. "You win."

That's it, whispered Janet, *play along and then cream the sonofabitch when he ain't looking. Just the way I taught you. You still got a little juice left in you, Franklin. Just enough to do something right for once in your miserable goddamn life.*

"Shut up, bitch," Frank muttered. "I got this." He slipped carefully into his sweatpants. He didn't want to do anything to undercut the blessed numbness in his urinary tract. His rash no longer oozed and the itching had abated, thanks to the healing properties of the slimy balm the Fungus God had slapped onto his crotch and belly.

He wished he could have one last double-shot of vodka with a beer chaser. See the sunrise one last time. But . . . fuck it. Janet was right. He had one last chance to do something right. Fucked if he was going to blow it. And anyway, there was no point in living when your dick was split open from the inside. He put his crushed pack of smokes and Zippo in his pocket.

He followed the limping dead scarecrow out to the hearse. "Need gas," Frank said as he grabbed the plastic gas can with a faded red rag tied to its handle from the bed of his truck. He uncapped the hearse's tank and fed it half the can's contents, then he soaked the rag in gasoline and stuck it into the mouth of the tank, turning the death wagon into a giant Molotov cocktail.

"Get in the back," he told the dead geezer/Fungus God, "so nobody can see your ugly fucking head."

That filthy fungal voice hissed angrily in Frank's head, warning him to show proper reverence and awe.

"Yeah, yeah, I hear ya. Not to worry. We're going south right now."

Frank flicked his Zippo open, lit his last cigarette and then held the flame to the gas-soaked rag hanging like a red tongue out of the vehicle's tank. He slid behind the wheel and keyed the ignition. The hearse's motor sputtered, coughed, and then rumbled to life. He slapped it into reverse and gunned the engine.

The death wagon lurched backward, rolled over the edge, undercarriage shrieking, and bumped and bounced down the steps and banged into the shallow end of the pool. Something snapped in Frank's back. He gritted his teeth and waited for the explosion.

The voice of the fungus screamed incoherent curses inside Frank's head.

The hearse rolled in reverse until the mound of sludge in the deep end stopped it.

"C'mon," Frank said around the Spirit clamped in his teeth, "blow!"

Then he saw the burning rag flame out on the shallow-end steps.

"Sonofabitch," he said, realizing his Molotov hearse was a dud.

What a fuck-up, said Janet.

When he heard the geezer bumping around in the back of the vehicle and then the creak of the rear door swinging open, Frank figured it was time to get the hell out of there.

But he couldn't move his legs. Couldn't move anything below the waist. The loud snap when the hearse bounced down the steps had been the sound of his lower spine cracking.

He would have to crawl out on his forearms. *Shit!*

He threw open the door, leaned left and fell out onto the sludgy floor of the pool. He heard the shuffle of the dead guy's bare feet behind him. Pain flared in his groin, renewing the hot-poker sensation in his devastated urinary tract.

Smoke from the bent cigarette still clenched in his teeth burned his eyes. He looked back at the open mouth of the gas tank on his left, and crawled toward it. *One shot*, he told himself. *Make it good.*

He sucked on the butt until its ember glowed bright red, then rolled onto his back, took aim and tossed it at the target. The remains of his last American Spirit struck just below the tank's mouth and fell harmlessly in a shower of tiny sparks.

"Fuck!"

He saw the walking dead man coming at him with arms outstretched, zombie-style. The voice of the Fungus God gibbered madly, but there was no mistaking its rage.

Give it up, Frank, said his ex. *You're fucked. And I'm outta here. See ya. Wouldn't wanna be ya.*

Since when did Janet speak in sports clichés? he wondered.

Easy answer: Since your maximum fuck-up landed you in this giant toilet bowl in the middle of a deserted suburb, trapped with a pissed-off talking fungus that fancies itself a god. Capische?

Frank screamed in frustration. Old Melon Head reached down for him. Frank grabbed both of the fungus-furred wrists and fended the monster off as best he could. But the geezer fell upon him and gave Frank a big, slimy kiss on the lips.

When he opened his mouth to spit and bellow his disgust, the thing vomited a gushing torrent of stinking slime into Frank's nose and mouth and down his throat.

Gagging, Frank flung the geezer aside and tried to catch his breath through the foul, viscous fluid blocking his airway. The putrid stuff wheezed obscenely in his throat.

That was when Frank knew he really was going to die here in this giant toilet. His remains might go on as something else, but Frank would be no more.

Defeated by fungus.

Then he remembered the Zippo in his sweats' pocket.

He dug it out as Melon Head was getting up to come at him again, no doubt to heave another barrage of fungoid stew at him. He flicked open the Zippo's metal lid, thumbed the roller and struck the flint. A slender flame danced in Frank's fist.

He rose up off his belly with a snake-like motion and lobbed the lighter at the mouth of the old gas tank. The flaming Zippo disappeared through the opening.

From the belly of the tank came a whooshing sound and then a blinding light—

Frank was grinning when the explosion flushed him out of the world.

*   *   *

Riding updrafts and thermals on dihedral-angled wings, the turkey vulture soars, then glides closer to the earth and begins to circle the manmade pool below. With its acute sense of smell it scents food, descends gracelessly and alights beside the dead thing in the bottom of the waterless pool.

Designated "peace eagle" by the Cherokee Nation because it does not kill, the turkey buzzard dips its bald red head into the broken skull of the dead thing that isn't as badly charred as its carrion companion. The vulture pecks brain tissue from the fuzzy fungus growing inside the shattered skull and eats with great appetite.

Two cold hands suddenly seize the bird's stubby neck. The buzzard flutters its wings and dances on air but cannot escape its captor's grasp. The dead thing vomits a thin stream of gummy liquid into the bird's mouth and eyes, then it releases its hold and the buzzard takes to the air.

Ruffled by the unexpected encounter, the buzzard nevertheless rises into the autumn air and catches a southwesterly current.

HALLOWEEN BASH

"God, I feel so foolish," Trixie said, stabbing a finger at the doorbell button.

"It's Halloween," said Tom. "Loosen up. Get in the spirit."

"Easy for you to say," she said. The porch light painted her pout yellow. "You're not the one who'll get arrested for indecent exposure."

"Sweetheart," said Tom, letting his eyes roam the swells of her cleavage, "the last thing you are is indecent. If you looked any hotter, we'd have to skip the party and go home and screw like newlyweds."

With a fragile smile, she tugged upward on the bodice of her French Maid costume in a futile attempt to cover more of her bosom. "I hope they're not fighting tonight," she said, lowering her voice. "Otto can be such a prick when he's drinking."

"He's all bark and no bite," said Tom. He dropped his voice to add: "It's Inga you have to watch out for. I wouldn't want to get on that woman's bad side."

"Inga won't be the one ogling my boobs."

"Ring it again," he said, nodding at the door. "Those storm clouds are right on top of us. All hell's going to break loose and I don't want lose the deposit on these costumes."

Trix pushed the button three times in quick succession. They heard the frenzied chiming on the other side of the door. Then footsteps.

A crack of thunder made Trixie jump. Tom barked a nervous laugh. The door swung open.

Otto Krieger crowded the doorway, grinning broadly and rubbing his beefy palms together. "Inga," he deadpanned over his shoulder, "the maid's here."

Trixie covered her breasts with her feather-duster prop.

"Bonsoir, mon cher," Otto said with a curt bow. "But who's this dastardly fellow at your side?"

Tom clicked his heels together, touched the brim of his stovepipe hat and said, "Dr. Jekyll, at your service."

"Bugger all," Otto said, affecting an English accent, "I was hoping for

Mr. Hyde. He's a bit uncouth, but the chap's great fun at parties."

"That your costume?" Tom joked, referring to Otto's terrycloth bathrobe gaping open on his broad chest, showing wiry coils of reddish hair.

Otto chuckled, then stood aside and said, "Come in before the sky pisses on you both."

As Trixie stepped over the threshold, Otto put his hands on her bare shoulders, leaned down and kissed her cheek. She turned up her nose at his boozy breath. "You look lovely, my sweet," he said. "And you, young Dr. Jekyll, you look like a smooth operator. Pun sarcastically intended."

He led them to a loveseat in the den and stationed himself behind the mini bar. "Name your poison," he said.

Trixie glanced at her watch. "What time are we supposed to be there?"

"Well, the festivities begin at eight, but Inga likes to be fashionably late, so we have plenty of time. It's just a thirty-minute drive from here. Wait till you see her costume. Magnifique!" He kissed his fingers, then flung them at the air. "For a bitter old broad, she looks damned sexy in it."

"Fuck you, Otto," Inga said, strutting into the room and slapping a rider's crop against her black leather boots. Sheer black stockings sheathed her long legs. A garter belt hugged her ample hips. She wore a black top hat at a roguish angle, and a waist-cropped tuxedo jacket clung to her heavy bra-less breasts. A choker with a faux bowtie and her short hairstyle rounded out the cabaret-singer's outfit, giving her an androgynous look Tom found surprisingly sexy. "I'll whip you till you bleed."

"Be still my foolish heart," said Otto. "See? I told you. Doesn't she look great?"

"Fantastic," said Tom.

"Wow," said Trix. "Great costume."

"Too bad she sings like a dying canary," Otto said, raising a bottle of Inverness. "Scotch all right?"

"Fine," Tom and Trixie said in unison.

"You two sound like an old married couple already," said their host. "You've been married how long?"

"Five years," they both said, then laughed, embarrassed.

Inga sashayed to the bar, put down the crop and poured herself a vodka-on-the-rocks. She took a big swig and said, "I've been strapped to this bozo for sixteen frigging years. Can you believe that? I can't."

"Sixteen years of blissful torture," said Otto as he delivered their drinks. "She could've had any man she wanted, but I was the lucky guy. And do you know why she chose me?"

"Shut up and go get in your stupid costume," Inga told him. She sat on a barstool with her back to her husband and lit a cigarette. Her stockings whispered as she crossed one lithe leg over the other.

"She chose me because from the very beginning she could see my weakness, my secret masochistic streak. She knew I would make the perfect victim of her sadistic urges. A normal person would've murdered her years ago."

"Ignore him," Inga said. "He's already soused to the gills. You always were a mean drunk, Otto. I used to think you would mellow with age, but you're the same passive-aggressive bastard you always were."

"You know you love me, shit dumpling. You can't help yourself."

Thunder boomed and rolled over the house, rattling the ice cubes in their glasses.

"If you aren't ready by the time we finish our drinks, we're leaving without you," Inga said. "I don't need you with me to have a good time at a Halloween Ball."

"Don't I know it. You'd be balling the first young stud you could sink your teeth into." Otto winked at Tom and Trixie as he was leaving the room. "When I return, I shall be wearing the prize-winning costume."

Inga made a spitting noise with her lips to show her disgust and disdain. "Right. If there's a prize for Biggest Butt of the Ball," she said.

"That's my little dominatrix," he replied with a dry laugh. "All mouth and no cunt."

Trixie literally gasped. Tom patted her bare knee as if he were comforting a child and glanced at Inga to see if she would return fire, but Otto was already bounding up the stairs, out of range.

Inga drew furiously on her cigarette, then noisily exhaled. "You have to forgive Otto. He's not been himself lately."

Trixie muttered to Tom: "More himself than ever."

"He would hate me for telling you this," Inga told them, "but his doctor found a brain tumor. Otto's scheduled for surgery next Tuesday."

"God, that's terrible," said Trixie.

"Jeez, I'm sorry to hear that," Tom said. "Is it . . .?"

"It's very serious. Dr. Crawford won't know till he gets inside his skull if he can safely remove it. The brain-imaging test results were inconclusive."

"So it's . . . affecting his behavior?" asked Tom.

"Oh yes. He's always been a pain in the ass, but now he's downright nasty. You heard him. Before the tumor, he wouldn't have dreamed of saying such things in front of guests. Now . . . well, I never know what he's going to do or say. Sometimes he really scares me. A couple of nights ago I locked myself in the spare bedroom all night because . . . I'm sorry. I shouldn't be burdening you with all this. We're going to the party to have a good time."

Trixie asked, "Should he be drinking?"

"No, he shouldn't. But who can stop him?" Inga shrugged.

"Maybe I could talk to him," said Tom. "He listens to me. Sometimes."

"Good luck," said Inga. "He won't listen to me or his doctor."

The phone rang. Inga excused herself and went into the next room to answer it.

"Now I'm really scared of him," Trixie confided. "I don't want to ride with them to the party. Not if he's driving."

"I'll drive," said Tom.

"The man was scary before he got a brain tumor. He's always been creepy. Anybody who writes such horrible books . . ."

"He's a horror writer, Trix. They're supposed to be horrible."

"Still . . ."

Inga returned to the room. Trixie caught Tom ogling Inga's sexy outfit and elbowed him in the side.

Lightning flashed in the windows. The rain came all at once, as if a malicious storm god had thrown a switch. An artillery barrage of thunder pounded the house.

"Great night for a Halloween party," said Inga, lighting another smoke.

"Talley-ho!" shouted Otto, thumping down the stairs. He stomped into the den and preened for his small audience, showing off his bizarre costume. From the waist down, he wore the legs, hoofs and horse-tailed rump of some gray-furred equine creature. A horsehair vest topped off his outfit.

"What, a horse?" said Tom.

"Horse's ass," Inga said. "Very fitting, don't you think?"

Otto stopped dancing about and said, "Don't you people know a satyr when you see one? The mythological creature of ancient Greece? Half man, half goat. Sometimes half man, half horse. Disciple of Dionysus. Usually pictured with a huge erection, but I have to supply my own, you see."

"Contest over, you win," Tom said.

Otto danced some more. "Let the debauchery begin!"

"Good Lord, Otto, get hold of yourself," Inga said sharply.

He grabbed at the sexless crotch of his costume and made an obscene gesture. "Shut up, Nazi scum. I've got my eye on a comely French maid. What say you, my lovely? Ready to ride the beast?"

"Cool it, Otto," Tom warned. "You're over the line."

Otto galloped over to where Tom and Trixie were seated. "There is no line, Dr. Jekyll. They've all been erased. This fine madness of mine has taught me that much. Oh, I know my better half—and I'm talking about my wife, not my costume—has told you about my condition. I know her inside out. There's a ghastly image." He shuddered for effect. "I know a lot of things now. For instance, I know your young wife here isn't getting enough cock. Fess up, sweetheart. Tell him I'm right."

Tom tried to stand, but Otto was towering over him and he fell back onto the loveseat.

Inga was coming off the barstool with the rider's crop in her hand. Trixie cringed in her corner of the loveseat, hugging her feather duster.

"Back off, Otto," Tom said. "I don't care if you are sick, we don't have to put up with this crazy shit. I think we'd better go."

"That's where you're wrong. Doc. I'm not crazy. I've finally gone completely sane. I think everybody should have a brain tumor. It opens the doors of perception."

Tom pushed Otto backward and stood up. Like a mother swatting a misbehaving child, Inga slapped the crop across Otto's back. Otto rounded on her and threw her toward the bar. She rode the barstool to the floor, losing her top hat.

"Stop it!" shouted Trixie. She jumped to her feet and shook the feather duster at the mad satyr. "Leave her alone!"

Laughing maniacally, Otto seized Trixie and crushed her to his thick chest. He pressed his lips to hers in a rough kiss. Tom tried to pull them apart, but Otto's grip was too strong, so he drew back his fist and swung it at Otto's head. At the last instant, fearing that a fist to the head could have dire consequences for a man with a brain tumor, he opened his hand and the would-be sock became a slap.

Otto said, "Ahhhh," as he released Trix and ripped the lacy top of her costume off her breasts, revealing a black push-up bra. "A real bodice-ripper, eh?" Otto brayed. "You have beautiful breasts, dear. You should display them proudly."

"Keep your hands off my wife," Tom said, balling his fists. "Are you all right, Inga?"

Inga was getting up from the floor. "That's it," she said with a demonic look. "I'm calling the police. And then I'm going to have you committed."

Otto stomped his hoofs and howled. "Here's Dr. Jekyll. Maybe he'll do the honors."

"Otto, settle down," Tom said, trying to reason with the madman. "This behavior is unacceptable. You can't go around attacking women. Jesus Christ."

Inga started toward the kitchen, presumably to use the phone. But Otto put himself in her path. "Get out of my way, goddammit," she said.

"I am in the way, all right," he said. "A real bad way. And all the king's horses and all the king's men can't put Otto together again. Don't waste your time trying."

Holding her torn bodice up to her breasts, Trixie said, "Take me home, Tom."

"We can't leave Inga like this," he said in a loud whisper. "There's no telling what he'll do to her."

Inga tried to get around Otto, but he moved sideways to block her. "I swear to God," she said through clenched teeth, "if you touch me again, I'll kill you."

"Oh-ho, a death threat," said Otto. "Now we're cooking. Is this a party, or what? Happy Halloweeeen!"

Inga feinted left, then darted to the right, but Otto grabbed her by the throat and rushed her backward until she banged into the wall. "Didn't know I had it in me, did you?" he said. "It's in me, all right. An insidious throbbing lump of death. But the really remarkable thing is, it talks to me. It makes demands. Right now it's telling me how hungry it is for a kill."

"Let go of her!" Tom shouted.

Inga's face was turning red. She worked her mouth like a fish out of water, trying desperately to breathe. Her eyes bulged from their sockets.

"Stop him," Trixie whimpered.

Tom picked up the barstool by two of its legs and swung it at the back of Otto's head. The rounded edge of the padded seat struck the occipital region of his skull and bounced off. He didn't go down, but he did let go of his wife's throat, and Inga slumped to the floor, wheezing and coughing.

Otto turned to face Tom. He grinned. His bloodshot eyes were bright with wicked madness. "So there you are, Mr. Hyde. I knew you'd show up for our little bash."

Tom backed away, feeling small and helpless before the big man. Could a brain tumor give a man superhuman strength? The barstool to the head would've put a normal man down, but Otto was still standing, crazier and more dangerous than ever.

Trixie was kneeling beside Inga, trying to see how badly she was hurt and keeping a wary eye on the psycho satyr. She was no longer concerned with her ripped bodice and exposed brassiere.

"Otto, I'm sorry I had to hit you, but . . ."

"Tut, tut, Hyde, bugger that. It's just your nature, n'est pa? I've got something to show you, something I know you'll appreciate, being who you are."

Christ, thought Tom, does he actually believe I'm Mr. Hyde come to life? No, he's just toying with me. Isn't he?

Otto went behind the bar, reached down and came up with a huge handgun. "Beautiful, isn't it? Desert Eagle .357 Magnum. You can see the power radiating from it, nicht wahr?"

"Otto, what are you doing with that?" Tom couldn't keep the tremolo of fear out of his voice.

"I was going to use it after my final fling tonight, but the way this is turning out, I see we won't make it to the Halloween Ball. This is too great an opportunity to pass up."

"Use it for what?"

"Don't be dense, dear boy. What do you think an old fart with an inoperable brain tumor might do with such a fine weapon?"

"But you're having surgery next Tuesday. You—"

"Surgery I'd never wake up from." Otto picked up the pistol and waved Trixie and Inga to the loveseat. "Sit down and get comfy. You sit between them, Mr. Hyde."

"Otto, don't do this," Inga said in a strangled voice. "Don't give up hope."

Otto smiled as Tom wedged his rump between the women on the loveseat. "I don't expect you to believe this, but this thing growing on my brain really does communicate with me. They call it a tumor, but that's not what it is. It's a little lump of god stuff. I think I've figured it out now, with its help, of course. The godlike intelligence behind the process of evolution tried to make its next leap in me, Otto Krieger, hack horror author. Wild, isn't it? Why it chose me, I don't know. Mysterious ways and all that rot."

"You aren't thinking clearly, Otto," said Tom. "This is delusion. It's not your fault."

Otto leaned his elbows on the bar and stared at the .357 in his thick fist. "Unfortunately, this great evolutionary leap for mankind is a failure, humanity's doomed attempt at godhood. Maybe next time." He shrugged. "That's how evolution goes. Trial and error. Hit or miss. But as the losers at the Oscars always say, 'I'm just happy I was nominated.' Can't all be winners."

"So you're going to force us to watch you blow your brains out? Jesus, Otto, think about it. Your wife doesn't deserve this. Neither does mine. Please."

"It wants to come out," Otto said. "It's demanding its freedom. What're you gonna do?" He shrugged again. "Who am I to argue with a god?"

Trixie said, "A tumor is not a god. It's an abnormal mass of tissue. That's all it is."

"Tumors don't talk, mon cher. But this thing . . ." he tapped the muzzle against his temple, "is a hell of a conversationalist. And smart? My God, if I had one tenth of its intelligence, I could save the world from itself. But, alas, I'm just a failed experiment. A talking lab rat that needs to be put to sleep."

Otto looked at his wife and said, "Inga, I'm sorry about our little dust-up while ago. I never wanted to hurt you. It made me do it. Truth is, it wants the three of you dead. It's smart, but it has a hell of a temper. It doesn't deal well with failure."

Trixie choked back a sob. Inga said, "Oh, Jesus." Tom's jaw dropped.

Otto said, "Sit quietly now while I try to convince it that we don't all have to die." He closed his eyes.

Trixie started to speak, but Inga placed her fingers to Trixie's lips. A whip-crack of lightning made them all jump. A tree, or perhaps a large limb, crashed to the ground in the back yard. Thunder shook the house. Bottles behind the bar clinked against one another.

Otto opened his eyes. "Good news," he said. "Only one of us has to die now." He pressed the muzzle of the pistol to the center of his forehead. "Sit still. I'm not sure what it will do when it comes out. Don't draw attention to yourselves."

"Otto, please," Inga moaned. Tom clutched at her hand.

"I love you, sweetheart," Otto said. And pulled the trigger.

The explosion resounded within the walls of the den, followed by a long roll of thunder outside. The lights flickered off, then came back on. Otto wasn't there, but his blood and bits of brain were splattered on the wall behind the bar.

Trixie shrieked once and covered her eyes with her hands. Inga jumped up and ran to the bar. Tom remained seated, looking at an eerie black mist rising over the mini bar. He knew the spectral fog wasn't smoke from the barrel of the gun.

"You stupid son of a bitch," Inga said to her dead husband.

"Inga . . ." Tom called.

"You goddamn stupid son of a bitch," Inga said, her voice breaking with a mournful sob.

"Get away from there," Tom urged her. "It's right—"

An ear-splitting crack of lightning knocked the lights out.

Trixie trembled at Tom's side, mewling like a kitten. In the next strobe-like flash from the storm, Tom saw the inky mist enveloping Inga's head.

He sat dead still in the dark for what seemed an eternity. Thunder rumbled in the distance as the storm moved east. The heavy rain became a drizzle.

In a silent flash of lightning Tom saw Inga's dark shape hovering over the bar, the big pistol rising with her hand.

"I see you," said Inga, her voice full of wonder. "I can see through the dark."

THE BONE TRAIN

McCobb was a haunter of railroad yards and lonely stretches of track spiked to the earth by men of mud-colored muscle long since in their graves. Seen at a distance, he was a dark phantom, an elongated shadow crowned with a ridiculous top hat, propelling himself along the rail bed with a black walking stick. Anyone familiar with the pantheon of voodoo deities would recognize his remarkable similarity to Baron Samedi, the Loa of the Dead, but McCobb knew nothing of that spectral patron of graveyards, nor of Baron Cimetiere's other names. McCobb avoided graveyards. The only time he ever set foot near a cemetery was when he was walking a beat of track at the outskirts of Vinewood, where the lay of the land had determined that the railroad track must pass within shouting distance of the old weed-choked churchyard beside an abandoned Negro church.

Seen up close, McCobb possessed no phantasmagorical aura. He was a rail-thin man with a long face and lackluster eyes sunken beneath a Cro-Magnon forehead. The black stovepipe hat scrunched down on his flaring ears was a remnant of his erstwhile affiliation with the counter-cultural underground, and was now a part of his personality, grafted on to his form to conceal and expand his misshapen skull, symbolizing nothing larger than itself. Hanging round his long neck by a black strap was his ever-present camera, a top-of-the-line model capable of shooting superb 35-millimeter exposures. The camera was the instrument with which he created his photographic symphonies of speeding trains. Frozen on film in grainy blurs of motion, these great locomotive beasts provided a chronological record of McCobb's debilitating obsession—his hunt for the mythical Bone Train.

He had first heard whispered intimations of the Bone Train's existence in the Catacombs. The pub was a favorite hang-out of bohemians, artists and anarchists, and McCobb was there most every night during the underground's golden era. I had become acquainted with him when I was covering the local art scene for the now-defunct periodical, *The American Spectre*, and we found that our mutual contempt for trendy performance art provided us fodder for delightfully acerbic conversations over pitchers of beer in the smoky shadows of the Catacombs.

The first time he broached the subject of his obsession to me, there was a near-naked poetess stomping about on the small stage, waving a straight razor at the buzzing audience. It was the night of the full strawberry moon, and the Catacombs' air-conditioner wasn't doing much to cool things off. McCobb folded his long frame into a chair at my table and launched into a diatribe on the sorry state of so-called performance art. At what I thought was the end of his rant, he said, "I mean, look at that cow on stage. She's actually drawing her own blood! If this passes for art, then I say bring on the Bone Train! We'll go quietly into that night."

"What are you talking about?" I asked him.

He propped his knobby elbows on the table and leaned toward me. With his hair sprouting like Spanish moss from under his top hat, he looked like a scarecrow come to life. "The Bone Train. Don't tell me you haven't heard of it."

I told him I hadn't. He gave me a look of incredulity. "Have you been hiding under a rock? It's the mythical mystery train, snorting through the endless night, coming to collect our sinful bones."

I put my hand over his mug of beer and told him he'd had enough.

McCobb smirked and said, "You've heard of the Rapture, surely. The Christian concept whereby the chosen few will ascend into Heaven in the blink of an eye?"

"Yes, of course I have. You can't go into a bookstore without seeing those damned books all over the place. At least the booksellers have the good sense to sell them as fiction."

The poetess was now flinging drops of her blood at the audience members closest to the stage as she chanted, "Menarche! Anarchy! Menarche!"

McCobb said, "Well, the Bone Train is the vehicle for the Damned. When the Bone Train rides into town, all us pitiful sinners will be gathered aboard and taken to the ovens of Hell. It's like the Rapture in reverse."

I bristled at the imprecision of his simile. "And where did you hear this nonsense?" I asked.

"Oh, it's whispered here and there. I think it leaked out of Sheridan Le Fanu College and found its way to our backwoods little town. Vinewood's a veritable hotbed of erudite gossip, you know."

With that satiric remark, McCobb tipped his top hat and shambled off into the night, presumably to patrol the local railroad tracks.

A few weeks later, the Catacombs was shut down by order of the police. The bloodletting performance artists were not going to be allowed to "corrupt the morals of our misguided youth."

I thought nothing more of McCobb's Bone Train until the following fall. A severe draught dulled the autumnal colors, and the inhabitants of Vinewood and its forested environs seemed themselves to be as brittle and drab as the season. While covering a grave-robbing incident at Vinewood Memorial Gardens, I encountered a black man who claimed to have witnessed a dead man walking out of the graveyard and into the trees beyond the tumbledown wrought-iron fence. "He heard the whistle," said the shaken man. "The ghost train called him and he had to go."

"Did you hear it as well?" I inquired, stealing a glance into the opened grave.

"No, suh," he said. "I'm still here, ain't I? I just heard the echo, and that's all I ever wanna hear."

He would speak no further on the subject and beat a hasty retreat from the cemetery. When I wrote up the story, I made no mention of a supernatural train or its siren call. Though my Atlanta editor would've loved it and it would've made good copy for *The American Spectre*, I couldn't bring myself to set it down on paper for fear of lending credence to the preposterous idea of a phantom train calling up the dead. In truth, I secretly harbored the superstitious notion that I could keep the thing at bay by denying its alleged existence.

That night McCobb showed up at my door. In spite of his haggard appearance, he was terribly animated in his recounting of a conversation he'd had with Dr. Goolsby, the founder of The Sheridan Le Fanu College of Alternative Medicine And Esoteric Philosophy. "Goolsby validated the whole thing," he told me. "It's all true."

"What's all true?" I asked.

"The dreams, the desolation, the Train of the Damned. All of it. It's true and it's already happening."

"Oh, your Bone Train. You're still on about that?"

He looked at me as if he were searching for something lost. Then he seemed to find it in my face. "You've had them too, haven't you? The dreams?"

"What dreams?" I backed away from him.

"The nightmares. The visions. You've heard it roaring through the night. You've felt the ground tremble at its passing. You can't see it yet, but you know it's out there, getting closer."

I led him to the study and offered him a strong drink, which he readily accepted. "What exactly did Goolsby say to you?" I asked.

"He said I've been wasting my time in train yards because the Bone Train doesn't run on manmade tracks. He said it isn't even what we would recognize as a train, that it's myth made manifest by the dreaming."

"What the hell does that mean?"

"Some gods are created by their worshipers' visions of them," he explained. "Other gods were always there, existing outside of time and space or known dimensions. The Bone Train started as a myth, but now it's built up a good head of steam, so to speak, and the old gods are using it as a vehicle to enter our reality. But it's not what I thought it would be. I had it all wrong, you see. It's not coming to take us away to Hell. It's coming to ride the rails of our bones! We *are* its tracks!"

I was stunned to silence by his delusional reasoning. McCobb had gone completely mad, and I wanted to be rid of him.

"Admit it," he urged me. "You've had the dreams. You know exactly what I'm talking about."

He was right in that I'd had unusual dreams, disturbing nightmares that left a foul residue of ill-omen and contaminated my waking hours. "They're just dreams," I argued. "They have no meaning outside themselves. Dreams lose their contextual logic when you try to apply that logic to the real world. Didn't the illustrious Dr. Goolsby mention that?"

McCobb shook his head in disgust. He rapped his black cane on the floorboards and said, "You're obfuscating. Where's your journalistic integrity? Your thirst for the truth?"

Belatedly, I realized there was no point in arguing with a madman. The human scarecrow's agitation had infected me, and I'd allowed him to lure me into his madness.

"Enough," I said. "You're absolutely right. I see now that you're onto something of great significance. Don't waste another minute trying to convince me. Surely, the gravity of this business leaves you with much else to do."

He raised his cane, and I thought he was actually going to strike me. His eyes blazed with murderous fire. His thin lips twisted into an ugly grimace, and he leapt to his feet and stalked out of my apartment. I poured myself another drink to calm my nerves, and then went to bed, fearful of what might be awaiting me in my dreams.

Sleep eluded me. I all but convinced myself that a formless evil was bearing down on me, charging out of the night like a runaway train. Worst of all was the idea that this external force was coming to ride my bones and use my mortal form as a means of conveyance to some unnatural end.

The next day my editor phoned to tell me that *The American Spectre* had declared bankruptcy and that I was out of a job. There would be no severance package. In the proverbial blink of an eye, my world of stability had crumbled beneath my feet.

To forestall eviction, I took a job as night watchman at The Sheridan Le

Fanu College. The small campus was nestled in a woodland hollow several miles outside Vinewood's city limits, but despite the bucolic tranquility of its surroundings, the melancholic aura of a mausoleum arose from the gray walkways and sinister buildings of somber stone. Decked out in an ill-fitting uniform, I took my first tour of duty as a security officer. Armed with a flashlight and a nightstick, I walked the beat, checking doors and windows for any breach.

By midnight, I'd fallen in love with the job. The pay wasn't good, but I relished the fact that I had the entire campus to myself, with no other living soul to bother me or interrupt my walking meditations. I had a set of master keys and could enter any building I chose. No place was off-limits to me; if I wanted to enter the library and pull down a leather-bound tome for my own perusal, who was to stop me? I was master of all I surveyed. The night belonged to me. I took to spending hours each night in the stacks, pouring over obscure volumes of esoteric philosophy, treatises on anthropological oddities, and field journals depicting the practices of pagan medicine men. The drawback of my night-watchman job was that I couldn't sleep in the daytime. I never got more than two straight hours of sleep at a time, but it soon dawned on me that this wasn't necessarily a bad thing. Sleeping in such short bursts, I rarely dreamed. My unease about the Bone Train quickly diminished. Of course, I was tired all the time, but not too tired to make my watchman's rounds or to pursue my clandestine scholarly interests.

After three months on the job, I was accustomed to my chronic state of fatigue, and I was able to use it as a seeker of enlightenment uses fasting and flagellation to purify himself and open his spiritual channels to the higher vibrations of the cosmos. If the Lord should happen to speak, I certainly would be one of the first to hear His words, I told myself—only half in jest. I never imagined that I would encounter something of supernatural origin so horrifying that I would faint dead away in the middle of night and not wake up till sunrise. But that was precisely what happened.

It was a moonless night in early spring. The air was frosty and damp. I slipped into the cozy warmth of the library, shucked my heavy coat and sat down with a book so old that the title on its leather spine was no longer legible. Its frontispiece was engraved with an indecipherable illustration that nevertheless filled me with foreboding. The longer I stared at the artwork, the more anxious I grew. Finally, an identifiable image emerged from the Rorschach-like patterns of darkness. It was unmistakably the image of a locomotive engine, somehow possessing the illusion of movement on the yellowed page. This would not have been so startling, but for the fact that the book was produced in the 1500s—well before the first train engine was ever invented.

I turned to the title page and read: *The Secret Sayings of the Wandering*

Monk. I slammed the book shut and jumped to my feet. I didn't know who the monk might've been or why I should be interested in his secret sayings, and at that moment I didn't want to know. I rushed outside and resumed my rounds, telling myself that my imagination had fashioned the image of a locomotive out of the illogical illustration. In my haste to leave the library, I'd neglected to grab my coat and flashlight, so I shortly returned to the stacks, shivering as much from the dead-of-night cold as from fear. I reached down to retrieve the book, but I couldn't resist another look at the haunting picture engraved on the frontispiece. My perception remained unaltered: the ominous locomotive was still there on the page. I began to tremble and shake as if in the throes of a grand-mal seizure, accompanied by dull roaring in my ears. Then it dawned on me that the whole room was shaking as well, and that the roaring sound, growing louder each second, was of external origin. Books not tightly shelved were jostled by the violent tremors, and the light fixtures on the ceiling buzzed like the warning clatter of rattlesnakes. The wooden legs of the table before me danced on the floor. The antiquated book bounced toward the table's edge. A horrific revelation bloomed like a poisonous flower in my mind: the earth was trembling at the approach of the Bone Train. It was coming for me! I turned to flee, but my turning went on and on as I spun round and round within a spinning room, upon a spinning globe within an expanding universe made of atoms circled by electrons, all in perpetual motion, everything whirling toward an inevitable doom. I fell to the floor, lost in the thunderous vibrations.

*   *   *

"Good Lord, are you hurt?"

I looked up at Dr. Goolsby. His balding forehead was creased with concern.

"No, I don't think so," I said, sitting up. He helped me to my feet. I dusted off my rump and straightened my uniform, hoping to make myself presentable to the founder of the college. We had never spoken before, but I knew him by sight.

"What happened? he asked.

"I'm not sure. It felt like an earthquake. You didn't feel it?"

"Certainly not." He looked at his wristwatch. "Well, you're off duty now, so you'd best go home and sleep it off."

Off duty? Had I been out that long? Did the man think I'd been drinking on the job? "I'm not drunk," I said, foolishly defensive. "I guess I fainted."

Dr. Goolsby noticed the book lying open on the table and picked it up. "Were you reading this?"

"No, sir. I was just looking at the illustration."

"And did you see it?"

"See what?" I averted my eyes.

He smiled. "You *did* see it," he said.

"The train engine? Yeah, I saw it. I felt it too. That's how I ended up on the floor."

"Really. How interesting." He rubbed his chin, looking very professorial.

Now that the cat was out of the bag, I figured I had nothing to lose by yanking its tail. "My friend said you talked to him about the Bone Train," I said. "He said you validated all of it."

"Oh, you mean the Mad Hatter. The young man in the top hat, of course."

"Lucian McCobb," I said.

"We did have a brief discussion of modern myth and how it's interwoven with ordinary reality. Are you sure you're all right? You look rather ashen."

"Wouldn't you be, if you'd had your lights put out by a train from Hell?"

"Follow me to my office," he said. "I'll give you something to help you sleep. It's a herbal remedy, perfectly safe."

Wondering if my chronic insomnia was so easily read in my face, I followed the guru of alternative medicine to his office and accepted his herbal offering. No further mention was made of the damned train. I went home, swallowed the capsule of herbal powder, and slept the sleep of the dead.

Later that day, I learned that Lucian McCobb had been killed on the railroad tracks near the old churchyard. His body had been cut in half, presumably by a speeding train. His legs were so badly mangled that the undertaker was unable to reattach the mutilated limbs. Nevertheless, his upper body was in good enough condition for the coffin to be opened for his funeral. I paid my last respects, regretting that his family had declined to outfit his corpse with his trademark top hat. I was sure he would've wanted it on for his final public appearance. I should have been shocked by McCobb's grisly death. I should've wondered how a seasoned train-watcher could've been caught short on the tracks. Instead, I met the fact and manner of his demise with numbed acceptance.

I kept my job as night watchman at the college and became Dr. Goolsby's patient. His herbal medicines worked wonders for my nervous condition and afforded me many wonderful hours of restful sleep. We never again spoke of the mystery train, and I quickly gave up my delusional thinking along those dreadful lines. Except for the unpublished text you hold in your hands, I have written nothing of consequence since the dissolution of *The American Spectre*. I seem to have found my true calling as night watchman.

I miss neither the journalist's never-ending quest for answers, nor his self-righteous search for some presupposed truth.

Now and again, I hear word of ghostly sightings along Vinewood's railroad tracks or graveyards, but I give them no credit. More than once I heard that a scarecrow of a man in a stovepipe hat had been seen prowling outlying stretches of railroad track, but no further word of the Bone Train has ever reached my ears.

I must, however, confess that there have been a few nights when the good doctor's herbs failed to keep my delusional fears in check. On those black nights the earth does tremble at the passing of something appallingly powerful, and I hear its terrible roar and feel its vibrations deep in my marrow. On such nights I find myself aching to hear the phantom train's mournful call, and I long to feel its wraithlike wheels ride my bones, for only then might I discover its unearthly purpose, perhaps to divine an ultimate terminus.

*   *   *

Now it comes. Its banshee shrieking grates on my skull. My bones want to rip free of my flesh. A blinding beam from a malevolent eye eats up black night and seeks to catch me in its cold gaze. My bones are hollowed out, fluted, scrimshawed by sinister feats of psychic engineering. Locomotives crisscross the night, bypassing death-camp destinations because death has become locomotion.

Bones shrieking, I go out to meet it.
Flesh follows bone.
Bones ground to dust.
Soul slipstreamed to silence.

MANHUNTER

Alabama Stamps sat his horse, struck a match to a cigar to mask the stench, and looked again at the naked woman hanging from the limb of the oak. She wasn't a pretty sight, probably never had been much to look at, but now she was overripe with death and her face looked more like rotten fruit than womanly flesh. Her tongue, purplish and unnaturally fat, protruded over her lower lip as if to signify her utter distaste with the way she went out of the world. Her left eyeball bulged from its socket like a glazed pocket of pus and the right eye was gone, likely carried off by a crow. Her chin rested on her chest, her head bowed as if in skewed prayer. Her teats were long and skinny, purple nipples pointing longingly at the ground. The patch of hair between her legs was scraggly as a hillbilly's beard.

Stamps kneed his horse forward a few steps for a better view of the noose around her neck and of the elaborate hangman's knot growing out of the back of her skull. The idiosyncratic knot confirmed that this was the work of his quarry, the man some were calling the Hangman of Goat Head Hollow. The standard hangman's noose had 13 loops. The Hangman's always had 12.

Puffing thoughtfully on his cigar, Stamps judged that the woman had been dead no more than two days. Springtime was late coming to the North Georgia hills this year, and the cooler temperatures had slowed the corpse's decay. Had she been hung in high summer, she would've been a hell of a lot riper and harder to look at.

Stamps reached into his vest pocket, pulled out the daguerreotype of Crookshank's wife and held it up to compare the photograph's likeness to the woman on the rope. The two didn't much favor now, but the scar over her left eye told the tale. The dead woman was indeed Mrs. Crookshank, wife, mother, and churchgoing Christian.

He cut her down, wrapped her in the spare blanket from his bedroll, then secured her over his horse's flanks so the stench wouldn't be right under his nose on the half-day's ride back to her family. Returning Mrs. Crookshank to her home would put him behind a full day, but the Hangman's trail was already as cold as the woman's corpse. One more day wouldn't much matter. The woman deserved a proper burial, and the husband would want to get her in the ground before she was completely unrecognizable.

*   *   *

At dusk he rode up in front of the farmhouse. Crookshank came off the porch, his eyes on the blanket-wrapped bundle on the back of the horse.

"That her?" Crookshank asked. His face was as constricted as his voice, the hurt in his eyes betraying his otherwise stoic countenance.

Stamps nodded.

"The son of a bitch hang her?"

"He did." Stamps dismounted.

"Reckon I shoulda had a coffin ready, but I didn't . . ."

"Winding sheet will do. I'll help you do the digging. We'll need a lantern."

Two small towheaded boys came out of the house. The older boy came running. The younger boy hung back, hugging his pet chicken. The older brother was the one who had seen the man in a black hood ride off with their mother.

Crookshank said, "Git back in the house and stay there. I got to bury your ma."

The stunned-faced boys reluctantly obeyed. The one with the chicken hugged the bird so hard it squawked in protest.

By the hazy light of a lantern the men dug the grave under a dogwood tree behind the house. "She loved dogwoods," Crookshank said, not missing a stroke with his pick-ax. "She said the dogwood was the Jesus tree because the red spots on the white petals stand for the blood of Christ on the cross. You think the bastard violated her before he strung her up?"

"I think it don't do no good thinking about it," said Stamps, pausing to lean on his shovel. "You got them two boys to raise and a farm to work. It were me, that's what I'd fix my mind on now."

"You believe you can catch up to him?"

"I expect I will."

Crookshank paused to catch his breath. "It true you rode with Stuart's cavalry?"

"For a time. Before they had me climbing trees to pick off Union officers with a long-range rifle."

"I want you to kill this son of a bitch when you catch him." Crookshank looked up into the night sky and quoted the Bible. "'And if a man lieth with a beast, he shall surely be put to death and ye shall slay the beast.'"

"Don't believe I've heard that one," said Stamps, using the sole of his boot to work the spade's blade deeper into the earth.

"Exodus 22:19."

The passage didn't fit the situation, but Stamps didn't say so. The new widower was dealing with his loss the best way he could. He had a right to be confused in his quotations.

When the grave was dug, they lowered Mrs. Crookshank into it and filled it in with rich dirt. Crookshank brought his sons out so they could pay last respects. The younger boy wouldn't turn loose of his chicken, so Crookshank snatched the ruffled bird from the boy's arms, wrung its neck and tossed the bird aside. "You got to learn to let go o' things, son," he said in a stern voice. "Now say goodbye to you mother."

*   *   *

On a winding road he met a peddler in a buckboard pulled by an under-fed mule. The peddler reined the mule to a stop and tipped his straw hat. Stamps touched a finger to his own hat brim and stopped beside the wagon; his horse raised its tail and dropped a pile of road apples on the red dirt.

"Could I in'erest you in some merchandise, friend?" The peddler gestured at the pots and pans and assorted wares piled in the wagon bed. "Ammunition for your hardware? I see you own a Winchester. A fine rifle. A man cain't have too many bullets these days, what with road agents and such. And then there's that Hangman feller goin' round hangin' innocent folks. I tell ya, friend, folks up and down this road is all het up about that murderin' fiend."

Stamps folded his hand across the pommel of his saddle and waited for the drummer to finish his spiel.

"That a sixteen-gage shotgun you got there? I got the shells for it, yessir. And for that Colt on your hip as well. Peacemaker, ain't it? Say, you wouldn't be a-huntin' the Hangman, would ya?"

"You got any news on him?" asked Stamps. "I don't want no gossip."

"Say I do. What'd it be worth to ye?"

Stamps gave the man a hard look, then said, "I don't see no newspaper and I ain't paying for what might come out of a man's mouth. Now you tell me what you know. Friend."

The peddler scowled, spat on the road, and said, "All right then. Yestiddy they found a man and a woman strung up from a pecan tree in front of their house outside o' Dalton. Nekkid as jay-birds. 'Course, that ain't nothin' to what he done in Goat Head Holler where he hung six men, women and children in a single night. Man at the telegraph office says a famous manhunter's done been called in to catch the sumbitch. Alabamy Stamps. Reckon you heard o' him, ain't ya?"

"That all you know?"

"Them's the only real facts. 'Course they's all manner of wild talk. They say the Hangman wears a black hood on account o' him havin' the face of a demon. Some say he *is* a demon. Hell-spawn, sho nuff. Other folks say he was hung his own self and set on fire but lived through it and now he's out for revenge on the whole human race and his face ain't nothin' but a mess of burn scars with two red eyes and nothin' but holes where his nose used to be."

Stamps nodded. He motioned at the peddler's wares. "You sell rope?"

The man nodded, a worried look creasing his weatherworn face.

"Anybody bought more than one or two at a time?"

"Oh, I see what you're askin'. You wanna know if the Hangman's done got his rope from me." He took off his hat and scratched his thin hair. "There *was* a feller on the road to Pine Bluff bought six coils o' rope off me. Said he was goin' to a rodeo in Tennessee. You reckon they have rodeos there?"

"What'd he look like?"

"Hard to say. There was a cold nor'easter that day and he had his collar turned up and his hat pulled down so's I couldn't see much of his face. You reckon . . .?"

"Was he on horseback?"

"He was. Big black stallion, biggest I ever seen. Mean lookin' mount."

"When was this?"

"Yestiddy, just before sundown. He was headin' north."

Stamps nodded. Touched the brim of his hat and headed up the road.

The peddler called after him: "They's a fine-lookin' young whore 'bout ten miles up the road. Works out of the shack with a red flag. A two-dollar ride ort to make you less ornery."

He looked back at the peddler. The peddler grinned and snapped his reins. The wagon lurched forward, pots and pans rattling.

When he came upon the shack with a faded red banner flapping above its rusted tin roof, Stamps stared at the two men sitting out front in the thin shade of the roof's overhang. The one in the bowler hat passed a jug to the other. A third man came out the door, hitched up his britches and crowed like a rooster, flapping his elbows. The lanky hatless man passed the jug to Rooster. A haggard girl appeared in the doorway, pulling down the skirts of her plain dress. "Git yer ass back in there, girl," the man in the bowler said, his voice sharp-edged and dirty. She said something Stamps couldn't make out, and Bowler suddenly sprang from his chair and slapped the side of her head. She fell against the doorframe, bracing herself for another blow.

Stamps reined left, rode up to the shack, swung down from the saddle and grabbed Bowler by the back of his collar, spun him around and slammed his head into the front wall. The man dropped facedown, his hat smashed over his ears.

The man still sitting came off his chair with a knife in his fist. Stamps drew his Colt and hammered its butt against the man's forehead and he went down too. Rooster dropped the jug and backed away, saying, "Whoa now, Mister, I ain't done nothin' to you."

Stamps looked at the straw-haired girl, jerked a thumb at Rooster and said, "This man hurt you?"

She shook her head, then glared at Rooster and said, "He ain't hardly big enough to know he's even there."

"Beat your feet on that road," Stamps told him. "I see you round again, you won't have a chance to run off."

Rooster ran.

"You done it now," said the girl. "When he wakes up, Larkin's gonna beat me bloody."

"Only if you're fool enough to wait around for it. He your pimp?"

She scrunched up her face and glared at him. "If that means whore-master, I reckon he is."

"You got someplace to go to get away from him?"

"I got people up in Pine Bluff but I ain't got no way to get there." She brushed a strand of hair from her eye.

"I'm going that way," he said. "I'll take you, if you don't mind riding on the back of my horse."

She cut her eyes at the two men on the ground and said, "I've rode worse."

*   *   *

Her name was Callie and she said she was twenty-one, but Stamps had his doubts, thinking she was likely closer to seventeen. Larkin was her stepfather. He'd forced her into whoring a week after her mother died of consumption. Callie ran away twice but both times Larkin caught her, beat her and put her back to work in the shack under the red flag.

She stared into the campfire's flames in silence after telling her story. After awhile she said, "You can have some if you want. Won't cost you nothin' Reckon I owe you."

"No, you don't owe me," he told her. "You ain't a real whore. Don't act like one."

She nodded, looking off into the surrounding darkness. An owl hooted. She asked him what his business was and why he was heading to Pine Bluff.

He told her. She said she'd heard of him from a couple of her customers.

"You gone kill him if you catch him?" she asked, taking a hot sip of coffee. "The Hangman?"

"If I need to."

"Ought to hang him up and set him afire so he'll know what's awaitin' him in Hell."

He lit a cigar with a piece of kindling.

"Just to look at you, I wouldn't think you was the famous manhunter," said Callie. "You're kindly old, and that gray beard makes you look sorta like a schoolteacher. Or maybe General Robert E. Lee." She chuckled. "But I saw you whup Larkin and that other pig like they was nothin' and send the other one runnin', so I know you're rougher than you look."

"Rough line of work. But it's the one I know."

"Alabama your real name?"

"It's what the boys called me in the War. It stuck. Lot of things did."

"'Cause you were from there?"

"No. My name's Alva Samuel Stamps. It went from Alva Sam to Alabam and on into Alabama. Nicknames were common in the War."

"It was a long time ago, wudn't it?"

"Thirty years," he said, drawing on his smoke.

She scratched an itch under her arm. "Seems like you ought to be out in the Wild West."

"I was, for a time. It was more monotonous than wild. I missed these green mountains."

She looked prettier in firelight than she had in the harsh glare of the sun. He didn't understand how a man could set such a young girl to whoring, and it made him furious to think about it even now. He regretted that he hadn't been more severe with her stepfather. Maybe he'd stop by the shack on his way back and impress upon the man the error of his ways. The impressions that stayed longest with a man were the ones that drew blood and left scars.

"You got a wife somewhere?" the girl asked.

"No. She died. Long time ago. Birthing our son."

"Did he live?"

"Not but three years," he said, gazing into the fire. "Mule kicked him in the head."

"I bet you woulda been a good daddy. I never knew mine."

He flung the coffee grounds from his tin cup and stood. "Time to turn in. You can use my bedroll. I'll use the poncho to keep the damp off."

Callie fell asleep by the roots of a magnolia tree. The campfire burned low. Stamps lay with his hands behind his head, looking up at the stars and thinking that somewhere out there in the night the Hangman was on the move under these same stars. The darkness seemed to shrink the world and Stamps sensed that the killer was not far off. Very soon he would have the man in his gun-sights. His sense of such things was seldom wrong.

*   *   *

The Hangman visited his dream. Two crimson eyes burned holes in his black hood and burned holes in the night as well. Shafts of red light shot out from the holes and held Stamps frozen in the monster's fiery gaze. The Hangman came forward, dangling his precisely knotted noose. Naked, the girl rose to her knees and offered her head to the rope. The Hangman looped it over her head and jerked it straight up to tighten it around her neck. Stamps groped for his gun, but it wasn't there. The hooded man tossed the free end of the rope over dead limb and pulled it taut. The girl whimpered as the noose stretched her neck and lifted her up on her toes. His hood black and shiny like slimed leather, the Hangman gave a nod to the manhunter, and then gave the rope a powerful yank and the girl flew straight up off the ground, dangling and twisting in the air.

He came awake with the Colt in his hand and the gunshot ringing in his ears. Callie yelped and jumped up from her blanket. "What're you shootin' at?" she shouted.

He shook his head to clear it. "Nothing," he said. "Go back to sleep."

She dragged her bedding behind the magnolia, saying, "If you gone be shootin' at nightmares, I'm sleepin' behind this tree."

*   *   *

He rose before sunrise and went into the trees with his rifle. He moved quietly, eyes up and searching the dark limbs against the gray predawn sky. He spotted a fox squirrel eating a pinecone, brought the Winchester to his shoulder and shot the squirrel off the limb. He hung the animal on his belt by the bush of its tail, then stalked deeper into the woods. He angled a shot into a nest in a forked limb and blew a squirrel out of it. He hung it from his belt and hurried back to the campsite, anxious about leaving the girl by herself. His dream was fresh in his mind. He could still see Callie dangling from the noose and feel his own helpless frailty at being unable to stop it.

"What was you shootin' at this time?" she asked when he came out of the trees.

"Breakfast." He held up the two squirrels. "Get the fire going while I skin 'em. And boil some coffee."

They roasted the squirrels in the flames and ate them with a couple of hard biscuits from his saddlebag. Callie seemed a little more relaxed in his company. He guessed it was due to her understanding he wanted nothin from her—unlike the men she was used to dealing with.

"Why you reckon he does it?" she asked, tossing away her licked-clean squirrel bones. "The Hangman."

"There ain't no good way to figure men's evil ways." He licked his fingers. "Don't matter no way. Sickness of the soul or the work of the Devil, they all come to the same end."

They broke camp, packed up, and Stamps reached down from his saddle to help her up. She hesitated and said, "My be-hind sure is sore. I ain't used to ridin' a horse's ass."

He blushed and looked away, thinking about the kind of riding she was used to. She smiled, took his hand and let him pull her up behind him.

"I surely do thank you for bein' so nice to me, Mr. Alabama," she said close to his ear. "I wisht I knew how to repay the kindness."

"You're pulling your own," he said. "You built the fire and made the coffee. And you ain't bad company."

"That ain't the way Larkin tells it. He says I ain't good but for one thing."

"That man's a fool. Forget what he said. Just remember how we left him."

She laughed. "Facedown in a smashed hat. I won't never forget that. No sir, I won't."

He dug his heels in and the horse started toward the road. She hung on to his hips with both hands, still laughing.

The music of her laughter made him smile to himself as they headed up the road.

*   *   *

They stopped at a general store on the outskirts of Pine Bluff. Callie trotted off to use the privy and Stamps went into the store to buy cigars and coffee. He stood in the doorway, waiting for his eyes to adjust to the store's dim interior. The proprietor was a slight man with a bushy mustache and a bent nose. He wore a blue string tie and matching suspenders. A frail-looking old woman sat in a rocking chair beside a cold woodstove. Her eyes were cloudy as clabbered milk and obviously useless. She cocked an ear and listened to his footsteps across the floorboards as if she were reading something from his creaking tread.

"Top o' the morning to ya," said the man, hooking his thumbs in his suspenders and strutting behind a long wooden counter.

Stamps pulled his pocket watch from his vest and consulted it. "It's straight up noon."

"So it is. Lost track. Well, what can I do ya for?"

"Grind me half a pound of coffee beans and sell me three of your best cigars."

As the man weighed the coffee on his scales, Stamps asked if he'd heard any news of the infamous Hangman.

"You ain't heard? They caught the son of a buck last night. Turns out it was a local man, Levi Cohen. Somebody tipped the sheriff and they searched his house and found his hood and ropes already tied into nooses. Got him dead to rights."

"Ain't him," said the old blind woman, rocking forward for emphasis.

Stamps turned to look into her milky eyes.

"I know that boy," she went on, "and it ain't him. Ain't got it in him to kill nobody."

"But they found the evidence, Mother Nora. They got the goods on him sure enough."

"Anybody coulda put it there. Levi's got more'n a few enemies in this town, don't ya know."

The man scratched his belly and said, "The vigilance committee aims to hang him, I know *that* for a fact."

"Does Cohen ride a big black horse?" asked Stamps.

Callie came into the store and began to browse the merchandise.

"Never seen him on horseback," said the counterman as he worked the handle of the coffee grinder. "He's usually afoot or in his buggy behind a dun mare."

"Ain't him," the blind woman repeated. "They're gonna hang the wrong man."

Stamps paid for his coffee and tobacco, then walked over to join Callie, who was looking through a rack of dresses. "See one you like?" he asked.

"Just this un," she said, fingering a dress of bright yellow cotton. The dress she was wearing was drab, dirty and too small, her budding breasts straining the faded red bodice.

"Try it on."

She looked up at him and smiled expectantly. "Can I?"

"You want to look nice for your relatives, don't you? Go on."

A minute later she came out from behind the curtain of a booth scarcely bigger than a coffin that served as a dressing room. The yellow dress brought out the sunny streaks in her hair. Grinning, she curtsied and said, "It fits real good."

Stamps paid for it, the girl tossed her old dress into a trash bin, and they went back out into the bright sunshine. Callie swirled around like a dancer, humming to herself.

"Thank you, Mr. Alabama," she sang.

He nodded, smiling. He realized she was about the same age his son would've been if the boy had lived. "My pleasure," he said.

*   *   *

They drew a few odd looks from some of the citizens of Pine Bluff as they rode through the center of town. Stamps ignored them. Callie snapped, "Why doncha take a pitcher?" to a fat woman in a high-collar dress who had stared a bit too brazenly for the girl's liking.

"Easy now," he said over his shoulder. "These folks ain't used to seeing such a pretty young gal on the back of a horse."

She giggled and playfully swatted his shoulder. "Hush," she said. Then: "I hope Aunt Dot ain't heard about what Larkin had me doin'. She won't let me in her house if she has."

"Then you just explain how he beat you and made you do it."

"She'd still look down that big nose of hers and shame me. That's just the way she is."

"I expect she could be made to feel some shame for leaving her niece at the mercy of a lowlife like Larkin."

"That's right! I hadn't thought of that." She leaned up against his back. "I wisht Mama had married a man like you. Too bad she didn't know you."

"I'd be a poor match for a woman. I'm well past my prime and I'm always having to go off on a hunt. A smart woman wouldn't put up with that. And I wouldn't want me a dumb one."

"Mama was dumb for hitchin' up with Larkin. She knew he wudn't no good. He was interferin' with me before she died. I told her but she didn't believe it."

"Or didn't want to," he said. "Sometimes people turn a blind eye to such things." He recalled the old blind woman in the general store and then got to thinking about an innocent man getting strung up as the Hangman of Goat Head Hollow. The sheriff's office was ahead on the right. Without further consideration he rode up in front of it and stopped at the hitching post.

"I've got to talk to the sheriff," he said. "Why don't you go sit in the shade yonder till I come back. And don't be yelling at nobody."

*   *   *

The sheriff of Pine Bluff was a barrel-chested man with thick graying hair and a puffy red face. He looked up at the lanky bearded man standing in front of his desk, and dropped his eyes to the pistol on the man's right hip.

"Damned if I don't know your face," the sheriff said, "but I can't think who you are."

"Alabama Stamps."

"Damned if you ain't! The famous bounty hunter." The sheriff stood up, remaining behind his desk. "If you're hunting the Hangman, you're too late. I got him in my jail."

"No, sir, I don't believe you do," said Stamps.

"Is that right?" His mocking tone was unmistakable. "Then what you reckon he was doing with an executioner's hood and hangman's nooses in his house?"

Stamps ignored the question. "I hear your vigilance committee aims to hang him. If you can keep him alive long enough for a trial, I expect I'll have time to get the right man and save an innocent one from hanging."

The sheriff laughed. Then his eyes went cold and he said, "I don't need no goddamn graybeard bounty hunter to tell me my job. Next time you waltz into my office, you best be wearing dancing shoes and no sidearm."

Stamps gave him a harsh stare. "You do your job, Sheriff. I'll see to mine."

*   *   *

Callie's Aunt Dot was a tall, bony woman with a severe face. Standing on the front porch of her white two-story house with her arms folded across her chest, she looked down at her niece and said, "What do you mean, you need to stay with me? That no-account Larkin trying to pass you off on me again?"

Callie glanced at Stamps, who remained on his horse. "He don't know I'm here. He's a bad man, Aunt Dot. I cain't stay with him no more."

"It's not my place to get in the middle of a family quarrel. You best go back home."

Stamps said, "The man was abusing your niece, ma'am. He's not fit to raise her."

"Who are you, sir?"

"Why, Auntie, that's Alabama Stamps, the famous manhunter," Callie said with some pride. "He's a-huntin' that murderin' Hangman. He come along when Larkin was beatin' me and smashed his hat against the wall with his head still in it. He was out cold when we left him." She grinned from the bottom of the porch steps.

"Larkin can't be trusted with a young girl like Callie, ma'am," Stamps said.

The woman looked at him, studying him a long moment and weighing his words. "Well, I could use some help around the house now that your cousin Jenny's gone to Atlanta with her new husband. You'll go to Church every Sunday, do your chores without sassing me and read your Bible every night. I'll make a lady out of you 'fore you leave here."

Callie bounded up the steps and hugged her aunt. The woman's face lost a measure of severity while she was in Callie's fervent grasp.

"Let go of me, girl!" Aunt Dot said. "You liked to knock me over."

"Ma'am," said Stamps, touching the brim of his hat. "Callie, you behave yourself."

"Yessir, I sure will. Will you stop by here after you catch the Hangman? You could have supper with us. Cain't he, Auntie?"

"Let the man be on his way. If he's quick enough, he might can keep Levi Cohen from the hanging tree. That poor Jew didn't kill anybody." She ushered her niece into the house and shut the door.

Stamps turned his horse and rode off into the warming afternoon. As he went down the road the prickling hairs on the back of his neck told him someone was watching him. He scanned the stand of trees to his left, then the greening meadow on the right; he saw no one. The sensation passed and he wrote it off as imagination.

*   *   *

He stopped at Pine Bluff's hotel dining room for a hot meal, then he fed and watered his horse and headed north because that was direction the mysterious man on the big black stallion had been heading when the peddler last saw him. When he was a couple of miles outside of town, Stamps recalled his feeling of being watched as he rode off from Callie's aunt's house. He'd had the same feeling several times during the War—once when he was waiting in a tree for a target to offer itself, just before an unseen Union sharpshooter had taken a shot at him, grazing his cheek.

He stopped in the middle of the road. He sat there, letting his jumbled thoughts settle, then he reined around and headed back to town at a gallop, disgusted with himself for not paying more heed to his neck-prickling warning when it came. Getting old, he thought.

Dark clouds scudded in from the west, and by the time he got back to the aunt's house, the late-afternoon sky had turned dark and threatening. Thunder rumbled on the backside of the mountains to the west; in it, he heard the thunder of phantom artillery. Rising winds raised dust from the road, and the few houses out here at the edge of town were already shuttered against the coming storm.

He was too late. The naked woman was hanging by a rope from the second-story gallery, twisting a little in the wind. He could tell by the angle of her head that her neck was broken, which meant she'd likely been unconscious as she slowly choked to death. The bastard had noosed her and dropped her off the gallery. A piece of paper was pinned to her small bosom.

He dismounted and ran into the house, calling Callie's name as he raced up the stairs. He didn't expect her to be there, and she wasn't. He pulled out his pocketknife and cut the rope. Callie's dead aunt dropped to the ground.

He went back down, picked her up and carried her gaunt body into the house. He put her on the sofa, pulled out the bloodied hatpin holding the note to her breast. Printed in a neat hand were five words: "Bounty Hunter, Goat Head Hollow."

Stamps stared at the note. Was the son of a bitch sporting with him? Had he counted on the news of this hanging drawing Stamps back here and left the note as a bold challenge? It could be that the Hangman was taking Callie to the place where he'd made his name, and he wanted the famous manhunter to come after him. It was one of the drawbacks of being too well-known. Newspapers and word of mouth broadcast your business like a planter scattering seed all across the land and alerted your quarry you were coming after him.

He had never sought fame, but he had apprehended too many fugitives to go unnoticed or remain anonymous. The name Alabama Stamps was nearly as famous as Bedford Forrest or James Longstreet in some parts of the South. A reporter had once asked him how it felt to be "a living legend" and Stamps had answered, "I reckon it's a little better than being a dead one." Now he avoided reporters as best he could, but folks knew his face, thanks to the invention of photography, and it was hard to go anywhere unrecognized—except for those backwoods mountain settlements where the papers didn't go and few could read anyhow.

So now the Hangman was inviting Ol' Alabamy to Goat Head Hollow. Why? Was the killer goading him there to find Callie strung up as a means to discourage him? Was he luring him there to ambush him? Stamps doubted that a man who liked to hang women—he'd hung men too, but seemed to prefer females—was the sort to lay an ambush. As far as anyone knew, the Hangman had never shot anyone. If he intended to hang Stamps, he would have to somehow get the drop on him first, and Stamps was confident that the man would want to avoid a face-to-face confrontation with a legendary manhunter.

He folded the note, stuffed it into his vest pocket, and then mounted up and rode to the sheriff's office to tell him the hangman had claimed another victim. Then he rode hard for Goat Head Hollow. Catching the Hangman was now secondary to saving Callie. In the short time he'd known her, he had grown enormously fond of the girl and had already formed a fatherly attachment to her. Seeing her so happy in the sunshine-yellow dress he'd bought for her had made him feel something close to a father's pride. The thought of Callie choking to death in a hemp noose was as dark a thought as he'd ever had.

*   *   *

He rode ahead of the rain for awhile, but it caught up with him on a mountain-trail shortcut to Goat Head Hollow. The rain poured off his hat brim and hammered his shoulders, but his poncho kept him relatively dry. He kept the horse moving at a brisk walk along the winding trail. It wasn't safe to go faster, and he didn't want to exhaust the animal too early while an all-night journey lay ahead of them. He hoped the Hangman didn't know of the shortcut.

The killer had little more than an hour's head-start and his mount was carrying two riders, so Stamps figured he had a good chance of catching up to them before journey's end at the hollow. He would know them at a distance by Callie's straw-colored hair and by the big black stallion they would be riding. *If* he could catch up to them.

"We got to catch 'em," he said to his horse. "Or that girl's as good as graveyard dead."

By nightfall the trail wound down to the muddy road. The rain had diminished and the night was turning cold. He paused to feed his horse some carrots from his saddlebag, then he drank a ration of water from his canteen while the horse drank from a rainwater puddle.

With the half-moon appearing through breaking clouds, Stamps stepped into the stirrup and hoisted himself back into the saddle. He spurred his mount and set off at a gallop.

*   *   *

An hour before dawn the road forked, and he took the left fork that would lead him into Goat Head Hollow. He'd expected to catch up to the Hangman and Callie before now, and he wondered if he'd been duped by the killer's note, or if the shortcut had put him on the road ahead of them. He glanced over his shoulder at the empty road at his back and shivered.

Stamps supposed the Hangman aimed to return to the giant oak from which he'd hung his first victims and hang Callie from the same tree. But that was just supposing. The son of a bitch could string her up from any number of trees in the hollow. He just as easily could throw a rope around a chimney of one of the empty houses there and hang her off the rooftop.

So far, he hadn't seen any fresh tracks in the muddy road, but that didn't mean his prey wasn't already ahead of him; the Hangman could've left the road so as not to leave fresh sign. One story going around painted the elusive Hangman as the ghost of a hanged man, come back for revenge against the living. Stamps didn't believe ghosts—if they existed—to be capable of murder, but the man he was hunting did seem to possess some will-o'-the-wisp qualities. Those who had seen him described a phantasmal man in a black hood, riding a giant black stallion with flaming red eyes—a hellish vision, sure enough.

He topped a rise and stopped to look down into the low-hanging fog of Goat Head Hollow. Dark shapes of trees seemed to be growing from a wide river of mist. As he descended into the hollow, the moonlit fog began to resemble otherworldly smoke rising from the earth, and it reminded him of how much he'd come to hate low places—sumps and swamps or any depression in the earth where things washed to and accumulated in wet darkness, to putrefy and decompose, life so often seeking its lowest level before finally passing over into the world of the dead. The low places on a battlefield were the worst. Blood pooled in them, and blown-off heads and detached limbs always seemed to end up cradled in those dreadful places, in disgusting prelude to the grave. They belonged to the Devil, those geologic depressions for the damned. Stamps detested them.

He pulled his rifle from its scabbard and rode down into the hellish hollow inexplicably named for the horned head of a beast.

*   *   *

A crow's caw echoed sharply through the hollow. The horse moved through the low fog in a slow, deliberate walk. Stamps levered a round into the Winchester's firing chamber and held the rifle in the crook of his right arm as his aging sharpshooter's eyes scanned the shadowy trees and fog-swathed underbrush and thickets. The moon had disappeared behind the mountains to the west, and the sky was beginning to brighten with the approach of sunrise, the hollow turning an eerie blue-gray. The early blossoms of dogwoods stood out stark white against the muted light, calling to mind Mrs. Crookshank's burial beneath her Jesus tree.

Stamps was lightheaded from lack of sleep, his senses dulled and unreliable. A sour knot of fear clenched his stomach like a burning fist. He belched and tasted the sawmill gravy he'd eaten on his cathead biscuits yesterday at the Pine Bluff dining room. He caught himself wondering if that meal had been his last on this earth; from that unpleasant turn of thought, his mind traced a straight line to Jesus and His Last Supper with the disciples, and from there to the Judas tree. Iscariot's beard-hazed face became the clear smooth face of Callie's, and with a will Stamps shrugged off his fears. His life had grown short and lost much of its value, but Callie's wealth of years lay ahead of her—if he could forestall her premature death.

He saw a slanting roof ahead in the thinning fog. He eased down from the saddle, mindful now that the creak of leather or the thump of hooves could be amplified by the great natural bowl of the hollow. If the man he sought was already here in the fog, the tiniest sound might give away one's presence. He tethered his horse to a small mimosa tree, and then went forward on foot with his rifle at the ready, stepping with the stealth he'd refined in the War.

The smoky fog was sulfurous, redolent of evil; he felt as if he were treading upon the earthen roof of Hell amid fetid vapors vented into the mortal world through invisible fissures. He'd experienced this same illusion on battlefields running red with blood, blanketed with the smoke of muzzleloaders and cannon, pitilessly greased with liquefied flesh and exploded organs. He shook off the illusion as he crept forward. The fog was good. It gave him cover.

Another house appeared out of the brightening mist. He slipped his finger inside the trigger guard and caressed the cold trigger, setting his mind more firmly upon his prey. The Hangman, if he was here, was going to die here. Stamps had already decided to kill him rather than take him alive. The self-appointed executioner would perhaps understand the symmetrical necessity of his own immediate execution—just as Stamps now understood that his own role in this passion play was but a mirror's image of the Hangman's. As a sniper in the War, Alabama Stamps had executed men from distances magically shortened by his assassin's telescope. The scope took him in for close views of their faces during their final moments of life. Those he killed never saw him, just as the Hangman's victims never saw beneath his black hood as he strung them up. They both killed from positions of anonymity. They both killed innocents, for who could say a soldier in service to a cause larger than himself was guilty of anything but soldiering? But the Hangman killed women, and Stamps never had, nor never would; in that way, at least, he was unlike his quarry. The Hangman might've made his kills in service to a sickness of mind or in servitude to Satan. Stamps saw little difference betwixt the two. And the only difference between himself and the Hangman that mattered now was that the Hangman was the one destined to die this day. And if he had caused grievous injury to his captive, then the masked killer was going to suffer the torments of Hell before he was dispatched thereto.

Now the morning light was more blue than gray, and he could see all of the log buildings of the tiny hamlet whose former inhabitants had been hanged. He wondered how the killer had managed to accomplish the mass hanging. Had he slipped into each abode to take them one or two at a time, hang them and then move on to the next building, or had he chivvied them all out at gunpoint, forced them to disrobe and to noose one another? Stamps figured the latter would've been the most efficient method. Maybe he would ask the blackguard before he executed him.

He crept through the dimming shadows, using trees as cover. He was counting on his sensitive neck to warn him of being watched, but so far, there was no prickling. *What if,* he wondered, *the note had been a ruse, or simply a signature rather than direct challenge? What if he never intended to come back to the place of his first kills? What if—*

Then he heard it—a sniffling whimper. He froze, cocked his ears and listened hard. There it was again! The sound led his eyes to the farthest cabin, about a hundred paces from where he now stood beside a live oak. He moved left until he had a clear view of the front of the squat building.

She sat astride the biggest horse Stamps had ever seen, its coat aglow with a blue-black sheen in the first light of day. Callie was as naked as the Godiva of Anglo-Saxon legend. Her new yellow dress lay in the mud at the stallion's feet. The tall man wearing a black hood over his head stood by, brandishing a pistol in his right hand. He wore a long black coat that reminded Stamps of an undertaker's garb.

The length of the rope noosed on Callie's neck stretched tautly from the loop it made round the stone chimney, its other end tied off to pine on the side of the cabin. If the great horse bolted, Callie would be left to dangle by the neck from the overhang of the roof. There wouldn't be enough of a drop to break her neck, which meant the hemp would slowly strangle her to death—unless Stamps could get her down fast enough to prevent it.

He crouched, unseen, behind a sapling apple tree and watched the Hangman, in hopes of reading his immediate intentions. Did the man intend to wait for his hunter's arrival before setting the girl to swing? Was he going to go ahead and hang her and leave her to be discovered, naked and dead?

Stamps could easily deliver a killing shot now, but his rifle's report would probably spook the stallion into charging off, and he wasn't sure he could run the hundred paces and cut the rope quick enough to save Callie from lasting damage. He'd heard tales of men surviving the rope as idiots due to lack of blood and air to their brains, and the thought of her living the rest of her life as an addle-brained beauty sickened him. He had to creep closer to shorten his distance to the pine tree the rope was tied to.

Callie whimpered again. She shivered, her meager breasts quivering. "I don't wanna hang," she said in a child's voice. "Please, Mister . . ."

Her captor's left hand lashed out and struck her bare hip with a quirt. The stallion danced, startled by the sharp slap so close to its own flesh.

Stamps moved quickly, while his adversary's attention was on punishing the girl. He crept forward in a crouch, keeping his eyes on the Hangman, who delivered a second blow with the quirt. Callie shrieked and he hit her again to silence her.

The great black stallion lowered his head and danced to the brink of an all-out bolt.

Stamps thought it odd that the man hadn't uttered a single word. Did he simply prefer to let his violent action speak for him, or was he incapable of speech? Had his tongue been cut out? His voice box so damaged as to render him speechless? Stamps had an inkling that the Hangman had suffered some catastrophic injury that had compelled him to vent the resultant rage upon the world.

Callie's shoulders shook as she silently cried. Her hands were bound behind her back by a leather thong. The hooded man reached up and caressed her breasts with the quirt. She responded with a convulsive shudder.

Stamps paused at the corner of a cabin thirty paces from his target. The fury within him threatened to prematurely explode as he watched the man take vile liberties with the helpless girl. The quirt moved down her belly to the place where the bare flesh of her sex rested on saddle leather.

Raising the rifle to his shoulder, Stamps straightened up and advanced at a quick, light-footed pace on the man in the long black coat. From his angle of approach, the Hangman was in profile, but the Hangman didn't see him—apparently because the hood obstructed his peripheral vision, as well as dulling his hearing. When Stamps was no more than ten paces from him, the man whirled round, raising his pistol. The tails of his clawhammer coat swirled about his legs like the black wings of a demonic bat.

Without breaking stride, Stamps aimed his Winchester at the Hangman's chest and said: "And if a man lieth with a beast, he shall surely be put to death and ye shall slay the beast." Crookshank's Bible quotation came as much of a surprise to him as it no doubt did to the Hangman. The strange biblical passage had stuck in his memory and now came out of its own accord, puzzling the Hangman and giving him pause long enough for Stamps to swing the rifle's stock from his shoulder and butt-stroke his adversary's jaw—but not long enough to forestall the pistol's firing. The close-range pistol-shot slammed into his left shoulder and spun him halfway around and dropped him facedown to the ground.

Stamps lost his rifle in the fall, and now he rolled—empty-handed—onto his right side to see the stallion thundering out from under Callie, leaving her to swing in front of the house, her neck small and delicate within the elaborate noose.

The Hangman was on his hands and knees, groping for his dropped pistol.

Stamps drew his Colt, cocked the hammer and shot the hooded man in his upper chest. The Hangman grunted but did not go down. He grabbed his own pistol from the ground, dropped back on his haunches and took a second shot at Stamps. The slug sang past his left ear as Stamps fired again, this time hitting the Hangman squarely in the head and toppling him backward.

Callie was kicking her legs as if trying to run away from the choking rope. Ignoring the deep pain in his wounded shoulder, Stamps stood, holstered his Colt and drew his bowie knife from his belt as he hurried to the side of the house and toward the tree to which the rope was affixed. Smelling the iron of his own blood, he grew dizzy as he sawed the thick hemp with his blade. He'd been wounded once in the War and had passed out before the skirmish ended. If he passed out now, Callie would surely die. He stole a glance in her direction. She was no longer kicking her legs, but hung limp as a rag-doll. A black fog crowded his vision. His ears started ringing and he knew he was losing the fight to stay conscious. He cursed his weakness and continued to saw at the rope, but he was no longer sure the knife was still in his hand. He strained to see the weave of the hemp unraveling, but the black fog swallowed him down to a low place.

*   *   *

He drifted up from darkness. He opened his eyes and saw her above him, her nakedness outlined against the bright blue sky. He squinted against the glare. "Oh Lord," he said, sitting up.

"I thought you was dead," she said, the noose hanging from her neck like a grotesque necklace.

"You're not?" He stood slowly, relieved to see that she was standing on the earth and not hanging above it.

"I almost was. But I woke up on the ground." Her hands were still tied behind her.

He looked at the trunk of the pine tree and saw that he'd succeeded in cutting the rope enough so that it had snapped from Callie's weight after he fainted. Then he looked around for the dead Hangman.

But the Hangman was gone.

"Where is he?"

"I think he rode off on that damned devil horse," she said, her voice hoarse with loosened phlegm "unless I dreamed it. I was 'bout half-dead at the time."

Stamps picked up his pistol. "That can't be. I shot him in the head. And chest."

"There's lots of blood there, but he ain't."

"If he's bleeding, I can track him easy."

"You're bleedin' yourself. You need doctorin'.

"How the hell can he be alive?"

"Maybe he ain't," she said. "Maybe he's a ghost."

Stamps holstered his pistol, removed the noose from her abraded neck, and then retrieved his knife. "Turn around so I can free your hands," he said. "Then put your dress on. It ain't ladylike running naked in the woods."

Callie laughed, then made a pained expression as she turned her back to let him cut her hands free.

"I'm sorry I nearly got you killed," he told her.

She turned back to face him, rubbing her reddened wrists. "Hush! If you hadn't come after me and shot the sumbitch, I'd still be hangin' there. Dead as Adam's housecat."

She hugged him fiercely, pressing her naked body against him. He knew it was an innocent expression of gratitude, not a whorish gesture.

He kissed the top of her head.

She pulled away, picked up her yellow dress and shook clumps of mud off it.

"We'll have to buy you a new one," he said.

She slipped into the soiled dress. "After you get your shoulder tended to, we'll go after the sumbitch."

"We?" He gave her a sidewise look.

"We," she said with a determined look on her face. "Soon as you're well enough, you're gonna teach me to be a manhunter."

*   *   *

"Don't you ever let up?" said Stamps, swinging his legs over the side of the bed and setting his bare feet on the hotel room floor. He wriggled his toes.

"Nope." She grinned at him, then opened the curtain to let in daylight.

"There ain't no quit in you," he allowed. "That's about the only thing in your favor."

"Nah it ain't. There's other things."

Stamps lit a half-smoked cigar. "I reckon I'll have to hear 'em now."

"Well, I ain't dumb. I know how to handle men. And I don't fall out when I see blood, which is more than I can say for some people."

"I passed out from losing blood, not from seeing it." He puffed on his stogie. "And the way you been handling men ain't much help in tracking them down."

"Shows what you know. You ain't had to do it. If I couldn't handle a man I'd be dead now, or all cut up wishing I was."

"Maybe so. But there just ain't no female manhunters."

"So? I ain't afeared of being the first. So you can add brave to the list. See? You cain't talk me out of it, Alabamy, so you may's well not waste time trying."

"I could teach you how to track and cut sign. What to look for. The hard part is knowing what to do when you find who you're looking for. You have to be willing and able to kill a man without hesitation."

"You don't think I could kill the sumbitch that strung me up?"

"What about the others?"

"What others?"

"The ones you ain't ever seen before and don't have a personal grudge against. Them."

"If it was me or them, I reckon I could do it all right."

"That's exactly what it would be. When they saw you was a girl, they'd soon as kill you as look at you. No self-respecting outlaw would let himself be brought in by a girl. See what I'm getting at? Just by being who you are, you'd force a man to violence. And get yourself killed."

She frowned. She looked out the dirty windowpane and at the dusty street below. Then she turned and looked him square in the eyes. "How many men you killed?"

"Too many to keep count."

"I don't mean in the war. How many since you been a manhunter?"

He shrugged. "Upwards of a dozen."

"More'n enough to get your reputation. That's what I'd have to do. Kill enough so I was took serious."

Stamps chuckled. "Got it all figured out, have you? Build your legend one dead man at a time."

"If that's what it takes, yessir."

"The fearlessness of youth," he said. The cigar made him cough. The cough made the bullet hole in his shoulder ache.

"We need to change that dressing," Callie said. "Blood's leaking through again."

"Why don't you be a nurse? You'd make a good one."

"I'd make a good whore too but I don't wanna be one."

"A whore is a damn sight different than a nurse."

She shrugged and pushed a strand of hair out of her eyes. "I don't wanna do no kinda waiting on nobody or tending to their needs. I done enough of that. I wanna go after people. Like you."

"You don't want to be like me, girl. It ain't no kind of life for a young lady. Old one either."

"My aunt thought she was a lady," she said. "I don't wanna be like her, looking down her nose at folks. I know it ain't right to speak ill of the dead, but she was a sour old biddy. I'm sorry, Lord, but she was. And lookit how she ended up. Looking down her nose from up in a noose."

"You couldn't be like her if you tried. You're you. You can't be like me or your aunt."

"See them gray hairs on your chest?" She pointed a finger and narrowed her eyes.

"What about 'em?"

"That's why you need me to help you catch the Hangman. On account of you're getting old and you been shot."

He rubbed a hand over his shirtless chest and scowled. "I couldn't catch anybody if I had to wet-nurse you along."

"Listen here, Mr. Alva Sam Stamps, I ain't no baby and I don't need no sugar-tit to keep me quiet." She cupped her hands to her breasts. "I got teats of my own, in case you ain't noticed. So I'll thank you not to talk about me like I'm a baby."

He tried to keep the grin off his face but he couldn't. He nodded. "I don't mean to insult you. I'm just trying to talk you out of this foolishness. If you had a daddy, he'd do the same."

"You ain't my daddy. My daddy's dead. And he weren't never no help when he was alive."

She stared at the floor. Then she said, "Besides, I ain't got no place to go. If you don't take me with you, I'll probably end up whoring again."

"You ain't that dumb. Don't run that bluff on me."

"See this?" She pointed at the rope burn and bruises on her neck. "I aim to be there when you catch the man that did it. One way or t'other, I will be."

"Is that a fact?"

"Yessir, it is." She stepped close and took the cigar from his fingers and took a puff. She blew smoke in his face. Then she gave it back to him and said, "I already know how to shoot. My uncle taught me before he died. He didn't have but one arm after the war but he was still a dead shot with a pistol."

With the cigar in his teeth he peeled the bandage away from his wound and looked at it. "Don't look too bad," he said. "That doc was better than some."

"When you reckon you'll be up to riding?" She sat on the foot of the bed.

"Hell, I'm ready now. But I don't figure we need to be in a hurry."

She screwed her face into a look of skepticism. "How you figure that? You think the Hangman rode off and died?"

"He might have. But I ain't counting on it. I figure he'll be staying close enough to keep an eye on us, if he's able."

She glanced uneasily at the window.

"Which means we don't have to go hunting him," he went on. "We'll let him come to us."

"What makes you think he will?"

"That's what this is all about. Whoever he is, he's got it in for me. That's why he hung your aunt and tried to hang you. To throw it in my face. Which means *he's* been tracking *me*."

"Why would he do that?"

"If I knew who he was, I could tell you. I've caught a lot of men and turned 'em over to the law. Most likely, he's one of 'em and he wants his payback. Some men you catch, they don't take it personal. Others hold a grudge. I reckon he's the type to hold a mean one."

"So we're just gonna set and wait on him to try to kill me again?"

"Something like that. Unless you ain't got the stomach for it. I wouldn't blame you if you didn't. Thing is, you'll be safer with me than without me as long as he's on the loose."

"So all that talk about wet-nursing me was bull. You never aimed to cut me loose."

"No. That was me trying to tell you why you can't be a manhunter."

She stood and folded her arms across her chest. "You're gonna eat them words, Alabamy. And then you're gonna eat crow for dessert."

"I wouldn't care for any crow," he said with a grin, "but I reckon it wouldn't hurt to show you the ropes."

She hugged him fiercely until he cried out for mercy.

MISS THANG

"Oooh, you're gonna do Miss Thang?" Shamika wrinkled her nut-brown brow and widened her eyes in disbelief.

"Shamika, show a little respect for the dead," Sue Ann scolded. "Besides, you're going with me."

"To the funeral home? Uh-*uhn*. Not me. No ma'am."

Sue Ann made a notation in the appointment book, then snapped it shut and turned her full attention to her shampoo girl.

Shamika was young, not more than twenty-two, attractive but rather boyish and flat-chested. Her short, wiry hair was dyed the color of a Yellow Cab, and her nails were painted a deep purple. The rims of her ears were studded with rows of flashy hardware, and her nose and tongue were pierced as well, bejeweled with faux diamonds.

"I don't like the idea any more than you do," Sue Ann said. "But I told John Cox I would do it, so I will. And you're going with me. All you have to do is shampoo her hair. I'll do the rest."

"I can't be touching no dead folks' head."

"For God's sake, Shamika. Grow up. Beauticians do this kind of thing all the time."

"You ever done it before?"

"No. But Miss Thang's—*Miss Trask's* sister insisted that I do it, because she knew Judy wouldn't allow anyone but me to touch her hair."

"I couldn't stand that woman when she was alive," Shamika said. "And I ain't gonna like her no better as a corpse."

Sue Ann nodded. "Judy had some harsh ways, but deep down I think she was a good person."

"She was always rude to me. Treated me like I was her house nigger. That's why I called her Miss Thang. 'Cause she thought she was *it*. Like her doo-doo didn't stink."

"I've warned you about your language. What if our clients were to hear you talk like that? Here in the shop I expect you to keep a civil tongue in your head."

"I don't have no silver tongue." She stuck out her pierced tongue. "Sthee? Red like yours. But with a gold stud."

Sue Ann laughed in spite of herself. "We'll close up early this evening and head on over to the funeral home. I'm sure there will be a nice tip in it for you. The Trask family's filthy rich, you know."

"They're not gonna be there, are they?"

"No, Susan Trask will probably drop the payment off here tomorrow after the funeral. And whatever the amount, I'll split it with you fifty-fifty."

Shamika made a sour face, then did some speculative arithmetic in her head. "Do I *have* to go?"

Sue Ann sighed. "No, I can't make you. But I'll be very disappointed with you if you don't. To tell you the truth, I don't want to be alone with . . . with the client. I've never worked on a dead person before, and I would feel a lot better if you were there with me. Will you do it this one time? For me?"

"Okay, then. Just this one time. You said fifty-fifty, right?"

Relieved that she would not have to go alone, Sue Ann smiled and said, "Absolutely."

Shamika chewed on her lower lip, then said, "Miss Thang ain't gonna be, you know, messed up, is she? Like something out of a horror movie?"

"No. She died of an accidental drug overdose. I think she'll look pretty much like she did when she was alive."

"Long as she don't look like one of those ghouls."

Sue Ann laughed. "I don't know why you watch those movies if they scare you so much."

Shamika shrugged.

"Well, let's get this place straightened up. My first client will be here any minute."

As she emptied the shop's waste baskets, Shamika recalled the last time she had seen Miss Thang alive. It had been over a month ago, and the snooty bitch had really showed her ass, acting like she was the Queen of Fucking Sheba, coming all up in here with her nose in the air and making catty-ass comments to Shamika, even to the point of making fun of her many piercings. What was it the bitch had said? "You're not in Africa now, girl. All that tribal jewelry looks ridiculous." Shamika had deliberately pulled the witch's hair while she was shampooing her, and Miss Thang had actually cussed her, shouting: "You little shit!" Shamika swore then that she would get even with the bitch for acting so ugly to her. She had checked the appointment book daily, looking for Miss Thang's name—Judy Trask—to appear, but it never did. Then came the news that the woman had died.

Shamika was at first shocked by the news, then disappointed that it was too late to get even with Miss Thang.

But now she saw that it wasn't too late.

She would have her revenge after all.

*   *   *

Shamika left the shop on her lunch hour and drove across town to her grandmother's house on the south side of Babylon, Georgia. The old woman was sitting in her rocker on the front porch, shelling pole beans. Her Persian cat was curled up near her feet, one eye open and watching Shamika come up the wooden steps.

"Hi, Grammy," Shamika said, smiling and keeping a wary eye on the cat. Something about that cat had always spooked her, though she couldn't say exactly what it was that made her afraid of the old tom.

"What is it, girl? Something wrong?" Grammy's voice rattled in her thin chest like dead leaves blowing over a sidewalk.

"No, ma'am. Nothing's wrong. I just came by to get some of your beauty oil. My skin's starting to feel like sandpaper."

Grammy regarded her with suspicion. "Humph. Skin looks fine to me."

"You don't have to get up," Shamika said. "I know where it is."

"You know I don't like you in my root cellar. They's things down there I don't want you touching."

"I know, Grammy. I won't touch anything. Just the beauty oil. I know right where it's at."

"You use too much of that stuff, you'll break out in a rash."

"I know. I won't use too much. Be right back."

Before her Grammy could argue with her, Shamika opened the screen door and was through the living room and on her way down the rickety steps to the root cellar. As she descended, she slowed her pace and lightened her step. The place still scared her, as it had since she was a small child. And even now she had the notion that she should tread very softly; it wouldn't do to stir up the pungent mysteries that lived down here in the musty dark.

At the bottom of the stairs, she hesitated before stepping onto the dirt floor. The cellar's walls were lined with shelves containing countless jars of murky glass. Inside some of the jars were grotesque things that looked like gnarled fingers or mummified organs long ago removed from unfortunate corpses; others contained dark powders, herbal extracts tinctured with strange liquids, or tiny seeds and dried pods. Now—as when she was a child—Shamika ran her eyes over the jars to make sure none contained anything like that two-headed baby floating in piss-colored liquid she had seen at a carnival sideshow. Not that she really believed Grammy would have anything like that. But down here in this creepy place, any horrible thing you could imagine just might jump out at you like a two-headed baby jack-in-the-box.

She stepped onto the black dirt of the cellar floor and went immediately to the shelves Grammy had always told her to stay away from. "Don't never touch any of that stuff," the old lady had warned. "It's dangerous."

"Like poison?" Shamika had asked.

"Thass right. Poison to a body who don't know how to use 'em"

"But why do you have poison, Grammy? I thought you said it was all medicine."

"They's all kinds of medicines. Not all of 'em good. Now stop asking fool questions, child."

And when she was older, Shamika had sneaked down to the cellar one night to read the labels on those forbidden jars. Most of them were labeled with letters and abbreviations that meant nothing to her, so she figured it was Grammy's secret code. But a few of the jars were plainly marked with things like, "Love Spell," "Baby Maker," and "Black Root of Damnation."

It was the Black Root of Damnation she wanted for Miss Thang. The woman was probably already damned by her own bitchy behavior, but Shamika wanted the satisfaction of having a hand in the damning of Judy Trask. The way she saw it, she owed it to the cracker cunt. And the bitch owed her retribution. Shamika reached for the jar, but froze when she saw what was written on the amber vial beside it.

"'Slave The Dead,'" she read aloud. Did that mean what she thought it did? *Slave The Dead.* Make the dead your slave? Or had Grammy misspelled 'salve,' meaning ointment? No, that wasn't likely; her grandmother was usually meticulous with the smallest detail, and she prided herself on her spelling ability. What would be the point of smearing salve on somebody dead? It had to be "Slave The Dead."

She picked up the vial and slipped it into her purse. Then she took down the jar containing the Black Root of Damnation, unscrewed the metal lid, stuck her fingers in the jar and broke off a piece of the dried, sooty root. She held it under her nose and sniffed it. There was a faint scent of earthiness that reminded her of the way peanuts smelled when you first pulled them out of the ground. With a thrilling tingle in the pit of her stomach, she slipped the thumb-sized bit of root into her purse, then turned toward the stairs. And froze when she saw the Persian cat sitting on the top step, watching her with knowing eyes.

"Shoo," she said. "Get on out from here, cat."

The tom didn't move. Holding her purse like a weapon, Shamika started up the steps. "Don't make me hit you with this. Go on, now. Scat!"

Finally the cat turned and walked off with a haughty twitch of his tail.

Grammy was still shelling beans when Shamika came out onto the porch. She bent over and kissed her grandmother's cheek. "Thanks, Grammy. I got to get back to work."

"Careful how you use that beauty oil, Shamika. Don't come crying to me if you break out in a rash."

"No ma'am. I won't."

As she slid behind the wheel of her car, she waved to Grammy, and the old woman raised a dark claw-like hand as if in benediction. The tom cat was back on the porch, sitting regally at the feet of his mistress, watching Shamika with his eerily intelligent eyes.

*   *   *

The autumn days were getting shorter, and dusk was turning the evening sky a deep blue, shot through with streaks of purple near the western horizon. Shamika rolled up her window against the chill as she followed Sue Ann's white sedan to Cox Funeral Home. John Cox, the owner and funeral director, was a long-time client of Sue Ann's, being too vain about his appearance to trust his full head of graying hair to barbershop butchers. Shamika had never liked the man's looks because he looked like what he was: a mortician. His long, sallow face with the ever-present five-o'clock shadow reminded her of Christopher Lee in those old Dracula movies they sometimes ran on cable. He seemed a nice enough man, but his looks gave her the creeps.

They parked behind the funeral home and entered the two-story building through the back door. Sue Ann led the way, hugging her make-up kit to her ample bosom like a school girl hugging her books. Shamika trailed close behind, carrying a plastic bag of shampoo, conditioner, and latex gloves. Her purse secreting the Black Root of Damnation and the vial marked "Slave The Dead" was slung over her left shoulder.

"Why we gotta use the back door?" Shamika asked, softly shutting the door behind her. "Like we're sneaking in."

"We don't have to," Sue Ann answered. "It just seems like we should, you know, preserve the client's confidentiality."

"Huh? You mean, like nobody should know she needed a make-over in the worst kinda way? Or that Miss Thang look like death warmed over?"

Sue Ann shushed her. "Don't call her that here. Behave yourself."

Shamika was no longer paying attention to her employer. She was looking down the long, dimly-lit corridor ahead of them, searching the darkened doorways for lurking shadows.

She shuddered. "It's quiet as a tomb in here," she whispered.

Sue Ann smiled mischievously over her shoulder and whispered back, "Let's keep it that way. We don't want to wake the dead."

"Don't *even* say that," Shamika said in a strangled voice that was meant to be a whisper. Then her heart made a leap for her throat when Dracula appeared at the other end of the corridor.

"Good evening, ladies," said John Cox, his well-modulated voice booming softly.

"Hi, John," Sue Ann greeted him. "Sorry we're late. I had a hair emergency show up at the last minute."

"No problem," he said, walking toward them with an oily smile on his bloodless face. "I don't think Miss Trask will mind."

Shamika snickered. An undertaker with a sense of humor was better than a blood-sucking count. At least the guy wasn't a total creepoid.

"She's right in here." John Cox opened a door marked: Private.

Shamika's heart fluttered, and she had the urge to turn around and walk right out the back door.

Cox flipped a wall switch and the room, with all its horror, seemed to jump out at her. Judy Trask was laid out on the stainless steel table in the center of the room. From where Shamika stood, she couldn't see the dead woman's face, but only the top of her head and the tip of her big nose. The slug-like toes of the corpse's bare feet pointed haphazardly toward the ceiling. Her feet were as white as a frog's underbelly.

Thank God she's not naked, Shamika thought, relieved that Judy Trask was already decked out in the navy-blue dress she would be buried in.

"She's ready for you," said Cox. "You ladies go ahead and work your magic. If you need me for anything, I'll be up front in the office."

Sue Ann nodded. Shamika could tell that her boss was as shaky as a cat stuck in a tree. Her hands trembled as she set her make-up kit down on the Formica countertop beneath glass-fronted cabinets housing an odd assortment of sinister implements, tools of the mortician's trade, no doubt. The scent of industrial-strength deodorizer was overpowering, but it did not completely cover up the smell of formaldehyde used in embalming; nor did it mask a darker odor Shamika recognized as the smell of death itself.

Cox paused in the doorway. "I know this is your first time, Sue Ann," he said. "But it's really no different than working on the living. Except that my clients aren't very good conversationalists."

Sue Ann tittered nervously. Shamika scowled at the vampirish undertaker, thinking that his humor was already wearing thin. Then Dracula disappeared into the shadowy hallway.

"Well, let's get this over with," Sue Ann said. "I'll help you push her over to the sink."

Together they wheeled the gurney to the sink so that Shamika could wash the dead woman's hair. Both avoided looking at the death-slackened face. Shamika went through the routine motions of her job as best she could, placing the plastic tray behind the client's head so that the water would drain off into the sink, then placing the drape over the shoulders and torso to keep soap and water from staining the client's burial dress.

"It's just another job," Sue Ann said, as though trying to convince herself. "That's all it is."

"Yeah, right," said Shamika. "A job for a ghoul."

"Don't start," warned Sue Ann.

Shamika got out her bottles of shampoo and conditioner, then slipped on a pair of latex gloves. She turned on the tap and reached for the hose with the spray-gun attachment.

"Shamika?"

"Ma'am?"

"You're still wearing your shoulder bag." Sue Ann grinned.

Shamika cut her eyes at Sue Ann. "That's so if she sits up and starts cussing, I won't be leaving my purse when I haul butt outta here."

Sue Ann laughed girlishly. "Ahh, I'm glad you're here. I don't think I could do this by myself."

Shamika was wondering how she could slip the black root to Miss Thang and anoint her head with the liquid from the vial, with Sue Ann hovering close by. Then the idea came to her. "They *do* have a blow dryer here, don't they? Mine ain't in my bag."

"I should think so. I wonder where—"

"Why don't you go ask Lurch while I get Miss Thang lathered up?"

"You'll be all right by yourself?"

"I'm not by myself," she said with false bravado. "I've got *her* for company. Just don't take too long."

As soon as Sue Ann left the room, Shamika dug in her purse for the Black Root of Damnation. She didn't really believe the gnarled root would have any effect on a dead person. It would be nothing more than a symbolic gesture, a last laugh, so to speak, on Miss Thang. A way to thumb her nose one last time at the mean bitch. She found the root and held it in her gloved fingers, wondering if there were any special words you were supposed to say as you administered the damning dose of root medicine.

Grammy had always said that a root doctor worked from the heart. So Shamika stood over the corpse and spoke from her own heart. "Judy Trask, I damn your sorry soul to Hell." Then she held her breath as she reached down and parted the dead woman's cold lips. The bitch's mouth wouldn't open. Her jaws were wired shut. *Damn. Now what? How do I get it in her? I sure ain't sticking it up her ass!*

"Stick it in her ear," she whispered. *Hell, stick it in both ears. I didn't want to stick it in her mouth anyway. Ears are better.*

She easily broke the desiccated root into two smaller pieces, then turned the corpse's head to one side and pushed one of the pieces into the left ear. To make sure it didn't fall out later, she used a ballpoint pen from her purse to tamp the root into the ear's canal, and as she did so, the root crumbled to powder and worked its way deeper into the dead woman's head. Then she used the same method to tamp the other piece of root into Miss Thang's right ear. Satisfied that the grounds of the root would go to the grave with the white bitch, Shamika quickly hosed and lathered her limp straw-colored hair. She was rinsing out the conditioner when Sue Ann returned with a blow dryer.

"You *can* work fast when you want to," Sue Ann said.

"Yes, ma'am. Be done in a minute." Shamika toweled the hair to remove excess water, then positioned herself with her back to Sue Ann and uncapped the vial of amber liquid. She poured half the vial's contents onto Miss Thang's scalp, then recapped the "Slave The Dead" vial, planning to return it later to Grammy's root cellar. She dropped the vial into her purse and used her fingers to work the oily liquid into the lifeless scalp. A strong musky odor wafted up from Miss Thang's head and made Shamika's eyes water. Without warning, she sneezed into Miss Thang's face.

"God bless you," Sue Ann said.

Shamika used the damp towel to fan the fumes away.

"She ready for me?" asked Sue Ann, coming over to inspect Shamika's work. "God, what's that smell?"

"I dunno. Must be something the undertaker used," she lied. "Embalming fluid, probably."

"*Pee-yew.* I hope I can cover that up with perfume."

"I think it'll die down before the funeral," Shamika offered.

As she was putting away the bottles of shampoo and conditioner, Shamika felt something cold and feathery touch the back of her neck. She whirled around only to see that there was no one there who could have touched her.

"What is it?" asked Sue Ann, spritzing detangler on the deceased client's hair.

She shuddered. "Somebody must've walked on my grave."

"Humph. You've done well so far. Don't have a fright attack now."

"I ain't. You just go ahead on and do your part so we can get outta here. This place is starting to get on my last nerve."

Sue Ann said, "Just a case of the willies. Why don't you take a walk outside. I'll be all right here. John Cox is right down the hall."

"All right, then." Shamika was already heading toward the door. "Fresh air's what I need."

As soon as she stepped out into the night air, she had the urge to rush back inside and wash that "Slave The Dead" oil out of Miss Thang's hair, but of course she couldn't do that without explaining to Sue Ann what she had done, and that would get her fired for sure. No. It was too late for that. What was done was done. And she would have to live with the consequences—if there were any. But there couldn't really be any consequences—could there? She didn't actually believe in this back-from-the-dead stuff. It was all just a harmless prank played on a middle-aged dead woman who wouldn't—couldn't—know the difference. Shamika didn't truly expect the corpse of Judy Trask to get up off that table to become her living-dead slave. There were no such things as voodoo zombies in the real world. That was the stuff of dumb black & white horror movies, impossible in real life. No matter what Grammy said or believed. *But* something *touched the back of my neck.*

"Just my imagination," she asserted aloud, trying to drown out the nagging voice in her head. "Or a chill."

But the sub-audible voice persisted: *Don't be stupid. You did something to that woman and it's coming back to haunt you.*

With trembling hands, she rummaged in her purse for her week-old pack of cigarettes. She was an occasional smoker, and this was definitely an occasion for a calming smoke. She lit the cigarette and inhaled deeply, savoring the hot-cool tang of menthol. She exhaled, releasing some of her pent-up anxiety.

"Nothing's coming back to haunt me," she told herself. "Miss Thang's dead. She's *embalmed.* And that's the end of it."

What about life after death?

"That's in the Good Lord's hands. That ain't got nothing to do with me."

The inner voice was finally silenced, and Shamika was satisfied that she had won the debate—with the help of the Lord. She vowed to go to church next Sunday to pray for forgiveness for the wicked prank she had pulled on poor Judy Trask. She had been an unhappy and bitter woman, old before her time, and now she was dead. If her sins needed punishing, the Lord would see to it.

She took one last drag from her cigarette, flipped the glowing butt to the ground, then went back inside the funeral home. Pleased with herself for allaying her superstitious fears with the power of logic and reason, she walked bravely down the corridor and opened the door to the room where Sue Ann would be applying make-up to the dead client.

But Sue Ann wasn't. She wasn't there at all.

Shamika's eyes swept the room, then settled on the body lying supine on the stainless steel gurney.

"Sue Ann?" she called out. "Where are you?"

"Boo!"

Shamika spun around to see that Sue Ann had sneaked up behind her. "Sweet Jesus!" Shamika hissed. "You trying to give me a heart attack?"

Sue Ann giggled. "I'm sorry. I couldn't help myself. I was coming back from the rest room and there you were. I just had to do it."

"I oughta whup your butt, girl." Shamika barked a nervous laugh, more to relieve tension than to express amusement.

"You owe me one."

"Damn right I do. That was mean, *Miss Thang.*"

"Don't call me that," Sue Ann said, suddenly looking hurt. "I said I was sorry. Jeez."

"I don't care. You pissed me off," said Shamika, seething, her anger growing. "Miss Thang!" It was meant to be a defiant jab at Sue Ann, just a taste of the payback she was going to get for scaring the bejesus out of Shamika.

But that last angry utterance had unintended consequences.

Sue Ann's jaw dropped and her eyes seemed to swell up in their sockets. She worked her mouth but no words came out.

"What the hell's wrong with you?" Shamika demanded. She didn't care that the woman was her boss. She didn't have to put up with this honky's bullshit. There were plenty other jobs out there.

Deathly pale, Sue Ann fell back against the wall. Urine dribbled down her leg and spattered on the tile floor. She raised a hand and pointed a shaky finger. Shamika turned to see what she was pointing at—and immediately regretted it.

Judy Trask was sitting straight up on the table, her dull eyes open and unblinking.

"No," Shamika croaked. "This can't be. This is a trick . . ."

Miss Thang slid off the stainless steel table and her bare feet slapped against the floor tiles as she—*it*—shambled forward.

Sue Ann started babbling incoherently.

Shamika said, "Lord Almighty, stop this. Make her lie down. *Please.*"

She wanted to turn and run, but her rubbery legs wouldn't move. Warm liquid flooded her underpants as her bladder let go.

Miss Thang raised her arms, reaching out with long, pale fingers.

Shamika's vision clouded with splotchy darkness, then the darkness blossomed and completely engulfed her.

* * *

She awoke on the cold floor, her drool pooling on the tile. She opened her eyes and tried to lift her head.

"She's coming around," said a faraway voice.

She managed to push herself up to a sitting position, then looked around. Sue Ann was lying on the floor a few feet from her, her eyes bulged out like little balloons. They were the eyes of the dead. But that wasn't the worst; the worst was her tongue sticking out like a pink slug caught between her lips.

"Come on. Get up," the voice said. Hands clamped around her arms and she was lifted to her feet. The hands and the voice belonged to a policeman. Standing behind the cop was the undertaker with Dracula's face.

"What happened?" Shamika asked, bewildered. "What happened to Sue Ann? Is she . . ."

"She's dead," said the cop. "Strangled, by the looks of things."

Then she remembered. She remembered Judy Trask coming at them with outstretched arms.

Shamika jerked her head around and saw the deceased woman lying on the stainless steel table. She started trembling all over. Her teeth chattered. But she managed to point a finger at Miss Thang and say, "It was her. *She* did it."

"Uh-huh," said the cop as he pulled down Shamika's arm and snapped the cuff around her wrist. Then he yanked the arm behind her back and cuffed her other wrist as well. "You can tell us all about it at the station."

"I didn't mean for it to happen," she insisted, panic rising with the bile in her throat.

"You have the right to remain silent," the policeman recited. "Anything you say can be used—"

"It was *Miss Thang*, goddamn it! I swear to God! She got up and . . ."

"—against you in a court of law."

HOGBUTCHER'S HEART

Cozy up and I'll tell you what you don't know.

Guy told me this story. Swore on his dead mama's soul it was true. Said he knew a guy who knew the dumbshit it happened to.

You heard a lot of bullshit tales back in Your Dick Cranked, aka, YDC (Youth Detention Center). But *this* one had that clapper-clanger ring of truth. I liked it so much I killed the bastard the night he told it to me. Smothered him in his bunk with his own pillow. He was too ugly to live anyway. Had a face looked like it had been branded with a hot waffle iron. Probably his mama did it.

That was back when I was knee-high to a wharf rat and had to look up to see a good set of tits. Guess I was pretty wild back then. Poor Impulse Control, the shrinks called it.

Anyway, the story. Told to me by a thirteen-year-old gang-banger, spawn of slaves and as fine a specimen of a Ubangee-American as you'd ever want to meet and kill. Called himself Tee Bo. I called him Sambo because his waffle face reminded me of that Little Black Sambo story where the tigers run around in a circle and turn to butter little Sambo uses on his pancakes. Whenever I see a tiger I get hungry for a stack of buttered pancakes—or waffles, which I like better cause of the way those little squares hold the syrup and butter. Could've licked syrup off Tee Bo's face if I'd had any.

You think I'm a racist, right? Well, I'm here to tell you I'm not. I don't discriminate on the basis on skin color. White meat, dark meat—it's all the same to me. Everybody's Crow meat, heh heh.

Okay, okay, the story. Keep your fucking pants on. And your dick in your pants.

There was this black dude worked on a hog farm in North Carolina. It was his job to herd the hogs into the slaughterhouse where this fat guy with a stun gun would pop those hogs in the head and send them to Hog Heaven. They called it a Penetrating Bolt Stunner. A gun with an exploding cartridge that would drive a penetrating rod through the skull and into the brain. The hogs never knew what hit 'em. Stunned those porky fuckers to death.

So the farmhand—call him Isaiah—did something to piss off the Stun Gun Man. Maybe ole Isaiah didn't show proper respect to the tub of white fat. Maybe he didn't bow and scrape low enough to suit the dyed-in-the-wool Klan man. Whatever it was, the Stun Gun Man casually raised his Penetrating Bolt Stunner, jammed it against the darkie's noggin and fired the hog-bloodied bolt right into Isaiah's brain. Ole Isaiah dropped like a hundred-pound bag of fertilizer and was dead before his face hit the shit-splattered floor. When the sheriff came, Stun Gun Man told him it was an accident, and the sheriff—also a Klan member—said it was a damn shame to lose a good nigger thataway, but what the hell, shit happens.

Soon as I heard that story I made up my mind to get one of those hog stunners and try it out for myself. On a hog of the human persuasion. Did too. Few months after I busted out of Your Dick Cranked. Hired on at a hog farm in Georgia, worked a couple of days slopping porkers, then caged myself a genuine Penetrating Bolt Stunner. It was a beaut. A fine piece of American craftsmanship. Good solid feel in my hand. I was hot to try out my new toy.

I lit out of there in the middle of the night, hitchhiked south, aiming to get to Florida in time for Spring Break in Panama City. The thought of all those college babes bare-assed in string bikinis and crack-kissing thongs got my blood up and the good old kill juice flowing.

Got a ride with a farmer in a straw hat and an old pickup just outside of Valdosta. He didn't talk much, which was good, but he smoked these stinking stogies looked like something you'd see floating in a toilet, too ornery to be flushed. I couldn't very well ask him not to smoke, since it was his truck and all, so I decided to use the stunner on him, then drive myself all the way to Panama City.

I reached into my gym bag and pulled out the gun.

"Whatcha got there, son?" he asked, glancing over at it.

"You ever seen the like?" I good-ole-boyed him.

"Well, it looks like one of them thangs they use in a slaughterhouse. That what it is?"

"Yes sir," I said, flashing him a countrified grin. "You're exactly right. Ever see somebody use one?"

"Naw. Don't reckon I ever did."

"It's a sight, I tell ya. I watched 'em zap them old hogs just the other day. Put it up to their heads and fired the sonofabitch and boom! them hogs go down all at once like a ton o' bricks. Made my dick get hard just to see it."

The farmer gave me a worried look. I knew what was going through the cow fucker's mind.

"Ort not to talk thataway, son."

"Don't worry, old dude. I ain't a faggot or nothing like that," I reassured him. "I just like to see things die hard. That's why I stole this beauty."

"They Lord . . ."

I put the Penetrating Bolt Stunner right up against his temple, just under the band of his straw hat. "Pull over," I told him.

"Wait now, son, you—"

"Pull over or I'll do you right now. There. See that dirt road? Turn there."

He wised up and did what I said. Pulled off the blacktop and onto the red clay road and followed it into the trees and out of sight of the blacktop, right where I wanted him. I told him to stop and he did. I pulled the gun away from his temple, took off his sad straw hat and ordered him to look at me. He turned his weathered whiskery face toward me.

I'll be goddamn if he didn't have pig eyes!

It was one of those times when everything seems to fall in place, like some divine hand had tossed the holyfucking dice and they came up PIG EYES. I saw the fucking light, brother. Praise God, it was right there in front of me. My true calling. My purpose in this suck-ass thing called life.

I smiled at the pig-eyed farmer.

I gently, *tenderly*, *lovingly* placed the stunner against his forehead.

And squeezed the trigger.

It made a sound I'll never forget. *Phzzzzzz-Thump!* That pressure-driven bolt punching a hole in a ripe melon.

The force of the bolt firing through his skull and into his brain knocked him against the driver's door and he slumped there, shrunken in his overalls like a puppet with its strings suddenly slashed. Blood jizzed from the neat hole above his pig eyes. Then it stopped, same as his heart.

And those eyes stayed wide open, wet but already drying out in the hot air. I shoved him out of the truck, then drove back onto the state road, heading for Florida.

At the age of seventeen, I knew who I was—*what* I was. I was Michael Wayne Crow, Hogbutcher to the world. Hunter and killer of the Hog People. They were out there waiting for me. I would know them by their close-set pig eyes or their heavy flanks and jowls. I would take them where I found them.

The Season of Slaughter was upon me. And the real butchery was just beginning.

I'll spare you the grisly details. Most of them have already been cataloged in newspapers and tabloids. I will say this: I butchered my Hog People with utmost care and consideration. Not a one of them suffered undue pain.

Nor did I in any way desecrate their bodies, as my skills with knives and cleaver are considerable. On that you have my solemn word.

My childhood? Well, I guess I'd have to say it was pretty fucking abnormal. I mean, how do you imagine *you* would've turned out if your old man was a mortician whose principle passion in life was fucking corpses? I wasn't into it myself. Not that I never tried it. When I was sixteen and full of rising sap, I greased up my pole and battered the cold vulval gates of one Enorma Biddy, dead of a heart attack at twenty-nine. But the hot blood drained from my root and my erection was lost before I could slip it to her. My cock, much to my adolescent sorrow, had a mind of its own and it refused to fuck anything without a pulse. Apparently I had not inherited my father's predilection for cold cunt.

I suppose the old man loved me in his own twisted way. He made me study hard and read all the literary classics—even poetry. Carl Sandberg's my favorite. You can guess why. But whenever I strayed from the old man's idea of the Straight and Narrow, he beat the living shit out of me. And I mean that literally, the "living shit" part. He beat me delirious this one time and after I shat myself I saw my lumpy feces *come alive* and come crawling up my body like it wanted to devour my ass. It was a Shit Monster—no shit. Anyhow, you get the sick picture. The Dad showed his love by whupping me senseless. By the time I was thirteen, I'd given up on winning his approval and invested my energies in avoiding his brutal beatings. In other words, I coasted along the prescribed path, doing my best to avoid his wrath. Sometimes it worked.

After a particularly nasty beating which left me with a broken nose, two busted ribs and a split lip, I nursed my wounds by fantasizing ten different ways I could kill the sadistic bastard. At the top of the list was cutting off the top of his head with a chain saw while he was bedded down for the night. Of course this was an implausible method of doing him in. The sound of the saw would wake him before it could take its first bite, and worse, it would wake my mother at his side and I would have to kill her too. I didn't especially want to kill the old lady, and I wanted to spare her the trauma of witnessing the old man's death. Maw had been traumatized enough already, not by spousal beatings but by the ravages of some unknown venereal disease the old man had passed to her as a result of his corpse-porking activities. She never knew the source of her strange ailment, nor did she suspect her hubby of necrophilia. Her doctor treated the "infection of unknown origin" with antibiotics, but the slow rot of her soft tissue was never completely conquered. I knew the origin of Maw's flesh-eating bacteria, but I couldn't reveal it without letting on that I had surreptitiously watched the old man fuck the dead—his "loved ones," as he called them. That would've been the death of me, for sure. Anyway, how do you tell your mother that her husband is a carrier of Corpse Rot? The cheating bastard was free of symptoms himself, so she wouldn't have believed me anyway.

My patricidal fantasies soon took on lives of their own, and I began to make concrete plans for his murder. But as it turned out, my father died of natural causes while engaging in unnatural acts with the unembalmed body of a sexy high school cheerleader. Sexy for a dead girl, I mean. His ticker wasn't up to the excitement of plundering that freshly dead pussy. So he croaked, and I was cheated out of killing him. I even covered up for him. I found him dead atop the stiff chick, so I pulled him off her and put his pants back on him and deposited him on the floor so it would look like he just dropped dead where he stood. I did it to spare Maw the pain and humiliation of learning that her husband had been the worst kind of pervert. The Corpse Rot eventually found its way to her brain and her behavior took a hard turn into real madness. She developed a taste for raw meat. She started talking to dead folks and even gave them tea parties in her gloomy parlor. What they talked about remains a mystery to me. But I swear there were a few times when I could actually feel the chilling presence of her dead guests. Up until then I had never really believed in life after death.

Now I know better. Now I know the souls of the dead are all around us, all the time. And some of them are not exactly thrilled to be here. Those are the ones you want to avoid at all costs. They are not at all nice. They are damned. And they're damned mean and nasty.

So you see, my early life was not exactly ripped from the pages of old *Leave It To Beaver* scripts. Even *The Addams Family* was normal compared to my family. I was screwed from the get-go, no doubt about it.

But I had a lot of heart. And it was my heart that led me into cannibalism.

Hah! Thought that would get your attention. Looked like you were dozing off there. Comfy now? Chains starting to chafe a little? You'll get use to them. I told you this was going to be a long night, didn't I? And then some.

So. Cannibalism. The ultimate taboo. Murder doesn't faze us anymore, but the idea of one human eating the flesh of another—well, that's the worst depravity of all, isn't it? Never mind that Holy Communion is symbolic of eating the flesh of Jesus Christ and drinking his blood, for Christ's sake. How could society go on if people were to run amok and start making Happy Meals out of their fellow citizens?

As butcher of the Hog People, I came to see that it wasn't proper to kill just for the sake of the slaughter. I needed justification for the killing. So I began to eat my kills. And that made all the difference. I know now that to kill without devouring the flesh of the victim is like having sex without reaching orgasm. It's unsatisfying. And mucho wasteful. When I partake of human flesh, I take a bit of the person's spirit into me and allow them to live on, in a sense. And you know the best part? It tastes good! Properly prepared, human flesh is the sweetest meat you'll ever put in your mouth. Granted, it's not very good raw, but then what meat is? Of course, my mother had a different opinion—but she was crazy. Before she died, she nearly drove me nuts the way she badgered me about her raw steaks. "Mikey, this meat's not bloody enough. I can't eat this," she would say. I think it had something to do with her Corpse Rot disease, like the bacteria that was slowly eating away her flesh had affected her own appetite. Almost like it had a mind of its own, you know? Intelligent bacteria! Hah!

What's that smell?

Jesus, you pissed your pants. You didn't—oh, I see. You're scared. You think I'm going to butcher and eat you. I'm sorry. I should've made that clear at the start. I didn't bring you here to my little mountain hideaway for that. If I had, you would already be in my belly by now.

No, I brought you here for an altogether different purpose. I'm going to honor you, and you in turn will do me a particular honor. That's why I'm telling you all this. So you will understand what this is really all about. That's what you do, isn't it? As an investigative journalist, you dig for facts and seek out the meaning below the surface of things. You have a sharp mind. That's why I chose you. I knew you would understand me and see that I'm much more than a cannibalistic serial killer. That "Butcher of Birmingham" business really rubs me the wrong way, you know? You're going to tell the real story—if you choose to live. And I think you will.

Let me explain.

When I looked in the mirror a couple of days ago, I saw something that I never knew was there. But there it was, no mistake, staring back at me. How could I have been blind to it for so long? Some sort of tunnel vision thing, I suppose. Being human, we see only what we want to see all too often.

Take a good look at my face. Go ahead. I won't bite.

You see?

Pig eyes! I'm one of them. One of the Hog People. Ripe for slaughter.

You realize what this means, don't you? There's really no other choice. I have to kill myself. A perfect ending to our story, don't you think? And you, my friend, will have the scoop. You will witness my demise. I'm going to put that Penetrating Bolt Gun right to my own head and drop dead at your feet.

But there is a catch.

After my death, you will remain as you are now, chained to the floor. You have plenty of bottled water, but no food. And no one will be coming up here for six full weeks. So, if you are to live to tell the tale, you will have to partake of my flesh. You'll have to eat me raw, of course. Sorry about that. There's no way around it. That leather case there contains my knives and cleavers. The tools of my trade. They are yours now, to use as you see fit.

So there it is. My death will save your life—unless you choose starvation.

This way I'll know that the person who tells my story will have first-hand knowledge of his subject.

Inside information, see?

A real bellyful.

THE KITCHEN WITCH

The girls tittered with amused excitement as Cherry Harper methodically removed the pink bow and ribbon from her last present. Gauging the devilish reaction of her two adolescent daughters, Cherry paused and said, "I'm not sure I want to open this one."

"Aw, Mom," the girls said in near unison.

"Gag gifts always make me nervous," said Cherry, eyeing the small package with raised brows.

"Who says it's a gag gift?" asked Sindee, the eldest daughter, remarkably full bosomed for a sixteen-year-old.

"Family tradition," Cherry replied. "Your father's legacy."

"If Dad was here you wouldn't be afraid to open it," said Sandy.

"Because I trusted your father. With you two, I don't know what to expect. I'm telling you right now, if something jumps out at me, I'll blister both your bottoms."

"Aw, Mom."

Cherry smiled and opened her last Mother's Day present, her long lacquered nails slicing the wrapping paper. She lifted the lid of the oblong box and squealed girlishly when she saw its ugly inhabitant. "A kitchen witch! Just what I always wanted. Yuck!"

Sindee and Sandy cackled, then howled.

"A witch for the witch," Sindee declared.

"Watch it, young lady," warned Cherry, pinching Sindee's cheek, "or I'll put a spell on you you'll never forget."

"Okay, okay. Jeez, Mom. That hurt."

Cherry regarded the doll-sized crone curiously. Its glossy black eyes gleamed from narrow slits and its nose was long, unmistakably phallic. The hag's lipless mouth was recessed between her nose and pointed chin. Two rounded cheeks at the base of the crone's nose reminded Cherry of the crude drawings of male genitalia that inevitably appeared on high school chalkboards. She wondered if the girls were aware of the symbolism. Chuckling, Cherry pinched the hag's prick of a nose.

"My God," she said, suddenly drawing her hand away as if burned. "That feels like real flesh. What's this made of?" Goosebumps popped up in her own flesh.

"Some weird kind of rubber or something," said Sandy, her stubby fingers palpating the face of the witch. "Ooh, it does feel creepy."

Then Cherry noticed the small card in the bottom of the box—a black card with white lettering.

THE ORIGINAL KITCHEN WITCH
HANG HER IN YOUR KITCHEN
FOR SPECIAL MAGIC
WORKS LIKE A CHARM!

"Well, come on, Mom," Sindee said. "Let's hang the old bitch up."

Cherry's open palm shot out and slapped Sindee's face. "You don't use that kind of language in this house," she said quietly.

With a stunned expression on her stinging face, Sindee pulled away from her mother. Tears welled up in her eyes, but she willed herself not to cry. She couldn't remember the last time her mother had hit her.

Trying to ease the tension, Sandy said, "Come on, guys. Let's hang it up. We could use some magic around here."

Cherry stood and carried the witch to the kitchen, her daughters trailing behind. She felt a pang of guilt at having slapped Sindee, followed by a gnawing feeling of sadness that her husband was no longer alive to help her with the girls. Phil had been a wonderful father and a good husband, devoted to his family. He had died over a year ago at the health spa while working out on an exercise machine. Heart attack, they said.

Cherry hammered a small nail into the bottom of the space-saver cabinet over the sink, then hung the witch by the black thread growing out of its humped back.

"There," she said. "Now I'll be able to do magic in the kitchen. Lord knows, my cooking needs all the help it can get."

"Amen," snapped Sindee, barely disguising her anger for her mother.

"And maybe it'll keep away evil spirits," Sandy said, reaching for a chocolate chip cookie. At fourteen, her body's march toward puberty was made sluggish by her abundant body fat.

"Too bad it won't keep the fat away," said Sindee, venting some of her anger at her sister.

"Be nice," Cherry said.

Munching on the cookie, Sandy gave her sister her meanest eat-shit sneer.

The kitchen witch slowly twisted on its axis of black thread as if moved by a phantom wind. The witch straddled a small straw broomstick, clutching the stick with little metal-hook hands.

"She looks like she's going to take off and fly," said Sindee.

"Spooky," agreed Sandy.

Cherry nodded, not taking her eyes from the hanging hag. A chill of apprehension brought back the gooseflesh, and she felt a tingling sensation at the back of her neck.

*　　*　　*

The next morning she packed the girls off to school and sat down at the kitchen table to relax with a second cup of coffee. She lit a menthol cigarette and gazed through the open window at the wind-dancing trees in the back yard. The overcast sky grew darker as storm clouds swept close to the earth. Thunder rumbled in the distance, then rolled over the house, rattling windows. The parted curtains billowed in the cool breeze like ghost dancers.

Pensive and preoccupied with remembrances of her late husband, she absently watched the cigarette smoke swirl around her. Since Phil's death, she had been a woman incomplete. She had sublimated her sexuality and poured her energies into motherhood. Now she was becoming acutely attuned to the biological storm brewing within her, and she was thinking of ending her extended period of celibacy. How, she wondered, does a thirty-six-year-old widow get back into circulation? Singles' bars repulsed her. Church socials were not her cup of tea. Most of her male friends had been friends of Phil's as well, so she had already ruled them out. She needed someone new, a fresh hunk of meat.

"Jesus," she said, "what an unladylike thought." She crushed out her cigarette in the ashtray, then stood and went to the kitchen sink to rinse her coffee cup.

The kitchen witch was stirred by the breeze coming through the window over the sink and appeared to be riding her broomstick over rough currents.

Cherry looked up. "What do you say, Hazel? Does your magic work in affairs of the heart?"

The witch seemed to mock her with a wicked smirk.

"Fuck you, too," said Cherry. As she turned away, there was a loud crash behind her, and something struck her in the small of her back. She spun around to see that the crock-pot had somehow fallen off the top of the cabinet and had smashed against the front edge of the sink. The pot's cover was in pieces on the floor, and the broken pot lay in the sink, its electric cord hanging out like a black snake with a forked copper tongue.

She looked up at the smirking witch and suddenly felt afraid. She shivered against the morning chill as the storm clouds released a heavy downpour of spring rain.

*   *   *

Cherry was sitting on the couch with her legs curled beneath her, reading the latest Stephen King bestseller. Sandy was sequestered in her room with her homework, and Sindee was in the upstairs bathroom, getting dolled up for her date with Buzz Sellers. The evening rain had tapered to a steady drizzle.

The doorbell chimed. Cherry put down her book and went to the door.

"Hi, Miz Harper," said Buzz. "Is Sindee here?"

"Come in, Buzz. Sindee's upstairs, making herself beautiful for you."

With an embarrassed smile, Buzz entered the living room. His six-foot frame was filled out with rippling muscles. He was a regional wrestling champion and was known as Super Jock at the high school. Blonde-haired, blue-eyed and square-jawed, he was becoming a beautiful hunk of manhood, Cherry observed.

"Would you like something to drink?" she asked. "Coke, tea or juice?"

"Juice would be good."

He followed her into the kitchen. Cherry flicked the light switch and there was an explosion of blinding light, followed by darkness.

"Damn," she said. "The bulb blew again. I just put a new one in last night." Fumbling in the dark, she found a new bulb in the drawer. "Would you change the bulb for me?"

"Sure, Miz Harper."

She dragged out a stepstool and positioned it below the light fixture. Buzz stepped up onto the stool and reached for the glass dome.

"Be careful," she cautioned. "That stool is not too sturdy. Better let me hold onto you. I won't have your athletic career ruined by an accident in my kitchen."

Standing behind him, Cherry placed her hands on his muscular thighs and gripped them firmly. As he unscrewed the light fixture, his hips turned slightly and Cherry's fingers brushed his crotch. A twinge of excitement shot through her. His hips turned a few more degrees and she felt a growing hardness through his pants. Her mind clouded, and her body acted independently. Her eyes closed as her fingers massaged the young mans' erection. She found his zipper and pulled it down.

"Mom?" Sindee called from the living room. "Where are you? Did I hear the doorbell?"

Buzz dropped the blown light bulb and it shattered on the kitchen tile with a loud pop.

"Mom?"

"Jesus," whispered Cherry. "I'm sorry, Buzz, I . . . I didn't mean for this to happen." Then she called to Sindee, "We're in the kitchen."

Buzz screwed in the new bulb and light flooded the kitchen. He had zipped his pants, but there was a noticeable bulge in his crotch and beads of perspiration on his face. He stepped off the stool as Sindee came into the kitchen. Cherry was already sweeping up the fragments of shattered glass.

"Whu . . . what the heck is that?" asked Buzz, pointing at the witch on a stick.

"That's Mom's kitchen witch," laughed Sindee. "Isn't she sexy?"

Cherry involuntarily glanced at the hag and thought she saw her wink an eye.

*　　*　　*

A foreign sound woke her. Her heart was racing, her stomach tightening into an acidic knot. Cherry sat up in bed and stared into liquid darkness. In a back corner of her mind was a vague memory of a sexually arousing dream. Had the sound been part of the dream? *Christ, what's wrong with me? I'm too old to worry about things going bump in the night. Unless it's the bumping and grinding of sex.*

She settled back into her thick pillow and closed her eyes. Her heart slowed its pace and the knot in her belly uncoiled. She was thinking of Buzz Sellers' hard thighs when she heard the scream.

She jumped out of bed and raced down the hall to check her daughters' rooms. A second scream came from Sandy's. She found her crouching in a corner, blood trickling down her cheek.

"What happened?"

"Something bit me!" said Sandy, touching her fingers to the small wound in her face.

Sindee rushed into the room. Cherry put her arm around Sandy and examined her bloodied cheek. Three tiny punctures formed a triangle in her flesh. "Not like any bite I've ever seen," Cherry said.

After cleaning Sandy's wound with alcohol, they searched the room, looking under the bed and in the closets, but found nothing.

"Maybe it was a rat," Sindee suggested.

"I'll call the exterminator in the morning," Cherry assured them. "Okay, girls. Back to bed. Tomorrow's a school day."

Unable to get back to sleep, Cherry read through the night and finished the King novel before sunrise.

*   *   *

While washing the breakfast dishes in the sink (the dishwasher had gone on the blink the night before) Cherry noticed the hands of the kitchen witch and felt a cold shudder. The metal hands gripping the miniature broomstick were triple-pronged claws. Not realistic at all but disturbingly menacing.

Sindee and Sandy came into the kitchen. A flesh-colored Band-Aid covered Sandy's injured cheek. "We're off, Mom," said Sindee. "Don't forget to call the rat killer."

"It wasn't a rat," insisted Sandy.

"Where did you get this kitchen witch?" asked Cherry, turning away from the sink.

"Oh, you wouldn't believe—"

"From a witchy old woman," Sandy interrupted her sister.

"Yeah, Mom. This spooky old biddy came to the door last week while you were at work. She was selling kitchen witches for Mother's Day."

"She was so creepy," added Sandy. "And she smelled bad."

"Had you ever seen her before?"

"No. I think she was a gypsy or something," Sindee said. "She was sure dressed like one. Why do you ask?"

"Just curious. You two better go on out to meet the bus. And take an umbrella. It looks like rain again."

"Bye, Mom," the girls said in unison.

Cherry didn't bother to finish the dishes; she went to the den and built a fire in the fireplace. Perspiring in the heat of the crackling fie, she unbuttoned her housecoat and added more firewood. She needed a roaring fire to do the job. Maybe she was being silly and superstitious, but she was beginning to believe the witch was evil. The ugly devil doll was working wicked magic.

A violent thunderclap rattled the house and a hard rain drummed on the roof and against the windows.

She returned to the kitchen. With her heart thundering against her rib cage, Cherry reached for the kitchen witch. "You're going to burn, bitch," she said in a husky voice.

The doorbell chimed.

"Damn."

She went to the front door, half expecting to find an old gypsy woman on her doorstep. Instead, she found Buzz Sellers, wide-eyed and anxious.

"Buzz? What are you doing here? Why aren't you in school?"

"I'm skipping. I had to see you."

"Listen, Buzz. You have to forget what happened last night. It shouldn't have happened. I'm sorry, but you have to go."

The young man stepped through the doorway and shut the door behind him. Then he threw himself upon her, mauling her breasts with powerful hands.

"No!" she shouted. "Stop it, Buzz!"

"You want it as much as I do," he said breathlessly. He crushed his lips against hers. The sweet scent of his cologne sickened her. She tried to push him away, but he was too strong. She kneed him in the groin and he released her, doubling over in pain.

"You bitch," he growled. With eyes reddened by pain and anger, he limped toward her.

Cherry snatched a large lamp from an end table and slammed it against the side of his head. Buzz crumpled to the floor. She stood over him, ready to bash him again if he tried to get up, but he stayed down, unmoving. She dropped the lamp and went to the kitchen.

It was time to end the witching. Time for a good old-fashioned witch burning.

She grabbed a kitchen knife from the wall rack and went to the sink to cut the hag down.

The witch was gone.

"Oh, my God," she gasped. She glanced into the sink, confirming that the kitchen witch had not fallen there. Near panic, she spun around, her eyes searching the room for the demon doll. Nothing was out of place. Nothing out of the ordinary . . .

A cabinet door swung open and the witch flew out, gliding silently through the air as if attached to an invisible string, flying straight at Cherry's face. She swung the knife, cutting nothing but air. The witch strafed her with metal claws and sliced the flesh beneath her left eye, then circled over her head for the next assault.

"God damn you," Cherry growled through clenched teeth.

The hag dived at her and Cherry swatted with the knife, the flat of the blade connecting with a solid blow. The witch bounced off the window and landed in the stainless-steel sink. The little broomstick dropped to the floor.

Holding the knife with both hands, Cherry cautiously approached the sink. Blood streamed down her face from the gash under her eye. As she was about to impale her adversary, the witch shot out of the sink and attached its metal claws to Cherry's throat. She screamed in intense pain and ran from the kitchen, her hands clutching at the thing hooked into the soft flesh of her throat.

Dizzy and stumbling like a drunk, she made it to the den and fell to her knees in front of the fireplace. She grabbed the hag with both hands and yanked it away from her throat. The claws ripped free of her flesh. Cherry flung the witch into the fire and watched the little creature writhe as the flames consumed its dress and melted its grimacing face. Finally, nothing was left but a pair of blackened metal claws.

A sudden wind screamed up the chimney.

Cherry removed her torn housecoat and used it to staunch the flow of blood from her throat. Then she returned to the living room to see about Buzz. *Christ, I hope I didn't kill him.*

He was sitting on the floor, rubbing his head. He looked at her with a dazed expression and said, "What am I doing here? God, you're *bleeding*. What happened?"

"Something wicked brought you here. But she's . . . it's gone now."

"The last thing I remember, I was on my way to school and—"

Cherry ignored his anxious rambling and went to the wood-framed mirror in the den. The scarlet wounds in her throat and beneath her eye would leave ugly scars, but for the moment, she was not concerned with them. From her haggard face her eyes shone in triumph. She turned toward the fireplace and stared into the dying flames.

A moaning wind from the throat of the chimney became a desolate howl. Then the howl died to a whisper, and the only sound was the cackling of the low-burning fire.

A WITCH IN FAERIE

Deep in Faerie Wood the stump witch brooded.

Someone—or some*thing*—was interfering with her spells. Her incantations tripped clumsily over her tongue, coming out all wrong, often with disastrous results. Her herbal cures and mystical prescriptions seemed of late to have no affect, and Catkin, her longtime feline companion, was off his feed, and his usual sweet temperament had turned nasty.

"Something's amiss, Mither Mawkins," the stump witch said to herself, "and I mean to ferret the cause of the malady."

She walked out of her little stone house, sat down at her willow stump and cast the runes upon the stump's burnished surface. The lettered shingles fell with an ominous clatter, but the runic symbols spelled nothing but gibberish. "Zook's thunder!" she cursed.

Next she cast the knucklebones of a troll, but try as she might (and mightily she did), Mither Mawkins could divine nothing from those jointed digits. She swept the knucklebones off the stump and onto the ground. Catkin eyed her warily, then sauntered away with an insolent twitch of his tail.

"Don't think I didn't see that, rat-breath," she shouted after him. "One more insult and I'll turn you back into a pussywillow." *If only I could*, she lamented.

She spat three times round the stump, then went into the stone house to get her cloak and willow-wand. Pulling the cowl over her iron-gray hair, she set off to make the rounds of Faerie Forest.

"When witchery won't do," said Mither Mawkins, "womanly wiles will have to."

*   *   *

Her first stop was Booty Hill, home of the thieving Spriggans. She rapped her willow-wand against the tiny mouth of their cave and called: "Spriggans! Mither Mawkins would have a word with you!"

They came roiling out of their cave, a tumbling scrum of arms and legs and ugly faces, biting and swatting one another for the sport of it. At last they disentangled and stood, all six of them, at the feet of the witch.

"What's the word, Mither?" asked Bir the Spriggan leader. The brown fur on top of his head stood up in spiky clumps like a matted headdress.

"Yes, Mither, tell us the word," chirped Tir as he picked a pebble from his bird-like beak and gazed up at her with slanty eyes.

Fir, Wir, Vir and Dir chorused: "The word, the word."

Mither Mawkins held up her willow-wand to silence the sassy Spriggans. She narrowed her eyes and gave them a look to remember in their nightmares (if they *had* nightmares).

"The word," she said, "is *skullduggery* . . ."

As all of one mind, the Spriggans simultaneously curled their rodent-like tails round their spindly legs in their instinctive posture of defense.

"Skullduggery," Mither Mawkins repeated, letting the word settle over the Spriggans like a dark cloud.

"We don't know nothing about that," said Bir finally. "Thuggery, buggery, muggery, sure. But duggery of the skull? Horse manure!"

"Watch your filthy tongue, Spriggan Bir," she warned with her best evil eye.

Bir stuck out his lizardly tongue and crossed his beady eyes to look at it.

Wir uncoiled his tail and gathered courage enough to speak to the stump witch. "Honest, Mither, we know nothing of this skullish business. We're simple thieves."

"Minor villains," added Vir.

"Sure, we kidnap babies sometimes," said Fir, "and leave a baby Spriggan in its place, but that's all for a lark, you see."

"We might blight a few crops here and there, or stir up a whirlwind or two, but that's all the magic we know," Bir said with all the sincerity he could muster.

"True enough," she said, "not a one of you is cunning enough to be behind this wicked business." She rubbed her pointy chin thoughtfully, then said, "Keep your ears to the ground and let me know if you hear anything out of the usual way."

"We will, Mither," pledged Bir with his bony hand over his heart.

"If you don't . . ." The stump witch raised her willow-wand high in the air.

The Spriggans cringed in unison, then scurried back into their dark hole, no doubt to keep close watch over their stolen treasures.

Mither Mawkins chuckled to herself, then proceeded to her next stop in Faerie Wood.

*   *   *

The Asrai sisters were shading themselves on the grassy bank of the emerald pool, relishing the seclusion and the deep shadows afforded by the overhanging trees. When the two naked faeries saw the human lumbering through the undergrowth, they immediately melted, leaving two tiny puddles of golden liquid on the ground where they had been.

"Wait, sisters!" the cowled human cried. "It's only me! Mither Mawkins. Come back."

Like two little waterfalls rising up instead of falling downward, the Asrai sisters reassumed their comely shapes, the last of the twin puddles disappearing into their feet.

"Wishes, Mither," sang Azri.

"Blessings, Mither," sang Azra.

"Yes, yes, thank you, ladies. I just wanted to ask you, have you noticed anything . . . untoward lately?"

Azra looked puzzled. Azri said, "Toward the *un*? Goodness, no. Unless . . ."

"Less the *un*?" queried Azra, looking even more puzzled.

"Unless," Azri continued her thought, "you mean yourself, Mither, when we saw you walking in the air."

Mither Mawkins sighed. She had forgotten how difficult it was communicating with the Asrai; their small brains were attuned to music no one else hears and little else. "You didn't see *me* walking in the air," she said.

"Oh, but we *did*," insisted Asra.

"We did," echoed Azri. "And when we asked you what you were doing, you growled at us."

"And frightened us so that we melted away for the rest of the day."

"Sisters, you are mistaken. I don't know how to walk in the air. I don't know any witch who does, though they say it is possible for one with power enough."

"But it looked like you, Mither," said Azri. "Except for the eyes."

"What about the eyes?" asked the stump witch.

"Oh, they were terrible!" Azra trembled.

"Red and shining!" Azri quailed.

"Well, my eyes are black, as you can plainly see."

As the Asrai sisters went on about the air-walking witch, earthbound Mither Mawkins ambled off, wondering what the little faeries had actually seen.

Next she stopped at the bank of the river that courses through the very heart of Faerie Wood. She bent down, picked up a rock, spit on it, then tossed it into the water. A moment later Peg Powler surfaced, her huge mouth opening and closing like a guppy's, her big eyes scouring the riverbank for prey.

"Hullo, Peg. I don't suppose you've seen anything strange hereabouts, have you?"

"None stranger than you, witch," Peg Powler said in a deep, watery voice.

"Meaning what, then?" Mither Mawkins scowled at the river-prowler and stealer of children.

Peg's long hair floated about her shoulders like flattened marsh grass, and the puffy, wrinkled flesh of her face hung like melting tallow from her oversized skull. "Strange it was to see you walking across the river without getting your feet wet," she said in a tone of disapproval.

"I never—" She stilled her own tongue. There was no point in telling Peg Powler that a mere stump witch has not the power to walk on water.

"Practice your black arts elsewhere, witch," Peg growled. "I'll not have you scaring children away before I get a chance to take them down."

Peg Powler disappeared below the river's surface, and Mither Mawkins turned and walked toward the road. Now there could be no doubt; someone who looked like her was abroad in Faerie Forest, performing feats of wizardry unknown to her.

"'LO, STUMPY," boomed a large voice behind her. She turned round just in time to be hit in the face by the wind from the giant's mouth. His breath was fouler than ditch water and twice as rancid.

"Don't call me that, you big oaf," she said to Jack-in-Irons, haunter of lonely roads and collector of bashed heads.

The giant raised his huge club in the air, rattling the chains that festooned his enormous girth. "JACK NOT 'FRAID O' YOU."

"Well, you *should* be," she bluffed. "I could shrink you down to the size of a flea."

Jack-in-Irons scrunched up his face into an expression of bewilderment. "JACK SEE RIGHT THROUGH YOU," he said, pointing a log-like finger at her. Then he laughed a booming laugh that gave Mither Mawkins a pain in her head.

Thundering Lord, how can this simple-minded behemoth know I've lost my powers? Then as she raised her willow-wand she saw what Jack was talking about: the hand holding the wand was becoming transparent! Near panic, she looked beneath her cloak and saw that her hands were not the only parts of her that she could see through. "I'm fading away," she whispered to herself. "All of me is going."

A Pixie appeared on her shoulder and spoke in a wee voice: "Come with me, I'll show you to safety."

She flicked the puckish sprite off her shoulder, declaring, "I'm not so foolish as to let meself be Pixie-led. Be gone, twit!"

Jack-in-Irons laughed his rolling-thunder laugh again, but Mither Mawkins ignored him and walked on down the road. There was powerful magic at work, and if she didn't soon discover its cause—and its remedy—she would slip into oblivion and altogether cease to be.

*　　*　　*

She reckoned there was but one chance to come out of this mess with her skin (and the rest of her) intact. *What I should've done to begin with*, she chided herself. She left the ancient road, cut through the wildest part of the forest and made her way to the forbidding barrow of the Will-o'-the-Wisp. Few Faeire folk understood that the Will-o'-the-Wisp was an oracle, and those few were reluctant to consult the mysterious flickering light, *the* ignis fatuus, for fear that its prognostications were actually curses, but Mither Mawkins had learned that the Wispy One's words were truthful so far as you didn't in some way anger the fiery oracle.

As she approached the partial clearing where the huge mound sat like an island amid a dark sea of trees, she heard a shuffling tread and a rustling of leaves behind her. She spun around and shook her willow-wand at the diminutive willow tree that was stalking her. "I've no time for your nonsense, stupid tree," she hissed. "Away!"

Muttering to itself, the uprooted tree shuffled away, its branches dangling in apparent dejection. The witch turned back to the shadowy barrow and knelt at the foot of the earthy mound. Gazing up at the twisted limbs of the dead tree rooted in the center of the mound, she reached into her mouth, grasped the loosened eyetooth and yanked it out. She ignored the pain, and tossed the bloody tooth onto the barrow as an offering.

"A bit of my blood and bone freely given," she said. "In return I would have your wise counsel, if it please you."

A dim light began to flicker near the exposed roots of the dead tree. The low-hanging limbs seemed to move toward her like the gnarled fingers of a giant hand, feeling the air around her. The eerie light shone brighter and gathered itself into a floating ball of cool fire.

Coming from deep within the barrow, the crusty low-pitched voice spoke: "Here you are not. At your home of stone, death from the shadow."

The fire flickered out. Mither Mawkins got to her feet, and started for home on travel-weary legs. She was too tired to even try to make sense of the oracle's words. All she wanted now was to go home—perhaps for the last time.

*   *   *

The sun was setting when she got home. As the day's light waned, so, it seemed, did she; her body was losing its substance, and her cloak felt as if it might at any moment fall off of what was left of her. Her grip on the willow-wand was tentative at best—as was her grip on life.

"I was wondering when you would show up," said the woman emerging from Mither Mawkins' little house of stone. Catkin rubbed himself against the stranger's ankles.

She stopped in her faint tracks, clinging desperately to the willow-wand. The woman coming out of the house was her double. Not a weakened, transparent Mither Mawkins, but one full of life and brimming with self-confidence. "This cannot be!" she cried. "Who *are* you?"

"I am the new you," her double said with a hearty laugh.

They stood facing each other over the witch's stump.

"A spitting image, sure enough," she said. "Except the eyes. Your eyes are full of red fire, just like the Asrai said."

"Dragon-fire," boasted the red-eyed witch. "That's right. I mastered the Dragon Spell."

"Then you've lost your soul." The willow-wand slipped from her grip, With great effort she managed to pick it up with both hands.

"I've lost nothing and gained everything. It's you who has lost."

"I don't understand. How can there be two of us?"

The crimson-eyed Mither Mawkins smiled, showing perfect teeth. "You are nothing but a shadow of the self I was," she explained. "And like a shadow, you will be gone with the last light of day."

"No!"

"Yes, my little shadow. When night falls, you shall be gone forever. But I, Mither Mawkins, shall live for hundreds of years."

The fading witch suddenly remembered the enigmatic words of the Will- o'-the-Wisp, and now she knew their meaning. Tightening her grip on the willow-wand as best she could, she leveled it, aiming its sharp end at her foe's chest, and thrust it with all her remaining might into the heart of the usurper. Blood splattered the stump, obscuring some of the sacred symbols carved into its burnished surface. With her eyes flaming fiercely, the wounded witch staggered backwards, mouthing angry curses.

"*Death from the shadow,*" Mither Mawkins repeated the Oracle's words. "And *I* am the shadow."

The dragon-fire in the dying witch's eyes spread like wind-driven flames, and very quickly the unearthly fire consumed her body.

Turning her back on the burning carcass, the shadow-self of Mither

Mawkins sat down on the bloody stump to watch the last light of day fade from the sky.

"Well, Mither Mawkins," she said to herself, "let's see what nightfall brings."

SPLIT FINGER

Stoked on Smokestack Lightnin' and throbbing like a relentless erection, Split Finger rolls off his bed of spikes and suits up for Opening Day. He snugs his cup over his testicles, having his usual difficulty with the low-hanging lefty, then pulls on his ragged jeans, shrugs into the Kevlar vest, ties on his baseball shoes and slips into his loose-fitting New York Mets windbreaker. After one last snort of Smokestack, he puts his soiled cap on his shaggy head and hangs his bulging gym bag from his left shoulder. He glances at the mirror over the yellowing sink and grins at his ghoulish reflection. Bloodshot eyes in sinkhole sockets. Skin touched with the pallor of death, stretched taut over his dented skull.

"It ain't over till it's over," he says.

Then he picks up the rusty gas can and splashes two gallons of regular unleaded all over his one-room hovel. He stands in the doorway and tosses a lighted match onto the bare wooden floor.

With a WHUUMP the gasoline ignites and the flames quickly engulf the windowless room.

Split Finger steps out of the burning hovel, shuts the door on the leaping flames and saunters along the New York City street, his steel cleats clicking against the sidewalk.

He is stoked, primed and ready-ready-ready-to-uh rock'n'roll.

Finger's Last Opener.

*   *   *

Jools Robinson never saw what hit her. Never even knew she'd been hit. She had just bolted down a jelly-filled doughnut and a cup of black coffee at the crowded counter in Cafe Java, had picked up her briefcase and had gone back out into the muggy morning air, glancing at her wristwatch as her high heels beat a business-like tattoo on the grimy sidewalk. Noting that she was running a few minutes ahead of schedule, she relaxed a little and allowed herself the luxury of actually seeing the world around her. Confident that she wouldn't be late for the morning meeting in the office of her boss, the genius ad-man with the Harvard education, Jools engaged in her hobby of people watching.

New Yorkers were a breed apart, that was for fucking sure. They moved to the beat of a demented drummer, hyped on adrenaline and fear, always on the edge of the fight-or-flight switch. New York City was the crucible and New Yorkers were the distillate of the world's humanity, cooked down to its primal essence and pulsing with stubborn vitality.

You could see it in their eyes, in the expressions that twisted their faces. If you were as practiced at the game as Jools was, you could see at a glance who and what they were. And they were legion. The were fast-track velocity junkies, power-player wannabes, bums-on-the-rush, victims-in-waiting, muggers, addicts, saints, sinners, old-timers, raw beginners, you name it—it was there on the street with you, breathing down your neck or groping your ass. The perverts, the lovers, the street-corner preachers and self-proclaimed prophets. The flatterers, the instigators, the public masturbators.

See it. Name it. Defend yourself against it. That was the nature of the game.

And Jools had to admit, she took perverse pleasure in playing it. It was more stimulating than sex and it cost you nothing—usually. Though it was true that there were some faces you shouldn't gaze into at all. The truly scary ones that, like the proverbial abyss, gazed back into you and touched you where you never wanted to be touched.

Like the creep you just passed, Jools mused. He looked like a refugee from one of those Night of the Living Dead flicks, deathly pale skin and filmy red eyeballs, looking right into you, violating your psychic sanctuary. Wearing track shoes on the street. *Cha-click, cha-click,* cleats making sparks. What a freak!

She shivered and decided to end the game. She looked up at the dirty sky and tried to clear her head. The early sun warmed her face and painted her with murky reddish light. Jools had a thought, one of those minor insights that sometimes flit into your head on the wings of a butterfly, leaving pollen on the delicate petals of your mind: the dome of polluted air over Manhattan was pure compared to the human pollutants moving about on two legs. This cynical insight led her to the realization that the city had indeed hardened the edges of her own humanity, tainted her with its oppressive amorality. She was just one of eight million worms burrowing toward the core of the Big Fucking Apple. And like worms, they were neither good nor bad. The simply *were.*

She tightened her grip on the plastic handle of her briefcase and for the first time in the six years she'd been living here she thought that perhaps she should move back to Virginia. With her connections and her impressive portfolio, she could land a job in the ad game back home, couldn't she?

A red light stopped her at the corner. The snarling traffic in the street in front of her suddenly made her dizzy. She closed her eyes. *I'm not a fucking cow. I don't belong in this herd. They haven't put their brand on me yet. I can leave anytime I want. I can click my heels together and say, "There's no place like home . . . there's no place—"*

Jools Robinson's life ended before she finished her homesick mantra. She was dead before she toppled into the street. But the people who had been standing with her on the corner didn't know that and they seemed to gasp with one breath and recoiled in horror when the beer delivery truck ran over her.

*   *   *

Split Finger sees her fall and the world seems to grind to a breathless halt. Nothing is moving but the falling woman and the growling truck whose front wheel goes over her head like it's a hairy speed bump. The truck driver slams on the brakes, but of course it's too late and the rear wheel, weighted with countless cases of beer, crushes her head as easily as it would a water-filled balloon. No, a *blood-filled* balloon is more like it, exploding with a red, wet splat. Then the braking wheel grinds the bloody skull fragments and brain debris into something you'd never see in a mortar with pestle on your druggist's shelf. As the truck skids and grinds to a stop, the woman's lifeless body twists and flops like a fleshy rag doll, and the rear wheel finally frees the doll's flattened head. Her scalp is largely intact and partially covers the lumpy pool of gore.

Split Finger knew she was the one as soon as he looked into her eyes. Striding along with her briefcase, sexy and important; yet her eyes told a different story. Her eyes said she wanted to be called home. He was happy to oblige, reaching into his gym bag for a brand-new regulation baseball, letting her get to the corner before he went into his wind-up. Knew as soon as the ball left his fingers that he had his best stuff today. Knew he'd just thrown a killer strike.

A hand grabs his arm and a man in a gay suit snarls, "Ya crazy sonofabitch!"

Split Finger snatches his arm away and gets another ball out of his bag. He cocks his arm, holding the ball high and letting the suit see the seamed sphere of death.

"Get him!" someone shouts.

Split Finger picks out a random target. A balding chunk in a sports shirt, chomping a turd-like cigar. The turd-chomper's eyeballs look like they're going to pop out of his skull when he realizes he is the next target, but he doesn't make a move to run. He is frozen by fear to his spot on the sidewalk.

And the ball flies.

THWACK!

It catches Turd Face in the middle of his bald forehead and he drops like a big sack of fresh shit.

Now the real panic hits the street. More screams, much crying, some whimpering, as everyone backs away from him. No one wants to be next.

Split Finger grins.

It's Opening Day and there's no joy in Mudville.

A young cop comes out of the crowd of cowering street people, a gun in his hand and fierce determination in his blue eyes.

Split Finger already has another ball in his right hand, his arm cocked and ready to unload without a wind-up.

"Drop it!" shouts the cop. The spectators draw farther back.

Still grinning, Split Finger hurls the ball. The cop fires his pistol just before the ball—traveling at close to ninety miles per hour—smacks into his throat and crushes his Adam's apple. The cop goes to one knee, clutching his throat, wheezing asthmatically.

The round from the cop's gun hits Split Finger squarely in the chest and knocks him on his narrow ass. Slowly, he gets up, gasping for breath. He feels a dull pain in his sternum but he knows the lead failed to penetrate his Kevlar-spun bulletproof vest.

He leers at the crowd, pulls a fresh ball from his bag.

Everyone is running now, fleeing in desperation.

Split Finger is alone on the sidewalk with the asphyxiating cop. He goes into a full wind-up, every muscle in his body coiling and twisting with dynamic tension, then he releases his best fastball. His aim is true and the ball pops the cop's face. The cop drops facedown on the sidewalk and doesn't move anymore.

Closing his eyes, Split Finger feels the sun on his face and hears the crowd cheering as he steps onto the mound. The scent of freshly mowed grass and damp earth fills him with delight.

God's in His Heaven and Split Finger stands at the center of the diamond, the fastest young gun in the East. The million-dollar arm of the Majors. Pitched a perfect game when he was twenty-one. The world was his baseball.

Until that cloudy day in Atlanta when he stepped up to bat against a wild pitcher with a white "A" on his cap. He was going to bunt a runner to second, but the pitch curved inside and struck him in the temple. That was the freak pitch that knocked God out of Heaven. Then things really went to hell and the ambulance zooming him to the hospital crashed into the rear of a MARTA bus and put him in a coma.

Brain damage, they said. You can never play ball again, they said. They put a steel plate in his head and started feeding him medication. Time passed, and he started medicating himself with street drugs. He tried everything, every type of shit known to man or beast. Then Scratch had turned him on to Smokestack Lightnin' and Split Finger saw the fucking light. He saw himself step onto the burial mound in the center of the shining diamond, saw himself calling the chosen ones home. Of course, he saw a lot of other things he didn't like to think about, but what the hell . . . it's Opening Day.

He opens his eyes. Turns his ballcap around to shield out the sun.

A man coming out of the pawnshop across the street.

Split Fingers laughs with absolute joy.

The dude is carrying a fucking baseball bat.

*   *   *

Mike Bellew had seen enough. The maniac was cutting people down like Kewpie dolls and somebody had to stop him. When the cop went down, Mike reached under the counter for his Louisville Slugger.

When he stepped onto the sidewalk, the freak looked at him and grinned. There was something real fucking familiar about the guy, but Mike couldn't place that cadaverous face. Wishing he hadn't let his wife talk him out of keeping a gun in the shop, he waded into the thick traffic, holding up his free hand to stop bewildered drivers.

The freak started walking down the sidewalk, glancing back and grinning at him. Mike didn't get the sense that the guy was afraid of him or trying to get away. The punk had just wasted an armed policeman. It wasn't likely that he'd be frightened off by a man with a baseball bat. What the hell was he up to?

Mike stepped onto the curb on the other side of the street, stuck two fingers in his mouth and gave a shrill whistle. The freak stopped and turned toward him, still grinning. Thirty feet of empty sidewalk separated them. A few brave souls watched from store windows and doorways.

Mike looked back at the felled cop and calculated his chances of grabbing the pistol off the sidewalk before getting creamed by a fastball. Having seen the power and accuracy of the freak's pitching, he figured his chances were slim to none. And because there was no blood on the freak's jacket, he also figured that the pitcher from hell was wearing a bulletproof vest. It would take a headshot to put him down to stay, and Mike wasn't much of a marksman with a handgun. *What the hell can I do with this bat?* The psycho can dust me off before I get close enough to bash his goddamn skull. Outrage had brought him out of his shop. He'd acted on impulse and now his ass was on the firing line. He'd never felt so naked in all his life.

The freak held up a hand as if to stop Mike's uncertain advance.

Mike stopped. *At least I've got the sonofabitch's attention.* Distant sirens gave him some cause for hope.

The mad pitcher adjusted the bill of his cap, then leaned forward as if reading signs from a phantom catcher.

Then Mike knew what the guy wanted. *He wants to pitch to me! Crazy freaking fuck! Okay, but what happens when I strike out? Or if I get lucky and hit the ball? Will the maniac take his balls and go home?*

Mike had little choice. He had to play out this crazy scenario and keep the freak distracted until the cops arrived.

He took a deep breath and went into his batter's stance. He went through the motions of a few half-speed practice swings, limbering up, just the way he'd done thirty years ago when he played for the Pasco High Pirates in Dade City, Florida. He'd been the best hitter on the team, but that was a hell of a long time ago. And the demon he was facing now was in another league altogether.

Okay, motherfucker, let's play ball.

The pitcher, still leaning forward, nodded his head and went into a smooth windup, just like a pro. Then his arm came forward and the ball came off his fingertips like a shot.

Ready to jump out of the way if he had to, Mike let the first pitch go by. The ball sailed over an imaginary plate, clearly a strike. The ball thumped against the sidewalk somewhere behind him.

Shouted curses and honking horns rose from the stalled traffic. The sirens were closer now, maybe three blocks away.

Mike tapped his bat on the concrete where home plate would be, challenging the pitcher to throw another strike.

The freak pulled another ball from the bag at his feet, pressed the ball between his hands, as if infusing it with energy, then went into his windup.

Mike watched it come. He swung the bat, putting everything he had into it. Catching nothing but air.

Strike two.

He felt himself getting into the rhythm of the "game" now. His muscles were working on memory of long-ago training, but his timing just wasn't there.

The look.

The windup.

The pitch.

He swung.

Pop!

The ball arced off the bat and went almost straight up, then dropped onto the roof of a blue sedan. Foul ball.

The screaming whoop of a siren filled the street, and Mike glanced over his shoulder and saw an ambulance. Where the hell were the police?

The killer pitcher seemed oblivious to everything but the bizarre game of street ball. He went into a fluid wind-up.

And here came the ball. Mike bent his knees and went for it.

Crack!

He caught it squarely and followed through perfectly, turning his wrists over just the way he'd been taught, and he watched the ball soar skyward over tops of nearby buildings, going, going, gone right through a window of a twelve-story office building a block away.

Jesus, I hope nobody was standing by that window, he thought, then looked back at the pitcher he'd just taken "downtown."

The freak tipped his hat to Mike, picked up his gym bag and slung it over his left shoulder, then turned and started walking away.

Mike wiped sweat off his forehead, relieved that the freak hadn't tried to bean him with one of his deadly balls. Exhaust from the idling traffic suddenly seemed very thick, and he thought he was going to choke on it, growing sick to his stomach. Then he saw the black kid sailing down the sidewalk on a skateboard, heading straight toward the freak with the bag of baseballs. When he saw the freak reach into the bag, Mike launched himself down the sidewalk and jogged as hard as he could toward the killer. He ran on the balls of his feet, his Reeboks soundless under the noise of the traffic. Quickly, silently, he closed the distance to his wiry target.

The freak didn't bother with a windup this time. He cocked his throwing arm, ready to cut loose on the kid who had just skated into the killing zone.

Mike Bellew awkwardly raised the bat over his shoulder as he ran. He saw the surprised look on the black kid's face, saw the pitcher's arm fully cocked and ready to shoot forward.

Mike swung early, and the bat made contact with the freak's right wrist just as Mike drew even with him. Because he was off balance, it wasn't a damaging blow, but it did knock the ball out of the pitcher's hand.

The kid crashed into a waste can and tumbled to the sidewalk. The freak had a stunned expression on his face as he watched Mike regain his balance and raise the bat for another hit. He was reaching into the bag when Mike went for the Grand Slam with the Louisville Slugger.

*   *   *

Split Finger knows he's made a big mistake. He should've called the batter home, should've cleaned his clock, but now it's too late. The bat makes a blonde blur in the air and Split Finger's world all at once explodes in a shower of fire-spitting stars.

The steel plate in his head chimes like a gong and his entire body vibrates like a cartoon figure, trembling and shaking violently. The gong hums in his skull and his eyeballs feel like they are going to splatter and run down his cheeks from the force of the vibration.

He's on his back, looking up at the man with the bat. *A little more Smokestack Lightnin'. That's all I need,* he thinks. But it's hard to hear himself think with that fucking gong ringing in his skull and putting all that sonic pressure on the backs of his eyeballs. And he begins to convulse, his legs kicking and thumping and his head bouncing against the concrete and his bladder and bowels betray him and fill his jeans with nasty.

Holy cow!

He brings his shaking hands to his face as the pain becomes unbearable. *Gotta stop that fucking gong.*

*   *   *

Mike watched in horror as the freak began to gouge his eyes, bony fingers with dirty nails digging into the aqueous orbs. The eyeballs burst and his sockets filled with a bloody substance that looked a lot like strawberry jam. Then the freak began to chew his tongue and blood dribbled from the corners of his mouth.

"Da-da-da-da-da-da . . ." he said as he mutilated his tongue.

Mike wanted to look away but he couldn't. He suddenly doubted that this guy was even human.

Three times the freak's body jerked violently, then was still. A final ragged breath hissed out of his mouth.

Mike poked him with the bat.

"Step away," someone said.

Mike turned and saw two cops behind him, their guns drawn.

"Drop the goddamn bat," said one of the cops.

He let the bat clatter to the sidewalk.

"Jesus," said the other cop, getting a better look at the corpse.

"I had to do it," Mike told them. "He was killing people."

A crowd of onlookers had begun to gather around them, and several witnesses backed up Mike's story, pegging him a hero.

Mike gagged at the ammonia-rich stench of foul urine wafting from the freak's body. He swallowed hard to keep from puking. He belched, then said, "Sonofabitch was good, but I got a hit off him. Caught up with an off-speed pitch and it was *gone*. Broke a fucking window too. Ain't that some shit?"

The policemen stared at him like *he* was the freak.

Mike didn't care. As he spoke, he watched the remaining baseballs roll out of the freak's bag, along the cracks in the walk and into the gutter. He squatted down and stared at them. One of them had Hank Aaron's autograph on it. On a whim, Mike picked up one of the balls, reached into his pocket, pulled out his ballpoint pen and signed it dead in the center in the horseshoe of stitches.

Ain't that some shit!

(3-D)

(You see the world through a telescopic lens & you know this otherworldly light never dies. You scope the seedy mole on the Bug Lady's nose as she prowls around the dumpster in search of sacrificial insects whose fate is written on the treads of her secondhand Nike running shoes, though if she ever broke into a run, her heart would break & her aortal light would shatter like a fake diamond. She broke a few hearts in her misplaced youth; now she breaks nothing but wind. Before her fat foot comes crashing down, you raise your sight to the window where the woman with the tabloid tits is on display in Venetian lines & shadows. You put the delicate crosshairs on her left nipple & you can almost see the slow spiral of the Earth & your breath catches in your arid throat. Crosshairs crawl down her belly & kiss the twisting vegetation of her pubic valley. Your damp lashes meet in an involuntary blink & the Venetian blinds slam shut in a quiet explosion of blue.)

*   *   *

Varmit told you you were crazy as a shithouse rat but you were near the end of your homicidal stretch & you knew he was actually the Fourth Stooge, a slapstick throwback to the black & white era of innocent comic violence, so you didn't break his face, didn't even spear his eyeballs with double-pronged victory sign fingers. Just told him to eat shit & die the death of the nobody he was, unmourned, unloved, & unknown to the sybarites of the ruling class. Varmit summoned every bit of his wit & wisdom & said: "Huh?"

(Metal music filters through the scope, Mega Death, you think but it could just as easily be the funeral march of the Dead Kennedys or the mindfucking strains of the Fascist Phallic Fury. Mood music for maniacs. You're in the mood for sounds that don't yet exist—Metaphysical Metal of Heavy Light pure enough to eat away a cerebral knot of cancer & powerful enough to etch visions in the minds of brain-dead dreamers. Sunset winds rise from the dark void, spawning dust devils of city debris, cold, swirling demons who chase winos into phone booths & whip tangles in the wild

hair of the big-assed hooker standing cock-kneed on the corner of Dead &
Gone. A diabolical wind whistles up the tower & claws at your trousers but
you keep your eye to the scope, waiting for the deathblow on Diablo Street.)

*   *   *

They may say it started when you were blue-shifted to the nightmare shift.
There will be much speculation about the sinister effects of your dubious
origin & a few apologists will refer to you as an impotent headline-seeker
deprived of paternal love, while others will simply label you a soulless monster. So many voices howling in the media wilderness! No one will know
what you see through the magic scope—those ghostly auras of enlightened
foreboding which form bas-relief halos around the heads of street people.

*   *   *

(A fish truck stops in front of the market & a family of felines emerge
from the Cat Condo dumpster like furry tumbleweeds in a desert wind.
Such graceful targets you could easily pick off, marksman that you are,
but you're after vermin, after all, feral-faced scavengers with vulture souls.
Like the one you zero in on now—the biggest, nastiest bastard you've ever
seen outside the ghetto.)

*   *   *

Ghetto Red was dead but the light had not yet left his eyes, even though
half his face was eaten away. Varmit took a slug from his pint of dark Port
& declared that Red had never looked better. You turned away from the
bloody site of the scavenger's banquet & puked into a garbage can. Varmit
drained his bottle & his lizard, then staggered back to the street to pan-
handle more change for more wine for lack of anything better to do. You
hung your head in the can & vowed revenge, your garbled voice amplified
by the smelly well of garbage & rat droppings.

*   *   *

(Crosshairs overlay the rodent's head with a 3-D death sign & you squeeze
the trigger. "Rat's eye!" you shout as the rodent's head explodes. A kid on a
skateboard shoots a sidewalk curl, points up at you & yells: "Sniper!" You
scoop the kid's head into the scope & you see a death's-head aura but you
don't squeeze off another round & the panicked kid skateboards into traffic
& is crucified on the evil grill of a delivery truck carrying a cargo of Final
Edition newspapers. You feel a twinge of sadness near your heart, then you
glimpse the kid's scruffy spirit leaving his crushed body & you figure your

twinge is just gas, an angry fart of the future. Faces crowd the scope, faces registering horror, disgust & primal fear. Death, The Divine Comedian, choreographs this sadistic sideshow & his chameleon cloak is sidewalk-gray but the scope allows you to see the grinning bonehead laughing at his own sick joke & trashing humorless humanity with satiric bites. You put the crosshairs on Death's forehead & wonder what would happen if you shot him in the head: A black hole sucking universal light into its perverse density & leaving nothing but the lonely sounds of canned laughter?)

*   *   *

Your fan letters to Lee Harvey Oswald never came back, so you were certain they found him on the other side of nowhere, but Varmit told you the FBI probably had them, had *you* in their files.

(Bethatasitmay, you feel Lee Harvey's deathless eyes upon you & you feel the approval of the Patron Saint of Snipers, so Varmit can go mindfuck himself & die of a terminal lack of imagination. The blue-light special is flashing on Diablo Street & the black-clad SWAT Team deploy with military precision. A disembodied megaphonic voice orders you to throw down your weapon & put your hands in the air & you think: Sure thing, pal, then you'll throw down on me. Can you dig it, Lee Harvey? Gangbusters, man! The paramedics are peeling the kid's remains off the grinning grill of the truck. A TV news crew busting balls for a video scoop zooms in with telephoto lens & you grin & wave & say: "Hi, Mom," though you never had a mother, either. Varmit appears on the street, his shabby coat the same sidewalk-gray as Death's cloak. He pulls a pint from his coat & as he unscrews the cap he mouths "Crazy as a shithouse rat," & you pull the trigger & blow away his bottle of rot-gut wine. You don't hear the barrage of rifle shots, echoing like 1/3 of a 21gun salute. You don't feel the rounds ripping into your skull. You aren't aware of your rifle leaving your hands. None of that can matter now. You watch yourself take flight, see your body falling from the tower & for a brief moment in eternity you feel your own ghost-light caught in the scope of the weapon that was your only possession. Then the sidewalk-gray cloak of Death opens & takes you.)

THE COFFIN

Charlie Kootch was forty feet above ground when it hit him. It came screaming up from gastric depths and struck with a gurgling rumble loud enough to draw a "Was that thunder?" from Woody Wilsap, who stood by the truck below, scratching a hemorrhoidal itch.

Clutching his belly, Charlie groaned and said, "That was me."

"What you get for eating them greasy tacos for breakfast," Woody observed.

Charlie left his handsaw in the groove he'd already cut in the limb overhanging the power line and came down the tree as fast as his cramping gut would allow.

Woody whooped, then guffawed.

They were working on the wooded outskirts of Dogwood, under contract to Georgia Power to trim troublemaking limbs away from power lines. As a seasoned tree climber for Tip Top Tree Service and crew foreman, Charlie felt he was due more respect than Woody was presently inclined to give him, but the urgent business of his bowels precluded a dressing-down of his underling just then.

Grabbing the emergency roll of toilet paper from the truck's glove box, he spied a derelict house in a nearby stand of trees and made for it in a knot-kneed trot, his gut still grumbling.

Satisfied that the house was indeed uninhabited, Charlie stepped up onto the long creaking porch, walked down to the end of it, undid his jeans and pushed them down to his ankles, then squatted with his hindquarters hanging over the edge of the porch boards. So great was his relief that he let go with an ecstatic "Ahhhhh."

In the distance Woody sent up another *whoop-haw-haw* but Charlie scarcely heard it; the thing at the opposite end of the porch had captured his complete attention and made his heart do a little skip-to-my-lu-my-darlin'. He blinked hard and then squinted at the oblong object.

Was that . . .?

Nah, couldn't be.

But sure as hell it was, for what else *could* it be but just what it looked like?

A coffin.

Resting there, pretty as you please on the front porch of this dilapidated house he was using as an outdoor toilet. A frigging coffin. Shaking his head in mystified wonder, Charlie wrapped toilet paper around his hand and wiped himself clean. He hiked up his britches and warily approached the coffin.

Every dumb horror movie he'd ever seen should've prepared him for such an eventuality; he should've known better than to get any closer to the coffin, and he sure as shit *had* to know better than to touch it, much less lift the damned lid.

But lift it, he did.

Very slowly. Because who knew what might be hiding inside? Some wild critter that could launch itself at Charlie and rip his face apart in a furious flurry of teeth and claws. Or a rotten corpse. Or Count-fucking-Dracula.

Yeah, right.

The lid creaked open and Charlie stared into the empty coffin, relieved, yet slightly disappointed that he hadn't found anything interesting inside, something that would've made a good yarn to spin for his wife and daughter. The inside of the coffin was lined with transparent plastic to protect the silk interior and contained nothing but a small silky pillow. This wasn't anything at all like a horror movie, but it *was* a mystery as to what a coffin—-even an empty one—was doing here on the porch of a deserted house.

The mystery required further investigation. Charlie decided to enter the house to look for clues that might solve the Mystery of the Empty Coffin. It was as good an excuse as any to avoid going back up the tree while his bowels were still in turmoil.

The house was a low, rambling building that might've once been a residence or just as easily a backwoods business establishment. Vines had grown up the sides and twisted their way onto the roof. The windows were opaque, hazed with grime, their corners festooned with cobwebs. The front door was dark oak, and when Charlie turned the doorknob it swung open on rusty hinges with an ominous groan. He passed some odoriferous high-octane taco gas and then stepped quickly inside to escape his own fumes.

The first thing he saw was an old wooden wheelchair in the center of the dim and dusty room. The skeleton sitting in it was unreal, supplied no doubt by his creeped-out imagination. Pushed against one of the tongue-and-groove walls was an old gurney with rusty wheels and a dusty black mattress of cracked faux leather. The decaying corpse that wasn't lying on it was there just long enough for Charlie to swear off horror movies for the immediate future. With an imagination as fertile as his, he decided to limit himself to chick flicks until further notice.

The footsteps behind him *were* real, and he spun around with his fists raised in pugilistic fashion, ready (he hoped) to confront any walking corpse or demented mugger.

"Whoa," said Woody. "It's just me, dude. What the hell kinda place *is* this?"

"Maybe it used to be a low-rent funeral home."

Woody strolled about the big room, taking in the odd sights with the same slack-jawed expression he always wore to the funky sideshow of freaks and unnatural oddities when the carnival came every year to Dogwood. His left eyelid had a permanent droop that made him look as if he were perpetually sighting down the barrel of a gun, drawing a bead on some unseen, defenseless creature—though Charlie had never known the man to actually hit anything he ever shot at with an actual gun. The sun's rays had stained his skin, leaving it not with a healthy glow but with a dull and dingy duskiness. His stumpy stature and his unvarnished tan made "Woody" the perfect name for him.

Charlie eyed the door in the rear wall and moved toward it with a modicum of stealth. The door was slightly ajar, inviting exploration of the dark room on the other side.

Behind him, Woody picked up an old cigar box from the floor, extracted a sheaf of yellowed papers, and said, "Bills and burial receipts from the forties and fifties. It *was* a funeral home. Hah! Postcards from another mortuary talking about the new hearse they bought. Spooky, huh?"

"Yeah," Charlie said as he slowly dragged the door open. The room was half the size of the one they were standing in. It contained an antiquated washer and dryer, odd pieces of cheap furniture, and a rusty casket-lowering rig for graveside services.

"Anything interesting?" asked Woody, peeking over Charlie's shoulder.

"Nah, just more funeral home junk."

"I wouldn't mind having one of them old wheelchairs."

"Why would you want that?"

"Why, hell, what if I was to fall out of a tree and break a leg? If I had me a wheelchair I could roll around the house and terrorize the wife."

"She'd roll your ass to the curb in it." Woody's wife Wilma was stout enough to do it, and mean enough to make it stick.

They explored the remaining two rooms, one of which appeared to be a waiting-room with a scattering of flimsy chairs; the other room contained three more closed coffins.

Charlie raised the lid of one and found it identical to the one on the porch.

Same for the next one he opened. But the last one was different. It was a plain pine box of the kind you see in cowboy movies. And it wouldn't open.

"Stuck," he said.

"Uh-oh, bro," Woody said. "That ain't good. Best leave it alone."

"Whaddya talking about?"

"Whatever's in there don't wanna be disturbed. Could be a blood-sucker holding it shut till nighttime. Anemic old dude with vampire fangs going: 'I vant to suck your blud.'"

Charlie pulled out his pocketknife and slid the blade under the coffin lid and tried to pry it open, but it refused to budge. Taking care not to break off the blade, he worked the sharp edge to the right until the lid came unstuck with a dry snap.

Then he lifted the hinged lid.

"Sonofabitch," Woody said when he saw the inside of the empty box. "What the hell is that?"

"Damned if I know," replied Charlie as he studied the strange markings on the underside of the lid and on all the inner walls of the coffin. "What-cha-call-it, hieroglyphics of some kind, I reckon."

"That ain't good. I mean, why would somebody put that shit there? Gives me a bad feeling, dude. That's some kinda hoodoo writing."

"Maybe so," said Charlie, contemplating the cryptic markings. "Go get the truck."

"*What?*"

"Get the truck. I'm taking this sumbitch home."

"No way."

"Hell yes I am." Charlie turned to his friend and grinned. "Halloween's next week, ain't it? I'm gonna scare the bejesus outta Harley. She'll *love* it."

Harley was Charlie's sixteen-year-old daughter who had a passion for all things *horror*. She loved Halloween more than most kids loved Christmas, and Charlie was going to make sure *this* Halloween would be one she'd remember for the rest of her life.

*　　*　　*

His wife Vivian was not much amused when she discovered Charlie in the basement with his funeral-home find.

With Puddles their rat terrier on her heels, Vivian clutched her hand to her bosom as she stared at the thing on top of his workbench. "Jesus, Charlie, that's . . . that's . . ."

"Just what it looks like," he said, beaming. "A coffin. A genuine antique. But wait till you see what's in it."

"I don't wanna see what's in it." Viv took a backward step and appeared ready to turn and flee up the stairs.

"Aw, come on. Be a sport. It ain't gonna bite you."

"*It?*"

"Them."

"*Them?*" She paled.

"The markings. Really weird stuff."

He raised the lid with melodramatic flair, then took her by the arm and gently pulled her to the edge of the coffin. Holding her breath, she peeked inside. Puddles backed away, growling.

"Oh my God, Charlie, what *is* all that chicken-scratch?"

"Dunno. Never seen the like. Kinda cool, though."

"Creepy's what it is." She shuddered. "Where'd you get this thing?"

"Found it on the job in an old building at the edge of town. Used to be a funeral home."

"You *stole* it?"

"Hell, the place was abandoned. Finder's keepers."

"Take it back."

He shrugged. "Maybe I will. After Halloween."

"Char-*lee* . . ."

"I got plans for this beauty."

"Scaring the stew outta your daughter," she guessed, scowling.

"Yeah. And now that you know about it, you're gonna help me pull it off."

"Uh-uh, no way."

"C'mon, it'll be fun." He stared a moment at a particularly dense jumble of markings inscribed on the inside of the coffin's lid and seemed all at once to lose himself in them.

"Charlie?" Viv touched his arm as if to bring him back to the here-and-now.

He picked up an old stepping-stool from the stacked clutter in the basement's corner, set it down beside the workbench and mounted the stool.

"What are you doing?" Vivian's tone turned cold.

"I'm gonna try it on for size."

"You better *not* get in that thing. It's bad luck. Like tossing a hat on a bed."

"Where in hell did you get that? Stephen King? C'mon, this is the *real* world, not some horror yarn."

"Don't do it, dammit."

Puddles barked at Charlie, adding emphasis to Viv's curse.

"Calm down, babe. It's just a wooden box."

Charlie carefully climbed into the coffin and stretched out on his back. He folded his hands sedately across his abdomen and shut his eyes.

"My God, Charlie . . ."

"How do I look?" He flashed a big grin.

"Like the biggest fool in two counties."

*   *   *

A weird dream woke him in the middle of the night. His heart hammered at his chest as if it wanted out NOW. The back of his head was soaked in sweat. His hard-on wanted out more than his heart and was straining against his old Darth Vader pajama bottoms with a cold-blooded vengeance. If Vivian hadn't been snoring softly beside him, he might've flogged the stiff little bishop for its uppity attitude. Instead, he tried to recall the disturbing dream.

He'd been scaling a tall oak with ease when he spied an upright coffin wedged between forked limbs. *What the dickens is a coffin doing in a tree?* Then it dawned on him that he was dreaming, so he figured it wouldn't hurt to investigate. He climbed higher with uncharacteristic recklessness. If he fell he'd wake up before he hit the ground, so he wasn't worried about dying in the dream; he'd never really believed that old wives' tale anyway.

When he reached the pine box, he opened the lid. The hinges creaked with a sound like the caw of an irate crow. He looked into the coffin and nearly took a header when he saw that the coffin was not a coffin at all, but a doorway to a long coffin-shaped corridor, glowing softly with a reddish-purple light. *Why, hell,* he thought, *that's as good as an engraved invitation.* So he unfastened his leather safety-harness and boldly went through the doorway.

And immediately regretted it when . . .

And that was when he woke up with a pounding heart and a raring-to-go hard-on. Whatever had scared him awake was lost back in dreamland.

Damn coffin in the basement's giving me nightmares. Harley would get a kick out of that little backfire.

Then he heard the crow-creak of hinges and knew somebody was down in the basement, messing with the coffin.

"Sonofabitch," he whispered as he crept out of bed. What the hell was Harley doing down there in the middle of the night? Spoiling his best Halloween trick ever, *that* was what.

He slipped down the hallway and glanced into his daughter's room. In the glow of her nightlight he saw that she was in bed, asleep.

Uh-oh. So who's in the basement?

He grabbed the baseball bat from the hall closet, did his best to steel his nerves, and then proceeded with stealth to the basement. He flicked the light switch at the top of the wooden stairs and the basement materialized out of darkness. As he slowly descended the creaky steps, he noted with alarm that the coffin was indeed open, and that the tarp he'd used to cover it was lying in a heap on the cement floor.

Oh Jeez.

He scanned the room to make sure no one was hiding among the shadowy clutter. No one was. He cocked the baseball bat over his shoulder and inched close enough to the coffin to see over the side. Empty.

Of course, it's empty, idjit. You didn't really expect to find anybody in it, did you?

"No," he answered himself.

So that means . . .

"It opened itself," he muttered.

Like a night-blooming flower.

"Blooming idiot," he chastised himself. He was not in the habit of talking to himself, and wanted to nip that sort of thing in the bud.

His eyes fell on a thick tangle of markings etched on the inside of the open lid. He *saw* something there. The longer he stared, the more he saw. Patterns began to emerge. If he looked long enough, he just might be able to decipher the markings' meaning.

He let his eyes roam the jumble of humpbacked crooks and sharp-angled swirls. He opened himself to them and waited for them to speak to him. His eyes fell out of focus and he grew light-headed.

The wind moaned in the backyard trees. The soft rattle of autumn leaves sounded like light rain.

He shivered. He had to pee but he couldn't take his eyes off those enchanting markings. He was too close to understanding what he was seeing to break off and go pee. Charlie Kootch was not one to piss away a revelation. This coffin was here for a reason. He didn't know what the reason was, but he was damned sure going to find out. Whatever it was, it was way beyond a silly Halloween gag.

Something important was about to be revealed.

"Ah," he said. "I know . . ."

And he stepped onto the stool and got into the box. Hugging the bat with one arm, he reached up and shut the coffin's lid.

*   *   *

Dark. Darker. Darkest.

Until those markings started glowing an eerie green.

"Gulp," Charlie said. It was something he picked up from all those comic books he devoured in his youth, and he still uttered it whenever the situation called for a good gulp.

He fought the urge to throw open the lid and jump out of the box like a hatless jack with a coiled spring up his ass.

One good thing: he no longer felt the urge to pee. But he did have to fart. His stomach hadn't been right since that greasy taco attack, and this one was of the variety that would not be denied. He raised his hips, parted his cheeks and gave vent to the foul gas.

"O foul and ugly mists of vapours!" said a disembodied voice.

Charlie said, "Whoa! Who said that?"

"Carrion monster," said the voice—a man's. "Away, you catpurse rascal, you filthy bung, away!"

The voice was coming from inside the coffin. How could that be? There was room but for one body in the box, and that was Charlie's.

"Out, dunghill!"

"Just a goddamn minute," said Charlie.

Spoken as an aside, the voice said: "I will smite his noddles."

"Say what?" said Charlie, clutching his bat with both hands.

"Pig-like, he whines."

"Who are you? *What* are you?"

"O illiterate loiterer!"

Charlie considered the possibility that he was dreaming. Or losing his mind. The lingering stench of his fart told him this was no dream, so that left losing his mind. He *was* lying in a coffin and talking to a . . . a what? A ghost? Not exactly the sign of a sane mind.

"Are you a ghost?" he asked.

"Let's talk of graves, of worms and epitaphs; make dust our paper, and with rainy eyes write sorrow on the bosom of the earth."

"Hey, I asked you a simple question. Yes or no, are you a ghost?"

"You smell this business with a sense as cold as is a dead man's nose."

"*Jesus Christ*, but you're starting to annoy me!"

"You are rough and hairy."

"Yeah and you're jealous 'cause you ain't got a body."

"Misshapen Dick. Whoreson loggerhead. Stuffed cloakbag of guts."

Charlie counted to ten so as not to blow up. He didn't think *he* was crazy but this ghost sounded certifiable. Better to stay cool when dealing with a nutcase. So he said, "So, what, you're haunting a cheap-ass coffin? Most spooks haunt houses. What happened to *you?*"

"They were devils incarnate."

"Who's they?"

"O that she were an open-arse and thou a poperin pear!"

"I don't understand a word you're saying," Charlie said with mounting frustration. "If you're not gonna make sense, just shut the fuck up!"

"Not so loud," said the ghost. "You'll wake *him*."

"Who?"

"That foulest of fiends. All the infections that the sun sucks up from bogs, fens, flats, on Prosper fall, and make him by inch-meal a disease!"

"Here we go again. Look, if you don't start making sense, I'll wake the sonofabitch for real."

"No, no, you mustn't."

"All right then. First off, tell me your name."

"Forgive my rudeness, but I at first thought you were a corpse. Even dead men pass gas."

"Okay," Charlie said, tentatively.

"Had Fate been kinder, you might've heard of John William Boot. I was fairly well-known in my day as a fine Shakespearian actor. If I'm remembered at all now, I'm remembered as a murderer."

Charlie bit his lower lip to keep his mouth silent. Now that his coffin-companion was finally making sense, he didn't want to say anything to send him off on another wordy tangent.

"In my defense, I must say I only killed those guilty of murdering the Bard's golden lines. O how they tortured his sublime language! Theatre in those days was a cut-throat business, marred by petty jealousies and venomous hatred. At any rate, I was hanged for my crimes on a rainy day in 1866, and that black voodoo queen of New Orleans cursed me to my soul."

"Voodoo queen?"

"Marie Laveau, the infamous Creole sorceress. She etched the markings inside this coffin to imprison my spirit so I couldn't do any ghostly mischief. I should've happily gone on to Hell rather than be stuck in this damnable box. But tell me, sir, why are you in here with me when you're not even dead?"

"That's sort of a long story. And not as interesting as yours. There's one thing I don't get. Where's your bones?"

"Once my spirit was trapped in the box, Marie Laveau burned my body and ground my bones to dust. In New Orleans the dead are entombed above ground because the city's below sea-level. That's probably why it's the most superstitious city in the country. And why the snobbish aristocracy paid that bitch handsomely to work her spells. Not just on me but on others as well. Once she'd destroyed my remains she went on to use the same coffin to trap the soul of another nefarious sod. That fiend I earlier mentioned. I'm afraid he's negotiated a partial release with the Devil and makes frequent sojourns in Hell. To what purpose, I know not, though I'm sure it's inherently evil."

"And he's sleeping?"

"In a manner of speaking. *Molting* is probably closer to the truth. He's just down the corridor there."

Charlie remembered the coffin-shaped corridor from his dream and the way the coffin served as a doorway to it. Then the dread that had been gnawing on his mind since Boot explained the etchings suddenly drew psychic blood and he blurted: "Damnation! What will that chicken-scratch do to a living body's soul?"

"Damnation, indeed. Probably just that." John William Boot's ghost chuckled hollowly. "But I don't actually know. There are more things in heaven and earth, Horatio, than are dreamt of in your philosophy."

"My name ain't Horatio. It's Charlie. Charlie Kootch."

"Pleased to make your acquaintance, Mr. Kootch. Very pleased indeed."

"Yeah, well, I gotta be going, pal. It's been real. At least I *think* it has. But I gotta get the hell outta this box before it steals my soul."

"Wait! I have a great favor to ask of you. Please."

"Make it quick. It's getting awfully damn close in here."

"Destroy this coffin. Burn it to ash."

"To free you up, right?"

"Up, down, whichever. But at least it would get me out of here."

"I don't know, man. I don't like the idea of getting mixed up in voodoo shit."

"You already are. It may be the only way to save your own soul."

"Hmm. You may have a point there." Charlie chewed his lip. "Tell me something. How would a man know if he's lost his soul?"

"I imagine you'd feel a deep sense of dislocation. Or perhaps the sensation of being in two places at once. Or you might simply feel a fathomless void where the human heart used to thrive, making you devoid of emotions of any kind. Devoid of your humanity, as it were. This is just speculation, since I can only speak for the dead."

"Yeah . . . okay. I'll light this mother up. But what happens to that other dude? The fiend."

"He's in league with the Devil, so I would imagine it would have little effect on *that* scurvy lord. In short, I wouldn't worry about it."

"Right, then. Catch you later. I'm outta here."

"You will do it right now, yes?"

"It's the middle of the night."

"It's *eternal night* in here. Please. Do it now. Your soul's survival may depend upon it."

Charlie pushed open the lid and climbed out of the coffin. He half expected to see Boot's ghost in the box, but he saw only the witchy markings faintly reflecting yellowish light from the naked bulb overhead.

*   *   *

He set the coffin crosswise on the brick barbecue pit in the backyard, emptied a can of gasoline on the bewitched pine box and set it afire with a kitchen match.

He stepped well back from the blaze, unsure of what might happen when that voodoo gibberish went up in smoke. One thing he was sure of: if the neighbors saw him in his Darth Vader pee-jay bottoms, burning an old-timey coffin in the middle of the night, they would think his trolley had run off the tracks. *Chucklehead Charlie's gone round the bend. Crazy Kootch has screwed the pooch.*

He folded his arms across his bare chest, hugging himself against the chill. The fire didn't seem to give much heat, though the old wood burned very quickly.

Something cold touched Charlie's bare ankle and he jumped away with a yelp. The rat terrier looked up at him and nervously wagged its tail.

"Puddles, how the hell did you get out?"

"You freed me," said the little dog. "I am in your debt, sir."

"Boot? How—"

"I don't know, exactly. The little cur was there and I just slipped inside him. All that open space scared me after my long years of confinement."

"Jesus, man, you can't be in my dog."

"Why not? It's rather pleasant, actually. I think I should like to roam those woods there. What time is breakfast?"

"Get out of my dog," Charlie scolded.

"Be reasonable, Mr. Kootch. I need a little time to adjust to my new-found liberty."

"I can't have you padding around the house, licking your dingus and watching my wife or daughter take showers. That's invasion of privacy. Suppose you got tired of being a dog and decided to possess my wife?"

"I don't believe it works that way. I don't have the power to evict a human soul and take over the body."

"You bullied the soul out of poor Puddles? That's cruelty to animals, by the way."

"He had but a rudimentary soul. Believe me, it's no great loss."

"I never should've let you out of the box. What the hell was I thinking? And you, a murderer. God forgive me."

"I'm no danger to you or your family," said Boot-Puddles. "But I'm afraid you have a bigger problem."

"Great," said Charlie, his bare shoulders sagging. "Now what?"

"The other . . . entity I mentioned?"

"The dude down coffin corridor? What about him?"

"Yes. Well, I'm afraid he's inhabited that brick cooking pit there."

"Hell, I'll just smoke him out."

Boot-Puddles stared at the barbecue pit, his big ears at attention. "I fear you cannot. You see, sir, your cooking pit has become a portal to Hell."

Charlie threw up his arms. "This is a fucking nightmare. Didn't you know something like this would happen? Christ Almighty! My dog's possessed by a murderer and my barbecue pit's a doorway to Hell!" Charlie resisted the urge to kick the little dog.

Then he said, "I'll take a sledgehammer to it. And then I'll take you to the pound. That ought to put an end to this hellish business."

Boot-Puddles whined. "You would pound me with a hammer? O monstrous! A burning devil take you!"

"No, no. The pound is an animal shelter. Where stray dogs and cats go. You'll like it. Three squares a day, free medical care."

"Charlie, what are you doing out here?" asked Vivian.

He whirled around and saw his wife standing there in her pink robe, curlers in her hair and an angry frown on her face.

"Uh, nothing," he said. "Just burning that damn coffin."

"It's three o'clock in the morning, for God's sake."

"Is it?" he said with all the innocence he could muster.

"Who were you talking to?"

"Puddles." He looked around for the dog, but Boot-Puddles was gone. He whistled. "Puddles, here boy."

"Uh-huh," Viv said with mocking skepticism. "Come back to bed. We'll talk about this in the morning. I just don't have the energy right now. You're wearing me out, Charlie."

"Sorry. You go on. I'll be in shortly. If you hear any hammering, it'll just be me knocking down the barbecue pit."

"*What?* Have you lost your mind?"

"Maybe," he said, smiling reassuringly. "But you know what? It's a hell of a lot better than losing my soul."

"I don't know what's got into you, but if you start hammering those bricks in the middle of the night I'll call the police. I'm not joking."

Charlie considered this. He looked at his lovely sleep-disheveled wife in the fading light of the smoldering embers and could see by the fire in her eyes that she was serious as inoperable cancer. "I reckon it can wait till morning," he allowed.

*   *   *

"Hey, Dad, since when did you start sleepwalking?"

"Whaddya mean?" Charlie asked Harley, who was sitting at the breakfast table in a golden shaft of sunlight.

She shrugged with exaggerated nonchalance as she took a bite of a strawberry Pop-Tart, some of the red goo dripping onto her chin. "Mom said you built a fire in the barbecue in the middle of the night for no good reason."

"She did, huh?" He poured himself a cup of coffee. "It's a deep, dark secret. If I told you, I'd have to take away your cell phone."

Harley grinned. "A fate worse than death."

"Exactly." He grinned back.

"Seriously, Dad. What were you doing?"

He decided a half-truth was better than an outright lie. "A Halloween gag gone bad. That's all I can say at this point in time."

"Hah! I *knew* it." She took a big gulp of moo juice, giving herself a cute little milk mustache. "Give it up, Daddybucks. You can't trick me. I'm not a dumb little kid anymore."

"I know, sweetie. But I'm a dumb big kid, so you gotta cut me some slack."

Harley laughed.

Vivian breezed into the kitchen and said, "Your father's not dumb, he just never outgrew his adolescence, and teenage boys do dumb things."

"Hey!" he said, pretending to be offended.

Harley downed the last of her milk, grabbed her schoolbooks, and hurried off to school.

"You're not dressed for work," Viv observed when they were alone.

"I'm taking a sick day."

She shot him a worried look. "You wanna tell me what's going on?"

"Nothing. But I *am* gonna tear down the barbecue pit so I can build a new one."

"There's nothing wrong with the old one and you know it. This has something to do with that foolishness with the coffin, doesn't it?"

"Maybe."

"Well, I *am* going to work, but when I get home, we're going to have a long talk about this crazy business."

"Yes, Mommy."

She flipped him off and stalked out of the room.

He shrugged to himself and polished off his coffee. Then he headed out to the backyard to once-and-for-all close the door to Hell.

*   *   *

He stared at the barbecue pit, the sledgehammer heavy in his hands. He had built it himself when Harley was three, had done a damned good job, too, considering he wasn't much of a stonemason. He fondly remembered how the cute little kid had liked to pretend the thing was her throne and she the Queen of Fairies. It *did* resemble a primitive throne if you imagined its squat chimney was the backrest and the grill the regal seat. How many times had he scolded her for sitting on the soot-blackened throne? He chuckled to himself. Then felt a pang of sadness for the loss of childhood innocence—especially his own.

He put on his safety goggles and stepped up to the erstwhile throne. He didn't stop to consider that he might be nuts, that only a dyed-in-the-wool lunatic would take the word of a talking dog that this mortared brick construct was a portal to Hell. He *knew* that the spirit of the hanged Shakespearian actor could not be the product of his own mind because good ol' Charlie could not have come up with those hifalutin Shakespearian insults. He just didn't have it in him to do it. The only Shakespeare he'd ever seen was Mel Gibson in *Hamlet* and he'd dozed off halfway through and damn-near missed the swordfight at the end.

He cocked the sledgehammer over his shoulder. Started to swing it, but then didn't. *What if,* he wondered, *I end up making the opening to Hell bigger by knocking down these bricks? So big it can never be closed.*

"Shit," he said. "I should consult a professional."

Preacher Bob came to mind. The Bible-thumping minister of The Church of Holy Christ was always spouting off about the End Times and the coming of the anti-Christ. Sure, he was probably a few bricks shy of a load, but the man knew his holy shit, sure enough. Maybe he could pray over the site and consecrate the ground. Trouble was, Preacher Bob probably wouldn't believe the story of the talking dog. Charlie didn't remember any talking dogs in the Bible. But if he substituted a burning bush for a talking dog, that just might do the trick.

"How now, coz," said the rat terrier, appearing out of nowhere at Charlie's feet.

"Where the hell have you been?" Charlie lifted the goggles to his forehead.

"I was making the beast-with-two-backs with that poodle across the street," said Boot-Puddles. "Wanton little bitch, she was. Though not much for conversation."

"Don't run off without telling me. Remember you're the dog and I'm the master."

"I am not your wag-tail, sir." He spoiled his indignant posturing when he turned to gnaw at an offending flea feasting on his hindquarters. He stopped chewing long enough to add, "You're the dogsbody, not I."

"Whatever," said Charlie. "Look, are you sure about this being the portal to Hell? I don't wanna knock it down if you're not a hundred percent. My wife already thinks I'm nuts, but I can't have this thing in my backyard, especially if that . . . that thing's in it."

Boot-Puddles said, "O, the blood stirs more to rouse a lion than to start a hare!"

"Don't start with that Shakespeare shit. Talk plain English."

"*Plain* English!" The dog's eyes bulged.

"Fucking-A, Jack."

"Whot, *whot?*"

"How now, brown cow," Charlie said with raised voice, "I could have you put to sleep, you know."

Boot-Puddles bared his teeth and growled.

Charlie growled in frustration, suddenly sensing there was no time to consult Preacher Bob. He positioned the goggles over his eyes again, stepped up to the barbecue pit and swung the hammer. The solid blow knocked a chunk of brick from the chimney and sent an electric current up his right arm.

"Don't do that," said the dog. "You might anger the fiend."

Pausing to rub his tingling arm, Charlie said, "What's he gonna do? Come out and kick my ass?"

"I don't know, but I *do* know you shouldn't poke a stick at one in league with the Devil."

"How 'bout if I cement it shut? Wouldn't that seal it up and keep Hell in its place?"

"I doubt it."

"So you don't really know. You're just farting in a whirlwind, same as me." Charlie rolled his eyes heavenward. "Lord, I wish I'd never found that damn coffin."

The air suddenly changed, turning so unnaturally cold that Charlie's teeth started chattering. Then the air seemed to tremble like a thin curtain fluttering in an ill wind. Charlie didn't want to see what was on the other side of that curtain.

"You've roused the thing," said the dog. "Fie!"

"Fo fum," said Charlie, cocking the sledgehammer over his shoulder.

"Come on then, cocksucker. No more fucking around. You want some of me? Step out here and let's see what you got. This is *my* house, by God. *My* yard, and I want you off my property." Then he remembered that catchy chant from *The Exorcist*, and decided now would be a good time to employ it. "The power of Christ compels you! The power of Christ—"

He broke off his moronic chanting when the knockout redhead shimmied out of the little brick chimney and fixed him with fierce green eyes and a beatific smile. The fact that she was naked as a jay-bird was less startling than was the fact that her feet were cloven hooves.

"Uh-oh," he said, and dropped the hammer.

Boot-Puddles whined, and then tore off into the patch of woods behind the house.

"Well?" said the woman, licking her pouty lips with an impossibly long and obscenely red tongue. "You summoned me."

"No I didn't. I was ju-just . . ." He shrugged and backed away.

"You mustn't lie to me," she said in a smoky voice.

He sprouted a murderous hard-on. It wasn't her perfectly-formed burgeoning breasts or the wild thatch of crimson pubic hair so much as it was the cloven hooves that so strangely aroused him. He couldn't keep himself in check.

She stepped down from the chimney and onto the iron grill—the seat of the Fairy Queen's throne. Her perfect body was covered with downy hair of deep scarlet.

Clasping his hands in front of his crotch, where his meat-rocket was nearing blast-off, Charlie said, "I'm not lying. Why would I summon you? I don't even know who you are. *What* you are. Can't a guy knock down his own barbecue pit?" *Without calling up a naked babe from Hell?*

A snarling dog barked in the near distance. Charlie's teeth chattered so hard he feared his fillings would fall out. He pushed his goggles up to his widow's peak for a clearer look at his backyard visitor. There were two flesh-colored bumps on either side of her forehead which were either humongous moles or stunted horns. *Baby* horns.

"You mustn't lie to yourself," she said in that smoked, seductive voice that was driving Charlie mad with unnatural lust. "You summoned me, I came. What do you desire of me?"

"Gulp," said Charlie.

The rat terrier came tearing around the corner of the house, running faster than Charlie had ever seen him run. A big black mongrel was in fevered pursuit, threads of thick saliva flaring out like jet-trails from both corners of its mouth. Boot-Puddles said something as he ran by, but Charlie wasn't sure what it was. It sounded like, "Bugger me."

"Christ on a crutch," said Charlie, turning back to the redheaded temptress. "This is all too much. You wanna know what I desire? Fine. I want my dog back the way he was. Dogs aren't supposed to talk. That's why they're Man's Best Friend, 'cause they don't talk back. You with me so far? I want my barbecue pit to *be* a barbecue pit, not a doorway to Hell. Which means I want you to go back to where you came from and leave me alone. Got all that?"

Again that obscene tongue flicked out; this time its forked tip touched the little dimple in her chin. Charlie shuddered.

"Those are wishes, not desires," she said, stepping down to the ground.

A slimy head with two inflamed eyes rose out of the chimney and looked at Charlie. Its face was covered with ripe boils and warts, its lips sewn together with viny black sutures.

"What the hell is *that?*" Charlie pointed at the hideous head.

"The tortured soul that opened the way for me. Pay him no heed."

"I know who you are!" Charlie blurted. "You're the Devil! Father of lies!"

"Hardly," she said with a sly laugh. "I am one of his many concubines."

"The hell you say," said Charlie.

"I know well the desires of mortal men," said Satan's concubine, staring at the bulge in his jeans, "and how to satisfy them."

"Yeah, and I know how that would turn out. I'd lose my soul and be damned to Hell—all for a half-ass handjob."

She laughed. "But you are already damned."

"Like hell I am." Charlie heard the lack of conviction behind his own desperate bravura. He glanced at the slimy wart-faced fiend's mug sticking out of the chimney and wondered if he would end up looking like that poor son of a bitch. *No.* He would not accept such a fate. If he had to go down, he would go down fighting. He did his best to stiffen his resolve and said, "*Hell* no, it ain't over till it's over, bitch. I didn't do anything wrong. All's I did was crawl into a coffin. You ain't getting my soul for that. Not without one hell of a fight."

She gave him a quizzically amused look. He stole a glance at the sledge-hammer at his feet and wondered what it would do to her head. She flashed him a crinkly smile. Between the smile's lines Charlie read a warning, a dare: *Go ahead, make my millennium.*

She said, "Men always think violence will solve their problems. I promise you, it will not help you now."

Charlie's shoulders slumped. "What exactly *is* my problem? Other than getting rid of you and your pimple-headed pal Slimeball."

"Look at your shadow," she said.

This caught him off guard, and of course he had to look. The morning sun was bright in the cloudless sky, and his shadow should've been dark and distinct, but it wasn't. It had the faded reddish tint of the moon in full eclipse, and its shape was ill-defined, amoeba-like. A chill crawled up his spine on skeletal fingers. Finally his killer erection began to flag.

"Yeah, so?" He tried to sound unconcerned.

"You lost much of your soul in the necromancer's box. And then you burned it." She chortled.

He thought he was beginning to understand. "How do I get it back?"

"Desire."

"Jesus, lady, I *do* desire it. I can't be without a soul. Tell me what to do."

"Since you've demonstrated desire for something above the carnal, you shouldn't have too much difficulty. All you have to do is go in there and retrieve it." She pointed at the brick chimney.

"Go down the chimney?" Charlie stared blankly.

The temptress smiled lasciviously.

"What about him?" He nodded at Slimeball. Charlie didn't want to be at close quarters with *that* warty guy.

She snapped her fingers and Slimeball did a speedy Whack-A-Mole disappearing act.

Without pausing to think about his actions, Charlie lowered his goggles over his eyes, climbed onto the grill, hoisted himself onto the chimney and went in feet-first, yelling: "Geronimo!"

*   *   *

He woke in claustrophobic darkness. His body ached and he remembered having a wild-ass dream in which he'd been grappling with . . . *something*. *Some*where.

He tried to sit up but he bumped his head on the coffin lid.

He panicked, threw open the lid and jumped out of the box.

Puddles was on the basement floor, licking his furry balls.

"Jesus, what a fucking nightmare," said Charlie, feeling a little like Dorothy just back from Oz. "It seemed so real!"

"How now, coxcomb," said the dog with a halfhearted wag of his tail. "We are such stuff as dreams are made of . . . and all that rot."

A sickly shadow slid across the floor and dashed out the basement door. Charlie reacted with alacrity and ran off in pursuit of his unmoored shadow, the dog yapping at his heels.

It was not a merry chase. He ran beyond the limit of endurance, the run becoming a loping slog, and in the end it was impossible to know if he was chasing his shadow or if his renegade shadow was dragging him down a haunted pathway to Hell.

AT THE EDGE OF THE WORLD

I, Hexus, boy, beast and mad prophet, do swear these words are true. As I can no longer hold a stylus, I am dictating my account to Jarl the eater of souls. My sketchy bit of history, like our world, may not long survive, but I'm compelled by my hybrid nature and dire circumstance to have it set down in writing in order to leave this little scrap of myself behind.

Here, then, is my story.

*   *   *

The holy ladies came at the red of the sun. I was playing closer to the cliff than I was supposed to, so I saw them floating along the narrow mountain path below me like ghosts in their white robes. The three ladies walked in front of two big men hauling a cart with a single body in it. The dead one was wrapped in a yellow winding sheet, so I knew it was somebody important they were bringing to the soul eater. I ran back to our stone house to tell my mother they were coming. We didn't get many visitors of consequence there at the edge of the world, so I was thrilled by their coming.

I threw open the door and charged into the house. Mother was stirring a big pot of soup over the fire and her smock bore spatters of her labor. She scowled over her shoulder at me and said, "Go back and wipe your feet, Hexus."

I walked backwards to the doormat, blurting, "The ladies are coming."

Her scowl deepened. "What ladies?"

"The Whiteskins. And there's a corpse cart. The dead one's wrapped in yellow!"

She hung the long metal spoon on the hearth hook and brushed the front of her smock with her coarse hands. "You calm down now. The good ladies should not be disturbed by a rambunctious boy. And keep your distance. I'll not have you spellbound for getting underfoot."

"Da says there's no such thing," I said, tempting her cookfire temper.

I knew she wouldn't hesitate to whack the crown of my head with her spoon—or worse, a ladle—but excitement limbered my tongue and I went on: "He said the ladies just like to scare people with their witchy ways so they won't be bothered. He said—"

Her hand shot out and smacked my jaw. It stung so, I wished she'd used the spoon. "Don't say such things!" she scolded. "You want them to hear you? They can, you know. They have ears like wolfhounds."

"But Da—"

She struck me again. "Hush. Now go find your da and tell him of the ladies. He'll need to get the temple ready for the ceremony."

Rubbing my jaw, I turned to the door. None of my excitement had been knocked out of me.

"Hexus?"

"Mum?"

"Make sure you're back before full dark."

"I know," I said, then hurried out to find Da. The sun was a deeper red now as it neared the wound in the sky. The people of the hamlet at the foot of our mountain always said that one day the great rip would eat the sun and end the world, but Da said the ignorant and superstitious should learn to hold their tongues. No one alive knew what the great tear was, what it meant or what caused it, but Da thought he knew what it wasn't.

I found him digging a hole behind the temple. His shirt was off and his wiry muscles glistened with the sweat of his labor. Since the coming of the xenolope, he'd dug a lot of these pits in hopes of catching the phantom beast. Once the hole was deep enough, he would cover it with a tarp, then sprinkle loose dirt and dead leaves over it so that the xenolope would think it was solid ground and step into the pit. Because the ruse hadn't worked yet, I suspected the creature was too sly to be thus fooled, but I wouldn't say so to Da. He would hear it as an insult and think I thought the xenolope was smarter than he.

He saw me and leaned on his shovel. "You should be inside," he told me. "It's almost dark."

"Mum said I should tell you the ladies are here. The Whiteskins. And they've got a yellow one in the corpse cart."

He held his tongue but I could see by his expression that he wanted to heap curses on the holy ladies. "Very well," he said. "I'll wake the old man and ready the instruments. You go back to the house and help your mother. We'll be expected to feed them all."

I hesitated there at the pit's edge. "Da? What does the xenolope look like? You said you would tell me."

"Not now, Hexus. I have much to do. Run along."

I did as he said and ran back to the house. I paused at the door and looked up at the torn sky. I liked to gaze into it at that time of day. When the sun sank below the horizon and darkness began to settle on the land, the great gash would glow with violet light and sometimes I could see things moving within the long slit. When I first told Da what I saw, he said it was only my mind making images the way it does when you see familiar shapes in clouds. Though I kept my thoughts to myself, I thought he could be wrong about that. The moving shapes I usually saw resembled those living things I'd seen in a drop of water under the old microfier in the temple's room of artifacts. Was it my imagination that I could feel the pull of the mysterious rip in the sky? Was it imagination that made the little hairs on my arms stiffen whenever I felt that those shapes wanted to draw me to them and consume me? No, the sweet terror I felt when gazing into that gash was well beyond any terrors precipitated by imagination. Some said it wasn't a rip at all, but a doorway to an alien world. I thought it might be both.

When I touched the door of our stone house, I remembered that I hadn't fetched the evening's bucket of water, so I turned and ran to the waterfall a thousand paces behind the house. Dusk hadn't yet thickened to full dark, so I wasn't much worried about being taken by the nocturnal xenolope. I filled the wooden bucket and started home with it. The holy ladies had arrived in front of the temple, and the two muscular men with shaven heads were wresting the yellow-wrapped corpse from the cart. Da had lit the temple's torches and stood ready to greet the priestesses. I took the bucket of water into the house, sloshing only a little on the floor, and told my mother that Da needed me at the temple. I wasn't in the habit of telling such easy lies, but the corpse in the yellow winding sheet drew me like a filament of iron to a powerful magnet.

I kept to peripheral darkness deepened by torchlight and made my stealthy way to the room of artifacts so I could spy on the ladies and see some of the communion ceremony. I hid there amid the ancient devices, odd gadgets and mysterious appliances—most with the rotting black tails that had once drawn energy from some magical power grid—and waited for the old man to come out of his austere lair and partake of the flesh of the eminent corpse.

Squatting behind a boxy thing with a glass front, I avoided looking at the reflection of the small phantom's face, lit by the eerie torchlight from the adjoining room. It wasn't long before Jarl sat himself at the stone table, the silver implements laid out before him. The High Priestess spoke the invocation in the language of the dead, then the two male servants set the corpse on the table and unwrapped the winding sheet, revealing a long-limbed male with pallid flesh and a long beard. His penis was impaled with the traditional chastity rod, as was the case with all males who served the holy ladies.

"This man is Prophet Wolfer," said the High Priestess, her words ponderous with gravity. "He was killed by an assassin sent by the Invisibles of the north. Prophet Wolfer's visions of things to come must not be lost to us. In the name of the Mother Most Holy, I charge you, Brother Jarl, with task of preserving this prophet's wisdom. Will you eat of his flesh and consume his eyes?"

Naked save for his white loincloth, Jarl responded gravely: "I will, Mistress. As you honor me, so shall I honor the bounty you have placed on my table."

Wearing his scarlet ceremonial robe, Da came forward and anointed the corpse of the prophet with the sacred oil of queensdrake. If consumed by itself, the oil would cause nightmarish hallucinations; when consumed with some of the flesh and the eyes of the dead, it would allow the essence of the deceased to survive in the mind of the consumer. In this case, the memories and visions of Prophet Wolfer might later be accessed by putting Jarl in a trance and questioning him. Da had told me that it was never a sure thing, but that more often than not, it did work. Jarl the Sensitive was indeed a repository of dead souls, but this was the first time in my life he'd been honored with the remains of a true prophet. I watched with queasy curiosity as he picked up his sharp implements and began to slice slivers of raw flesh from the corpse and eat them. With her long fingers, the High Priestess made the sign of reverence for the Holy Matron, then turned and led the other two ladies from the ceremony room. The two servants remained to witness the consumption of the dead prophet, and Da followed the ladies outside, his scarlet robe billowing behind him.

I knew I had to run through the darkness to beat them back to our house, but as I shifted my cramped legs to get up, my right foot struck a stack of artifacts behind me, altering the weight of the pile, and my foot was caught fast. I tried in vain to free it; I was caught like a rabbit in a trap. I twisted my body around and pushed against the stack of antiquated and useless gadgets with my other foot, trying to take enough weight off the trapped one to free it, but it was no good. The more I struggled, the heavier the stack became, and my ensnared foot began to throb with pain. If I cried out for help, the two muscular servants could easily free me, but then I would be caught spying on the sacred ceremony. Not wishing to be so doubly caught, I kept quiet and continued to struggle for my foot's freedom. My eyes filled with tears of anger and ache. Da would severely punish me for this intrusion, but what would the Whiteskin witches do to me? What if they *did* have the power to curse me or weave some horrible spell about me? Panic fed my anger and I delivered a violent kick to the stack with my unfettered foot. The little tower of artifacts toppled and crashed to the floor. I snaked my foot out and jumped up to run for darkness before I was seen.

Then I heard the scream.

I froze in my dusty tracks and looked through the doorway to the ceremonial room. One of the servants was flying through the air. The other one had drawn an arc from the sheath on his hip and was swinging it at a large, dark shape before him. The thing appeared to be a glowing shadow. Its shape was reminiscent of those powerful creatures that roamed the woodlands thousands of years ago, furred beasts whose roar filled hunters' hearts with fear. But this thing was transparent, as though it was not entirely in our world. When it effortlessly swatted the armed servant to the floor, I knew I was looking at the shadowy xenolope.

Jarl ran screaming from the temple. Both servants were down, apparently unconscious. The xenolope reared up on two legs over the stone table, then came down on the body of the dead prophet and began to eat of it. I don't know if it was fear or fascination that held me there, but I remained crouched in the shadows of the room of relics, watching the meat of the corpse disappear piece by sundered piece.

The mind thinks strange thoughts at such times, and the thought that came to me was that the holy ladies would hold Da responsible for this blasphemy and banish us from our mountain and send us into the wastelands of the south. Perhaps it takes such strange thoughts to give one the presence of mind to act precipitously in time of danger. Act I did. I ran out of the room of artifacts, past the feasting beast and out the temple doorway. I closed the heavy wooden doors and secured them with the iron bar. I didn't know if the barred doors were strong enough to hold the xenolope inside, but I thought trapping the creature was the only way I might redeem myself in the eyes of my family and the Whiteskins.

I raced around the temple and similarly barred the back entrance. It was then that I realized I had trapped the unconscious servants inside with the monster and might be held responsible for their deaths, were they to be eaten.

Da came running toward me, calling my name. He was brandishing his arc, though I knew he would be no more effective at subduing the alien beast than the two servants had been.

"It's the xenolope!" I shouted. "I've shut it up inside! It's eating the dead prophet."

The three holy ladies drew up behind him, their long white robes making it seem that their feet didn't touch the ground; at this point, I was not at all sure that it was an illusion. My mother and Jarl were not among them.

"Good boy," said Da.

I saw the fear in Da's face then. He glanced at the ladies, then made toward the barred door. I felt overwhelming pride for him then. Frightened though he was, he was going into the temple to fight the beast, fully prepared to give his life.

"Wait," said the High Priestess. "If the beast has eaten of the prophet, it must not be harmed. We must subdue it."

"It ate most of him already," I blurted, anxious to keep Da from harm. He glanced at me with relief, then sheathed his radiant arc.

"Are my footmen within?" asked the High Priestess. Her eyes were aflame as she looked at me, yet her face bore an expression of serenity.

"Yes, mum . . . good lady. I don't know if they're dead."

The two lesser priestesses had closed their eyes and appeared to be in meditative prayer. The High Priestess reached within the folds of her white robe and withdrew a small black box, which she cupped in the palm of her long-fingered hand. "Unbar the door," she told Da.

Without hesitation, he lifted the iron bar and threw the door wide. The High Priestess stepped forward, but Da touched her shoulder as if to restrain her, touched the handle of his arc with his other hand and said, "I should go first."

"No," she said. "You must stay behind me when I activate the elicitor."

What manner of magic was this? I wondered. Was the little box in her hand a witchy charm to neutralize the beast? It resembled something from the artifact room, one of those non-functioning relics whose purpose had been lost with so much of our history and had no value now except as a dubious link to a dark era of the past.

We followed her into the temple's rear entrance. Da made no move to stop me from tagging along. She moved with the regal grace one would expect of a High Priestess. We trailed her through the room of artifacts and on into the ceremonial room where the xenolope was gnawing the bones of the prophet. The creature appeared more substantial now, and I wondered if its eating had caused it to become less transparent and more a part of our world.

The High Priestess raised her arm and pointed the palm-held box at the beast.

The xenolope tossed the bloody skull of the prophet at her feet and reared on two legs. Da drew his arc and held it at the ready.

An amber ray of light shot from the little box, then the beam fanned out and painted the great length and breadth of the beast. The creature seemed frozen within the eerie sheath of light.

"Brother Wolfer," the priestess called. "In the name of the Holy Mother, I compel you to speak."

The xenolope opened its great maw and emitted a whining growl. The grumbling was continuous, as if the thing were trying to speak to us. Then, within the guttural sounds made by the xenolope's vocal cords, the distorted voice of a man echoed as from a distant mountaintop: "Mistress . . . I am here . . . to serve . . ."

The High Priestess said, "You must speak your prophecy and tell what you have seen. Quickly!"

The growling of the beast took a tone of mournfulness as the prophet's voice spoke in odd harmony within it. "I have seen . . . the world in conflagration. Our end will come from the place . . . where time is born . . . where space knots and bends back upon itself . . . and our world and all of heaven must conform . . . to its shapeless shape. When the stars spiral . . . and ether's strings bend and sing . . . we will be consumed. The destruction . . . of creation . . . will be—"

The fanned cone of light from the high lady's hand flickered and died. She shook the little box and jabbed at it with her thumb, but the magical light didn't reappear. Freed from its photon imprisonment, the great beast dropped to four legs and charged forward, knocking the High Priestess aside and dodging Da's slashing arc. The monster was coming straight for me. I had no time to react. I was of a sudden in the air, in the mouth of the xenolope. My right shoulder and underarm were locked in its toothy vice, and the beast carried me through the door and into the night.

Darkness rushed by us as we fled. The creature's mouth was neither hot nor cold, so I was sure the warm wetness trickling from the tender flesh of my underarm was my own blood rather than my sweat or saliva from the monster's maw.

"Hexus!" I heard Da shout after me. He was pursuing us, but I held no hope of being rescued from the otherworldly beast. I knew my short life on this world was about to come to an early end.

*　　*　　*

The stars were unusually bright, as was the quarter moon in the northern sky. Watching the heavens wink down at me, I became detached from my peril. I had made a not-so-conscious decision to enjoy the last few moments of my life. I looked at the stars and imagined my soul soaring among them for eternity (as souls did in some of the half-remembered stories of old). The waterfall roared pleasantly on my left, and cool spatters kissed my bare arms and legs. I thought of the last bucket of water I'd carried to the house and imagined my parents dipping from it and thinking of me. Then the sound of the falling water faded away behind me, and the only sound was the chuffing of the xenolope as it lugged me through the night.

The world dropped out from under us and we fell into the earth. My head thudded against the wall of the pit and the beast released me. I lay there, stunned and confused. The xenolope paced within the confines of the deep hole Da had dug, but it didn't step on me. It dawned on me that the beast was finally caught, but I was afraid it would eat me before Da could find us and kill it.

"Don't eat me, don't eat me, don't eat me," I chanted. The stars winked behind scudding clouds. I looked at the paling quarter moon and thought about those old bedtime stories of men walking on it. From my tenuous position in the bottom of the pit, the old myths seemed less than fanciful and I began to believe that men had indeed once capered on old Luna. In fact, I *knew* they had. I felt as if a hole had been opened in my skull and a wealth of knowledge poured into my brain. What was happening to me? Was my head going to burst like a melon with the sudden influx of information? Many of the things I all at once knew to be true were beyond the ken of man, so how could I know them? Then I knew that too. The xenolope's teeth and tongue had been coated with a residue of queensdrake oil, and when its teeth sank into my arm and shoulder, some of the oil entered my bloodstream, along with remnants of the prophet's cellular tissue and minuscule bits of the xenolope's own coded matter. Like an eater of souls, I had absorbed some of the essence of Prophet Wolfer and of the beast itself—though it wasn't dead. The memories and perceptions of the xenolope were too exotic for my brain to make much sense of them.

"Why would I eat you?" the xenolope asked, not with its mouth but with its mind. Its eye slits appeared empty, yet recessed in that emptiness was the same violet glow I'd seen within the rip in the skin of the night sky.

I stammered, "Yu-you won't hu-hurt me?"

"No. I do not eat living things. Only dead."

"Then why did you take me?" I asked with my voice, though I could've done it just by thought. Somehow, the creature was able to translate its thoughts in such a way that I could grasp their meaning.

"Because the one who sees is within me now and I see what he saw.

The dead one."

"You mean the prophet."

"Yes. Now I know why I am here."

The xenolope's voice in my head made me feel warm and trusting. "You came from there, didn't you?" I pointed at the glowing rent in the night sky. "You fell through it!"

"Yes, something like that."

My mind was racing to process my newfound knowledge. "And you're . . . a scout, an explorer."

"I am a seeker of knowledge. I and others like me have been trying to fathom the meaning of the meeting of our two worlds. Yours and mine."

"But why did you take *me?*"

"Because you are young and malleable. You may survive the crossing of the bridge of worlds." The creature looked longingly at the great gash in the heavens.

"You're taking me there?"

"Yes. It must be so. In the interest of science."

I understood that his "science" encompassed much more than what we lost-civilization humans meant by the concept. For the xenolope science was inextricably bound with religion and philosophy. In its world, science was indistinguishable from imagination. The xenolope could imagine worlds and make them manifest. To my youthful way of thinking, that made it a god. I was conversing with a god from beyond the heavens! And it was going to fly me through the rip in the sky and into the realm of gods.

I suddenly felt a chill having nothing to do with the night air or the coolness of the pit. "Those things the prophet saw . . . Is our world really coming to an end?"

"Yes. He cast his eyes into the stream of time and saw what is to come. Such change is immutable. But we may be able to guide the change and shape what is to replace the old. We will know more once I get you back to my world. There is much we don't know. Until the nexus opened, we did not know we could cross into your world. We knew it existed, but we thought it impossible to transverse dimensional boundaries. It is all more wondrous than we ever imagined."

I heard approaching footfalls and the faint babble of excited voices. Da and the others were coming. "My father will try to kill you," I warned. "He thinks you're a monster."

The xenolope rose up on its hind feet and leaned against the wall of the pit as though listening to the noisy approach. Its skin was at once transparent and reflective; though I could see through it, I also saw the stars of the night sky reflected in it. I remember thinking that I was beholding a true being of the cosmos, and I was awed by the mere fact of its existence.

"He has a weapon, yes?"

"Yes," I answered. "It's an arc. It drinks and stores energy from the sun and discharges it when it strikes. It can cut through stone after a sunny day."

"Then we must go now. I do not wish to harm your progenitor."

"Hexus!" Da called from just beyond the lip of the pit.

I answered on reflex. "Da! I'm here. I'm all right! I've made friends with the xenolope! Don't hurt it!"

"Hexus!" he shouted once more. I heard fear in his voice.

The xenolope whirled round and encompassed me with its massive arms. I felt coolness akin to a morning wind on wet skin. Then an oily slit opened in the creature's torso and it drew me inside and closed behind me. I couldn't breathe, but I knew no terror. Being swaddled like a babe inside the creature was oddly comforting, and after a few moments, I could breathe again. I could see only blackness, so what happened next I learned later from those who witnessed it.

The xenolope leapt from the pit in the earth and my father struck its belly with his arc as it sailed over him. The weapon's discharge sparked with a thunderous roar and the creature's entire body was illuminated with a blinding white light as it rose higher into the night sky (and here I was rendered unconscious). Higher and higher it soared toward the great glowing rent in the heavens. Da and the holy ladies watched as the xenolope receded, becoming a dot of light, a shooting star without a fiery tail. Then it was lost to their sight. Da saw the empty pit and assumed I had been eaten by the beast. His wail of anguish was interrupted by the startled cry of the High Priestess. She pointed skyward and Da looked up to see that the opening in the sky had become a cauldron of molten liquid, bubbling and roiling. He later said that it looked like a misshapen sun, though a sun without heat.

The holy ladies fell to their knees and began to tear their hair. Da stared into the cauldron until its fire faded and the great rent returned to its usual magnitude. From the glowing slit a star fell toward the earth. Da was the first to see that the falling star was the xenolope returning, floating as slowly as a leaf falling from an autumn tree. It landed with a soft thump in front of the temple, and Da ran toward it, intending to strike again with his arc, but when he reached the beast he thought it was dead, so sheathed the weapon. Assuming that my masticated remains were in the beast's belly, my father dropped to his knees and began to say my name. My mother joined him and wailed in despair.

I awoke in thick darkness and heard my parents' lamentations. To my astonishment, I was hearing them with the xenolope's auditory organs. I made to open my eyes, but it was the xenolope's eyes that opened, and I saw Mum and Da kneeling beside me.

Seeing that the world was not yet ending, the holy ladies recovered their wits and came to stand over my sprawled form. "It lives," said the High Priestess. She stayed my father's arc-wielding hand. "We must entreat the prophet to speak again," she said. She used her little box again and illuminated my huge body. Just as I was finding that I had motor control over the alien body, the dancing, fanning light from the lady's box paralyzed me. She bade the prophet to speak. His presence made itself known as if in a back crevice of my mind and I knew his madness. I knew that the visions he'd had of the future had loosened his grip on the material world and sent his mind to the brink of sanity and beyond. I fought him for control of the xenolope's thick vocal cords. A groaning roar escaped our mouth. "Da . . ." I managed to say. "Mistress . . ." Prophet Wolfer bellowed.

"Hexus?" Da cried.

"My son!" cried Mum.

I sensed no presence of the xenolope's mind. Had the jolt from the arc erased it? Was I now trapped forever in its body with the memories and mad visions of the prophet? What had happened to my physical form? Had it been absorbed by the creature's internal organs?

"The great fissure . . . eats our world," the prophet said, "like a hungry mouth."

"I'm here," I said, competing with the prophet for audience. "I am one with the xenolope."

"There are heavens beyond the heaven of the Holy Mother," Wolfer ranted. "Gods above our Goddess."

"Blasphemy!" cried the High Priestess. She turned off the light from her little box and the prophet's presence faded like red rays at sunset.

I, however, did not lose the power of speech. Though my words from the xenolope's mouth were distorted by its foreign voice box and broad tongue, they were coherent to human ears. I knew with certainty that my body had merged with its body, that my molecules had somehow found accommodation within their new host. "I think you killed it with your arc," I explained as best I could. "It's body lives, but I think its mind has died. Now I am he . . . it. It wanted to take me there"—I raised my great arm and pointed thick digits at the glowing rent in the sky—"so their scientists might save our world."

"It lies," said the holy lady. "Kill the unholy beast!"

"No!" I cried. "Mum! Da! I *am* Hexus. If I can find the creature's memories, I can cross the bridge in the sky and go to its world. They can help us."

The High Priestess screamed at Da to kill me, but he raised his arc to her and drove her and her subordinate Whiteskins away. My mother touched my snout with tentative fingers. I believe she felt the inner presence of the one born of her loins. Da sheathed his arc and touched my massive shoulder. We were a family altered, but a family still. Had I been capable of making tears, I might've cried at that moment to express my joyful sadness.

Six seasons have turned since then. My days are spent in the temple, out of the sun's rays which would burn my bestial body, and at night I roam freely, trying to jar loose more of the xenolope's cellular memories so that I might discover how to fly into the great rip and cross the bridge to that other world. I do my best to quiet the annoying chatter of the mad prophet, but he is always here with me, nagging like an aching tooth. The land south and west of our mountain has been eaten away day by day, and in its place is a yawning void of alien darkness, so that now we truly are at the edge of the world.

I know we haven't much time now. For all his hysterical vexation, the prophet's visions of catastrophe and conflagration are legitimate. I have decided to attempt the heroic leap without benefit of the xenolope's lost knowledge. When the creature's mind was still vital, I learned that in its world what could be imagined could be made real. So as I vault at the sky, I shall imagine myself soaring into the damaged heavens and crossing the bridge to that world where scientists are as gods.

It will require a great leap of imagination, but it is our only chance at having a hand in shaping our destiny. I pray I am up to the task and that my imagination will not fail me.

I, Hexus, boy, beast and mad prophet, bid you farewell.

The future, I should imagine, will be fantastic.

UNDERTAKEN

"How's he look?"

"Like death warmed over."

"You sure he's still breathing?"

Jolene sucked on her cigarette, then answered, "Oh yeah. He's breathing. Breath smells like a dead man's fart."

Ray-Ray was sitting hunched over the wheel, head craned toward the windshield because he couldn't see shit in this night fog. Jolene was in the passenger seat, turned sideways so she could keep an eye on Dean and report any obvious changes in his condition to Ray-Ray. She wished he would hurry up and die so they could dump his gut-shot ass, but the poor bastard was hanging on to life with the tenacity of a pit-bull in a Mississippi dog fight, and Ray-Ray was bound and determined he wasn't going to let his old cellmate die on him.

"You ought not to talk like that, Jolene," Ray-Ray said.

"Like what?"

"Dead man's fart! That's my friend you're talking about."

"Well, that's what it smells like."

"You ever smelled a dead man's fart?"

"No. But if I did, it would smell just like Dean's breath."

"You're a cold-hearted broad, you know that? Light me a smoke."

Jolene dug one out of her crumpled pack of Camels, lit it with her butt's ember and passed it to him. "Thank you, Jolene," she said, because he didn't.

He ignored her and concentrated on keeping the '46 Studebaker on this winding mountain road somewhere in the North Georgia sticks. The car was in good condition for a twelve-year-old relic. It had hardly been driven during Ray-Ray's six-year stint in the State pen. His mother back in Memphis had used it to drive into town now and then, but after she died of a stroke the Studebaker sat in the shed long enough for the battery to go dead from lack of use.

Jolene knew how that was—how things could go dead from lack of use. While Ray-Ray was doing time, she'd nearly gone dead herself from lack of loving. There had been times when she thought her female parts had closed up shop and called it quits for good. Until B. Rowe Tice came along and got her juices flowing again. A smooth-talking vacuum-cleaner salesman, B. Rowe would put his mouth on her, *down there,* and suck like a Hoover until she was delirious with lust. Then he would stick his humongous thing in her and ride her like a rodeo bronco buster until her passions were spent. She didn't love him the way she loved Ray-Ray, but she did love how he rode her into the mattress and left her walking bowlegged for days afterward. When he found out Ray-Ray had escaped from the chain gang and was coming home for his girl, B. Rowe hit the road for good. It was nice having Ray-Ray back, but Jolene missed those wild rides with B. Rowe Tice. And now she couldn't Hoover her floor without getting a hot tingle between her legs.

She was wondering how she could convince Ray-Ray to use his mouth on her, *down there,* without making him suspicious or sounding like a slut, when he suddenly blurted, "Bucksnort."

"Buck *what?*"

"Snort. You know, like a buck when it snorts. That's what it said on that sign. Bucksnort. Name of the town we're riding into."

"I didn't see a sign."

"Name like that, it must be a town full of deer hunters," he said. She couldn't tell if he was making a joke. If he had a sense of humor, he kept it well hidden beneath his tough-guy exterior.

Dean moaned in the backseat, but he didn't appear to be coming out of his feverish stupor.

"We got to get him some help,' Ray-Ray said, his voice raw with desperation. "Somebody to get that bullet out of his belly and clean the wound. I think it's already infected."

"Ten o'clock at night? I doubt Bucksnort's doctor keeps such late hours. If they even have a doctor."

"After we pulled that bank job in Alabama we found a vet to patch up Dean's arm where the bank guard popped him. That horse doctor did a damn good job too."

"You need to get a new partner. One who won't get hisself shot every time you pull a job."

"I told you, Dean's family. He's like a brother to me."

The road snaked down into the tiny town of Bucksnort. Streetlights in the dense fog made the hick town look unreal, like the storefronts were floating on clouds. Jolene absently wondered if they had stores in Heaven.

"Momma . . .?" Dean suddenly shouted as he lifted his head off the seatback. "What day is it?"

"I ain't your momma," Jolene snapped.

"Musta hit my head on the goalpost." He grimaced, then put his head back down and shut his eyes.

"He's reliving an old football injury," Ray-Ray explained.

"No wonder he ain't right in the head," she said.

"Dammit, Jolene, lay off, will ya? He can't help it. Spoze that you was back there, gut-shot?"

"I wouldn't be crying for my momma. Jeez, what a baby."

"You're starting to piss me off."

"Is that right? You pissed me off way back when you two geniuses decided to stick up that country store after I told you not to. If you'd listened to me, your butt-hole buddy back there wouldn't be bleeding all over the backseat."

"How was we spoze to know that old lady was packing heat? She looked harmless enough."

"Shows what you know. Soon as I saw her I knew she was bad news. She had Indian blood in her, plain as day. We're lucky we didn't get scalped."

"Well, she's a dead Injun now, so let's just forget it. It's over."

"No, it ain't over. Not while we got Crazy-legs Dean dying in the backseat."

"He ain't dying. We get him fixed up, he'll be fine."

"Fixed up where? I don't see nothing but a rolled-up town."

Ray-Ray grinned. He pointed a finger at a two-story building ahead on the right side of the street. "Right there," he said. "Claxton Funeral Home. Lights are on, so somebody must be home."

"Are you kidding me? A funeral home?"

"No, I ain't kidding. Morticians know all about the human body, don't they? I 'spect he'll fix Dean up 'bout as good as new. And keep his mouth shut about it unless he wants to get shot his own damn self."

He turned into the driveway and drove around to the rear of the building. Two hearses were parked under a vine-covered shed in the back. He parked next to a late-model Ford coupe and killed the Studebaker's engine.

"See? I was right. That'd be the undertaker's car," he said. "Come on."

"You expect me to go in there?" Jolene dug her fingers into the armrest.

"I do. There might be more than one of them and I'll need you to cover 'em while I convince 'em to do what I say."

"But there'll be dead bodies in there. Why else would they be working so late."

"Why, hell, Jolene, it's a mortuary, ain't it? What would you expect 'em to have? Rump roasts and hog jowls?"

"Funeral homes give me the heebie-jeebies."

"It ain't like we're renting a damn room here. Stop your bitching. Come on, now. Dean needs seeing to."

They went up the dank back steps. A glowing cone of fog hung from the back porch light. Ray-Ray tried the door. It was unlocked. It swung open with a muttering creak. He tiptoed in and she followed. They both had their pistols out. A long, dimly-lit hallway loomed ahead of them. A door on the right was marked "Private." They heard someone whistling a tune on the other side of the door. Jolene recognized the song. "Happy Days Are Here Again."

Great, she thought, *a happy undertaker.* And what would make an undertaker happier than having a corpse to work on? She shuddered, and then shot eye-daggers at Ray-Ray.

He looked at her and nodded, then he threw open the door. It banged against the inner wall, startling the gray-haired fat man bent over the naked corpse laid out on a long metal table.

"Jesus God," said Jolene, her eyes unnaturally drawn to the huge dead cock lying limp between the corpse's pale, hairy thighs.

"Don't move!" shouted Ray-Ray, waving his .38 around in the room's cold air.

"What the hell . . .?" blurted the mortician, reeling several steps backward.

"You the only one here?" asked Ray-Ray as he put the gun right up to the mortician's nose.

"Y-yes. Ju-just me . . . and Mr. Tilley there." He pointed a shaky finger at the corpse.

"Good. Just do what I say and I won't hurt you." Ray-Ray looked down at Mr. Tilley and said, "Goddamn! Look at that thing!" He pointed his pistol at the dead man's penis. "Now that's what I call a king-size tallywacker. Bet there'll be lots of ladies crying at *his* funeral."

Ray-Ray shot a sly glance at Jolene and said, "Imagine what that would look like with hard-on."

"I don't wanna think about it," she said, finally able to look away from the flaccid loggerhead.

"Mr. Tilley's tallywacker could put this shit-splat town on the map," he said. "Pickle it in formaldehyde, put it in a jar and charge a dollar to see it. Folks be lined up around the block."

Jolene didn't think he was joking.

"Hell, *I'd* pay a dollar to see it," he added.

No, he was serious, all right. Humorless moron. "Can we hurry this up?" she said, rolling her eyes at him.

"Yeah, yeah." Ray-Ray turned back to the mortician. "We got a man in the car's been gut-shot and you're gonna get the slug out and patch him up. Get me?"

"I'm not a doctor," said the undertaker. "I can't—"

"I know you're not a doctor. I look like an idiot to you?"

The undertaker looked at him, probably thinking: *Yes, an idiot's exactly what you look like.* But he shook his head, no.

"Come with me." Ray-Ray waved the man out of the room with his .38. "You're gonna bring him in and work on him. And remember, he ain't dead, so don't go tossing him around the way you do your dead customers. He dies, you're dead too."

Jolene followed them out into the hallway and was going to go out to the car with them, but Ray-Ray told her to check the front office to make sure there was nobody else in the building.

"And don't get no ideas about Tilley's tallywacker," he added.

"I'm not staying in here by myself."

"Christ, Jolene, a dead man can't hurt you. Do like I said and I won't hurt you either."

She gave serious thought to shooting him right then. She had the gun in her hand. All she had to do was bring it up and pull the trigger. The urge passed, and Ray-Ray followed the undertaker out the back door and into the foggy night.

She muttered a curse and started down the long hallway. The floor creaked and groaned beneath her feet and she thought she heard someone whispering. She froze and listened to the thick silence.

No whispering.

Imagination.

She walked on, finger tight against the trigger. She glanced over her shoulder to make sure Mr. Tilley wasn't creeping up behind her with a rigor mortis hard-on and a taste for some strange (*live*) pussy. He wasn't, but that didn't make her any less afraid of being alone in this house of the dead.

She glanced into the small chapel on the left and saw nothing but empty folding chairs arrayed in front of a small alter, then she rounded the corner at the end of the hall and crept into the well-lighted office. No one else was there. Two desks, some chairs, a scenic Claxton Funeral Home calendar on the wall, and an electric coffeepot. Mounted on the pine-paneling over one desk was a big buck's head with a full rack of antlers. The deer's glass eyes gave her the willies the way they seemed to follow her as she moved. At least the undertaker had told the truth about being alone. That was good.

Maybe Ray-Ray wouldn't feel compelled to kill him when they were done with him. Jolene had seen enough killing for a while. She worried that she might already be damned for her part in those crimes.

She picked up the phone from the larger desk and yanked the cord out of the wall, then dropped the phone in a trash basket. As she exited the office Jolene saw a small girl in a white summer dress dart across the hall and disappear into the embalming room. No, *dart* wasn't right. What the kid did was *float* across the hallway, like a bright leaf caught in a stiff breeze.

The back of her neck prickled. *Imagination,* her mind whispered reassurance. There might be a flesh-and-blood little girl down there, but she *did not* float above the floor. Jolene proceeded with nervous caution down the hall to the embalming room. She stopped just short of the open doorway.

"Get a grip," she whispered to herself. "You don't wanna shoot a little girl."

She took a deep breath and started to walk into the dreaded room where the dead guy with the enormous prick was laid out on the metal table, but the back door burst open and the undertaker staggered in, carrying Dean in his arms. Ray-Ray came in out of the fog behind them.

"Make way, dammit," said Ray-Ray, further pissing Jolene off with his bossiness.

The undertaker grunted past her and then stopped in front of the embalming table. "We should've moved Mr. Tilley first," he said, breathless with exertion.

"No problem," Ray-Ray said. He walked over and rolled Mr. Tallywacker off the table and onto the floor.

"Hey!" the undertaker protested. "Show some respect for the dead."

"Shut up, pal, or you'll be joining him." Ray-Ray brandished his pistol. "Now get to work on my buddy. And don't use no dirty instruments."

The undertaker laid Dean on the table, pushed up his shirt and began to examine the gunshot wound in his abdomen. Dean's eyes fluttered open to take in his surroundings. "I'm dead," he said in wonderment. Then shut his eyes and smiled.

Standing in the doorway, Jolene scanned the room but didn't see a little girl in a white dress. "I thought I saw a little girl come in here," she said. "A child with curly blonde hair."

The undertaker looked up from Dean's blood-encrusted belly. "You saw her?"

"I saw . . . something."

"You're not the first. I've never seen her myself, but a few others have."

"So, what is she, a ghost?"

He shrugged. "So they say. I had her here a year ago. The coroner turned her over after their investigation. She was murdered by her parents. Sacrificed, actually. To the devil."

"The hell you say," said Ray-Ray.

The undertaker nodded. "Parents belonged to a satanic cult. They're on death row now, waiting to ride Old Sparky. I never believed in ghosts, but if you've seen her . . . You're not from around here, are you?"

Jolene shook her head.

"That surely puts a new light on things. Surely does." He nodded thoughtfully.

"Never mind the ghost stories," Ray-Ray said. "Get to work."

"I'm not equipped for surgery. That's what taking the bullet out of him will be, you know. Surgery. It could kill this man. He could bleed to death. He needs to go to a hospital."

"He ain't going to no hospital. Now shut up and do it. And he better not die."

"I've never seen a ghost before," Jolene said.

"And you still ain't," Ray-Ray insisted. "You just flush that shit out of your pretty little head right now. This place is spooky enough without you saying you seen a damn haint."

The undertaker went to a cabinet and got a handful of shiny metal tools and set them down with a clatter on the edge of the embalming table. The only one Jolene recognized was a scalpel. She felt queasy just looking at those things. "I can't watch this," she said.

Ray-Ray told her to go up front and make sure the door was locked. "And then get your ass back in here," he added. "You might have to assist the doc." He grinned. The bastard.

She went back to the front of the building and bolted the door, then she turned around to confront the long shadowy hallway. She didn't want to go back to the embalming room, but she didn't want to be by herself either, not with that girly ghost roaming around. She tried walking with her eyes closed so she wouldn't see the ghost, but that was scarier than keeping them open. She made it back to the room without any further supernatural sightings.

The undertaker had already made an incision on the site of Dean's wound and was digging around in his belly with a long, skinny pair of forceps. Dean didn't react at all to the invasive probing in his gut. Jolene feared he'd already died until she saw his chest rising and falling with shallow breaths.

"Ever do any deer hunting?" the undertaker asked Ray-Ray.

"Not lately." Ray-Ray was looking a little pale.

"I love to hunt, myself. Bagged that nine-point buck hanging in the front office back in '48. One shot to the heart. Bam!"

Ray-Ray and Jolene both flinched at the *Bam!*

"I can hardly wait for the season to open so I can get back out there and shoot—"

"Shut up," Ray-Ray told him. "I ain't interested in your bullshit hunting stories."

Bent close to Dean's belly, the undertaker dug deeper with his shiny instrument. "Ah, there it is. Made a mess of his liver, but I think I can . . . Yep, got it, by gum!"

Suddenly very dizzy, Jolene had to lean against the wall to keep from falling down. Ray-Ray had gone several shades whiter and was weaving unsteadily. The undertaker dropped the bloody slug on the table. It hit with a metallic *thunk.* He looked appraisingly at his two armed captors. "I know who you are," he said. "You the ones murdered Maggie Bird yesterday and cleaned out her cash register. I heard it on the radio."

"You don't know shit," said Ray-Ray, his voice sounding a little weak. "If you did, you wouldn't let on you knew we was killers. Stupid is what that is."

He shrugged. "Before I sew him up I need to flush the wound with alcohol. I don't keep it in here. The dead don't have much use for it. It's in the bathroom, down the hall. May I?"

"Go with him," Ray-Ray told Jolene. "I need to sit down a minute. That barbecue we ate ain't agreeing with me."

She didn't want to give up the support of the wall but she thought she would feel better if she could get out of this stinking room of the dead and the dying. She followed the undertaker into the hall.

"So you saw little Megan," he said. "That can't be good, you know. She was killed in a satanic ritual, her soul offered to the devil. If you're seeing her ghost then that probably means Satan is near."

"Shut up with that shit," she said, jabbing the muzzle of her gun into his back.

"If I were you, I'd get the hell out of here fast. You could be up Hell Creek without a fireproof paddle. In danger of losing your soul."

"One more word and I'll blow the fuck outta you." She jabbed him again, harder.

The undertaker shrugged his beefy shoulders. He pointed at the door to the rest room and gave her a raised-brow look.

She nodded. He stepped into the small tiled room, opened the mirrored door of the medicine cabinet. The door swung to a stop and Jolene saw her reflection framed in the hazy mirror. She looked awful. Like reheated death, herself. Purplish bags under her eyes and deepened wrinkles in her forehead made her appear ten years older than she was, spoiling her good-looks. She no longer much favored a young Jean Harlow. Her blond hair looked limp and listless.

"I take it you don't believe in the devil," the undertaker said as he reached into the cabinet for a bottle of rubbing alcohol.

Jolene scarcely heard the man. The looking-glass had captured her attention. Behind her haggard face, something moved in the murky reflection's background. Something in the hallway behind her. Something too massive to be the ghost of the murdered girl. She spun on her heels and pointed her pistol at the empty hallway.

"What is it, dear? Something got you spooked?" The undertaker's tone was boldly scornful.

She stepped into the hall and looked left and right. Nothing there. Imagination again. Imagination colored by disorienting queasiness leftover from having to witness part of Dean's embalming room operation. She turned back to the undertaker. "I told you to shut up," she said, seeing her ugly sneer in the mirror. "Stop trying to spook me, you sonofabitch."

He chuckled. He unscrewed the bottle's cap and sniffed the alcohol's fumes. "Yes, this should do the trick," he said, and suddenly flung the bottle in her face. Alcohol splattered her eyes, blinding her, burning fiercely. Before she could react in any useful way to the first volley of alcohol, a second splash assaulted her, hitting her eyes and going up her nose and dribbling into her mouth.

Shoot him! her mind screamed. But before she could squeeze the trigger, the undertaker wrenched the gun out of her hand, snapping the bone of her index finger. She went to her knees, clasping her injured hand with her left armpit, alternately cursing and sobbing bitterly.

She felt him brush past her as he glided out of the cramped bathroom. Heard him say, "You should've steered clear of Bucksnort, lassie. Things have a way of evening out here. Past debts come due and restitution must be paid. You see? No, I guess you can't. That must burn something awful."

His hollow laughter faded down the hall with the sound of his footsteps.

Doing her best to ignore the sharp ache in her broken finger, Jolene crawled to the sink and pulled herself up, turned on the tap and flushed her eyes with cold water. She glanced in the mirror. She was a wet, blond blur in the glass, but at least she could see *something.*

Ray-Ray. She had to warn him. As she hurried out of the bathroom and down the hall toward the embalming room, she heard gunfire. A single pop. Then another. And another. Then a metallic crash followed by a heavy thump.

The long hallway was blanketed with fog nearly as thick as the fog outside. But the interior fog wasn't real; it was just the effect of having her eyes chemically scorched by alcohol. Nevertheless, she was half-blind, hardly able to see the door at the end of the corridor—the door out of this damned haunted place. The car was out there waiting to take her to freedom, but Ray-Ray had the keys in his pocket, and he was . . . screaming.

Never mind the keys, just run for it. She ran for the door.

The undertaker appeared in the unreal fog, blocking her escape route. He aimed the gun at her chest and smiled. "This way, lass. You have to see this."

She skidded on her heels and stopped a few feet in front of the big man. "Please," she said, "just let me go."

"You would desert your friends? What happened to honor among thieves? Or doesn't it apply to thieving murderers?"

Ray-Ray called out to her, raw agony in his voice.

"He's having a devil of a time," the undertaker said with mock concern. "I put a bullet in his lumbar spine and one in each knee. I'm afraid he's quite immobilized. Completely at my mercy. So the question is, does he deserve mercy? Did he show mercy to Maggie Bird? I'm curious. Which one of you shot her?"

"Ray-Ray. But that was after she shot Dean. He had to do it or she woulda shot us too."

"Oh, so it was self defense. Except for the pesky little fact that you were robbing her store. And that, little lady, makes you all guilty of murder. Come along now. I'm anxious to get started."

"Started on what?" Her pulse raced. The taste of fear was stronger than the lingering taste of rubbing alcohol.

"What you came here for. Trust me, you don't want to keep the Devil waiting."

*   *   *

He tied her to a chair he'd dragged from the office, using the velvet rope undertakers use to rope off seats at funerals or whatever they needed to rope off. Ray-Ray was sprawled on his stomach, head turned to one side. He alternately groaned and cursed the man who'd paralyzed him with well-placed gunshots. The undertaker casually walked over to him and stepped on Ray-Ray's face, giving him a taste of shoe leather. "Quiet," he said, "or I'll break your neck."

Then the undertaker said to Jolene, "Now it's time for your anatomy lesson, lass. Watch closely and you'll see the true essence of a man."

The undertaker stripped Dean of his clothes and set to work with a scalpel. He made a long Y-shaped incision in Dean's torso, slicing deep, and then deftly peeled back the bloody flaps of flesh to reveal Dean's ribcage and internal organs. Dean's heels beat a desperate tattoo on the table, his back arched, he heaved a great sigh and then lay still.

Jolene sobbed. She couldn't stop sobbing. When she looked away from the butchery, the mortician walked over to her, took her chin in his bloody mitt and said, "I told you to watch closely. You don't want to make me mad."

A moment later the butcher was unreeling Dean's intestines and holding them up like a proud fisherman showing off the catch of the day.

Jolene passed out.

She came to with the taste of vomit in her mouth and a shrieking buzz in her ears. The undertaker was using an electric saw to take off the top of Dean's skull. Then he switched off the saw and said, "Handy little thing, the bone saw. Never have much cause to use it in my line of work, but it's good to have on hand." He lifted off the top of Dean's bloody skull, exposing the brain. He set the round little bone cap on the table and peeled Dean's face down to reveal red muscles attached to facial bones. A tuft of dark hair from Dean's scalp hung to his chin, giving him a bizarre little goatee.

Jolene passed out again.

When she awoke, Ray-Ray was strapped to the embalming table, naked from the waist up. A washcloth was stuffed in his mouth to keep him quiet. His eyes were bugging out in panic.

"Please," she gasped. "Please stop." Her vision was clearing a little, though she wished it wasn't. Right now, foggy eyesight would be a blessing.

The undertaker said, "He's here now. I can't see him, but I feel his presence. You feel it too, don't you? Satan is here. Just for you."

"You're crazy," she said. "You—" She broke off when she saw the little girl—Megan's ghost. She was standing—or floating—beside the mortician, looking up at the gory spectacle on the table. She was smiling. It wasn't a nice smile.

The undertaker picked up a long metal tube attached to a flesh-colored rubber hose. "This is an aspirator," he explained. "The sharp steel piece is called a trocar. We use it to vacuum fluids out of the abdominal cavity. The fluids drain into that sink at the foot of the table. I warn you, it smells something awful. You might want to hold your breath." He flicked a switch and a noisy motor geared up. Then he pressed the sharp tip against Ray-Ray's belly and punched it through.

Ray-Ray's face went through a series of horrific contortions as his guts began to gurgle through the steel tube attached to a rubber hose. The back of his head hammered against the table and his upper body went into convulsions.

The stench was overpowering. Jolene wanted to pass out, but she didn't. She could do nothing but watch the stinking life being sucked out of her man.

Megan laughed soundlessly.

When Ray-Ray's belly collapsed on itself like a deflated flesh balloon, the undertaker clicked off the aspirator and withdrew the trocar. "Two for the Devil and one to go," he said, beaming.

"No," she said, hardly above a whisper.

He folded his big arms across his chest. He looked like a doctor about to give his patient bad news of a terminal illness. "Maggie Bird was my wife's second cousin," he said. "My Sadie's all torn up over Maggie's murder. Just last week we had Sunday dinner with her, at her new house in Dogwood. She worked hard for that house. And look what happened. She never had a chance to enjoy her new home. Thanks to you and your murdering cohorts."

She shook her head. "I told 'em. Told 'em not to do it, not to rob that store. It's not my fault what happened. I told 'em."

He nodded his big head. "So you're innocent. Done nothing wrong to nobody. That it?"

Megan had drifted over to Dean's body on the floor and was trying to poke a ghostly finger into his brain.

Jolene said, "Turn me over to the cops and let the law decide if I'm guilty. I won't tell 'em what you did. Call 'em. There's probably a big reward."

"You're in Bucksnort, little lady. We don't have cops. What we have here is Bucksnort justice. In your case, that means putting your pretty little ass on the line to see if the Devil bites. There's blood in the water now, and he's circling. If he wants you, you're his. It's out of my hands."

Jolene couldn't hold back her anger. "You're a fucking devil worshiper yourself! Giving me all that High and Mighty bullshit! You evil fucking butcher!"

"I'm a God-fearing man. A good Christian. If I wasn't, I would be scared to death now, knowing Satan is close to coming up from under."

She suddenly had an idea. It was an idea born of desperation, but it was the only one she had. The deck was stacked against her and it was the only card she could play.

So she played the ghost card.

"Megan," she said, trying to act surprised. "She's not happy with you. She's fingering you, you fat fuck. Pointing you out to the Devil." This, of course, was not true. Megan's ghost was still trying to poke a misty finger into Dean's brain, for some reason fascinated by the cauliflower-looking thing that had served Dean so poorly in life.

The undertaker laughed.

Jolene went on with her fear-driven performance: "It's your fat ass on the line, not mine."

"I know a piss-poor bluff when I see one," said the undertaker.

"I ain't bluffing, Mister. I was you, I'd be beating feet outta here. He's coming!"

"Bravo," he said, clapping his hands. "Good show. But now I'm afraid it's curtains for you. Hell's gate is about to open."

Megan soundlessly clapped her hands with ghostly glee.

Jolene's bowels vented something foul in her panties.

*   *   *

The elevator opened in the basement. The undertaker rolled the chair Jolene was tied to toward a big metal chamber that reminded her of a giant iron lung. Then she realized what it was and what the guy had meant by Hell's gate.

A cremation chamber. He was going to burn her alive.

He rolled her to a stop in front of the crematory's iron hatch. She struggled against the velvet rope, to no avail. The undertaker hit a switch and turned a gage, and the muffled *whoof* of the fire inside the chamber filled Jolene with terror.

Megan's ghost capered in front of the hatch, no doubt overjoyed that she might soon have a new playmate.

"This cost me a pretty penny," said the undertaker, "but it's already paid for itself. At 1,400 degrees Fahrenheit in there, you could say I bought me a little piece of Hell on earth."

He opened the hatch so she could see the flames building in the chamber's belly and feel the intense heat. "Now you contemplate your future while I go get the remains of your murderous pals."

He went up in the elevator. Ghost girl was studying a bit of Dean's brain matter stuck to the tip of her finger. This was a revelation to Jolene. It meant that a spirit could actually touch things in the world of the living. Jolene did some fast scheming. Then she spoke to the ghost. "Megan, that bad man means to burn me alive. You can't let him do that. If you untie this rope, I can get out of here and take you with me. You can be my little girl. Would you like that? You don't have to stay in this bad place. You don't belong here. Please, honey. Untie me."

Megan looked up from her gooey fingertip and into Jolene's eyes. The girl appeared more solid than before, and that gave Jolene hope. Megan looked at the flames in the crematory.

"Do you understand me, honey?" asked Jolene. "I promise you can come with me. I always wanted a little girl like you."

Megan nodded. She drifted behind Jolene's chair and tried to untie the velvet rope. Jolene felt a slight tickle where the child's spectral fingers touched her, but the rope held fast. Megan made girlish sounds of frustration, her voice seeming to come from far away. "You can do it," Jolene said. "Don't give up."

Above the roar of the furnace she heard the rumble of the elevator coming down.

The rope went slack beneath her breasts. She bolted out of the chair. *Free.*

A rake with ash-dusted tines leaned against the wall by the fiery chamber, and she grabbed it and stood in front of the elevator shaft and waited for the car to come down. When the elevator door opened, she stepped into the doorway and swung the rake straight down off her shoulder. It struck the undertaker across the face, one of the tines burying itself in his left eyeball and the rake going *spoong!* as it quivered in her hands. When she yanked it back, the man came with it, falling forward over the edge of the linen cart bearing the grisly remains of Ray-Ray and Dean. She hit him again, this time on the back of his melon head. Then again and again. Megan squealed in delight.

Jolene dropped the rake and pushed the cart and the unconscious undertaker up to the door of the crematory. With considerable effort she wrestled the big man onto the chamber's metal rack and then pushed a button on the control panel and watched as the motorized rack took him into the fire.

The undertaker came to, screaming and flailing amidst the flames.

Jolene shrieked and slammed the hatch shut, the afterimage of what she'd just seen in the fire still glowing inside her eyes. "I *saw* him," she said, as much to herself as to Megan's ghost. "I saw the Devil's face in the fire."

Megan nodded, a sly smile on her face.

Shaking off her shock, Jolene held her breath and foraged in the bloody cart until she found Ray-Ray's car keys in his pants. "Hallelujah," she said. "Come on, honey, let's blow this dump."

Jolene started toward the elevator, but Megan held back, sucking her gooey finger. "What's the matter, sugar? Don't you wanna come?"

She nodded her head. Then she said in that faraway voice, "He's coming too."

"Who is?" Jolene asked the little ghost.

"The Devil."

Jolene lurched backward as the iron hatch swung open and the Devil slithered out of the fire. She gaped at the fallen angel, towering over her with something like a smile on his fire-reddened face and the satisfied look of a man who's just eaten a hearty meal and is ready for a good cigar.

"Swell," she said, figuring to get on his good side. "You know, your pictures don't do you justice. You're much better-looking in person."

Lucifer laughed.

His booming laughter was infectious and Jolene laughed along, going at it so hard she snorted, which of course made her laugh even harder. When her laughter finally subsided, she looked down into the linen cart at what was left of her former partners in crime. "You guys fancied yourselves big bad outlaws, but look how you ended up," she said. "And look who it is gets to ride with the Devil. So long, chumps."

She waggled her fingers at them and then stepped into the elevator with her new companions. It occurred to her that she might be going a little loco but who wouldn't, given what she'd just been through. And anyway, maybe the Devil would look after her, take care of her. If she treated him right. Hell, she could be as evil as anybody. Sure, he would like that about her.

"Whaddya say we get the hell outta Bucksnort," she said with a snort and cheerfully hit the button with the upward-pointing arrow.

Her cheer disappeared when the elevator seemed to drop out from under her, taking her . . .

. . . down.

And down.

Deeper into mounting pressure.

"God damn it," Jolene said, though it was hard to talk because something was sucking the air out of the enclosed space of the elevator car.

Then she knew her one-way ride with the Devil was taking her to the last place she wanted to go, *down there*.

LIFE AFTER LIVING DEATH

Lazarus here. That's my Christian name so don't get any wrong reeking ideas. I don't know too much about my family tree but I've been given to know that its Old World roots ran deep. My missionary parents had the bright idea that we all came from one big divine family tree, roots deep in dirt and branches high in Heaven. Who knows? Maybe they were right, maybe they weren't psychotic zealots after all. But that was way before the rise of the Deaders, back when we were sitting on top of the world and didn't know the planet was destined to be overrun with the walking dead or that we were to be the favorite food of zombies teetering at the top of the food-chain.

Brother Pythagoras had his own ideas of how things should be. He saw himself leading the walking corpses to God. He was convinced that the Deaders had souls and that he was their spiritual compass, the divinely-tuned instrument of their salvation.

Sister Sybil was his right-hand gal, a lovely vision in faded white frills and as true a believer as you'd ever meet. She'd been a registered nurse before the Clysm and did a decent job of treating the minor nicks and knocks suffered by our ragtag cadre.

For all her piety, I sensed in Sybil a deep passion, silent as empty graves. Her wheat-straw hair was long and she wore it up in a thick bun on the back of her head for services. Her face was waxy white and gave her the look of a classical statue. But for her, I would've left the mission long ago and headed for the highlands where the Deaders didn't like to go. I saw in her a sunlit purity and a promise of better days ahead. At night she sometimes came to me in dreams that weren't so pure.

"It ain't right," Pynch said, his rifle hanging by a soiled canvas sling from his shoulder.

"So you've said," I said.

"You saying it is?"

"I'm saying so you've said."

"That ain't saying nothing."

I said nothing.

"Shit." He came down a step so he was on the same step I stood on, his boots rasping against the gritty stone. He locked his eyes on mine and opened his mouth to say something else but the pealing anthem of the pipe organ surged out of the wide church doors behind us and Pynch unslung his rifle as I unslung mine.

The church bell tolled and we watched the empty street and waited for the dead to straggle in from their Ghost-town hidey-holes.

"We could stop it," Pynch said. "We *should* stop it. Cohen is one of us. Or was."

"He's as good as dead already," I said, keeping my eyes on the town's main street. "There's no cure for what he's got."

Pynch persisted: "You don't actually believe this lead-the-zombies-to-Jesus crap, do you?"

"What's it matter what I believe? Me or anybody else?"

"Cohen is one of us," he said again. "He's a Jew, but still."

One of us. Whatever that meant. I didn't know anymore. Maybe never had. All I knew was that *us* was the living and *them* was the reanimated dead. Pythagoras occupied some mystical middle-ground no-man's land and he held it with a spooky come-to-Jesus fervor. And now Cohen was there too, suspended above it in his dying delirium.

"Jesus was a Jew," I said. "Cohen's the perfect stand-in."

"Yeah, well, he ain't got no res'rection waiting at the end." He turned his ballcap backwards and said, "Wish we could pop a few like we used to. Need the practice." He brought his rifle up and fired imaginary bullets at make-believe Deaders. "Pough, pough, pough . . ."

I watched the street. The wind kicked up and I smelled them coming.

"You ain't a Jew, are you, Laz?" Pynch asked me.

I gave him a shrug. "Christian. Got a Jew name but that's as far as it goes."

"Just the same, don't go getting sick or old Pythagoras might take a notion to offer you up on the cross."

"That'd be the day I put one in his head."

Pynch chuckled, then said, "Here come the chunks."

As Deaders go, this bunch that made up our current congregation didn't smell so bad. Most of them had been dead a long time. The fresher Deaders were the ones that stank to highest heaven. These older skinbags were as leathery as an old lady's cowhide purse. They were easier to handle too because they moved slower, like the walking stiffs they were, with eyes dulled and deeply fixed in their sunken sockets. You could see that whatever dark miracle kept them going was losing its grip on them as they were slowly winding down like rusty clock springs. If Brother Pythagoras was going to save their souls, he had to work fast before they went to ground and then to dust. You'd see the fallen sometimes on the side of a road or lying in a field, too desiccated to walk or crawl anymore, their jaws still working as if trying to eat the earth. Seeing them like that, I didn't see how they could still have souls—if they ever had. I didn't like to think too much about that; the idea that I might be nothing more than a glorified meat machine myself didn't exactly fill me with joy or give me good reason to go on living in this dead damned world. Pythagoras saw those pathetic earth-eating zombies as the ultimate insult to the natural order of things. That their souls might be trapped in their clockwork bodies, he said, was too terrible to abide.

A dozen Deaders ambled toward the church steps. The choir inside began their choral reading.

"That crap gives me the creeps," Pynch said. "Ain't like the chunks know what the words mean. Don't know myself, far as that goes."

The choir's reading drifted out in broken pieces: " . . . thank Thee for mercies of blood . . . martyrs and saints . . . enrich the earth . . . create the holy places . . ."

"Sounds like T. S. Eliot," I said. "Sybil gave me a book of his shit."

"Fucking creepy is what it is."

" . . . fear the hand at the window . . . than we fear the love of God . . ."

"It's about what you'd expect from Brother *Sly*-thagoras. High-tone doubletalk, smooth as shit through a goose. You know he keeps a Deader's head in a birdcage and uses its jaws for a nutcracker?"

I watched a naked Deader shamble out of the gutted drugstore and shuffle after the others. She was fresher than most of them, veins showing through her sallow flesh like blue highways on a yellowed road map. She fell in behind the others as they made their way toward us.

There was a whisper of bare feet and I glanced back to see Sister Sybil standing behind us, resplendent in the folds of her white robe.

"Such terrible beauty," she said. "God's wayward souls, our orphans of the Last Judgment."

"Spawn of Satan, you ask me," Pynch said.

"O no, don't you see? It's their very souls that keep them going. What else could animate dead flesh? They're hungry for the Holy Spirit."

"Everybody wants a free lunch." Pynch spat on a lower step.

She ignored him and said, "Such a glorious day! Those puffs of clouds look like cat's paw prints."

Pynch nudged me with an elbow and said, "Let's herd these damn dead cats, Brother Lazarus. It's showtime."

The sunlight on Sybil's skin and hair smelled so sweet I almost didn't notice the moldering reek of the advancing dead. I did a quick headcount: eleven Deaders. The usual gang plus the new naked one from the drugstore.

As they straggled to the steps, I glanced up at the morning sky. The clouds *did* look like paw prints and I tried to imagine the angelic cat that might've made them.

* * *

I don't want to say what happened inside that pathetic sanctuary but there is no way to stop the bleeding now. Like murder, it will out.

Damn them all and let it bleed.

* * *

The dead are dropping clumsily to their knees at the altar rail. He of the slick silver hair, Brother Pythagoras stands behind the altar and in front of unclothed Cohen, who has been roped to the tall wooden cross, his chin on his chest, mouth slack and drooling. Cohen's fever has ravaged him so badly that there isn't much meat left on his bones. Shocking to see how quickly a man can waste away. Three days ago he was fine. Now he's living death, deader than Deaders.

Sister Sybil stands to the left and a step behind Pythagoras, a tarnished silver platter in her hands. A slender stainless-steel carving knife rests on the platter, pointing at Sybil's belly.

Like armed ushers, Pynch and I have stationed ourselves on opposite sides of the chancel. A squadron of flies buzzes about the heads of the dead. The Pope twins stand ready with cattle prods, in case any worshipper should stray.

The organist plays a single sustained bass note that resonates deep in my belly. The tension is visceral, aching to break. I swat a fly out of the air.

Pythagoras lifts his hands and then says, "Whoso eateth my flesh and drinketh my blood hath eternal life and I will raise him up at the last day." He turns to Sybil and takes up the knife.

I close my eyes. I'm a child of six years, hiding in the bulrushes of Djibouti and watching fanatics with long knives murder my father and rape my mother before cutting her throat. I freeze in fear, and the shame will never leave me. The killers are so fierce in their dedication to their dark god's death cult that they've become single-minded demons. I want to cry for help from Heaven but I can't without giving myself away. I watch the slaughter in silence, swallowing the evil like a bitter seed. As a final insult, one of the demons stuffs my mother's silver crucifix into her mouth and says, "Here is your Christ, choke on him."

Cohen's shriek snaps my eyes open and I see that the blade has sharpened his senses, at least for the moment. Blood is streaming down from the wound in his side. Pythagarus places a sliver of the sacrifice's flesh on the silver platter and then surehandedly takes another cut of meat from the sick man on the cross. Cohen shakes his head in confusion and calls out for his mother. A couple of impatient Deaders rise up from their knees and try to clamber over the altar but the Popes zap them back into place with the cattle prods.

I look away and silently curse this church and everybody in it, living and dead. I could stop this sick show if I had the will. I'm the guy with the rifle. I could end Cohen's suffering with a headshot. I could punch Pythagoras a ticket to Heaven with a well-placed bullet. But I lack the will. The will to kill. Killing is not what it used to be. And Sybil would hate me for sabotaging the service.

So I do nothing.

Pynch is antsy. He shoots me a look of disgust and just for a moment I have the faint hope that he will intervene, but then he just shrugs and stares off and loses himself in a stained-glass window of haloed saints, and I know there will be no escape from the suffering of the flesh.

"Body of Christ," Pythagoras says as he shoves a piece of Cohen into a grizzled Deader's mouth.

"Body of Christ," he says as he goes to the next ghoul, Sybil following with the bloody tray.

Time crawls slow as a snail, making a bloody slime trail. When Pythagoras comes to the last Deader at the altar rail, Sybil suddenly squeals and drops the platter. Wearing the expression of a wounded and bewildered child, she holds out her hands to show the bleeding holes in her palms. Blood trickles from her scalp and drizzles down both cheeks. There is a bright red stain on her white dress, below and to the left of her breast.

I crane my head to see that her bare feet also bear bleeding wounds.

"Praise God!" Pythagoras shouts to the ceiling.

Sybil's face changes, fear and confusion replaced by a look of rapture.

The Deaders get frenzied at the sight of her blood. One of them, a leather-skinned woman with large hips and breasts like deflated basketballs, grabs Sybil's left wrist and yanks her halfway over the rail.

I raise the rifle and fire, the round smacking the Deader bitch right in the ass. Stunned by the shot, the ghoul lets go of Sybil's arm, but Sybil says, "No, Lazarus, it's all right. It's meant to be this way, don't you see?"

"God's will," Pythagoras declares.

With exaltation etched in her face, Sybil leans against the alter rail and offers her bleeding hands to the communicants. They receive her ravenously, lifting her over the rail and ripping off her dress to get at her appetizing flesh and sacred blood.

Pynch says, "Jesus fuck," spits on the floor and then walks down the aisle and out of the church.

I can't follow him. I owe it to Sybil to witness her sublime sacrifice, no matter how sick inside it makes me. The Deaders go at her like pigs in a trough, snorting and snuffling and gnawing her flesh.

Pythagoras presides over the gluttonous slaughter like a fiery-eyed prophet. He raises his arms in demented benediction and says, "Do this in memory of me. If you eat my flesh and drink my blood, you will abide in me and I in you. The words I have spoken to you are spirit and life."

His eyes fall on me, as I knew they would. There is not a glimmer of grace in them. I shoulder my weapon and put one up his nose that pulps his head. He falls over the altar rail and becomes the next course of the Deaders' holy feast.

For Sybil's sake, I make the sign of the cross and say, "Godspeed."

Outside on the steps, Pynch says, "You killed him?" I nod. He nods back.

With no look backward, I walk out of that godless ghost town and light out for the highlands.

THE GOD OF BROKEN WORLDS

The God of Broken Worlds poked his bulbous head through the rip in the cosmic veil, looked down upon the world and saw that it was bad. "Extraordinary," He said to his aide. "This surpasses all expectations."

"Very good, sir," said the aide.

"To the contrary, Satchel," boomed GBW, "it's very bad."

"It's Hershel, sir."

"What's that, Satchel?"

"My name, sir, it's Hershel." The deity's adjunct maintained his deadpan expression because he wanted the Old Boy to think he had the patience of Job. The truth was, his job and his deity sorely tried his limited patience. Acting as GBW's functionary and metaphorical appendage was a tribulation he would not have wished upon The Old Testament's most exalted hero of affliction.

"Yes, well, as I was saying, it's very bad down there. Worst I've seen in ages. Isn't that wonderful, Hershey?"

Hershel sighed and rolled his eyes. "As you say, m'Lord."

"Look at it! Running like an ill-oiled machine. Wound so tight the whole thing's ready to fly apart in utter [He pronounced it "udder"] chaos!"

Hershel winced at the mental image of bovine teats flying in chaotic formation, but he held his peace. Best not to disagree with the Old Man when He was on a tear.

"I think this world is just about ready for me to make my presence known. Don't you agree, Hereford?"

Hershel slapped his own cheek and replied, "Certainly, sir."

"Excellent! Make the necessary preparations. And while you're opening the way, I shall be choosing my outfit. I'm leaning toward the Raiment of Fire."

"Perfect choice, sir."

As the God of Broken Worlds stormed away amid a happy crackling of static electricity, Hershel gazed down upon the out-of-kilter world and allowed himself a moment's lamentation for his lost mortality. Then the moment was gone, and with a shrug of the spirit he turned his full attention to his assigned duty: the opening of the way for his erratic Lord and Master.

*   *   *

Certified Wreckmaster Buckley Butts was no stranger to bizarre situations, but the one in which he now found himself was certainly the most unnerving in recent memory.

He had nothing against dead people—some of his best friends were dead—but that didn't mean he liked riding at the head of this funeral procession, hauling the broken-down hearse with his raucous wrecker. By virtue of his surname, Butt's Wrecking Service was already the butt of too many lame jokes; teenagers with too much time on their hands never tired of phoning his place of business with snappy one-liners such as, "Wrecked any good butts lately?" Or "There's a crack-up on Route Six, time to haul butt." It was all very tiresome and made him long for the simpler days of Prince Albert in a can. But this—leading a funeral procession to Sunset Garden Cemetery—was sure to inspire the town's half-wit wags to new heights (or new depths, depending, of course, on one's perspective).

Buck glanced in the rearview at the hearse and the trailing line of cars and said, "Sumbitch."

"Which bitch?" inquired the voice from the wrecker's radio. It was Buck's dispatcher, Billy Moss. Buck had forgotten he had the mike in his hand keyed to transmit.

"Disregard," Buck told Billy.

"Hey, Buck?" Billy's voice crackled with static. "Are they gonna pay you extra for being in the carcass caravan?"

Buck shook his head in disgust. The first half-wit had spoken.

Howling at his own joke, Billy continued. "Got yourself a cadaver convoy."

"Billy?" Buck maintained a matter-of-fact tone, low-keyed and controlled as he led the parade for the dead through the cemetery gate.

"Yeah, boss?"

"Get your ass off the radio and stop polluting the air waves with your stupid jokes."

"Roger that, Wrecker One," Billy guffawed. "Or should I say, Meat Wagon Dragon? Get it? Dragon . . . draggin'?"

"Lord, deliver me," Buck muttered, casting his eyes upward in what he supposed was the general direction of Heaven.

"Perhaps He will," said the dapper man in a white suit who had just materialized on the seat next to Buck. "Pull over."

Buck jammed on the brakes and looked askance at his sudden passenger. "Who the hell are you?"

"Hershel the Harbinger, emissary of God."

Buck's mind suddenly slipped its cogs. He tried to get it back in gear, but the best he could come up with was: "The God?"

Hershel the Harbinger chuckled. "Not precisely. Just one of the many who make up the whole blessed pantheon."

"The what?" The ringing in his ears was the sound of his mental gears grinding, seeking purchase on reality.

"The God of Broken Worlds," said Hershel with an obvious air of exasperation. "See here, my good man, there is no time to explain further. The Old Boy is ready to come through and He doesn't take kindly to unnecessary delay. Believe me, you don't want to get on His bad side."

"Broken worlds? That would explain a lot. Are you . . . an angel?"

Hershel gritted his teeth and thought: Millions of souls on this planet, each containing at least a spark of the Divine, and I have to team up with this dim bulb. He wanted to slap the obtuse mortal, but that was against the Rules of Harbingering, so he slapped himself instead. "I'm the closest thing to an angel as you're likely to see. No more questions. Just do as I tell you and just maybe this god-awful scheme will work out for the best."

"Uh, mmm . . ." said Buck, resigning himself to enforced ignorance. "What do you want me to do?"

Hershel smiled sweetly, attempting to soften the force of his next words. "I want you to go get the corpse out of his box and lean him against that grotesque statue of an angel. I'd do it myself but I'm not allowed to touch dead things."

"I can't do that. There's such a thing as respect for the dead, you know."

"There's no time for pissing about," Hershel raised his voice. "The bugger won't be dead much longer. Just do it."

"Whaddya mean, he won't be—"

"Tch . . . tch . . ." said the harbinger, holding up a staying hand. "You're wasting God's time."

A beefy hand suddenly rapped against the driver's window of the wrecker, and Buck turned to see Porter Fields, the owner and operator of the funeral home, fuming and mouthing unheard words. Buck cranked down the window and caught the tail-end of Porter's rant.

" . . . to know what in God's name you think you doing."

Hershel snickered. Buck turned to the harbinger and said, "You tell him, wise guy."

"You, sir, are about to witness a divine miracle," Hershel said grandly.

"Who might you be?" Porter demanded.

"You might think of me as the left hand of God."

Buck wanted to get the whole thing over with, so he pulled a lever to drop the hearse onto all four wheels, got out of the wrecker, pushed past Porter Fields and went after the corpse. This whole mess was Porter's fault anyway; if he'd had his other hearse in good running condition, Buck wouldn't be here now with his revered wrecker hooked up to Porter's broken-down hearse.

Several family members of the deceased were out of their cars and stood staring in disbelief as Buck opened the coffin and dragged out the corpse of Maxwell Biddy. Biddy's widow fainted dead away, falling into the arms of her brother-in-law, who had been secretly sampling the forbidden fruits of her womanhood on a weekly basis for nearly two years.

Buck dragged Max Biddy's heavy corpse over the grass and propped it against the tall statue of an angel, feeling less than confident that he was actually doing the will of God. Hershel was out of the wrecker now and was urging everyone to "draw near and bear witness to the miracle of God Almighty."

"I'll have you arrested," Porter Fields threatened Buck. "You and your faggy little friend."

"Stand back, heathen," Hershel warned the undertaker. "Too close and you'll be consumed by divine fire. I assume no liability here."

"You pompous little—"

The air around the corpse seemed to waver, and a sharp sizzling sound filled mortal ears. Then the air itself appeared to catch fire and a muffled thunderclap made Buck jump several inches off the ground.

"Behold!" shouted Hershel. "The Lord is come!"

Surrounded by blue flames, a tall figure with an enormous head appeared next to the corpse of Max Biddy.

"Jesus," said Buck, awestruck, "look at the size of that head."

"That's the Godhead, you ninny," Hershel whispered. "Best keep such comments to yourself. The Old Boy is rather vain, and He's sensitive about His big head."

The God of Broken Worlds blew a fiery breath over the corpse, singeing Max's hair and brows. "ARISE, MY SON," God commanded. "SPEAK THAT ALL MAY KNOW YOU LIVE AGAIN."

Max opened his eyes; he looked like a deer caught in the headlights of an oncoming eighteen-wheeler. His lips parted slowly.

"Uh, there may be a problem, Hershel," Buck whispered. "Old Max can't talk. He lost his tongue to cancer."

"Bloody hell," said Hershel.

"Arrgh uhh ooh," said Max.

Two more family members fainted. Porter Fields pissed his Armani pants and reeled away from the reanimated corpse.

The Holy Flames circumscribing the deity all at once grew intensely brighter and a look of obvious panic appeared on His face. "HEREFORD! HELP ME!"

"Ooooh uuuh arghhh," said Max, shambling toward his unconscious wife.

"Go back, sir!" shouted Hershel. "Go—"

The God of Broken Worlds was enveloped in ravenous flames, and He began to flap His arms wildly like a chicken trying to fly, spinning round and round like a flaming top. His head exploded like an unpunctured potato in a microwave oven. The fire quickly burned out, leaving in its fiery wake a melted lump of smoldering goo.

Those spectators who had not fainted began to flee in terror.

"Bugger all," said Hershel. "This has never happened before."

"What the hell is that," asked Buck, pointing at the quivering lump of goo.

"Godstuff. It's what you get when God goes up in flames."

"You mean God's dead?"

"In a matter of speaking, yes."

"No, God can't be dead," Buck insisted.

"Dead is a relative term," explained the former harbinger. "You might say He's relatively dead. But not destroyed. Energy merely changes forms. There's always a danger of something like this happening whenever a deity takes physical form in your world. It was that Raiment of Fire. I should've checked its molecular structure before He suited up."

"What happens now? I mean, look at Him. He hardly looks up to ruling over Heaven and earth."

"Just for the record," said Hershel, "He never ruled anything. He only existed because enough people believed in Him. Take away all the parlor tricks and pyrotechnics, and all you had was a semi-supreme being created by the faith of misguided mortals. His only job was to give people hope, hope that there were better days ahead. A better place than this. Without such hope, your world would degenerate into violence and chaos the likes of which you can't imagine. That's the theory, anyway."

"Isn't there something you can do? You said there are other Gods. Can't one of them take over?"

"It doesn't work that way." Hershel rubbed his pale chin thoughtfully. "But there is something you might do."

"Me? What could I do?"

Hershel smiled thinly. "How would you like to become a god?"

"What?!"

"I'd do it myself, but that would violate the harbinger's code. What say you, young man? Why not be all you can be?"

Buck watched helplessly as the raised-from-the-dead husband dragged his unconscious wife behind an ornate mausoleum, the obscene bulge in the stiff's pants indicating that Max was hard-up for some wifely affection.

"Come, come, Mr. Butts," said Hershel. "This chaos will surely spread if you do nothing. Is it not time for decisive action?"

Buck's shoulders slumped in resignation. "What do I have to do?"

Hershel pointed at the lump of Godstuff. "Eat that. Eat it and be transformed. He who consumes Godstuff becomes godly."

"You're not kidding, are you?" Buck kept his eyes fastened on the heap of holy goo. He thought he detected a hint of movement within the amorphous lump, perhaps a pulse of life.

"I'm am not, sir." Hershel seemed offended at the suggestion that he would use such an occasion for foolishness. "The ingestion of Godstuff is hardly a joking mater. It is Holy Communion in its purest form."

"But I'm not . . . God material," said Buck. "Surely you can find a better candidate for Godhood."

"You will do. But you must do it now. Wait any longer and it will be too late. The stuff has a very short half-life, chemically speaking. Seize the moment, Mr. Butts. Now!"

Buck warily reached down, picked up the Jell-O-like lump and began to eat it. "Hmm," he said with his mouth full. "Not bad. Tastes sort of like . . ."

"Chicken?" Hershel chuckled at his own infrequent joke.

"No. More like 'possum. Wish I had some sweet potatoes to go with it."

"Don't talk, just eat," Hershel advised.

As Buck crammed the last of the Godstuff into his mouth and licked his fingers, a terrible screaming arose from behind the mausoleum.

"Oh dear," said Hershel. "I think the former widow has awakened from her swoon to find herself being ravaged by her resurrected husband."

"I s'pose we ought to rescue her," Buck said as he swallowed the last slimy morsel and belched a small thunderhead.

Mrs. Biddy's screams became cries of orgasmic passion.

Hershel smiled wistfully. "I don't believe she wishes to be rescued just now. There's an apocryphal saying of old: 'In every resurrection there lies a sturdy erection.' That certainly tells the tale."

Buck laughed and the unexpected force of his laughter knocked over three marble headstones and shattered the stone wings of a cherubic statuette. "Good Lord, did I do that?"

"It would seem so, sir. The transmogrification is taking place."

"The what?"

"The change, m'Lord. It's working its way through your body and soul."

All at once Buck's head inflated like a helium-filled balloon, and his feet were floating several inches off the ground. "Hershel!"

"Don't be alarmed, sir. All is well. Just relax and go with it."

"Easy for you to say." Buck pressed his hands to the sides of his swelling head. "My head. I think it's going to explode!"

"No it's not," Hershel reassured him. "It's just the Godhead taking shape. Nothing to fear, sir."

"I . . . I . . ." Buck began to stammer. Dark clouds scudded in from the west. Thunderheads formed with impossible speed.

"Yes?" Hershel looked up at him with unmistakable reverence.

"I . . . CHOO!" Buck sneezed and lightning flew out of his flared nostrils.

"God bless you," said Hershel.

"I AM LORD." These words issued from his mouth of their own accord.

"Indeed, sir." Hershel clapped his hands together and held them prayerfully beneath his chin.

Jagged bolts of lightning flashed across the black sky and thunder shook the earth to its molten core.

The new God of Broken Worlds flung open His arms and shouted: "I AM LORD."

"Very good, sir," Hershel said. "But let's not be tedious. Your worlds await."

"I UNDERSTAND."

"Best lower your voice, sir. You could be causing tidal waves in Japan."

"Right, right. I DO understand, Hershel. EVERYTHING."

"You do?" Hershel was skeptical. The previous GBW had been rather simpleminded in his understanding of the cosmic workings of the worlds He oversaw. His reach far exceeded His feeble grasp.

"I do. Come, good servant. We have worlds to put to rights."

The new God of Broken Worlds clambered into the cab of His wrecker, and Hershel obediently followed Him.

Leaving the broken-down hearse behind on the ground, the wrecker lifted off on wheels of whirling fire and flew into the tumultuous sky with all its multi-colored lights flashing—or as one stunned witness would later recount to the media, "They flew off into the storm, all lit up like a Mexican whorehouse."

Buck stuck his big head out the window and shouted: "Hi-yo Silver, away! Wreckmaster Buck to the rescue!"

MORTAL

Some days I believe I am the last human in the world. Most nights, I fear I'm not.

When it's dark I often hear their dead echoes a moment before the hollowed words slough harmlessly off into deep silence, and I fear someone may return and lay into me for trespassing. Daytime is hardly better. In daylight I see shadows fleeing into the trees as soon as my eyes snag on their edges. Just a glimpse of a gloomy outline and I'm terrified till nightfall. Shadows of *what?*

The old cathedral-shaped vacuum-tube radio plays nothing but static. I don't know if these gigantic trees block radio waves or if there is no one left out there to broadcast; whichever the case, I'm utterly alone here. Cut off. Hemmed in by these leafy mammoths too intelligent to be mere trees. It's hard not to believe they're plotting against me. Stealing closer when darkness is deepest.

I found this cabin in the clearing by following a clear-cut path through the dark woods, having lost my past along the way. So where is that path now? Gone. Disappeared as if by dark woodsy magic. It should've taken years for the woods to reclaim that snaking path and yet, here is it—or isn't—gone in a fortnight. It's an empty log cabin—a small hunter's lodge, by the look of it. With plenty of canned food and bottled water. Blankets, towels, coffee, woodstove, ax, coffeepot, oil lamps, to name but a few artifacts I spy with a cursory glance about the room. Many of the comforts of home, if I had one, which I must've, at some point, or I wouldn't know the concept, but damn me if I can remember a home that's anything *more* than a cold concept, an empty mold.

And books. Mustn't forget the books, or give them short shrift. Where would I be without this wall-length shelf of dusty tomes? I'd be lost without them. (Ha ha.) There they are, lined up and dressed right like little soldiers with ramrod spines. Books on philosophy with portentous titles. A few scattered books of poetry—slim volumes all—Frost being the only name I know. A book on television repair, absurdly useless without a TV. I could use one on radio repair, but alas, such is not to be. There's a preponderance of books on obscure religions and little-known cults, books with words like "Pantheism," "Cultic Delusion" and "Deification" in the high-toned titles. Books I wouldn't have picked up in a bookstore in a million years. But here, it's a different story. *They* are different stories. Here, I can little afford to be finicky about my reading material.

Don't think the books can't terrify me. In the dead of night I hear them whispering and fear they're plotting an all-out invasion of my skull. Pervasive psychic warfare. Endless battalions of words stealing a march on my mind. A skullish plot designed to undermine my dreams and turn them against me like insidious cancer cells.

*   *   *

There are no mirrors here, no quicksilver surfaces to return a reliable reflection of my facial features. Darkened window panes and kitchen pots make me out a deformed ogre. I avoid them when I can.

There's a lengthy section on ethics in one of the fat philosophy books, on the Good (good with a self-important uppercase *G*). I struggled and thrashed my way through it but all I got out of it was a headache and the conviction that philosophers are merely obsessive experts on semantics, anal-retentive little lords of dubious nobility. They know no more about reality and what it means than I do. Reality for them is an abstract *concept*. For me, it's something that can take a bloody chunk out of my hindquarters, a voracious something that can smother me in my sleep, or turn me out in a godforsaken wood where the leaves conspire against me, the vines want to devour me and the trees want to stomp me into the ground.

I stare at the rifle hanging on wooden pegs next to the fireplace. I don't know much about guns, but the one there on the wall looks absolutely evil. It exudes dark power. If I look too long, it makes me tremble. It raises too many hard questions. Is it loaded? Could I take it down, hoist it to my shoulder and actually fire the thing in my own defense? Could I put the muzzle under my chin and pull the trigger? That would make more sense than shooting at shadows.

Bedtime. Frost is forming on the panes. I'll read Frost, of course. I'll read until I fall asleep or until a way out of these vines and trees opens and I follow it back to wherever I came from and dream myself awake there.

*   *   *

I'm ambivalent about the cabin's walls. The first solid things I see when I wake in the morning and the last before I go to sleep at night, the walls are comforting in their rusticity, yet they frequently fill me with dread. For surely this cabin was made from trees cut down from the surrounding forest, and those lofty mammoths must have very long memories. They must, because they are centuries old, the tallest of them. How must they feel about a puny human inhabiting the mutilated and oddly-fashioned remains of one (or more) of their own? Do they see it as sacramental or sacrilegious? One hopes they see it as tribute to wood's finest enduring qualities, as a natural shrine, of sorts.

I have to depend on the cabin and its fireplace, on these walls to keep the elements out and the hearth's heat in on those coldest of nights when I would freeze to death outside.

My firewood is running out. The woodshed was well-stocked when I came here. Now I'm down to the last few logs.

*   *   *

I remember things from before in random pieces. I believe I once had a working knowledge of basic brain functions and could tell you exactly how memories are stimulated and subsequently remembered, but I can't quite remember any of that now. If my brain had a tongue, those memories would be lost on the tip of it.

Dead leaves rattle against the windows and scrabble against the door. The temperature is falling fast. I grab the ax and venture outside and into the trees to look for fallen limbs. Maybe the somber mammoths won't take it too unkindly if I chop only dead wood for my fire.

*   *   *

I follow the power line into the woods. It's the only line running to the cabin, and the cabin has electricity, ergo, this has to be the power line. There are no unsightly poles; the line is loosely attached to random tree limbs, draped or wrapped round them before running on like the world's longest vine. In fact, the power line looks more like a shaggy vine than an electric cable. The power vine will lead me back to the cabin. (I once followed it as far as I could in hopes of finding a way out but then it went underground, too deep to disinter and follow farther.)

My feet crunch crisp leaves. The forest floor gives off a grave scent of disturbed earth.

I see her in what little light the trees allow in. I stare, frozen as still as she. A wooden statue—a woman with absolutely stunning features. In the faint light, it is difficult to tell if she is nude or if the one who carved her wanted the thinnest suggestion of clothing, a flimsy gown or toga.

I take several cautious steps toward her. She is inches taller than I. Her feet are embedded in the ground, giving the impression that she grew from the earth and remains rooted to it. Her flesh is burnished blond wood with a honeyed glaze in some spots, depending on how the meager light hits it. Her breasts are full, her belly pleasingly rounded.

It takes me several hurried heartbeats to realize I'm standing before the statue of a goddess. I let the ax fall to the ground. I don't want anyone or any*thing* to wrongly suppose I intend to strike down their idol.

The wind rises, sighing in the trees. Brittle leaves rattle like tiny bones. I reach out to touch her cheek. The wood is smooth, cool yet vibrant, too. I sense life in it. Can it really have grown naked from the ground in this perfect womanly form? *Does* it have life-sustaining roots beneath? My index finger encounters something wet and sticky on her cheek. I snatch my hand back. Something glistens on my fingertip. I sniff it. I touch it to the tip of my tongue. Sweet, like tangy honey. I resist a sudden lascivious urge to touch her heavy breasts. I suck the sap off my fingertip and a sense of peace blooms in my chest. My fear flies away.

I make a slight bow to the woman of living wood and then go on with my desperate search for deadwood. I no longer fear that the trees will reach down to punish me for gathering their discarded branches for firewood. The goddess will afford me a measure of protection; her sweet promise is still on my tongue.

Later, before a crackling fire, I ponder the implications of feeling desire for a god, or in my specific case, lust for a woodland goddess, particularly one made of wood. The Greeks could probably enlighten me, but I have no books on Greek mythology. All I have are my unfinished memories of their myths. I go to sleep feeling as if a truce may have been struck with the woody mammoths, thanks to my unexpected encounter with My Lady of the Weeping Wood.

*   *   *

When I first came to this place, I sometimes saw a low, slinky shadow that made me remember my dead cat Gus. The cat-shadow would appear near my ankles as I heated food, made coffee, or washed dishes. But then he went away and other, more sinister shadows now demand my vigilant attention.

*   *   *

I return to my Lady early next morning. I kneel before her and lay offerings at her feet—I take it on faith that her perfect feet lie buried just below the soil into which her slim ankles vanish. I picture slender toes descending as long roots deep into the earth.

My offerings are, of necessity, modest. A pocket knife. Several kernels of uncooked rice. An empty food tin filled with purified water.

"Thank you, for allowing me to be here," I say with a bow.

Next morning I find a dead rodent outside the cabin door.

I lay the rodent before the goddess. The offerings of the previous day are gone. I mumble: "If it's all right, that is, if you don't mind . . ." I say as I touch a fingertip to the golden jellied streak on her left cheek and then bring it to my mouth. "To honor you, you understand," I say, licking my lips.

Early each morning I visit my Lady to pay tribute with my meager offerings, and then follow the shaggy power vine back to the lodge, already looking forward to my next day's mumbled communion.

*   *   *

Then one frigid indigo morning I find a naked infant lying on the ground in front of my Lady. The baby—a male—doesn't cry, doesn't coo. He simply stares at the wounded sky or seemingly at me when I get in the way of his infinite gaze. His skin is tinged blue from the cold, but he seems completely unconcerned, unaware of his peril. A thin snow begins to fall.

"How . . .?" I fall silent and look into my Lady's placid face. It doesn't matter how. What matters is that the infant can't stay there to die. It's up to me to rescue him.

I set down my humble offerings of a brass button, a piece of string and a paperclip, and then I carefully scoop the infant up in my arms. I look askance at the goddess and I notice the golden nectar seeping from her nipples, and it is blindingly clear what I must do.

I offer the infant to her bosom, cradling its tiny head in the L formed by my thumb and index finger. The baby's mouth immediately latches on to the left nipple and the little lad gives suck. I secret the sated child inside my ill-fitting fur coat and take it back through the thickening snow to the lodge. The infant's existence raises questions but one look into his beatific face blows them all away with the snow. Nothing matters now but seeing that the infant survives, thrives.

Before the warmth of the fire I rip bed sheets to make diapers and put one on him, using paperclips to fasten it. I have no milk to offer so the lad must subsist on bottled water and nectar from my Lady's breasts. This means frequenter visits to the goddess. My heart thrills at the prospect.

*   *   *

I dreamt that my cabin in the clearing was the center of a mandala—one of those spiritual maps used as an object of focus during meditation. (It took me awhile to arrive at the right word in my memory fragments, having first run an amusing gamut of murmuring m's, including Mandinko, Manderley, and medulla oblongata.) I came awake with the realization that my physical surroundings might indeed represent the very landscape of my soul as well as the cosmos itself, but before I could meditate further on the idea, an abrupt commotion across the dim room stole my attention: A huge white crow was aflutter, pearly plucked feathers flying as it barely escaped the clutches of the infant. The baby had grown to toddler size overnight. The crow alighted upon the rifle on the wall.

The bird is perched there still, affronted in his puffed-up feathers, and the infant lies on his bed glaring at me with eerie firelight in his eyes. What have I brought into my lair? He appears to have sprouted so much body hair that I suspect he might be a werewolf's whelp, but closer examination reveals that it isn't hair at all. The lad's pores have sprouted tiny stalks with miniscule heart-shaped leaves. Leaves with little dots of blood on their tips. And a spindly snip of a tree is growing from the center of his chest.

"Shadow," says the white crow, looking beady-eyed at the boy. "Shadow-shadow."

Of course. A talking crow. But I don't know if it is a warning or a curse.

Too much enigmata, avian and otherwise. Now the toddler has his makeshift diaper off and slings it at me. Too late, I duck. Hit full-force in the face with feces, I fall to my knees gagging. But then a wondrous thing occurs: I see to the very heart of reality. It is only a glimpse, a lightning-strike of enlightenment which leaves me in immediate darkness, but the afterimage is indelibly tattooed on my retina. I am at the heart of this forest primeval, caught in the clearing by time and circumstance . . . and in an inadvertent act of unlikely communion I am tasting the food of the gods after it has been filtered through the innards of a sacred son. I am at the threshold of understanding, at the precipice of seeing my way clear, from here. A way out of the primeval maze. Just there—then gone. And . . .

. . . I am a lost little man eating sweet shit.

*   *   *

The shadow-things have come out of hiding to set about corrupting the wee lad in earnest. They circle his bed, spinning round him like blackest oil swirling through transparent spiraled tubing. Silently, they spiral, shading his form with their gloom. Painting him in darkness, mortifying his flesh. He laughs! Laughs as if tickled. I can't watch. Are they are stealing the boy's light—his soul? I grab my pillow and take a swipe at the shadows, to no effect. I grab the boy up, or try to, but he is stuck to the mattress and

I fall beside him. The shadows are icy, swarming my flesh. I ignore them and drop to my knees to see what's holding the kid to the bed. Thin roots growing out of his back have grown into the mattress and snaked around the box-springs, holding him fast.

The shadows cocoon us both in cold gloom. When I awake, they're gone.

*   *   *

I make marks in my flesh to number the days since I discovered him. The bloodletting is ritualistic, signifying . . . what? Six marks so far, left forearm. Carved by a kitchen knife. The pain is nothing. Nothing to what the boy must feel with that tree growing out of the festered wound in his chest. The roots growing out of his back have gone from underneath the bed, into the floor and below, presumably rooted in the earth. He never cries. But I can read the suffering on his face. See it in his shining eyes, oh yes.

Last night an angel came. She materialized above me, her beautiful face filling the whole sky. Perfect facial features burned away the roof of the lodge, disintegrated the dense canopy of trees and beamed down at me for the longest. Time.

Then. She. Was. Gone.

And the roof and trees came back.

*   *   *

Thing is, I've seen that angelic face before. Somewhere. Certain details—the subtle hook of her nose, the way she pursed her lips before she spoke—were terribly familiar. She did speak, yes, but her words were lost in high cosmic winds.

When an angel translates itself to this realm, a lot may be lost in translation—in this case, her entire message. What good is an angel without a message?

The boy's unnatural growth matches the tree's anomalous development. Now its trunk has the circumference of a soccer ball. How the kid survives with that thing growing out of his chest cavity, I cannot imagine. What sort of displacement of organs must such a thing necessitate? How can any of this be real?

Yet I do bleed when I'm cut. My little finger is lying there on the floor, blood-sacrifice to earthbound gods. Real enough.

Time to visit my Lady and demand answers. I don't like the way the kid looks at me now. Like lunch. He's the size of a wiry adolescent and he looks strong enough to uproot himself and come after me. I've taken to sleeping with the ax.

Ain't no flies on me. Not yet, anyway.

*   *   *

The goddess is gone. This strikes sphincter-puckering terror in me. The ground where she stood has been disturbed, so I know this is the right spot. If this foreshadows what the lofty mammoths can do, I'm flat dead. Did I mention the ax goes everywhere with me now? A righteous convenience to this current circumstance, since I forthwith decide to sacrifice another finger to appease my Vacated Lady. The thought of her roaming free through the forest in her woodenly seductive form terrifies as much as it thrills me. I lay my left hand against the massive trunk of the nearest tree, spread my fingers, raise the ax and shed another bloody offering.

*   *   *

Coming to. The pain. The place, forsaken by the errant goddess. I touch my bloody hand to the hole in the ground where she used to stand. The soil is alive with her memory. Will it remember the taste of my blood when I'm gone?

Death lives inside me now. I feel it mounting, mortifying.

I'm not long for this place.

*   *   *

I stopped feeding the kid days ago. I want him to die. Because he is an abomination. The bed has collapsed beneath the weight of the tree growing out of him. Earthbound roots sustain him. His flesh has taken on the cast of fine-grain wood, blondish and vibrantly statuesque. He never makes a sound, though I know he must suffer. His eyes are utterly black now, piercing orbs of evil. Those death-shadows are inside him, eating at him, transfiguring him in the worst way. He glares at me as if he knows what I intend to do to him.

*   *   *

I scrupulously sharpened the ax blade because I want to end him quickly. One good stroke to the neck. If I wait any longer, his flesh will harden like wood and the beheading will seem as crudely unceremonious as splitting logs.

I honed the steel outside, in dead of night, out of the sight of his pitch-black eyes. He sees it well enough now. A few words are in order before I dispatch him.

"Look," I say. "I'm sorry I brought you here. Sorry I interfered. If I'd left you where I found you, you might've turned out better. Instead of like *this*. But I thought you would die out there. I didn't know you would take root. I meant no harm, you see. I intended nothing but good. Now I have to . . . undo my . . . put a stop to your . . . I commend your spirit . . ."

I deliver the blow with all my might behind it. His black eyes bulge in comedic outrage as the blade easily glides through his thin neck, mattress and rusty springs, and embeds itself in the floor with a hollow thump. His head tumbles to the floor.

The white crow says, "Uh-oh, uh-oh." It lands on the favored branch of the tree growing out of the beheaded boy's trunk. The branch has a small blood-orange hanging from it.

Bloody sap leaks from the stump of the kid's neck.

My eyes go back to the blood-orange. How long has *that* been there? The head is upside-down on the floor. Black eyes sparkle. That frown upside-down is a hungry smile. I snatch the blood-orange and rip off its skin with dirty fingernails.

I dig a blood-red section out of the orange's heart, cram it into my mouth. A sweet tang bursts over my tongue. A shriek explodes from the severed head. I run outside to escape the excruciating sound. When the pulp is gone, I choke down the peel and greedily lick my fingers.

The world wavers. The air trembles. Time bends back upon itself. Thunder throttles the depths of the earth.

*   *   *

They languish in the belly of a faraway bunker, remote viewers on the other side, surreptitiously tucked into their seedy trench-coats. They can't locate me, their lost number. I am the one sent to find myself.

As I turn deaf ears to the dead echoes of all those interminable prayers, the giant trees begin to fall, one by one, jarring the earth anew each time a lofty mammoth crashes down. Faster and faster they fall and crumble to dust, burying the cabin in sepia clouds and eclipsing the small citadel of assumed safety. My terror evaporates in a luminous flash.

The scales flake and fall from my eyes. I *see*. *My* blood gave the fruit its color, its mystical properties. *My* sap fed the goddess that birthed the infant, fed the tree that corrupted the child. *I* made the shadows and the light.

The game is up.

The books in the lodge have already collapsed into themselves, unable to resist the suicidal gravitas of their own weighty words, and are now nothing but dark holes in an invisible grid. The whole wrathful history writ small in my being, I *know* this without looking back. As I know everything else now, all at once, and perhaps once and for all, perhaps not, as I easily fall victim to my own whirlwind whims and numinous notions.

The landscape shifts. A severe rift in the denuded forest primeval gives rise to the dark crosshatched canvas upon which I hung the stars.

The trench-coat angels have found me at last. They come in the guise of empty coats to suit my present frame of Mind. A host of ghost-floating trench-coats.

"Well played, milord," says the foremost angel.

Drunk on my own starry blood, I wave away the servant's remark and the last fleshy remnants of the forlorn illusion fall away. The trench-coats disintegrate and the archangel appears in his familiar form.

"Perhaps I should give them another go," I muse, moody from my imitation mortality. "A fresh start. These self-deluded gambols no longer delight me. Hiding from myself in remembered flesh and mortal brain has become repulsive. What think you, Metatron? Shall I create humanity anew? Make them less imperfect perhaps?"

"As you wish, milord."

"Assemble the Sefiroth. There is much to be done. And this time, there shall be no trees. Make sure Lilith gets the word. No trees, no wood of any kind."

HELLBENT HOUSE

She stopped at a roadside country store on the outskirts of Vinewood and parked next to the lone rust-flaked gas pump out front. A blowsy old man in a straw hat was sitting in a chair balanced on two legs, leaning against the faded boards of the storefront. He didn't look up from his whittling, the blade in his hand haphazardly peeling curlicue slivers from the ill-defined piece of wood in his lap. A red-clay embankment to the right of the store seemed to be holding back the shade-dark woods behind it.

She studied the antiquated gas pump. Most of the paint had peeled off the plastic ball on top of the pump so it was impossible to know what brand of gas might be in the underground tank.

"Excuse me," she said. "Does this pump work?"

The old man looked up from his carving. "Yep. Most times."

She lifted the nozzle in one hand, pulled down a metal lever with the other, and fed ten dollar's worth into her tank, a sluggish bell dinging with each gallon pumped. A big truck blew by on the blacktop, leaving eddies of ocher dust dancing on either side of the road. The afternoon sun glared down from a hazy sky.

"Do I pay you?" she asked as she stepped into the shade of a rusty awning.

"Yes ma'am," he said, holding out a weathered palm. His fingertips were scored with scars of old nicks.

She dug two fives from her purse and laid them in his hand. He stuffed them into the pocket of his bib overalls and said, "Thankee." He resumed his whittling.

"Maybe you can help me," she said. "I'm looking for the old Manchester House."

He angled his head up so she could see his eyes beneath the brim of his misshapen hat. His leathery face was splotched with liver spots. His nose was crooked, road-mapped with tiny broken blood vessels.

"Well?" she said after a long moment of silence. "Do you know where it is?"

"Why you wan' know that?" he asked with an arch of bushy brow.

She glanced at her car as if weighing something in her mind, and then looked back at the old man. "It's a long story," she said. "Do you know or not?"

"Long story," he said with a nod. His murky eyes swam in sunken sockets. "I bet that's right."

Losing patience with the old man, she turned and started toward her car.

"Go down the road to Shaw's Barbecue and take a right," he said, pointing with his knife. "Go 'bout two miles and take the first dirt road on yer left. Take ya right up to it."

"Thank you," she said with a wave of her hand. She slid behind the wheel and shut the door. She buckled the seatbelt and adjusted the shoulder harness so that it crossed between her heavy breasts. She punched a number on her cell phone and waited for an answer. She got a recording and left a message. "It's me. I'm just outside of Vinewood and I've got directions to the house. It's just a few minutes from here. Call me on my cell. I know you think I'm crazy, but this is something I have to do. Talk to you later."

She turned the key in the ignition, put on her sunglasses and pulled back onto the blacktop. She gunned the engine, anxiety feeding her speed now that she was close. She left the paved road just past the redbrick barbecue place. She passed a beat-up logging truck to escape its dust trail. The truck's horn hooted behind her: Hello and goodbye. Woodlands and scrubby fields unreeled alongside her vehicle. In her rearview, the truck disappeared in reddish-orange clouds of dust. Past an abandoned farmhouse and derelict barn, the trees closed in on the road. Here the woods were deep, the land overrun with wilderness. The dirt road narrowed and she slowed down.

Her tires rumbled over the planks of a short bridge spanning a shadowy creek. The cool scent of creek water and wild flora filtered through the vents. She rounded a curve and saw the house ahead on the right. She took her foot off the accelerator, unable to take her eyes off the looming edifice. She drew even with the house and turned onto the weed-choked ruts of the driveway and drove right up to the front of the old plantation house.

She cut the engine. Filtered through the lens of the dirty windshield, the Manchester House had the look of an impressionistic painting, darkly ominous even in the glare of cloudy sunlight. She didn't need to take out the photo and compare it to the actual house; she knew this was the house that had been haunting her dreams.

It was a two-story building of scabrous brick. The four columns in front had once been white, but now they were the color of very old bones, a dirty gray stained yellow like the fingers of a heavy cigarette-smoker. The front porch ran the length of the building, shaded by the second-story gallery.

Only one of the tall front windows still held glass. Overhanging live oaks shaded most of the house, the shade suggesting darker depths within.

She retrieved the cell phone from her purse, stuck it in the pocket of her denim shirt, stepped out of the car and dropped the keys into her jeans pocket. She shut the door very softly, as if afraid of waking a sleeper. The grass was waist-high and she angled through it with her arms raised above the spindly shoots, making her way to the side of the building. A grasshopper flew past her face and she swatted air. When the outbuildings behind the house came into view, she stopped and stared. She guessed that the two rows of tumbledown shacks, overrun with kudzu and dwarfed by oaks and pines, had been the slave quarters. She was all at once disoriented, feeling as if she somehow had moved backward in time. Her scalp tingled and her pulse quickened. The land itself seemed to pulse with renewal, as if the heart of its history had begun to beat back to life. Something rustled in the undergrowth.

Snaky, she thought. She turned and followed the path she'd just made through the tall grass back to the front of the main house, relieved that she hadn't stepped on a snake. She folded her arms across her chest and stared up at the shadowy building. "What are you?" she whispered.

The phone chirped and vibrated against her breast like a captive bird. She dipped her fingers into the shirt pocket, fished it out and answered.

"Ava?" said the disembodied voice. "Darlene. Where are you?"

"I'm standing right in front of the place," she said.

"Really? Well, I finally tracked down the owner. Thomas Skaggs. He owns most of the land in that area, but he doesn't know much about the house. He said the previous owner had planned on renovating the place and getting it certified as a historic site, but he died before he had the chance."

"That's it?" Ava was staring at a second-story window where she thought she'd seen a shadow move.

"He said some of the older folks in Vinewood tell a lot of tall tales about the place, but he doesn't put much stock in them."

"What sort of tall tales?" Satisfied that nothing was moving in the window, Ava shifted her gaze to the front door.

"Not the sort you want to hear if you're going in there by yourself. I wish you'd let me go with you."

"I know. But it's like I told you. This house has been calling to me in my dreams. Whatever this is about, it's between me and the house. If I brought someone with me . . ." Her voice trailed off.

"I know. It's personal," Darlene said with more than a little sarcasm.

"Yes, it is." A sudden wind filled the trees and stirred their gray beards of Spanish moss. The sky darkened. "Tell me."

"All right. I'll give you the *Reader's Digest* condensed version. Matthew Manchester built the house just before the Civil War. He wasn't a wealthy man and his was one of the smaller Georgia plantations. He bought a handful of slaves to work his cotton fields. He took a liking to one of his slave girls and got her pregnant. His wife found out, and in a jealous rage she killed the poor girl. She couldn't have children herself and apparently she didn't want to see a little pickaninny born with her husband's likeness. The murdered girl's mother took it upon herself to punish Mrs. Manchester, so she—"

The signal carrying Darlene's voice wavered and broke with static.

"You're breaking up," Ava said. "Darlene?"

" . . . a curse . . . the house . . ."

"I'm losing you," Ava said into the phone.

Then the signal was completely gone.

"Shit," she said. She punched Darlene's number but the call didn't go through. She waited a few minutes for Darlene to call back, but she didn't.

Ava stared at the house. Her imagination supplied images of a white woman killing a slave girl in a variety of ways. With a gun. With a kitchen knife. With an ax.

She shut her eyes and tried to make the mental pictures go away. She grew dizzy. The drone of singing insects shrilled in her ears.

When she opened her eyes, she was standing on the front porch. She spun around to look back at the spot on which she'd just now been standing. "How did . . .?"

No, this wasn't possible. She hadn't moved from the yard in front of the house, but here she was, standing on the creaky floorboards of the front porch.

The phone trilled again. She answered.

"Ava? Can you hear me?" asked Darlene, her voice scratchy with static.

"Yes, I hear you now." Still lightheaded, Ava sat down on the cool boards of the porch and leaned back against the rough brick.

"Where was I?"

"You were saying something about a curse, but that's when I lost you."

"Okay. Apparently the girl's mother used some sort of African magic to curse Mrs. Manchester. The witch told her she'd never leave her house again. Not even death could free her. Creepy, huh? And apparently she was right. Mrs. Manchester never left the house again. She went mad. But there was cruelty in her madness, and she made life miserable for her husband. Drove him out of his own home. He moved into the overseer's cabin until his wife died several years later. Then he moved back into the main house but his wife's ghost drove him off again. There are a few other stories, but that's the best of the bunch."

Ava said, "So her spirit is still trapped in the house."

"Imprisoned within those old walls and mad as a hatter." Darlene chuckled. "All in all, it's your run-of-the-mill Old South ghost story. Just the same, you wouldn't catch me going into that house."

"She must be buried here somewhere."

"Most likely. But the house is her *real* tomb. If you believe the local legend."

After a long silence, Darlene asked, "Have you heard from Rob?"

"No. And I don't expect to. It's over. We both know it."

"Still, it's a damn shame. Ten years of marriage down the tubes just because—"

"I don't want to talk about it, Darlene."

"I don't want to get in your business, hon, but at the same time I feel like it's my duty as a friend to be honest with you."

"Don't."

"Dammit, Ava, I have to say this. You can bless me out if you want to, but I think this business with the Manchester House is somehow related to your losing the baby. Think about it. That's when you started having those dreams, and your . . . obsession with the house didn't do your marriage any good."

"Good bye, Darlene," she said. She hit the END button. Tears welled up in her eyes but she would not let herself cry. She'd done enough crying in the six months since her miscarriage. She hated that word. *Miscarriage.* It implied negligence on the part of the expectant mother. You *miscarried* your baby and delivered it dead. You killed it. No one to blame but yourself. Rob hadn't blamed her; he'd done his best to be supportive. But once she saw the photographs of the Manchester House, their marriage was doomed.

Ava's sister Alice had spent months traveling the back roads of Alabama and Georgia, taking photos of old barns, farmhouses, covered bridges, and any other rustic icons she thought suitable for her proposed coffee-table book of Southern Americana. When she showed her collection of photos to Ava, the glossy image of the Manchester House seemed to leap off the photographic paper and grab her by the eyeballs. She couldn't breathe. Her heart raced. This was the same house that had been inexplicably invading her dreams. With disturbing regularity, she had visited this house during sleep, wandered its dim rooms and gloomy hallways, unable to find her way out. Though she was sure she'd never seen it before in her waking life, the house, for some reason, became the claustrophobic province of her dreams. And now here was glossy proof that her dreamscape house existed in the real world.

When she could breathe again, she insisted that Alice tell her everything she knew about the house. Alice knew only that the antebellum building was known as the Manchester House and that it was on the outskirts of Vinewood, Georgia. Rob already knew of Ava's recurring dream of the mysterious house, so when she held up the photo and proclaimed *This is the house*, he threw up his hands and finally vented his frustration with her "obsession with that damn house and your silly-ass dreams." This led later that night to a hurtful argument and the release of pent-up feelings they'd both been harboring. Things were never the same after that. The emotional gulf between them grew wider, their silences colder, and eventually they agreed to split up. Ava knew the loss of the baby was at the heart of their discord. She couldn't look into Rob's eyes without seeing a reflection of her failure to give him a living child. The terrible emptiness she'd felt since losing the baby still throbbed deep within her.

She rested the back of her head against the front of the building and closed her eyes. The house moaned in the summer breeze, its vibration gentle on the back of her head. The low-pitched hum was soothing, and her anxieties began to drain away. There was another sound hiding within the windy hum, like the faraway music of a violin. The cool shade of the gallery above the porch insulated Ava from the summer heat. Her muscles released tension they'd been holding since she'd first set out from Atlanta this morning. The groaning wind and the distant sawing of the phantom violin's strings harmonized a somber lullaby, and she drifted into something like sleep.

*　　*　　*

"Wake up, girl! Don't make me take a switch to ya."

Pearl's eyes popped open. Delilah stood over her like an oak too strong to bend to the wind. Pearl rolled off her moss-stuffed pallet on the dirt floor without taking time to stretch her young bones awake. She knew she had about two shakes to get up and get moving before her mother switched her bare legs with that hickory branch clutched in her thick fist.

"Cow needs milkin' right now," Delilah said in her rumbling voice. "Miz Manchester in a foul mood this mornin'. You can eat ya grits when ya done."

"Yes'm." Yawning, Pearl shrugged out of her nightshirt and reached for her sun-bleached yellow dress. Too late, she realized her mistake.

Eyeing Pearl's budding teats, Delilah said, "Mercy, you done growed a set of udders, ain't ya. We gone hafta bind them thangs up to keep you out of trouble."

"What trouble, Mammy?" Pearl self-consciously held the thin dress against her chest.

"Man trouble."

Pearl looked at the cabin's dirt floor. The big woman grabbed Pearl's arm and turned her sideways. "Lord, you done done it. Look at that belly. Who done it to ya?"

Pearl felt tears flood her eyes. "Marse Manchester," she stammered. "He made me do it, Mama. I didn't want to."

Delilah shook her head. "Lady ain't gone like this. Not one bit. How you think she gone feel? She cain't give her man no babies and here you is wid his child in ya belly. We got to git rid of it. That woman li'ble to do any kinda meanness."

Pearl looked up with trembling lips. "How you git rid of it?"

"I know some ways. Some roots you can chew. Make you sick as a dog, but it make you spit out that baby. Lawd, I hope so."

"I'm sorry, Mama," Pearl blubbered.

Delilah crushed her daughter to her huge bosom and stroked her hair. "Ain't yo fault. I take care of it. You jus' stay away from Miz Manchester. Maybe she won't never know about it. Now go do ya milkin'."

Pearl wiped away tears, slipped into her dress, kissed her mother's broad cheek and ran out into the cool dawn. She trotted toward the barn, her bare feet kicking up dusty sprinkles of dirt. The field boss with the lightning-bolt scar down one side of his face was already marching the pickers out to get started on the cotton. Ol' Scarface scared her and she always tried to keep a safe distance from him.

As she entered the barn, she heard Marse Manchester tuning up his fiddle on the front porch of the big house. Most every morning around sunup, he sat on the porch and played his fiddle. Sometimes the man looked like he had the devil in him when he played. His eyes would roll up in his head and his face would scrunch up like a man in torment, but he could make that old fiddle sing sweet enough for the angels. Pearl wished he would teach her to play. She knew better, but since that first night he'd made her spread her legs for him in the barn loft, she sometimes daydreamed about living with him in the big house and being his wife. He didn't scare her the way Ol' Scarface did. She'd been scared the first time he stuck it in her, but it got better after that, and she had grown to like doing it. And she could tell that he liked her by the way he held her and stroked her skin after he'd put his stuff in her. She liked his pouty lips, soft and full like a girl's. A flinty hardness around his eyes kept him from being pretty like one.

Pearl thought he was a good man, but Delilah said it just seemed that way because the overseer did his dirty deeds for him. Pearl wasn't sure about that. She thought Miz Manchester was the one Ol' Scarface really answered to. When he whipped Clubfoot Sam 'til his back was bloody, it was the lady who ordered it done. Pearl knew that for a fact. Sam was always causing mischief, but he didn't deserve to be torn up with a bullwhip. The lady just didn't like him. And for that, Clubfoot Sam was made to suffer.

Pearl said good morning to the milk cow and was bending down for the pail when she heard the ragged, fleshy whistling close behind her. She froze with her fingers on the cool rim of the pail. She knew who it was without looking. Miz Manchester's add-noise was acting up again. Pearl didn't exactly know what add-noise was, but she knew it made the woman's big nose whistle like a teakettle when it acted up. The woman sounded like she needed some more of Delilah's root medicine. Pearl straightened up and turned around with the empty milk pail in her hand.

Miz Manchester's big eyes seared Pearl the way leaping flames scorch raw meat. Her mouth twisted down at the corners and her jaw jutted out, her small teeth showing in a possum's snarl. "If you ever let my husband touch you again," she said in a voice as cold as her eyes were hot, "I will kill you."

Then Pearl saw the big butcher knife in the woman's hand and her jaw dropped.

"You understand me, you filthy little slut?"

Pearl remembered the milk pail in her hand and decided she would defend herself with it if the woman tried to gut her with that knife. "Yes'm," she said.

Miz Manchester's fierce eyes dropped to Pearl's belly straining against the tight dress. "Jesus God, you're with child," she said in a hoarse whisper.

"Oh, no ma'am, I jus' been eatin' too much o' Delilah's cookin'. I ain't wid no chile."

"You're a lying little whore." The woman raised the knife so its wide blade pointed at Pearl's round belly. "You've got my husband's bastard inside you."

Sad music from the front-porch fiddler found its way into the barn. A tear rolled down Pearl's cheek. She didn't want to cry in front of this woman, but she couldn't stop herself. "I ain't done nothin'," she sniveled.

"That man will never lay his defiled hands on me again." The lady's eyes burned with hellfire, and Pearl knew the woman had the Devil inside her now. "And you will never give birth to his bastard."

The blade was inside her before she knew what had happened. She'd been distracted by the woman's wild eyes and hadn't even seen the knife coming. She looked down at the blade buried in her belly and watched the pale yellow of her dress turn bright red. Then the dull pain down there where the baby slept sharpened in a rush and sliced through the surprise of finding herself stuck. The pail slipped from her fingers and clattered on the dirt floor. The woman's face was inches from Pearl's, grinning like a skull. Her nose whistled with each breath, fluttering the little hairs in her nostrils.

Pearl wanted to turn and run but her legs were too weak to move, so she opened her mouth and started to scream. The Deviled woman pushed Pearl backward and the blade tore loose and Pearl was lying on her back. Before she could scream again, the woman fell upon her and started slashing at her throat. Pearl couldn't catch her breath. A blanket of red darkness wrapped itself around her, offering no warmth.

Then Pearl was alone, her pain gone now. Marse Manchester's sweet fiddling called out to the angels, but the angels never came.

*   *   *

Ava came awake gasping for breath. She jumped to her feet too quickly and the sudden vertigo forced her to lean against the brick wall for support. She listened for the dirge arising from bowed strings she'd heard in the dream, but she heard nothing but singing cicadas, crickets, birds and tree frogs.

The house. The house showed me what happened. It wants me to know.

The dream—or vision—must've seeped into her mind through the house's humming vibrations, just as the house had released the ghostly violin music stored within its walls and "played" it in her head. This *was* a haunting house.

But why was it haunting *her*?

When her head stopped swimming she walked to the end of the porch and looked out over the wild grass and chokeweeds to where the barn had been in the dream. It was not there now, but she had no doubt that the ground on which the slave girl had died was out there in the weeds, where skeletal moss-draped limbs bent close to the earth. She turned and walked back to the center of the porch. A dead squirrel lay on its belly a few feet from the heavy wooden door. Ava was sure the little creature hadn't been there before her "dream."

Why would a squirrel suddenly drop dead like that?

She shuddered. She nudged the squirrel with the toe of her shoe. It didn't move.

It got too close and the house killed it.

She backed away from the door. She turned and looked at her car in the yard, then started toward it. When she was halfway down the porch steps she stopped. "No," she said, turning to face the house. "You invited me. You won't hurt me." Even as she said the words, she knew how crazy they sounded, but she knew she was right and that she was supposed to be here. She didn't understand why that was so, but she knew she had to go inside. As long as she did what the house wanted, she was in no danger.

She strode to the door, turned the doorknob and stepped inside. The door shut softly behind her. The entrance hall and the adjoining rooms were empty, the old furniture long gone. The place held nothing but dust and mold and dead leaves blown in through the windows. And gloomy darkness. Ava went to the foot of the wide wooden staircase and placed her hand on the newel post. Something not unlike an electric current moved through her hand and up her arm and into her shoulder, then it climbed up her neck and her ear filled with fierce ringing. She spun around and sat on the bottom stair step to keep from falling, but the sensation of spinning continued unabated. Darkness spiraled into her dimming vision and she felt herself falling into a faint.

Through the crowding dark Ava saw Pearl's mother standing before her, a look of hatred etched into the ashen mummer's mask of her face. The woman raised her arm and pointed a dark, stubby finger.

"You kilt my li'l girl," Delilah said with venom in her raspy voice. "Murdered her baby. Now you got to reap what you sow. You won't never go out this house again. Dyin' won't do you no good. This house be yer soul's prison. You damned forever."

Ava tried to tell the apparition that she was accusing the wrong person, but she was unable to speak. Nor could she move. She could only stare into the old slave's pallid face and listen to the angry voice echoing through time.

"Yo man shun you in life an' hate you in death. But you ain't gone be lonely, no. The Devil send you some comp'ny." Then Delilah said something in another language that sounded like: "Doomba ho-tay tu tu see doo say."

Hearing these foreign words, Ava's stomach clenched and her bladder let go and she dribbled in her pants.

The apparition faded into the rich gloom of the entrance hall, its dark-skinned phosphorescent face finally shrinking to a lingering dot of light, then vanishing completely the way a TV screen goes dark when the power is switched off.

Ava's command of movement returned and she stood on unsteady legs, leaning on the newel post. Her panties and the crotch of her jeans were warm and wet, reeking of concentrated urine and making her briefly wonder if she had a bladder infection.

No, this is no infection; it's a physical effect of that old woman's poisonous curse. It wasn't meant for me and I had to let it pass through me and out.

Now that she was no longer confronted with the ghost, Ava realized that the old slave hadn't mistaken her for the Manchester woman. The house had simply shown her what had happened from the cursed woman's perspective. For whatever reason, the house wanted her to experience it as the murdering woman had.

Unless . . . something else had been going on during the ghostly visitation. Something she didn't want to think about, not now. Not here.

It was time to go. Whatever this whole thing was about, this obsession and her unexplained relationship with the house and its history, Ava wanted no more of it.

I didn't come here to get the piss scared out of me. It's time to get the hell out of here and forget I ever saw this place.

Even as these thoughts ran through her head, she knew she was kidding herself if she really thought she could leave here and forget all about it. The house had reached across two hundred miles and invaded her dreams to issue its summons. It would not let her go until it got what it wanted of her.

She turned and allowed her gaze to go up the staircase and into the thick shadows of the second-story landing. Something was trying to draw her up those stairs. Something too strong to resist. Without intending to, she placed her right foot on the first step and dragged her left foot up behind it. Like iron drawn to a magnet, her body yielded to the pull of whatever was up there, and she plodded up the wooden steps.

She was halfway to the top when the thing she hadn't wanted to think about moments ago forced its way to the forefront of her thoughts. The considered possibility stopped her cold. She white-knuckled the banister. Her breath caught in her throat.

"No," she managed to whisper. She sought to reassure herself that such a thing couldn't happen in the real world, but the attempt died in place when she was compelled to acknowledge that until a few minutes ago she hadn't believed in ghosts.

So how could she be sure that the cursed spirit of the Manchester woman—the brutal killer of a slave girl and her unborn baby—couldn't slip into Ava's mind and body in some sort of diabolical possession? When Delilah was pointing at her and issuing the curse, hadn't she felt a foreign *presence* trying to center itself within her, in the region of her belly?

She had definitely felt *something*. Something so invasive it made her piss her pants.

Her left foot took the next step up.

"What do you want from me?" she sobbed a shout, eyes filling with tears. She mounted another step.

The phone in her breast pocket chirped again. She pulled it out and read Darlene's name and number in the little lighted window. "Hello," she said, her response little more than automatic.

Darlene's voice was faint and tinny. "I'm sorry, hon. I should've kept my mouth shut. Forgive me?"

"You were right, I shouldn't've come. It's doing something to me. I . . . it won't let me leave. It's . . ."

Ava was almost to the landing now.

"What do you mean? What's it doing to you?"

"I can't stop," said Ava, distracted by the syrupy darkness at the top of the stairs. The air up here was stuffy and hot, pungent with the scent of rotting flesh. Another dead animal?

"Ava? Talk to me."

"I don't know what it wants," she sobbed into the phone.

"What? You mean the house?"

"I don't know." Ava stepped onto the oak floor of the second story.

"Listen to me, hon, you just march right out of there right now, get in your car and come home. You hear me?"

"*Help me*," she said, then her fingers would no longer hold the phone, and it fell to the floor, the green LED light winking out.

*　　*　　*

She watched from her bedroom window as Ira Stoner tied the hoodoo woman to the whipping post and sliced her dress open with his buck knife, exposing her broad, brown back. The overseer turned and looked up at her, touching a finger to the brim of his hat. The scar down his sweaty face glistened like a streak of silver in the sunlight. She nodded, and he uncoiled his cowhide whip, flicked it a few times as if preparing to cast a fishing line into water, and then he proceeded to lash Delilah's back. The woman whimpered under the whip, but she never screamed or cried out. The whip opened crisscrossed lacerations, and soon the slave's back was a canvas of mad, bloody art. Her body slumped against the post. Stoner paused to look up at the window again.

"Continue, Mr. Stoner," she told him. "I won't have that black bitch witching any more white people."

Stoner resumed. The sharp cracks of leather on flesh echoed in the trees behind the house. A hundred or so lashes later, Stoner paused to refresh himself with a ladle of water, and then stuck his fingers beneath Delilah's slumped head. "She's dead, Miz Manchester," he told her.

"Are you sure?" she yelled down.

"Yes ma'am."

"Bury her yourself. And don't mark the grave." She left her post at the window, brushed her hair in front of the mirror and said, "That should be the end of that nigger's curse." Then she went downstairs and boldly stepped out the front door.

It was a fine afternoon of bright sunshine. A breeze whispered through the trees and purred around the eaves of the house. She walked down the front-porch steps and into the sunlight. She glanced up at a single dark cloud hanging low overhead. A chill went up the back of her head when she saw the way the black cloud was wildly roiling, an isolated tempest feeding on itself, growing with unnerving speed. Something hard hit the top of her head and she furiously looked about for a rock-throwing culprit. Then a cannonade of hailstones pelted her head and shoulders. She screamed as she turned back and ran for the shelter of the overhanging gallery, but a ball of hail as big as a ripe apple bounced off her head and sent her sprawling to the flagstones in front of the house. The rain of hail punished her outstretched body as she crawled toward the porch steps, skirts dragging in the dirt. Blood trickled from her scalp, into her eyes, but she managed to climb the steps on her hands and knees and collapsed on the boards of the covered porch. "God damn that black witch," she said through clenched teeth.

She was crawling into the murky mouth of the wide hallway when she came to herself. Her head throbbed with a dull ache. Her vision was blurred—or maybe it just seemed that way because the outside light seemed unable to penetrate the house's interior gloom.

The phone! She remembered dropping it. At the top of the stairs. Knew it was her only link to the world outside this hell-bent house. Ava stood up and started back to the second-floor landing. She was not at all certain that her movements were entirely her own. She had felt the cold, prickly presence of another inside her, and she feared the damned woman's spirit was still there, still pulling invisible strings.

Her cell phone lay at the edge of the floor at the top of the stairs. Ava bent down to pick it up and kept going . . .

. . . down . . . blood rushing to her head and making everything spin madly about her as she went spinning and tumbling down and down the bumpy steps . . .

"It's a terrible thing you've done, Maggie," her man said. "The blood of those two women is on your hands."

"Two nigger slaves!" she said, spittle flying off her thin lips. "And the sin is on your head. If you'd kept that little one in your britches, none of this would've happened."

He looked at the bedroom floor. Night pressed close against the windows and the oil lamp's flame danced inside its glass bell, setting shadows to play in the hollows of his eyes.

"The little slut had your child in her belly," she said. "And that wicked bitch Delilah cursed me with her black magic. I did what had to be done. I cleaned up the mess you made and now I'm paying for my trouble. I'm a prisoner in my own house!"

"You didn't have to kill them. I could've sold them off. If you—"

"Stop your whining, Matthew. It's done. And it's not just me that's cursed. It's our marriage. You'll never touch me again. You'll sleep no more in my bed. Now get out! This is my room and you are not to set foot in it again."

He slunk toward the door, looked back once with a pitiable expression, and then left her alone in the room.

But she wasn't alone. Something skulked in the shadows, unseen but surely there. She could feel its vile presence. She smelled its graveyard scent. She sat on the bed, opened her Bible in her lap and began to read aloud. That black sow Delilah had said she would have company, and Maggie Manchester now feared the truth of those words.

She read until her voice gave out, trying to keep the fiend at bay. Exhausted, she fell back on the bed and shut her raw eyes. She no longer felt the evil presence. Either the holy words had banished the foul thing or she was too tired to discern its presence. She drifted toward sleep.

Without prelude, the unseen entity wrenched her legs open and slammed into her with such force that the wooden slats beneath the mattress snapped and the bedposts battered the wall as if the Devil Himself were demanding entrance.

Before the brutal assault took her mind away, Maggie knew that the Devil had indeed entered her—and impregnated her soul with something utterly demonic.

The banister rail had stopped Ava from falling all the way to the bottom of the stairs. Her neck was bent forward, chin on her chest, and she moved her head slowly, fearing her neck might've been broken. Apparently it wasn't, but it hurt like hell. The edges of the steps dug into her back in two places, but she was able to push up to her feet and knew her spine wasn't broken either. With the dreamlike images of unearthly rape fresh in her mind, she walked carefully up the steps to retrieve her phone. She hoped to God it still worked. She didn't believe she could ever leave this house without outside assistance.

Fearing that she was already beyond help, she picked up the phone and touched the button to activate it, but the LED window remained dark. She shook it and tried again.

Dead.

She dropped the phone in her breast pocket, sat down on the landing with her feet resting on the second step, buried her face in her palms and cried. A cavernous sense of loss overwhelmed her. The loss of her unborn child, the loss of her husband, perhaps even the loss of her soul—all of these losses caught up with her, accompanied by wrenching sadness. Despairing, she raised her head and gazed up into the hazy air, and then looked down the stairs at the front door.

She had lived this very moment before! This was a scene from her recurring dream of being trapped within this house. She'd felt this same despair in the dream, just before realizing it *was* a dream and that all she had to do was wake up and be free of this place.

Is this a dream?

Ava stood, resting a hand on the banister. She stared at the front door. "This is a dream," she said. "And I'm going to walk out that door and out of this dream and wake up at home."

She locked her eyes on the door and descended the stairs. She turned the doorknob and yanked the door open. At a steady—almost casual—pace, she crossed the porch boards, half expecting the upper gallery to fall on her. No ghostly hand seized her to snatch her back into the house. She stepped out into the failing light of late evening and walked toward her car.

The house let her go.

As she slid behind the wheel and stuck the key in the ignition, she pulled the phone from her pocket, punched Darlene's number and hit SEND. The call went through.

"Are you all right?" asked Darlene. "I was afraid something—"

"I'm okay. I'm on the way home."

*   *   *

The first thing Ava did when she got home was shed her grimy clothes for a near-scalding shower to wash away the musty scent and gritty residue of the Manchester House. The water jetting from the showerhead stung her skin and made her bruises ache, but she persevered until she felt clean. Then she used a floral-scented douche because the vision of Maggie Manchester's otherworldly rape had left her feeling soiled inside, but she knew it had been more than a vision or dream; she had relived the woman's experience from *her* point-of-view—from inside the cursed woman's skin.

As she toweled her hair dry, she thought she could still smell the faint scent of the old house, but she wrote it off to imagination. Now that the ordeal was over, she still didn't know why the house had chosen her to witness the heinous acts committed there so long ago. Nor did she know if the house and its restive spirits were done with her. She knew only that she had gone there to face her fear of the nightmare house and had broken free of its imprisoning walls—something she'd never been able to do in her dreams, short of waking up. She got on her knees, clasped her hands together and prayed that she had broken its stubborn hold on her and that she was finally free of the cycle of the recurring dream as well.

Bone-weary and emotionally drained, Ava crawled into bed, turned out the light and immediately fell into a foggy twilight world just this side of sleep. The drive home had been a fast cruise through misty darkness, and she imagined she could still feel the humming tires as they sped her over asphalt and away from the haunting house. Her bed was flying through the fog like a clunky magic carpet, transporting her of its own volition. The motion was hypnotic; there was no thought of resistance. All she could do was ride it out and see where it took her.

Then a dream that wasn't a dream took her back to the dreaded house and deeper into a dead woman's madness.

Ira Stoner came in out of the fog and stood before the fireplace, his damp clothes steaming in the heat of the roaring flames. He looked at her and grinned, the long scar on his face aglow in firelight. She watched him from her bed and held the blanket to her bare breasts. "You sure he won't be back tonight?" he asked, his tongue flicking over his lower lip.

"Does it matter?" she said as she let the blanket fall away. She cupped her pendulous breasts with both hands and gave him a provocative smile.

"No way in Hell," he said, coming toward her as he unfastened his breeches.

She fell back into the pile of pillows and kicked the blanket off her legs. Stoner climbed naked onto the foot of the bed and came forward on his hands and knees until he was poised above her, knees straddling her hips and engorged phallus dangling inches from her loins. He leered down at her, his scar now a shadowy rut in his rugged face.

"You filthy beast," she said as she reached up and grasped him as she would the udder of a milk cow. "I want you to ride me hard, the way you ride those darkies in the field."

Stoner snorted. "Yes ma'am, that's just what I intend to do."

She opened her thighs and he descended into her, crushing his muscular chest against her breasts and burrowing his angular face into her neck. He nipped her with his teeth, and she wrapped her legs around his thin hips.

He rode her hard, just the way she liked it, but as she approached the point of passionate release, something dark and bestial broke loose within her; she began to growl and rip his back with her nails. He cried out, then cursed her and tried to escape her wildcat clutch, but she only raked his flesh harder, drawing rivulets of blood.

"You bitch!" he shouted, then cocked his fist and socked her jaw.

She spat and hissed and ripped at his buttocks. He tried to withdraw but she held him as tight as a steel trap, cackling with inhuman laughter. Stoner's pain spurred him to climax and he shuddered and groaned with release. She made a sound as shrill as an eagle's cry, then finally ceased her attack and went limp on the mattress, eyes rolling in shallow sockets. He rolled off and flopped beside her, catching his breath.

"What in Hell got into you?" he said.

Dirty laughter rumbled in the back of her throat. "Your seed, fertile and stinking of sinful rut. Now you're damned too, Ira Stoner. Damned to Hell, same as me. It wants your bastard in me and now it will have it."

"You're *mad*," he said, sitting up. "What manner of affliction is this?"

She angled away from him and pushed him off the bed with her feet. He hit the floor with a thud and a curse. "Get out," she said. "And don't come back. I won't need your services any more."

After he was gone, she went to her mirror and looked long into the dim depths of her reflection. The looking-glass became a pool of water and tempted her to dip into it, but she resisted, intent on finding the vile thing hiding behind her eyes.

After awhile it showed itself, and the house rang with screeching laughter.

She was lost in the mirror. Her eyes were raw and bloodshot, but she would not blink. She expected to see the face of Maggie Manchester looking out at her, but she saw only her own face, familiar yet somehow strange. She touched her fingertips to the cool glass. Her reflection rippled. Her hazel pupils sparkled like sunlight on the restless surface of a lake, then suddenly dulled to the somber gray-black of moist stones. The lines of her face deepened. Her eyes seemed to be sinking into bottomless sockets. A scream caught on the back of her thick tongue.

The ringing phone shattered the looking-glass illusion. The would-be scream came out as a heavy sigh as she turned away and went into the bedroom to pick up the phone.

"It's me. Rob," her estranged husband said, as though she wouldn't have recognized his rumbling drawl. "What the hell was that message about?"

"What message?" She sat heavily on the edge of the bed. Her eyelids were heavy and she wanted to fall back into the mattress and go to sleep.

"That crazy shit you left on my machine."

"I don't know what you're talking about. I didn't call you."

"Bullshit you didn't. Are you . . .? Christ, what's wrong with you? You think this is funny?"

"I didn't call you, Rob. I don't know what you're trying to pull, but I sure as hell *don't* think it's funny."

"You didn't call me?" he said with indignant skepticism. "Then what's this?"

She heard a sharp click, followed by a muffled recording of her own voice: " . . . meant to happen. It had to be that way. We weren't supposed to have a child. Because of the curse. But I had this other soul growing inside me, and when I lost it, it left this . . . vacancy in me, like, I don't know . . . a soul hole, and that's why it wanted me in the house. That has to be it, see? I think it wanted to come into me to escape the house. Trust and believe, that house really is haunted. By more than one ghost. But this other thing isn't a ghost, doesn't have a soul. It's something from a terrible place. The curse . . . I think it—"

There the taped message ended. And Rob's voice, live and tight with tension, came back in the earpiece. "What the hell was that?"

"That wasn't me," she said just above a hoarse whisper. "I never said that stuff."

"You need to see somebody. A professional. I can't help you with this. This is too . . . fucked up. I gotta go."

Another click as he hung up. She sat unmoving for a long moment, still holding the phone to her ear. Over the dead line she heard the faint whine of bowed strings.

She remembers the torturous contractions, how they came faster and faster, and the terrifying sensation of something tearing loose inside as her water broke and came out in a wet rush. She remembers a thin black face hovering between her bent knees and feeling as if her insides were sliding out of her. She remembers the screaming and cursing, followed by mewling cries of the wrinkled red thing disgorged from her gore-smeared loins. How hungrily the tiny monster sucked at her breast! Its toothless mouth worked her sensitive nipple until she finally cried out in pain and thrust the infant into the black woman's hands and said, "Take it to the woods and leave it. Let the wolves have it."

She briefly surfaces from a deep dream and finds her fingers tightly clamped around something hard. Thinking she must've had the phone in her hand when she fell asleep, she rolls toward the bedside table to hang it up and sees that it isn't the phone. It's a woodcarving, a figurine of a pregnant woman. A fertility goddess? She looks closer and sees her own face on the statuette. She remembers the old man in a straw hat, the crooked-nose whittler in front of the roadside store outside of Vinewood.

This is still a dream.

The dream-sea closes over her head as she slides below the murky surface, wishing upon an unseen star that this dream wouldn't return her to the nightmare house.

She is crawling down the wide hallway. A terrible screeching echoes all through the house. An infant wails. A badly played fiddle yowls. Something with dark wings shrieks overhead. She hugs the floor, her face pressed against the cold, gritty surface.

I want to wake up now. Please, God, let me wake up!

The chirping in her ear brought her around. She mumbled into the phone.

"Ava? I just wanted to make sure you made it home all right." Darlene's tinny voice hung in the darkness.

"Yeah, I guess I did."

"You want me to come over?"

"Uh, no. I'm okay."

"You don't sound okay. You sound like you're out of it."

"God, I hope I'm out of it. That place . . ."

"Rob called me while ago. He said he was really worried about you. He asked if I knew what was wrong with you. Why don't you give him a call?"

"He called me." She remembered the answering-machine message he'd played for her and her skin prickled with a feverish chill. "He said I need professional help."

"No."

"Yes. The prick. He's not worried about me. He's only concerned about his own peace of mind."

"I don't know . . ."

"I do. I have nothing to say to him. And I wish you'd stop trying to get us back together. It's pointless."

"Sorry."

She looked at the glowing numerals floating in the darkness of the bedroom. A quarter before midnight. "Darlene . . ." she began, then faltered.

"Yeah?"

"That house did something to me. I . . . it's . . ."

"What, hon?" Her friend's tone turned sympathetic. "You can tell me."

Her own breath fed back into the earpiece like a ragged wind. "I was adopted. I don't know my real parents. Who they were. I think that's what this is about. I think I'm a descendant of the Manchester bloodline and that's why the house called out to me. It's the curse."

"Ava, you don't want to be thinking that kind of thing. Stop torturing yourself."

"I'm not doing it! *It* is! Not me. It got inside me. It's in my dreams. It's like I never really left that house. I'm not even sure I'm not back there dreaming all this." She laughed and heard madness in the giggling cackle. "You're probably just somebody I dreamed up."

"That's not funny, Ava. I think Rob's right. You should see somebody."

"I *did* see somebody," she said in a rush. "I saw somebody in the mirror who's not me. And you wanna hear the kicker? The best fucking part? I think something raped me."

"Jesus!"

"Guess again." More mad laughter from her own mouth.

"I'm coming over there, hon."

"Don't waste your time. I won't be here. I'm going back to the house."

"Do you know how crazy that is?" Trembling fear edged into Darlene's voice.

"It's a crazy old world, Dar. And you won't believe the next one."

Come midnight, she was on the road.

Going home.

She waits at the window. Insubstantial, yet filled with dreadful anticipation of what is to come. These dreams that aren't dreams writhe like snaky vines back upon the dreamer and hold her fast, a captive in her own home. These dark corridors and doomed rooms echo sinister whispers of her murderous sins.

The thing lurking, largely unseen, in the luminous darkness exists outside of time, bestowing the illusion of boundless patience. It can wait for aeons and never waver in its vengeful intent.

She truly understands timelessness now.

She has waited an eternity and waits still. She has glimpsed the world's future and knows it holds no place for her or her blood kin—the one summoned, en route, the one who will take her place so she can at last sink into eternal darkness and beyond: into blessed nothingness.

Insubstantial and solitary, she watches from the window of the hollow old house.

Save for herself and the vaporous thing with black wings, no one is here. Not a living soul.

END {Read on for the . . . }

. . . ALTERNATE ENDING

Ava nosed the car up to the front of the house, left the headlights on and stumbled out of the bucket seat without bothering to shut the door. She sensed that she was treading the rim of the world, stepping along its treacherous edge, mindful that the smallest misstep could lead to everlasting damnation.

The night wind conducted gloomy music from a faraway fiddle. The Manchester House hummed like a giant bassoon. As she mounted the steps to the front porch, a hazed shape appeared in the open doorway and seemed to waver in and out of this world. She stopped dead-still with one foot on the porch boards and one hand knuckled against her teeth.

You go in there you never come out, said the shape, flickering erratically like faded footage from an early Hollywood talky. Then the shape became more solid, more in the world, and Ava recognized the murdered slave girl. Pearl.

"But I have to," she told the ghost. "I can't—"

You ain't got no baby in your belly. No demon seed.

"The curse . . ."

That curse only for the damned. Ain't for you. You ain't did nothin'.

Then Pearl came forward, holding something small and glowing in her dark hands. *Dis my baby,* she said with motherly pride. *My li'l girl.*

Ava stepped forward and looked more closely at the radiant infant. "She's beautiful," she said with a sob catching in her throat.

Pearl beamed a proud smile. *Yes'm, she sho is.*

"But how . . . I mean, you died before she was born. How did . . .?"

She a pure soul. She d'serve a mama's love. Now she always have me.

From within the house came the harsh flutter of demonic wings beating dead air and the whispering murmurs of a voice as soft and repulsive as a mushy skin of rotting fruit.

Pearl held her baby at her breast and said: *You go on now, ma'am. That ol' hag cain't touch you. Leave her to her torment and go home. Dis ol' house leave you 'lone now, long as you never go in it again. Never wuz nothin' but a bad dream. A dream borned out of sorrow.*

Tears trickled down Ava's cheeks. She wanted to believe the profound relief she felt was real, but how could she be sure? How could she be sure *any*thing was real?

Go on. And don't never try to come back. Dis house be gone soon, gone on to Hell, and you be free jus' like me and my baby.

Pearl and her tiny daughter glimmered darkly within their hazy aura, flared brightly in the headlights, and then they were gone.

Ava turned her back to the house, went down the steps to her car, and then drove away. The haunting fiddle music rode with her a little ways, then finally fell away behind her in the dust as she drove onto the hard road and on into the deep night.

STORY NOTES

The Stain. What better way to start than with the invocation of a muse by the twisted mister in this unsightly tale? I think of it as an off-center Mark of Cain story, but it wasn't God who made *this* mark.

Kudzu Man. This story is sort of a black-sheep cousin to my novel DAEMON OF THE DARK WOOD. In fact I'm sure the elderly Leatherwood ladies are related, but the one in this story isn't so nice. For readers unfamiliar with kudzu, it might be worth your while to check out some of the many online photos of nature's creeping green "sculptures." Stare at those giants and hedge animals long enough and you'll swear you saw them move.

Manchine. I originally titled this tale "Necrography" but Larry at EOTU changed the name to fit the theme of that particular issue, which was The Exoskeleton of Manchine. My brother Bill thinks this story is a masterpiece. I don't know about that, but I think you have to take seriously a guy who scouts Georgia locations of "The Walking Dead" *after* the scenes have been shot. He gets some cool photos too. Zombie mania runs in the family. (And real zombies *don't* run.)

Devils. I really became quite fond of the women in this story. I felt terrible that they had to come to such bad ends. But you know devils. This tale is sicker than I remembered. But after all, I wrote it for the anthology SICK THINGS. I think it fits right in.

River Rats. Dumb rednecks and a yucky monster that looks like a "humongus intestine with a big ugly asshole for a mouth." What's not to like? It was refreshing writing as a semi-literate river rat. I think I may have missed my true calling.

Twister Man. One of my favorites. Not exactly horror, not precisely fantasy. This is one of those "dark wonders" promised in this tome's title. A sadly sweet story, to me. The twister man and the widow always touch my heart. Call me a twisted old softie.

The Handyman. If you've read my novel BAD JUJU, you probably know I have a thing for sinkholes. The one is this story might be another haunted hole or it could just be that the preacher and the handyman are haunted men. Either way, sinkholes are not to be trusted, especially ones that whisper things to you. Keep well back.

The Spook. You're not paranoid if they're really out to get you. Unless you are. You think they couldn't be out to get a paranoiac? Sure they could. Like Captain Draven and Rippy the spook. By the way, the captain is the brother of the Draven in "Deadside In Bug City." Hard luck brothers, to be sure.

Deadside In Bug City. Zombies. Nuff said.

Terra Incognita. When your time as one of the walking dead is done, then your resurrected body might end up in Terra Incognita, as Draven and his companion do here. This story was suggested by the surreal blues of the late Chris Whitley. Before lung cancer killed him, he created some great soulful music. His songs are dark wonders unto themselves. This album wrote this story in my head: *Living With The Law* [Released 07-02-91] 1. Excerpt. Living with the Law 3. Big Sky Country 4. Kick the Stones 5. Make the Dirt Stick 6. Poison Girl 7. Dust Radio 8. Phone Call from Leavenworth 9. I Forget You Every Day 10. Long Way Around 11. Look What Love Has Done 12. Bordertown 13. Excerpt II.

Death Comes Calling. Before the advent of Kindle, Amazon offered short stories for $0.49. You could read them on your screen or print them out. This story was one of those. Then last year it reappeared in DARK LIGHT, the anthology to benefit the Ronald McDonald House charities, edited by Carl Hose. Somehow it still strikes me as a little funny to have horror stories helping out clown house kids and their families. But, hello, he's a clown, so I guess it's OK. And this story is a little funny too, so it all balances out. Death is coming for all of us, so why not have a little fun with him in the meantime? I just hope he doesn't come wearing clown shoes. That would *not* be funny.

The Grind. Introduces my hapless hotel dick Trench in the first of three stories, each one taking him deeper into evil. Big Daddy Thug put this one up at *Thuglit*.

Lipstick Swastika. S&M. The vision of the "field full of dead soldiers with bloated boners" that haunts Trench is not fiction; the scene is described in historian Rick Atkinson's excellent WW II Liberation Trilogy.

Devil In 206. Trench is the type of guy who hits the bottom and keeps going. I think he and his demon may have one more creepy caper to come.

Flesh And Word. The premise of a fictional character coming to life isn't new, but I think I did manage to give it a new twist here. And though the writer/protagonist is a bit of an asshole, he did grow on me. But who needs an extra asshole?

Deathless. This story also appeared in the homemade chapbook *Books of Flesh*. The readership of that ugly-as-homemade-sin little book was probably no more than 10, so I'm happy this tale gets a shot at a second life. Maybe that does make it sort of deathless. At least for now.

Jacked. What can I say about a sci-fi sex dramedy starring the O-Max 3000? Don't look for a sequel. Too much of a good thing is not so good.

Fungoid. Actually this should be Fungoid 2. My first small-press horror story appeared in a crude little zine called *Doppelganger* in 1986. It too was titled "Fungoid" but was a completely different tale; I like the title more than the story. The "Fungoid" reprinted here began my long and happy association with Red Room Press editor/publisher Cheryl Mullenax. She invited me to contribute to VILE THINGS. This was the vilest thing I could offer at the time. Thanks, Cheryl, for thinking of me. When you think vile things, think of me. :)

Halloween Bash. While a brain tumor might make you nuts enough to think it was talking to you, something more than a tumorous Halloween trick was involved here. With apologies to Donald Pleasance: Why yes, as a matter of fact it *was* the boogeyman. If not the boogeytumor.

The Bone Train. Though I couldn't find any record of it, to the best of my memory, this story appeared online at Horror World during Andy Fairclough's reign. It's an odd little tale that exists in its own preposterous world. I wasn't sure I should include it here but something at its core always creeped me out so it made the cut. Call it fantasy and maybe it works. If not, then I'm sure the Bone Train will take me to hell soon enough.

Manhunter. Alabama Stamps and young Callie will ride again. The Hangman is still haunting the hills, so what choice is there? I am quite taken with these two characters and I don't believe they will let me rest until I go adventuring with them again. Big bounty ahead...

Miss Thang. Brian Keene accepted this one when he was fiction editor at Horrorfind. What I remember most about it is that in our e-mail exchanges I finger-fumbled the same typo several times, calling him Brain Keene. I'm sure he's been called worse.

Hogbutcher's Heart. If memory serves, "Brain" Keene also accepted this one for Horrorfind. Let the record show that in this story I had a killer using a Penetrating Bolt Stunner before Cormac McCarthy did in NO COUNTRY FOR OLD MEN. One pop and they drop.

The Kitchen Witch. This was my first story at *Grue Magazine*. The original ending had the witch winning out but editor Peggy Nadramia suggested I change the ending and defeat the witch. So we burned the witch in the fireplace. Still works for me.

A Witch in Faerie. I've always felt that this is one of my best stories. It's the only traditional fantasy I've ever written, and I enjoy revisiting Mither Mawkins now and then as she tours Faerie Wood.

Split Finger. For readers who aren't baseball fans, the split finger is a type of pitch thrown with forked fingers, an off-speed fastball that drops at the last second toward the batter's knees. But of course, my psycho pitcher liked to go for his victim's heads. By the way, smokestack lightnin' is a drug I made up, named after the Howling Wolf blues classic.

(3-D). This was my first story to appear in EOTU in its early days before it went Ezine. Tim Winter-Damon liked this little psycho sniper story so much he suggested we write a novel together. The result was DUET FOR

THE DEVIL. A lot of folks hated that novel, and I don't blame them. It's not everybody's cup of grog. Nevertheless, that depraved novel has never gone out of print since it made its debut splat in The Year of Our Lord 2000.

The Coffin. This story is based on actual events. It happened pretty much as described, except for the mysterious markings and the haunted coffin concept. A guy named Charlie did find a coffin on the porch of an abandoned funeral home while he was taking a dump off the porch. All the rest is, of course, *my* shit.

At The Edge of The World. Another one of my rare attempts at science fiction. Another in the old Amazon Short stable, at $0.49 a pop this one must've made me a grand total of S10.00 in royalties. Still, it has a certain charm for me. I wonder what happened to Hexus after his leap.

Undertaken. Another comedy of crooks tale. I was proud that HellBound Walt Hicks included it in DEATH GRIP: EXIT LAUGHING. I love the cover with the Grim Reaper coming out of the cemetery Port-A-Crapper.

Life After Living Death. Saving zombies one soul at a time...

The God of Broken Worlds. I confess: I wrote this one after reading Terry Pratchett. Could you tell?

Mortal. This story was written for the anthology HOLY HORRORS, which never quite became a book. It appears here for the first time. The notion of a deity hiding from itself in humanity and rediscovering itself there is not new. You find it in certain Eastern belief systems and perhaps even in the "secret sayings" of Jesus in the Apocrypha.

Hellbent House. So what's with the alternate ending? you may well ask. The first ending was bleak so I wanted to see what a happier ending would look like. And alternate endings on DVD's can be fun. So I did it. Most of the readers who gave an opinion prefered the the bleak ending. I like the second. I felt I owed it to Pearl and her ghost baby. But most likely the best ghost stories never really end.

ABOUT THE AUTHOR

Randy Chandler is the author of the novels *Dime Detective, Daemon of the Dark Wood, Angel Steel*, and of two previously published novels *Bad Juju* and *Hellz Bellz* (all now available on Kindle). He also co-authored *Duet for the Devil* with t. Winter-Damon (God rest his soul) and  has contributed short stories to numerous anthologies. Randy has been an Indy magazine editor/publisher, a freelance book reviewer, a mental health worker, a gas-pump jockey, an ambulance attendant, a soldier in Vietnam, and a funeral home flunky. He often haunts fields of carnage where angels and devils do battle.